JAGUAR
WIND AND WAVES

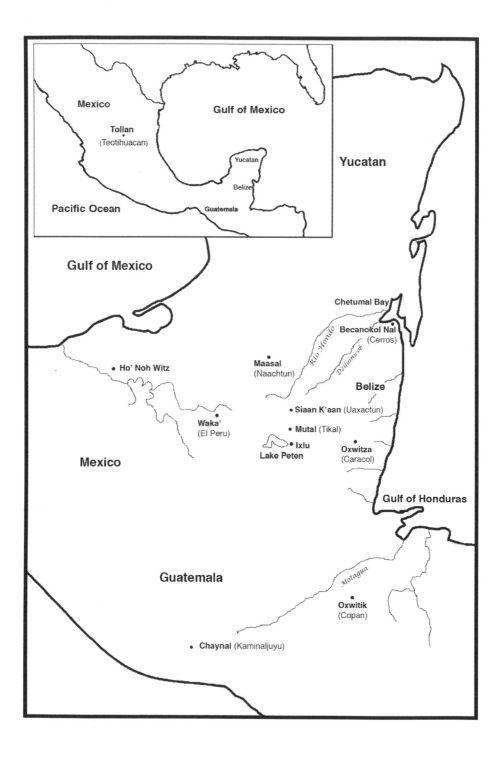

Mexico

Gulf of Mexico

Tollan
(Teotihuacan)

Pacific Ocean

Yucatan

Belize

Guatemala

Gulf of Mexico

Yucatan

Chetumal Bay

Rio Hondo

Dzilunicob

Becanokol Nal
(Cerros)

Maasal
(Naachtun)

Ho' Noh Witz

Belize

Siaan K'aan (Uaxactun)

Mutal (Tikal)

Waka'
(El Peru)

Ixlu
Lake Peten

Oxwitza
(Caracol)

Mexico

Gulf of Honduras

Motagua

Guatemala

Oxwitik
(Copan)

Chaynal (Kaminaljuyu)

JAGUAR
WIND AND WAVES

A novel of the Early Classic Maya

DAVID L. SMITH

THE PATH OF THE JAGUAR
Book Two

Also by David L. Smith

Television (www.Amazon.com)

Video Communication: Structuring Content For Maximum Program Effectiveness

Television That Matters: A guide for writers and producers

Novels in the series, The Path Of The Jaguar (www.Amazon.com)
Jaguar Rising: A novel of the Ancient Maya

Fine Art Photography Series (www.blurb.com/bookstore)
Auto Reflections
Flowers
Milestones
Patterns
Reverence For Light
Wisdom Of The Spheres

To Linda

Vocabulary and Spelling

The thirty or more Maya languages spoken today vary considerably from one another, but all derive from a common root. Scholars differ regarding the language spoken in and around Tikal in the late fourth century, but specialists have adopted Yukatek as the convention because that is the Mayan dialect found in most Colonial era documents. The language spoken at Teotihuacan (Tayoh-tee-wahcahn) in Central Mexico, another site featured in the story, is not known. Certainly it was not Nahuatl, the language of the Aztec. Teotihuacan was abandoned when the Aztec moved into what is known today as the Valley of Mexico.

In order to maintain the sensibility of pan-Mesoamerican languages, the names of principal characters, places, buildings, and natural features such as trees, plants, flowers, beverages, and foods, are rendered in either Yukatek or "Classic Mayan," the prestige language of the hicroglyphic inscriptions. The spelling conventions used in this book derive from two primary sources:

The Ancient Maya (Sixth Edition) by Robert J. Sharer and Loa P. Traxler. (California: Stanford University Press, 2006).

Chronicle Of The Maya Kings And Queens, Second Edition by Simon Martin and Nikolai Grube. (London: Thames & Hudson Ltd., 2008).

Grammar

Maya languages incorporate a glottal stop, a quick hesitation as if the breath is withheld for a moment. Their use and placement effects meaning: *K'an* ("Yellow") and *Kan* ("Snake"). Vowels arc similar to those in Spanish. Plurals end in *-ob*. Pronunciation is usually on the last syllable: The protagonist's full name and title is Ix Bahlam Ich'aak K'awiil (Eesh Bahlam E-<u>shock</u> K'ah-<u>wheel</u>.

Cast of Characters

Ix Bahlam Ich'aak K'awiil (Eesh Bahlam E-shock Kah-wheel)
"Lady Jaguar Claw K'awiil" is the second daughter of the Lord of Mutal, Chak Tok' Ich'aak. She married Jatz'om Kuh, the son of a Tollan lord.

Jatz'om Kuh K'awiil (Haats'oom Kuh Kah-wheel)
"Spearthrower Owl" is Ix Bahlam's husband. He is the son of a Tollan lord, a holy man and prophet.

Ajaw Chak Tok Ich'aak (Chaak Tok E-chaak)
"Great Lord Jaguar Claw" is the beloved and powerful, fourteenth ruler of Mutal. He is Ix Bahlam's father.

Sihyaj K'ahk' (Seeyah K'ahk')
"Born Of Fire" is a zealous and ruthless Tollan warlord, Jatz'om Kuh's emissary and enforcer.

Yax Nuun Ahiin (Yash Noon Aheen)
"First Crocodile" is the son of Ix Bahlam and Jatz'om Kuh. He is three years old when the protagonist's family moves to Mutal.

Ix Chab' Ich'aak (Eesh Chaab E-chaak)
"Lady Honey Claw" is the daughter of Ix Bahlam and Jatz'om Kuh. She is nine years old when the family moves to Mutal.

Gray Mouse
Ix Bahlam's attending lady.

Lady White Gourd
A middle-aged Maya shaman who has a very active healing practice in Ixlu, a village located south of Mutal by a morning's walk.

Standing Squirrel
Sihyaj K'ahk's highest-ranking lieutenant.

Naj Chan
"Far Sky" is a Maya holy man who served Ix Bahlam's father as spokesman and oracle.

Yajaw K'inich Bahlam (Ya-how Keeneech Bahlam)
"Underlord Sun-Faced Jaguar" is the ruler at Waka'. He was given his title and authorized to rule on behalf of Ajaw Chak Tok Ich'aak.

Long Stroke Macaw
A painter of ceramic vessels.

Ix K'inich (Ecsh K'eeneech)
"Lady Sun-Eyes" is Yax Nuun's wife.

Shining Flint Tapir
A Maya blind man who had been a daykeeper for Ajaw Chak Tok' Ich'aak. He performs Fire Entering ceremonies.

Ik'an Chak Chan Kuh K'awiil (Eek-ahn Chahk Chaan Ku Kah-wheel)
"Dawn Red Snake K'awill" is supreme commander of the Owl warriors and one of the three joint rulers of Tollan.

Ix Chak Kaab (Eesh Chac Kahb)
"Lady Red Bee" is a Maya commoner, the wife of a farmer.

Nakach Kaab (Nahkach Kahb)
"Knotted Bee" is a Maya farmer and husband of Ix Chak Kaab.

Nakal Kaab (Nahcaal Kahb)
"Opossum Bee" is the thirteen year-old son of Nakach and Ix Chak Kaab.

Nakoh Kaab (Nahkoh Kahb)
"Puma Bee" is the eleven year-old son of Nakach and Ix Chak Kaab.

Lady Lime Sky
A Tollan woman who supervises the cookhouses for both the royal residence and the palace at Mutal.

Turtle Cloud
Gray Mouses's husband. He is the head gardener who maintains the grounds at the royal residence and palace.

Tenan (Taynahn)
"Our Mother." The great goddess of Tollan. (A large, wooden, talking idol).

Primary Sources

Braswell, Geoffrey, Ed. *The Maya and Teotihuacan: Reinterpreting Early Classic Interaction*. Austin, TX: University of Texas Press, 2003.

Harrison, Peter D. *The Lords of Tikal: Rulers of an Ancient Maya City*. London: UK: Thames & Hudson, 1999.

Martin, Simon and Nikolai Grube. *Chronicle of the Maya Kings and Queens* 2nd Edition. London, UK: Thames & Hudson, 2008.

Pasztory, Esther. *Teotihuacan: An Experiment in Living*. Norman, OK: University of Oklahoma Press, 1997

Sharer, Robert J. and Loa P. Traxler. *The Ancient Maya*. 6th Edition. Stanford, CA: Stanford University Press, 2006.

Principal Locations

Ho' Noh Witz (Ho' Noh Weetz)
"Five Great Mountain." (Location not yet identified).

Maasal (Maa-sahl)
(Glyph not yet translated). The site known today as Naachtun in Northern Guatemala.

Mutal (Moo-tall)
"Hair Knot." The site known today as Tikal in Guatemala.

Oxwitik (Osh-weeteek)
"Three Roots." The site known today as Copan in Honduras.

Siaan K'aan (Seeahn K'ahn)
"Born In Sky." The site known today as Uaxactun in Guatemala.

Tollan (Toe-lahn)
"Place of Cattails." The site known today as Teotihuacan in Central Mexico.

Waka' (Wahkaah)
"Centipede Place of Water." The site known today as El Peru/Waka' in Guatemala.

The face of our father will not be extinguished, nor will it be ruined. The warrior, the sage, the master of speech will remain in the form of his daughters and sons.

Popol Vuh, Ancient book of the K'iche' Maya

The Previous Incarnation

MY FIRST INCARNATION IN THE LAND OF THE MAYA OCCURRED on the cusp of a great turning. According to White Grandfather, a great prophet and my guide in that lifetime, the lightning lords heeded the pleas of the rulers to end their trials—round after round of drought and fami ne—and establish the rounds of abundance that had been foretold in the Nube prophecy. White Grandfather said the gods delivered abundance and prosperity because the rulers fed them properly and the people praised their names.

More and regular rains, larger masonry plazas and buildings to capture the runoff, deeper reservoirs, and more canals carrying water to distant fields brought more and better harvests and more people to the lowland centers where temples rose to the clouds and residential districts expanded to hundreds of families beneath the forest canopy. The clothes on our backs, word-signs, paintings on ceramics, mural depictions of men and gods, the layout, scale, and alignment of temples, even the god-faces looking out from them were not only expressions of our gratitude, they brought us into harmony with the order in the sky and the Makers who established it.

In that lifetime Father gave me the name Seven Maize, in honor of the day I touched the earth. After initiation my brothers at the Lodge of Nobles called me K'akich Bahlam, Fire-Eyed Jaguar, because I'd faced down a jaguar with a torch.

The man who raised me until I became a man was a long distance merchant called Thunder-Flute Rabbit. My blood father, however, was Lord Jaguar Tooth Macaw, ruler of the great highland center of Chaynal. My mother was Lady Purple Dawn Sky, maker of regal garments and regalia. My wife, Butterfly Moon Owl, had three children. Females. Eight of our ten grandchildren survived.

When a man died, we said he took the dark road, made his descent into the Underworld. For me, that was literally true. Within days of celebrating my forty-second birth anniversary, I went to repay a debt to a neighbor by helping him harvest lily pads and stalks. As it happened, I fell victim to a curse put on the Mouth of Death, an ancient cave I entered with White Grandfather. I slid into a deep hole. I struggled with the straps on my back-basket, but I couldn't get loose. The weight held me down and I drowned.

I understand my first appearance in the land of the Maya to be an awakening. Here I offer the account of my next important advance—a cleansing or purification that happened at Mutal, Hair Knot, the largest of the lowland centers where my father was ruler. Curiously, the happenings in both eras were greatly influenced by prophecies: the first given to White Grandfather's ancestors by a lightning lord, the second given to my husband's ancestors by a goddess named Tenan, Our Mother.

The Prophecy of Tenan, Goddess of Tollan

Sons and daughters heed these words.
*Heart of Sky, Heart of Earth, the Makers and Modelers are angry. In all
directions they see arrogance and conceit. The rulers seek praise and ven-
eration. They claim to be our equal. They want songs sung and dances
danced to their glory. They erect monuments carved in their likenesses, to
honor their deeds. They demand tribute for their palaces. They feed the
Makers empty praise. In this way they are walking the path of destruction.*

Sons and daughters heed the decision of my brothers.
*They held council. They decided to end this, the fourth world, and begin
anew. The Chahkob will withhold their rain for an entire season. Everywhere. The Locust Lords send their warriors to devour everything green.
All who fly, walk, crawl, slither, and swim war on one another. With
branches bare and soil turned to dust, Lightning Lords burn the remaining
wood. Famine and disease force the human beings to scatter. The rulers
rule in vain. Ajaw Witz makes the ground tremble beneath their feet.
Houses and temples fall. The storm god releases a torrent of water that
floods the land. Those who reach the mountaintops plead on their knees.
Brothers eat the flesh of their brothers. This is the termination of the
fourth world. The face of the Earth is wiped clean.*

Sons and daughters heed the words I spoke to my brothers.
*"Brothers," I asked, "is it proper to punish those who are ruled for the
forgetfulness and wicked ways of those who rule? The ruling lords walk
the path of destruction in ignorance. With respect, my brothers. Hold the
destruction for a time. Let us give them a warning. Let us see if the rulers
can turn—and turn their people. Let me remind them how to feed us properly, praise our names, and offer respect and gratitude."*

Sons and daughters heed these words.
*Heart of Sky, Heart of Earth, the Makers and Modelers all granted my re-
quest. They will hold the termination until the rulers in all directions have
heard my warning. If they see the human beings walking the path of humil-
ity, gratitude, and respect, abundance will be theirs once again.*

3

AD 378
Waka', Guatemala

Roots

IT WAS WELL KNOWN AMONG MY PEOPLE THAT CHILDREN inherited their *ch'ulel*, the spirit essences that made them who they are, from their grandfathers. Just as the new crop of maize replaces the previous crop, so the sons and daughters of men replace their grandfathers, walk for them on the face of the earth. As long as we remember the ancestors, they are present in both *our* lives and the life of the *caah*, the community. As I was growing up I could see that this was true for everyone around me. It certainly was true for my brothers and sister. But it was not true for me. Although I knew my grandfather, respected him and laughed with him, I was my *father's* daughter.

Apart from the little red jaguar claw tattoo on my cheek, the hair on Father's upper lip and the differences in how we wore our hair, our reflections on the water were much alike. Both our foreheads had been flattened, shaped to look like maize cobs. We both had long noses, broad cheeks, deeply folded eyelids, and our skin was the color of brown maize. Another difference, one I kept secret, was a white spot, about the size of a small lime, on my left side, under my ribs.

I delighted when visitors to the palace spoke of the likeness between Father and me. I hoped it went beyond our appearance and that, when I became a woman, I would have his manner of talking and gesturing, especially his determined yet kindly manner in battling the everyday storms that rained down on the Mat and flooded palace life. Although I'd seen him stern and demanding in the audience chamber, I knew him as a gentle and playful father, the man carried me on his shoulders, danced to entertain me at court, and planted the thought in my head that I would make a grand contribution to our beloved Mutal. Among foreign dignitaries, long-distance merchants, and his underlords, Father's courage and ferocity as a warrior earned him the title, Ajaw Tajal Chaak, Lord Torch and Rain. At his accession he took the name, Ajaw Tok Ich'aak, Lord Jaguar Claw. Twenty years later, celebrating his accomplishments on the completion of his first *k'atun*—twenty years—on the Mat, the Chilam introduced him as Ajaw Chaak Tok Ich'aak, Lord Jaguar Claw The Great. He and Mother had seven children. Five survived. He also had a daughter by another woman, and they sometimes sat with us at court.

We never knew Mother's first born because he took the dark road four months after his arrival. My sister came next. She was introduced to the court as Ixway Ich'aak, Lady Dream Claw, a name that suited her because her manner was soft and her steps small, making it seem like she floated across the floor, particularly when we wore long ceremonial robes. When my brother Naway, Dreaming Claw, arrived the ancestors said he had the spirit of a warrior. I arrived after another son who only stayed for three days.

After me came Kachne', Knotted Tail, who, perhaps because he almost didn't survive or because his skin was lighter than ours, was a worrier. He was afraid of everything, but by the time he was nine he could outrun his brother and count faster than any of us, except for Father. He and I often sat on the branch of a cedar tree overlooking the marketplace where we predicted the exchanges for feathers and flowers. That's how it happened that at ten, I was the only flower among the Jaguar Claw who could sum, place, and takeaway numbers as high as twenty-four thousand, the number of *kakaw* beans Father received twice a year from both his underlords.

Twelve days after I touched the earth, Father named me Unen Bahlam, Infant Jaguar, after the twelfth ruler of Mutal. But as early as I could remember, he called me Palm Flower, the odor of which was said to take a person to other worlds. When I was four, and it came time to present me at court, he decided to give me the house name in honor of the new palace he built. At the dedication he introduced me as Ix Bahlam Ich'aak, Lady Jaguar Claw.

As it happened, the name fit. I was clearly more *claw* than *infant*. Naway called me Jaguar Mouth for a time, but it didn't stick. Between my sister and me, I was the fearless one, more determined than my brothers to have my way and make Father proud. It wasn't until he sent me to Tollan in fulfillment of his alliance with the lords there, that I took the title I came to share with my husband, Jatz'om Kuh, Spearthrower Owl. When they anointed him Kaloomte' U Cab Quetzal, Supreme Anointer Land of the Quetzal People, they made us both—together—custodians of K'awiil, the god of lightning who bestowed the authority to rule. From then on I was formally introduced as Ix Bahlam Ich'aak Kuh K'awiil, Lady Jaguar Claw Custodian of K'awiil. I didn't know it then, but that title and the office and rituals that came with it, including an audience with the Great Goddess of Tollan, gave birth to the clouds that would grow into the thunderheads that brought me down.

According to Mother, when the *aj k'in* spread the seeds, beans, and crystals to divine my birth prophecy, it came clear, definite, and without hesitation: the ancestors said my path would be "the path of the jaguar," and that "amidst powerful winds and waves," I would battle "a mighty demon." Father said that, unlike my wild temperament, the path of the jaguar was a path of listening and watching before pouncing. He said this would be my strength, and that, like the jaguar I would "roam free and without fear in the forest of men." As for the demon, neither the *aj k'in* nor my father knew what he would be like, but on the long journey to Tollan I kept an obsidian blade in my litter—the knife Mother used to cut the shell from my waist-cord when I became a woman of the *caah*. As it happened, not even Father could have dreamed that the man he sent me to marry would unleash the demon.

I proudly stood beside my husband and his forest of relatives, ministers, warriors, and noble friends for thirteen years, first at Tollan where the seasons alternated between dry heat and wet cold, and then at Ho' Noh Witz where the longer season was hot and wet. Thirteen years I kept his household and bore his children—of the five, two survived—while he took council with his father and the other lords of Tollan. Through it all, even at Ho' Noh Witz where he ruled, he layered well and rose in the favor of the Tollan lords, especially Tenan, their goddess. Jatz'om didn't regard me so, but I often felt like I was the house servant.

At Tollan I tried to be more like my older sister: soft and pleasant. Especially on formal occasions and when we visited with Jatz'om's very large family. It was only then that I became grateful that Father had required me to live at the Tollan settlement through the rainy season before my leaving Mutal. What I learned of their ways of dressing and speaking, their hand-signs, manners at court, their gods and the ritual rounds, especially their beliefs about how the world was made and what was needed to sustain it, helped me greatly. Later on, Father's advice that I would do well to listen and watch was also helpful. The more I learned about the Tollanos, the more I saw how our people differed, the more difficult it became to not speak up.

After three years of nodding my agreements and respectfully accepting my husband's ways, I could no longer tread that path. Late on a frigid and windy night, Jatz'om came through the doorway. He entered so quietly it was only his breathing that distracted me from my altar. I turned abruptly, knowing how he felt about the little ceramic likeness of the god I had brought with me from Mutal. Itzamnaaj, Far Seer, was revered as one of the world Makers. Father taught me to honor him and seek his wise council. Jatz'om grabbed the hook-nosed figure, smashed it on the pavement and ground it with his sandal. "I told you to get rid of that," he said. Jatz'om's manner of scolding was not like other men. His words could be as harsh, even cruel, but because of his soft voice and slow manner, criticisms and demands came out slowly, as if the Great Goddess and the lords of Tollan were listening to every word.

I knelt and picked up the largest shards, bits of the serpent headdress. "With respect husband, I kept it because it came from my father. It reminds me — ."

"Your blood may be Maya, but your allegiance is to me now. And Tollan. In this household we kneel and pray to the storm god and the great goddess. Is there anything else you are hiding?" I shook my head.

"Dear One, you have been here long enough to know that our gods and the Goddess are the only true gods. They alone can give you what you want."

Fearing the complete loss of my Maya ways, I pounced. "Husband, my father's gods are as true as your father's gods! They just have different names. Neither you nor your father will tell me which to favor."

8

"You dare speak to me in this manner? Where is your respect, woman?"

"I have been silent long enough..." The frustrations I'd been keeping down erupted in a litany of disagreements and complaints. In that moment I was glad that my husband, unlike his brothers who aspired to become warlords, was a *k'uhul winik*, a holy man. Surprisingly, he took a seat on his wicker bench and let me tell him that, although I had adopted the Tollan appearance, speech, and manners, in my heart I was and would always be Maya. He listened to me without interruption, got up and walked into the hallway. At least I'd had my say. That was when I learned, or so I thought, that Father was wrong about one thing: listening and watching, holding back before pouncing was not my way.

I continued to present myself as soft and reserved in formal situations and when I was with my husband's family and companions, but when we were alone I didn't hesitate to let Jatz'om know my disagreements and upsets. Unfortunately, one of the consequences of this was that he became silent on all matters other than the household, the children, and how we presented ourselves.

Still, I was a proper wife. Both at Tollan and Ho' Noh Witz I maintained a clean, orderly, and respectful household. I fulfilled my husband's needs, saw to his comforts, supervised the servants, raised his children, and stood beside him at ceremonies. I had my duties and he had his.

One of the things both Tollanos and the Maya agreed upon was "Once bound always bound." Commoners considered a man incomplete without a woman, and a woman incomplete without a man—as long as they walked the face of the Earth. Tollan males born to carry the burden of a *caah*— rulers and holy men—could have as many wives as they could support, but once they were bound they were bound forever, even beyond the grave. Maya women born into noble families stayed with their husbands—no matter the burden or difficulties—for the sake of the *caah*.

WHEN THE LORDS OF TOLLAN CHARTERED JATZ'OM TO PUT down roots at Mutal and from there deliver the goddess's prophecy to the lowland lords, I was excited beyond speaking. After thirteen years of sitting quietly among loud and ambitious men, of witnessing horrible methods of sacrifice and bracing myself and the children against cold western winds that often carried illness, I would be returning home. That alone would have given me great joy, but to be bringing with me the opportunity for Father and Jatz'om to make a contribution together that would extend throughout the lowlands, made those years away seem worthwhile.

The journey east to Waka', our last resting place before a four-day trek through the jungle, took forty-two days. Along the way I thought about how much I'd had changed. Father's little Palm Flower was more like a palm nut now: hardened, leathery, and lacking in fragrance. Except for the slant of my forehead and claw tattoo on my cheek, would he even recognize me?

I dreamed about telling him how, to bear the strains of living at Tollan, I'd built a home inside myself, a place of memories—Mother and him sitting and talking while she molded clay, Naway besting Kachne' in a contest to see who could chop the most wood from first to last light, Ixway getting us lost in the forest overnight, our walks and conversations on the reservoir trail, and the secrets he told us about growing up with a father so strict he lived in fear of his life. I wondered if I should even mention these things. Would it make him feel bad or regret that he sealed the alliance with Jatz'om's father?

Dreaming such dreams on the long journey east, remembering and talking to Father, Mother, Ixway and my brothers had kept them alive and real for me. The anticipation of being with them again, of seeing their faces and hearing them speak again distracted me from the jostling and rocking litter and the monotony of the canoe broken only by pounding on shoals. It all seemed like a dream. Nights, lying on a bed of blankets on the hard ground, I could still feel the rocking.

Fifteen loud and smelly men paddling down an endless snake of a river made it nearly impossible to string together a line of thoughts long enough to keep my eleven year-old son and nine year-old daughter—and me— from bouts of alternating irritation and boredom. Spotting birds and animals gave us something to do for a handful of days, but after that we more often slept or pretended to sleep. Sometimes, huddled under a blanket so I wouldn't have to talk, I took comfort in imagining our greeting at Mutal— the smiles on everyone's faces, presenting Yax Nuun and Ix Chab' to their grandparents, hearing what happened while I was gone and telling about life at Tollan and Ho' Noh Witz.

I imagined the pride in Father's eyes for fulfilling his promise—my "grand contribution." Presenting him with an heir to the Mat would please him greatly. And I couldn't wait to see his face when my husband told him how together they could deliver the prophecy of Tenan to his underlords and the other lowland rulers. After thirteen years of paddling against the current, these were the thoughts that kept me steady in the winds of change.

The First Wave

JATZ'OM COULD SLEEP ANYWHERE AND FALL ASLEEP ALMOST instantly, confident that the goddess would wake him when he was needed. Whether at home or on the trail, after Ajaw K'in made his descent into the Underworld, Jatz'om would start watching for the Great Tree. As the sky darkened and the tree of stars shone brightly with the Crocodile near the horizon, then and only then was it proper for us to take to our sleeping benches. His insistence that the children and I follow this "holy order" infuriated me because it meant I never got enough sleep.

Night after night at Tollan, he would be snoring and I would be lying beside him, eyes wide open, watching the light from the hearth grow dim on the ceiling, thinking about what had gone wrong that day, what could go wrong the next and how to prevent it, all the while worrying that Gray Mouse, my attendant, wouldn't wake me before the chacalacas so I could oversee the cooks. Jatz'om warned me that, because the house servants were slow to understand and couldn't be trusted, I needed to show them what needed to be done and then watch their every move to see that it was done properly. He was right. I especially had trouble with the cleaners, sweepers, and except for Gray Mouse's husband, the groundskeepers. I cannot say how often I found spider webs in the corners, leaves and mud tracked onto the audience chamber floor, and roots coming up through the patio masonry.

Although Jatz'om was the third son of the supreme Owl who ruled Tollan with two other lords, he held no office and had no authority there. We lived in a multi-chambered, less than regal dwelling some distance from the sacred district. Even so, I would have thought that the son of a ruler deserved to have servants who knew and put into practice the manners, customs, and behaviors—to say nothing of the beauty and order—that set our residence apart from those of their noble fathers. I thought it would be different at Ho' Noh Witz, but the more spacious compound with more servants was just more for me to do with even more aggravation. Gratefully, Lime Sky who saw to the procurement of our food and supervised the cooks came with us. As did Gray Mouse and her husband. Having been raised in noble households at Mutal, she and her husband understood that those burdened with caring for the *caah*—including those related to rulers and holy men deserved respect, not only in speech and manners but also in the order, cleanliness, and elegance of their living quarters, the patios and plazas where we spent most of our days.

According to Jatz'om's holy order, the proper time for rising for everyone but the cooks and me, was when the chacalacas began calling for the sun. To insure that Lime Sky and her attendants had the fires going, water boiling, and maize being ground, I had to get dressed in the dark and make my way down the portico and across the patio well before the birds started waking the others. Because the timing of their call changed with the seasons, one of Gray Mouse's tasks was to know when that would be, so she could wake me before they started up. The worry of not being able to depend on her hearing the birds meant many nights with very little sleep. As the sky brightened—or on cloudy days when the chacalacas stopped calling for the sun—the household, including servants and attendants, would gather with Jatz'om in the patio. On our knees facing Ajaw K'in we crossed our arms over our chests and bowed while he offered gratitudes for the day, afterward petitioning the goddess—he addressed her as Mother Of All—to keep us safe and healthy and keep the rulers everywhere on the path of abundance.

DESPITE THE SMOKE AND THE ODOR OF FISH AT WAKA', staying in one place was a welcome relief from the litter and the canoe, especially the worry of possible attacks which was worsened by the searching eyes of warriors with weapons in hand. Having slept for four nights with a solid roof over my head, a warm hearth, masonry walls with a doorway drape to keep out the mosquitoes and scorpions—and people—I was beginning to feel some stability again. It was short lived.

Midday on our fifth day at Waka', Jatz'om said he wanted me to accompany him to the river that night because the first wave was leaving for Mutal in the morning and he wanted to offer them our blessing. I was not pleased and I said so. They may have needed his blessing for protection from bandits, but they didn't need mine. I needed my sleep. Besides, my place was with the children when they rose. Jatz'om insisted, knowing that even with guards brandishing weapons and carrying torches, demons take women off the trails at night. "The spouses are all going," he said. "My duty is to show the men the face of gratitude and offer my blessing. Yours is to show their wives the face of courage." When Jatz'om insisted, I knew it was useless to argue.

So in the middle of the night, Gray Mouse tied red and black ribbons in my hair and made me presentable with the *kaloomte'* necklace, jade ear spools and wristlets. Because this was neither a ceremony nor a formal procession, I wore the smaller owl headdress with cattails—the sign of Tollan—emerging from the cluster of eagle feathers. Coming down the steps, I glanced at Jatz'om and nodded my surprise and appreciation for his having arranged to have me carried in a four-man litter rather than the usual two. Once in the litter, I took the knife out of its pouch and laid it across my lap, under the blanket. As "duty" required, I showed the women the face of courage. What they didn't see was how tightly I gripped the knife handle all the way to the river. And how hard I prayed to Ix Chel, the Maya goddess, with a pounding heart and wide eyes.

Gratefully, the long trip to the river was uneventful, helped no doubt by the drummers who likely scared away both demons and beasts. The bearers set me down thirty paces from the busy riverbank. I wrapped the blanket around my shoulders and they escorted me up a grassy knoll to a place where there were waist high boulders. Preparations were well underway below. Cargo boats, one for each of the six manned canoes had already been loaded, covered with broadleaves, and securely tied.

It was good to be out from under the forest canopy and somewhat protected by the rocks. Up river to the West, mountains of white, yellow-tipped clouds rose above dark green clumps of oak, ziricote, and palm that narrowed to the black horizon. Closer in, the calmness of the water with patches of fog along the banks somehow let me breathe a little easier, as did the squawking of scarlet macaws down and on the other side of the river. It was thrilling to watch them fly to a rocky cliff, peck at roots and then fly back to the arms of a giant cedar on our side of the river, their feathers turning from brown to fiery red as they broke out of the shadows and into the sunlight.

I had a vague memory of those cliffs. When I left Mutal I was eager for adventure, completely ignorant of what life was like beyond the four *ahkantuun* stones that marked the directions and her boundaries. Besides the heat and the burning thirst, my most vivid memories of the journey to Tollan were feeling proud to be fulfilling my father's promise, desperately wondering what my husband would be like, and worrying that I would not be suitable.

The water was deep by the bank, requiring the men to board their canoes from the side while others held the cords tight, front and back. For those in the boats, hand-to-hand packing from the side required balance as well as strength, attributes they exaggerated with clowning postures, grunts, and wordplay for the benefit of the giggling women who stood back and watched. Although it was undignified, it seemed to hurry the loading and ease the sorrow of parting.

Typical of Tollan women who'd never been outside the great valley, many of them weren't dressed for the jungle and they didn't know how to protect themselves from the biting flies and mosquitoes. So while they complained about their wet sandals and cold feet, smacked their bare arms, necks, and legs, and darted about wildly, I stood firm. Double-thick sandals kept my feet dry. A tightly woven mantle kept my shoulders warm. And a palm fan kept the insects away. My only complaint was the dew that collected on the bottom of my embroidered gown, but there was nothing I could do about that. The dampness, the smell of rotting wood, the squawking macaws, the drone of howler monkeys in the distance, purple-and-white orchids and bromeliad clusters hanging from the trees, the things the others found annoying—or barely noticed—were for me signs that I was close to home. Three days down river, two more on the jungle trail.

As the sky brightened and the canoes shoved off, I envied the men. I had expected that we would all go to Mutal at once, but on the approach to Waka' Jatz'om announced that while we waited for the other three waves to arrive—six canoes, each carrying sixteen people—he would send another messenger to my father to let him know we arrived at Waka' and were five days out. He sent the first messenger from Tollan a moon before our leaving but we hadn't heard back, Jatz'om decided that, because there were so many of us and not wanting to overwhelm my father or presume our welcome because of me, we would enter Mutal in groups, the first led by an emissary who, according to custom, would ask his permission to enter. Had this been anyone else, advance permission would have been necessary.

I had to admit, there was a complication. We were escorting K'awiil, the god of sustenance and royal descent, with the intention of having him take up residence at the Tollan settlement south of the Mutal's central district. Having made a pilgrimage to Tollan to take the K'awiil anointing—and as a consequence enter the alliance involving me—it was reasonable to assume that my Father would welcome the lightning lord, but as a courtesy and to be certain, Jatz'om wanted to secure his permission before we went in. Although it delayed my homecoming, I understood and appreciated his consideration of my father.

One of the benefits of Jatz'om's decision was that I wouldn't have to share a canoe with his emissary, Sihyaj K'ahk', a former Tollan warlord whose brash manner and brutish demonstrations were embarrassing. At times offensive. The name, Born Of Fire, suited him. The second night after our arrival at Waka', as part of the amusements following his performance of a fire ritual at the *Wi Te Naah*, the Root Tree House, he boasted that he could defeat fire. To prove it he walked down a path of burning coals without being burned. Jatz'om and I had witnessed this before at Tollan, so I was neither impressed nor surprised. As much as I tried to avoid even his gaze, Jatz'om kept him close, regarding him as he would a brother for demonstrations of loyalty at Ho' Noh Witz that Jatz'om never disclosed to me. When I suggested that my husband send someone better mannered to meet with my father, he raised his hand and that was the end of it—his way of reminding me that decisions concerning his charter and how he was carrying it out were his alone.

Holy men had their heads in the sky. I understood that. Coming down from there was difficult for Jatz'om. Frustrating for me. Even Sihyaj K'ahk' and the others with whom he discussed his charter must have been annoyed by my husband's snail pace and soft voice. Whatever the topic, he made everything seem simple or obvious, allowing no room for discussion. "It is in the hands of the goddess," he'd say. Or "The goddess knows best." In this way he unrolled his thoughts as if the goddess had painted them on a reed-mat. "This is how it is," he would say. I once commented to Gray Mouse that if the drape across our doorway was on fire, Jatz'om would sit and watch while fifteen men ran back and forth with buckets of water. She laughed. She understood.

The canoes disappeared behind the trees. Jatz'om and I got back into our litters and we entered the jungle again, now brightened by shafts of sunlight streaming through the canopy, the sounds of orioles and thrushes, and the chattering of spider monkeys in the distance. *Five or six more days at Waka', another five to Mutal and then I can stop worrying.*

On our return to Waka', at a place where the forest trail opened onto a broad Savannah, the wife of Standing Squirrel, an Owl first spear, told her bearers to bring her alongside Jatz'om's litter. "With respect, Jatz'om Kuh Kaloomte'," she said with the customary bow to him and nod to me. "Will there be trouble on the river?"

Her bearers matched their steps with ours. "Only if the canoes leak," Jatz'om said. The woman chuckled, but he meant it. Although hewn from enormous amapola, the canoes at Waka' were much like their handlers—old, rough, and dirty.

"Respect, *kaloomte'*," she said. "I wondered because there were so many warriors."

When I'd asked that he gave me the dismissive hand. Now he thought nothing of burdening a young and finely tattooed round face with a reasonable answer. "It would be disrespectful to overwhelm our host," he said. "Did you notice—even the Owl are wearing their ceremonial costumes? I want the *ajaw* of Mutal to see that his daughter married a man who knows how to show proper respect. Sihyaj K'ahk' will enter with music and dancing—and open hands. We bow to the lord on his Mat. And we come bearing gifts—as well as his daughter."

Open hands. Tollanos never tired of talking about their goddess and how she dispensed abundance and good fortune, even water, through her open hands. The woman nodded and smiled revealing jade flakes in her teeth. After a word of gratitude to Jatz'om and a parting nod to me, her bearers slowed and they fell behind us.

Trust

BY MY COUNT THE MESSENGER THAT SIHYAJ K'AHK' WAS supposed to send from Mutal was late by two days. I couldn't sleep so I wrapped myself in a blanket and went to an adjoining patio beside the place where we were staying. Ladders and scaffolds pressing against the facades of three buildings cast dark shadows onto the pavement. By situating myself in the center of the steps of the largest building, a council house judging by the woven mat motif over the doorway, I could see across the dark expanse of plaza to the *we te' naah*, Root Tree House, where Sihyaj K'ahk' had built and danced his fire shrine. Women weren't permitted but Gray Mouse's husband heard that the purpose of the dance on this occasion was to bind the Centipede warriors of Waka' in brotherhood with the Owl, Wolf, Rattlesnake, Eagle, Falcon, and Puma of Tollan. Torches at the sentry posts across the plaza lit the smoke from tall censers that sat beside large faces on a pyramid façade, apparently former Centipede lords, who looked out menacingly on both sides of a broad stairway.

The scaffolds and shadows surrounding me were eerie, but the quiet was delicious. No children asking for favors. No servants offering excuses or begging for favors. No screeching cicadas. Not even a breeze to ruffle the leaves. Overhead the bright arch of the Great Tree marked the journey of the ancestors. Grateful for Father's teaching, I quickly located the cluster of stars that enshrined Heart of Sky.

Thirteen years. Mutal will be very different. Her temples will rise higher and there will be new ones. Father will have expanded the palace, perhaps the residence as well. We'd heard much about the happenings at the Tollan settlement at Mutal, but little about the happenings in the central district. Thirteen years. Everyone would be thirteen years older. *One of the first things I will tell Father—I may look and sound like a Tollano, but I am still his daughter and a daughter of Mutal.* I remembered his parting words to me, words I had repeated nearly every night since I left home. "Palm Flower," he said, "you will always be my daughter and a daughter of Mutal. We will never forget you. Walk tall inside yourself. Remember your ancestors. They are always with you. Your mother and I are always with you. If you get off your path, trust your *ch'ulel* to guide you back. There too, inside, you will find your *chac patan*." Father's most fervent desire for all of us was that we make a "grand contribution" to the *caah*.

I looked up at Heart of Sky and made a promise. *When I become settled, the first thing I will do for myself will be to find my chac patan.* I asked my *ch'ulel* to guide me on my path and offered words of gratitude to Ix Chel and Itzamnaaj for seeing us safely to Waka'. I returned to the guest compound, found my sleeping chamber and got under the blanket relieved that someone else would be up early preparing food for us in the morning.

TOWARD DUSK ON THE FOLLOWING DAY I COULD RESTRAIN myself no longer. Either Sihyaj K'ahk' hadn't sent a messenger or something had happened to him along the way. "Husband," I worried, "should we send someone?"

"Sihyaj K'ahk' knows what he is doing," he said.

"What if something happened to the messenger?"

"The goddess will protect him."

"I told you there are too many of us."

Jatz'om breathed his impatience. "Dear one, you must learn to trust the goddess. You see how she delivered us here without incident. Whatever the delay, it is for the best."

Trust the goddess. Trust the goddess. I'd been hearing that since his father tied our garments together. He tended to forget that I'd knelt with him before his precious Mother of All. That she lived in a dark niche inside a mountain and stood taller than two men didn't bother me. Having seen her likeness painted on the palace walls, her arms with dripping hands poking out from a moss-covered cloak with a great tree rising above her quetzal headdress was no surprise. What frightened me to the bone were her piercing yellow eyes and fangs, especially her muffled and gravely voice. "It is easy for you," I said. "You grew up in her shadow. She speaks kindly to you. After my audience with her she spoke not a word to me—except through you. What worries me most is the power she has over you."

"That is my concern, dear one, not yours."

"It is *not* just your concern. As your wife what affects you affects me."

He turned his back to me. "There is nothing I can do about that."

"You can talk to me. I would worry less if I knew what was happening."

"You will know when the messenger arrives." I'd grown accustomed to Jatz'om's calm nature, but since leaving Tollan even his countenance had turned grim. He stopped, closed his eyes and pointed to the sky. "Little Flower," he said. He called me that—and referred to himself as "we" whenever he spoke the goddess's words rather than his own. "We understand this is difficult for you. In truth, our path is your path. There will be trials. There will be sacrifices. There will be burdens, great burdens for all of us. But you know the prophecy. Our warning is a healing wind. And it will sweep through these jungles. No matter how terrible, it will eventually bring abundance and good fortune to all. Your people will be stronger for it. Mutal will be stronger for it. The lowland centers will prosper and many more will rise up."

"Must there always be suffering before bounty?" I asked. "Why did the gods make it so there would be—."

Jatz'om thrust his finger skyward, which meant that he—the goddess—had not finished. "Tend to your household and the children, Little Flower. Leave the affairs beyond the doorstep to your husband. Though you may not approve of his ways, know that he cares for you, he respects you and will keep you from harm. Worry strangles the heart like vines on a tree. Loosen your grip. His charter is just, a privilege and burden beyond your imagining." Jatz'om put his hand down, opened his eyes and inhaled deeply.

"Have you asked the goddess about Sihyaj K'ahk' and why we have not heard from him?"

"I told you, Dear One. We will receive his messenger the moment he arrives."

Ajaw K'in was about to make his descent over the eastern trees, so we went to the plaza to join our host and his family to express our gratitude for the day.

The Report

A DEEP VOICE STARTLED ME AWAKE. WITH THE TORCHLIGHT raking across the face of Jatz'om's attendant, he looked like an Underworld demon. "Forgive me master," Cave Frog said. "He is here. You wanted me to wake you."

Jatz'om pulled his blanket aside and sat up. "Standing Squirrel?" he asked.

"He is on the steps catching his breath. He ran all the way from the river."

My insides tensed. The attendant set his torch into the wall-holder and turned to help Jatz'om into his kilts. I pulled the blanket around me and tied it, slipped my feet into the nearest sandals and rooted through a bundle to find something for my head. "Did you notice if there is a fire in the patio brazier?" Jatz'om asked.

"A little."

"Is anyone there?"

"Not that I could see, master."

I approached the doorway tying the strands of my head-cloth. "You are not going go out there like that," Jatz'om said. "We receive no one, not even a warrior, wrapped in a blanket. Make yourself presentable, woman."

Our host's ceremonial shields and banners hung on the wall pegs, so our bundles and regalia were on the floor making it difficult to move around and find things in the torchlight. Jatz'om told Cave Frog to get

Standing Squirrel some water and the roasted squash seeds we'd left sitting on the bench outside. "Tell him we are coming," he said. "Go quietly. Leave the torch. There is no need to wake anyone else."

"Should I raise the flame in the brazier, master?"

"Just enough to see his face."

The red, ankle-length sarong I'd worn for the evening's gathering at the brazier had been laid neatly over two bundles. Offering a mental gratitude to Gray Mouse, I wrapped the soft cloth around me and tucked in the end at the shoulder. Cave Frog got Jatz'om's jewel box and held it out to him so he could take the *kaloomte'* necklace and jade tubes for his ears. Without Gray Mouse I had to push some bundles aside to find my jewel box. Because the *kaloomte'* necklaces were strung with large jade beads, mine was so cold against my skin I had to hold the largest stones between my hands to warm them. The shell tubes for my ears were nearly as cold. But being eager to get out of that dark and confined chamber, I allowed it. Cave Frog pulled aside the doorway drape and was gone. *Ayaahh. Just once I would like to go out wearing nothing but a sarong.*

Judging by the darkness and quiet, it was nearing the middle of the night. Without a torch or moon, we had only the stars behind some clouds to light our way. Jatz'om took my hand and we went down the dark masonry steps. On the other side of the visitor's compound we passed between two buildings and a long ball court. We followed a long path to the the place where travelers gathered to refresh themselves and share stories. When he saw us, Standing Squirrel stood and bowed. Jatz'om put his hand on my wrist. "Dear one, I need a word alone," he said. "Just give us a moment."

"Husband, I have been waiting for this."

"You shall hear the full report. First, I need a word with him. Alone."

I didn't want to argue in front of Standing Squirrel, but I would not be shut out. "Say what you have to say quickly. You know what this means to me."

Jatz'om greeted the first spear and led him by the arm into the shadows of the cookhouse at the far corner of the patio.

I cannot believe this. The man travels for five suns, runs the better part of a k'in, and in the dark. Now Jatz'om wants to speak first? What could be so important it cannot wait? My husband's "moment" turned into a conversation. Finally, my grumbling and impatience reached its limit and I called out. Jatz'om responded with a glance and two gestures, one demanding that I keep my voice down, the other that I sit and wait.

Logs, benches, and mats of all sorts were strewn about on the grass. I preferred to pace and try to hear what they were saying—to no avail. Finally, Standing Squirrel bowed to Jatz'om. Then Jatz'om did something I'd never seen him do before: he gripped the warrior's shoulders with both hands. It might have been gratitude, but it seemed more like insistence or "take courage."

As they approached, the flame in the brazier revealed gravity on Standing Squirrel's face. "Jatz'om?" I demanded. "What is it? What happened?" Jatz'om took me by the arm, pressed me onto one of the flattened logs close to the brazier and whispered in my ear. "Never again speak to me in that tone in front of a guest." He turned to Standing Squirrel and gestured for him to pull one of the benches closer to me so the flames from the brazier would not separate us. Jatz'om went behind me and put his hands on my shoulders. "Dear One, Standing Squirrel will tell you everything. He will answer all your questions. I—"

"Me? What about you?"

"I heard all I need to know. For now. Standing Squirrel knows how you are about the truth. Be assured. His report will be complete and true."

My heart began pounding. Standing Squirrel steadied his bench in front of me and sat. "Complete and true, my lady. Whatever you want to know."

Jatz'om took his hands off my shoulder. I turned and was shocked to see him leaving.

"Husband, are you not—"

He took a few steps backward. "I will hear the full report in the morning. In private." I couldn't believe he was leaving. "Everything that happens," he said turning toward the steps, "happens for the best. "Praise and gratitude to Tenan. All for the best."

WITH BOTH HANDS ON MY CHEST I TURNED TO STANDING Squirrel. "I cannot wait another moment. Tell me what happened? How is my father? What did he say?"

The first spear warrior bent toward me with his forearms close to his knees and his hands clasped. He looked into my eyes. "With respect, Ka-loomte' Ix Bahlam, it grieves me to tell you—. Your father and the others, your mother, your two brothers and your sister—. They are all gone. They have all taken the dark road."

I turned but Jatz'om was gone. I stopped breathing. "What are you saying—they are dead? All of them?" Heartbeats thumped in my ears and thoughts that had been darting in my head like deer catching the scent of a jaguar, suddenly stopped. Standing Squirrel started to speak but I raised my hand to hold onto the silence and the faint hope that I'd either heard wrong or misunderstood. Desperately, I wanted to return to the moment of not knowing, of not waking one of the terrifying possibilities, the "what if's" that had been stirring in the dark caverns of my heart.

The silence ended violently when I choked on a dry swallow and coughed uncontrollably. Standing Squirrel ran over to the steps and came back with a gourd of water. When I was composed a bit, I faced into the path of knowing. "Tell me," I demanded. "What happened? An illness? An evil wind? Were they attacked?"

Standing Squirrel squirmed. He sat back with his hands on his thighs and spoke slowly, as if to measure his words. "Your family was sacri-ficed."

"Ayaahh!" I blurted. There it was, the word I'd dreaded for as long as I could remember. The water pooling in my eyes broke over the dam. I pressed one hand against my chest to keep my heart from bursting through my skin, the other over my mouth to keep from retching it up. I didn't want to know where or how, not at the moment. Gratefully, Standing Squirrel kept his eyes to the ground, allowing the waves of shock to sub-side until I could speak. "When did this happen? How long have they been gone?"

"Forgive me Ix Bahlam, your husband wants me to tell you everything. He said to tell you it grieves him greatly—." I nodded. I suddenly under-stood why Jatz'om had left. He would rather face a snarling jaguar than a storm of emotion. "With respect, I must tell you—. The deeper truth is—. They were attacked. We brought them down."

"Attacked? We? What do you mean?"

"All of us my lady. All who went in the first wave. The Owl, Wolf,

Rattlesnake, all of us. Our orders were to—." His hesitation and the look on his face caused me to cover my mouth with both hands. "Our orders were to join with the Centipede who'd gone ahead of us over land—two hundred of them came from Waka'. Another hundred came from the Tollan settlement south of Mutal. We entered from all four directions. After we took down the warrior compounds and the men's houses, we defeated the sentries and guards at the palace. Then came the regal residence. The order was to sacrifice the *ajaw* and his—your—family." Standing Squirrel hung his head. "None of the Ich'aak were to survive. We seized all weapons, took down or bound the resistors, and restored order."

It took a while before I could speak. "You said they were sacrificed—."

"That was the order, my lady."

"Whose order? Sihyaj K'ahk'?"

"I pleaded with your husband not be the one to tell you, but he insisted." Typical of fourth-generation Tollanos trained from infancy to take their place in their lineage's brotherhood of warriors, Standing Squirrel was well spoken. As an Owl warrior, his feathered headdress nearly covered the patches of his hair cropped in steps across his broad forehead. His scarred young face and the longer and darker scars on his bulging arms and legs explained his rapid ascent to first spear.

"Then it was Sihyaj K'ahk'?"

"Forgive me, dear lady. As I said, it was all of us. He led us."

I still couldn't imagine. "But I saw you off at the river. Fewer then ten or twelve of you were dressed as warriors."

"We only received our orders down river. We suspected there was more to it at the fire shrine ceremony—when Sihyaj K'ahk' ordered us to pack our shields, weapons, and battle regalia in the provision canoes the night before.

"So the fire shrine was part of the preparation? How long do you think he was planning this?"

"Since your husband received his charter."

"My husband knew about this?"

"Sihyaj K'ahk' said his charter required it."

"Then Jatz'om—." Standing Squirrel extended a hand to me but I pulled back. "He wants you to know he labored terribly under this burden.

He had no choice. It was the will of the goddess."

I didn't want to cry, but I couldn't help it. Standing Squirrel waited until I could speak again. "Help me understand," I said. "Are you saying my husband gave the order to execute my father, my mother, both my brothers, and my sister?" He nodded. "And then Sihyaj K'ahk', with the help of the Waka' ruler and the warriors at the Tollan settlement carried it out? Is that what you are telling me?"

"You have my deepest sympathy, dear lady. That is the truth. But no one, not your husband or Sihyaj K'ahk' ever used the word 'execute.'"

I got up and walked into the darkness of the patio. *How could he? How could any man—? This is why he would never talk to me about his charter. This is why Sihyaj K'ahk' never looked me in the eye. This is what he came for. Ayaahh, even farther back—this was the reason for the alliance in the first place. It goes back to Father's pilgrimage.*

My thoughts flickered in and out like fireflies. I returned to the bench and sat. "I want to hear how it happened," I said.

"With respect dear lady, I think it best—."

Everything. "If it takes the rest of the night, I need to know what you did. And I want the full truth. Tell me now and leave nothing out. How could you possibly reach the central district without meeting the full force of my father's warriors?"

"With respect, I have never seen such a well-planned, well prepared and well executed—. Such a large gathering of warriors. On the third day out, Sihyaj K'ahk' told us the plan and gave us our orders—different for each of the warrior houses. We put ashore well above the Mutal trailhead, removed our clothing and painted ourselves with mud and leaves. Under cover of darkness the Wolf, Puma, and Rattlesnake entered the forest and went east to meet up with the Centipede coming from Waka'. The rest of us went south through the forest, to the trailhead."

"Father's men would have been looking for you," I said. "Jatz'om sent a messenger so he would know when—." I stopped myself. "He never sent the messenger, did he?"

Standing Squirrel tightened the corners of his mouth and took a breath. "The Eagle and Canine took down the sentries and guards at the *ahkantuun* stones. While we were taking our positions north and west of the central district, closing in on the warrior compounds and men's houses, the Centipede, Wolf, Puma, and Rattlesnake approached east and south and joined with the warriors from the settlement. An *aj k'in* attached to each of the warrior houses, all eleven of them, kept their eyes on the bright wanderers, one rising from the Southeast through the Great Tree, another even brighter one rising in the West. By the time the wanderers were four fingers above the trees, we were in position. When the moon was about to clear the trees, the *aj k'inob* gave the signal to advance."

"This was before the call of the chacalacas?"

"Well before. We ran on the warrior compounds and the men's houses. Sentries and guards fought bravely, but our spearthrowers were no match for their axes, not even their throwing-spears or maces. Even we were surprised at the skill of the warriors from the settlement."

"Why would they betray my father? He did so much for them." We'd heard that he let them expand the settlement and dig a reservoir with long channels to their fields and orchards.

"All I know is the settlement warriors fought bravely. They cleared our way to the Great Plaza. That was where we met our greatest resistance."

"How many were you?"

"Over a hundred men came from the settlement. We were nearly that many. The Centipede who went overland from Waka' numbered three-hundred."

I guessed, but I had to ask. "Who led the Centipede?"

Standing Squirrel took a breath and folded his arms. "K'inich Bahlam."

"Father's underlord." *Our host.*

"Apparently he, your husband, and Sihyaj K'ahk' had been preparing for this for several *tunob*."

That explains Jatz'om's "seclusion." And why the central district seemed abandoned after Sihyaj K'ahk's fire shrine. "This is hard to believe. Father seated him on the Mat and established Waka' as the great trading center between Mutal and Tollan. Why would he betray him?"

"With respect, they are saying Waka' was the better trading partner."

"Even so, why destroy my family? My father learned about the prophecy when he went to Tollan on pilgrimage. I cannot believe that anyone would say he was walking a path of destruction. Why not take council with him and come to some kind of agreement?"

"You will have to ask your husband dear lady, I have no knowledge of that."

"But you can guess. I see it in your face. Why would Jatz'om have my father killed rather than talk to him?"

"It seems the lords of Tollan want to grow roots at Mutal, probably because of your son."

"Yax Nuun? He is only eleven. What could he have to do with this?"

Standing Squirrel's raised eyebrows said it was obvious. "With respect Dear Lady, he is the only male left carrying the Ich'aak blood. Although he has not yet received the title, he will surely receive the Ajaw Le title." I knew that someday my son would become the Succession Lord, but it never occurred to me that it could happen before he even became a man. "The grandson of a Tollan lord, raised by a Maya mother," the warrior continued. "He can recite the prophecy. And he speaks both tongues. The Tollan lords are far seeing..."

Standing Squirrel's words made it clear to me. Jatz'om's father had arranged my marriage with the hope of producing an heir to succeed my father, a grandson who would favor the Tollan ways so when he became seated he would open the gates to the other lowland centers allowing increased tribute and trade to flow west. "His father trained him well." I hadn't intended to say this out loud but I did.

"With respect, Ix Bahlam. Has your husband spoken to you of the *noh tzol*?"

I'd overheard Jatz'om talking about the new order, but I thought nothing of it. To me it just meant how things would be once the lowland rulers learned about the prophecy, how it would be when—and if—they choose to walk the path of abundance. "What of it?" I asked.

"Just that Sihyaj K'ahk' speaks of it as *his* charter."

The brightening sky reminded me that I was still at Waka'. I got up and walked aimlessly outside, as if I'd awakened from a horrible dream. I stopped and turned back because I'd walked onto the tall grass and, in spite of my sandals, my feet were getting wet.

Standing Squirrel stood and stepped back. "With respect, my lady. You should know that Sihyaj K'ahk', Yajaw K'inich Bahlam and the others above me are humbled before your husband. He is great man, a *k'uhul winik* who seeks only to serve the will of the goddess. If there had been any other way for him to carry out his charter, I am certain he would have chosen it. It grieved him greatly that he had to do this."

I stopped and thought a moment. "The men who came with us from Tollan, the noblemen, tradesmen, and the others—did they know this was going to happen. Did their wives know?"

"It seems that no one knew. As I said, my brothers and I only learned of it when we were down river. Looking back, I see now why your husband choose Sihyaj K'ahk'. And why together—."

I finished his thought. "Why they chose noblemen and tradesmen who had distinguished themselves as warriors."

"They were told they were being trained with spear-throwers to protect themselves and their families from possible bandit attacks."

"How many did you loose at Mutal?"

"All houses combined, seventy-eight men. Many more were wounded."

"My husband lied to me."

"He could not risk what you would do if you knew."

"I would have found a way to stop him."

"With respect Ix Bahlam, had that happened the destruction foretold in the prophecy might be fulfilled."

"So you believe in the prophecy?"

"You do not?"

I was about to ask about the manner in which my father and the others had been executed, but I became lightheaded. Seeing me wobble, Standing Squirrel lurched forward, took my arm and eased me onto a bench. I covered my face with both hands, preferring the darkness and refusing the tears. "They are truly gone?" I asked. "Did you see with your own eyes? Father, Mother, Nachan, Kachne' and Ixway? Are you certain? All of them?"

"I assure you my lady, they rest together now. Your husband knew you would want to give them a proper burial, so we placed their bodies in temporary graves. Respectfully."

I felt so weak I could barely lift my arms. Standing Squirrel went to get me some water and the calabash of squash seeds. I was going to dismiss him when he returned but he said he had something more to tell me, something he hadn't yet told Jatz'om. "There is a fuller truth regarding your brothers and your sister," he said. "As it happened, they were away when we entered Mutal. Sihyaj K'ahk' learned that they were visiting your aunt at Siaan K'aan, so the following *k'in* he left me and a contingent of Centipede and settlement warriors to hold the order while he took the Owl, Wolf, and Falcon to Siaan K'aan. Apparently it is not far—."

"A morning's walk north. Continue."

"I thought you should know, your brothers and your sister were sacrificed there, at Siaan K'aan. Not Mutal. You should also know, they put down the Siaan K'aan *yajaw,* and his family."

"His wife was my mother's sister." Across from me, strung between the legs of a bench, dewdrops hung like tiny pearls on the arching arms of a spider web. I was exhausted. "Is there anything more?"

"That is everything, my lady. Is there anything I can do for you?"

Standing Squirrel helped me up. I took a few steps and turned. "You can find my attendant, Gray Mouse. Send her to me. Then go to my husband and tell him I do not wish to see his face. All I want to do is sleep. Gray Mouse will find a place for me. Tell my husband that he, not I, will be the one to tell Yax Nuun and Ix Chab'. I want them to know that he was the one who gave the order to execute their grandparents and the rest of our family. I want them to hear it from him. No one else. Do you understand?"

Standing Squirrel nodded. Because the guest compound at Waka' had four clusters of buildings, double-sided ranges set on platforms with rows of sleeping chambers facing the patios, I had to lead him to the compound and point to where he would find Gray Mouse and Jatz'om. "Standing Squirrel, I realize the burden this was for you. It took great courage. While I despise what you and the others did, I am grateful to you for speaking the truth."

Standing Squirrel bowed. "My burden is a leaf compared to your forest of grief," he said. He took his leave and turned. I went back to the tapir patio, collapsed onto the longest bench there and put my feet up hoping not to be disturbed. Thoughts of my parents and the others being attacked broke the dam of restraint and I cried more forcefully than I thought I ever could.

The Report

GRAY MOUSE CAME RUNNING WITH A FRESH PAIR OF SANDALS. Without saying why, I told her I had been awake most of the night and needed a different place to sleep. She'd noticed an empty chamber at the end of one of the range buildings on the side facing the forest. Inside, the freshly plastered space was only three arm-spans long and two wide with a beam roof, but it was clean except for some leaves on the floor. And the doorway had a drape. I sent her to get blankets and a pillow at the house, *keyem* and water at the cookhouse. While she was gone I got rid of the leaves, wiped off the stone bench with some leaves and settled onto it.

"Mistress?" I was nearly asleep. "You are frightening me. I noticed Standing Squirrel is back. Can you tell me what happened?"

"I will tell you everything later. I want your husband to hear as well. For now, go to the children. Tell no one, not even them, where I am. If you can find some *chih* bring it. Wake me if you need to. Watch that no one sees you coming. I do not want to see anyone but you." Gray Mouse left. I pulled the drape across the doorway and tied the straps. By the light slicing through the cracks between the drape and the doorframe, I dropped a ball of maize dough into the water gourd, stirred it with my finger and drank the thick gruel. I laid out two blankets on the bench, pulled the *ka-loomte'* necklace over my head, removed the ear tubes, and set them in the corner above the pillow.

Without removing my sarong I pulled the blanket over my head to shut out the light. There was nothing I could do to silence the warrior's report. *Your father and mother, your two brothers and sister are gone. They were sacrificed... Sacrificed... The Centipede warriors... His charter required it. He had no choice. It grieved him greatly...* I turned toward the wall. *Yax Nuun and Ix Chab' will grow up without ever knowing their grandparents. Father and I will never again walk the reservoir trail. Mother, I want to see your face again. I want to hear your voice.* I could see my mother sitting on her heels, her toes all in a row, as she bent over a mound of clay, kneading it with her fingers as if it were maize dough. *They were sacrificed. His charter required it.* With these thoughts washing over me like waves of mud, I sunk into blessed darkness.

The screeching of a spider monkey woke me. I opened my eyes but stayed still. The blanket no longer covered my head. The fateful report and the "never agains" rolled in my head. To drown them I recited Father's parting words to me. *Palm Flower, you will always be my daughter and a daughter of Mutal. We will never forget you. Walk tall inside yourself. Remember your ancestors. They are always with you. Your mother and I are always with you. Palm Flower... my daughter... daughter of Mutal...*

Gray Mouse called. I untied the drape and pulled it aside, inviting her and her husband to come in. I gestured for them to set the baskets, pouches, and gourds they were carrying on the floor. We arranged the pillow and blankets in front of the bench so we could sit on them. "You have been crying, mistress," Gray Mouse said. "Your eyes are puffed out and red." They hadn't brought calabashes to drink from, so I unstoppered the gourd of *chih*, took a long drink, and passed it to them. After two more long drinks I told them what happened at Mutal and who was responsible.

"I am deeply sorry," Turtle Cloud said. "This is a terrible loss. What will happen to Mutal?"

I shook my head. "It is a terrible thing," Gray Mouse said. She knew what I was feeling. Her parents and two brothers had died in a fire accident. "I have no words—. Your father and your mother were so good to me. To us. They were my family as well." My father had taken her in after the fire. When the old woman attending me died, she began attending me. She was twelve, already a woman of the *caah*. I was eight. It was because she attended me so well and had no family that Father asked her to escort me to Tollan. When Turtle Cloud heard, he could not let her leave without him, so my father tied the ends of their garments together ten days before we left.

While she attended me at Tollan, her husband tended our garden and, as was required, trained as a warrior with the Rattlesnake. When we moved to Ho' Noh Witz they came with us and Jatz'om, being the ruler, raised Turtle Cloud to Keeper of the Palace Grounds, a title that came with a house and a strip of land to farm. Out of habit we observed the formalities of speech and manners of court, but Gray Mouse and Turtle Cloud were much more to me than servants. And Jatz'om knew it. "What will you do mistress?" Turtle Cloud asked.

I shook my head. "I know what I *cannot* do. I can no longer sleep in the same chamber as my husband. If he or the children ask about me, tell them I am in seclusion and do not wish to be disturbed. You need not say why. Especially, do not say where. I want to be alone."

"I understand, mistress," Gray Mouse said. "Would you like us to leave?"

"Stay. Let us finish the *chih*. You—both of you—are the only ones I can talk to now."

The Second Wave

DESPITE JATZ'OM'S ATTEMPT TO TALK TO ME, I AVOIDED HIM. I might have killed him. Three days after my seclusion Gray Mouse brought the children to me and we had a daylong conversation about what their father had done. In years to come I occasionally referred to that day as the Day Of Tears.

Toward dusk the following day, Gray Mouse became ill. She complained of being cold, but her flesh was burning hot. Her moaning and violent shaking left me no choice. I sent Turtle Cloud to Jatz'om to ask his help. He found a healer and, without a word about the tension between us, he escorted him to our little chamber.

The *aj men* who attended Gray Mouse said a cold wind had crossed her path causing some of her *ch'ulel* to go wandering. Being weak and vulnerable, a demon saw an opportunity and entered. The *aj men* needed the chamber so I got Yax Nuun and Ix Chab' to help me get some fresh blankets, pillows, cushions, and ceramic wares from the guest house and I moved into the chamber that backed on hers. Jatz'om was appalled by the condition of the little room and the weedy patio that it faced. He said he would not have me sleeping in a "scorpion's nest." I wanted to say that I preferred the scorpion nest, the fallen plaster, musty odor, broken stairways, and torn door-drape, to living within the sight of him. Instead, I turned my back on his complaints and eventually he went away.

The *aj men* needed a brew for Gray Mouse that required leaves from the *yax nik*, a tall tree with blue blossoms. After giving me instructions, he pointed to the forest south of the compound where we could find them, so I took the children and we gathered three large bundles. At the cookhouse we cut the leaves, mashed them into a thick green paste, and then boiled them in water with a dab of honey.

When we returned with the brew, a messenger who had been waiting greeted us. Jatz'om had sent him to tell us the second wave would be leaving for Mutal early, not the next day but the day following. He said if Gray Mouse was not well enough to make the journey, she and her husband could enter with the third wave. He hoped, however, that the children and I would accompany him in the second wave. I sent the messenger back to tell Jatz'om he would know my decision by dawn the following day. Either way, I would come in the morning to gather my bundles and baskets and remove them. I told the messenger to emphasize to my husband that I wanted no interruptions while I was there.

The next morning, even before I met the children at the guest compound to gather our belongings, Turtle Cloud reported that Gray Mouse was feeling better and wanted to go with us in the second wave. Since learning that Ajaw K'inich Bahlam had betrayed my father, the ground I was walking on had become, as the Owl say, "foul territory." To my eyes Waka' was and would forever be tainted, a *caah* no longer deserving of respect—or anything else. The sooner I could leave, the better.

Removing our clothing from the bundles, refolding and repacking them with Ix Chab', and not talking about what happened at Mutal helped to distract me from the many thoughts that made me want to cry, thoughts that made me want to take an axe to my husband and his dog, Sihyaj K'ahk'.

FOUR DAYS DOWN RIVER THE DEMON THAT HAD ENTERED Gray Mouse entered me. As quickly. On the approach to some rapids I began to feel dizzy. Crossing them I vomited over the side. By the time we reached deeper water I was sweating and shivering under two layers of blankets. Jatz'om had the canoes put in so I could be transferred to the one carrying Gray Mouse and the *aj men* tending to her. Despite the weakness and chills, the muck and rot tumbling in my stomach, the luxury of being able to stretch out with the blanket over my head dampening the singing and the stinging brightness helped me to breathe.

Awakened at first light to be bled and take the *yax nik* brew, I noticed that my head was no longer pounding. But when I tried to sit up the world started spinning. Unlike the demon who attacked Gray Mouse, mine had squeezed my throat so tight I could barely whisper. Except for a portage where they carried Gray Mouse and me in litters, we lay huddled under blankets in the shade of broadleaves that some of the men had fashioned over the canoe like a domed canopy. Past another run of rapids where we held tight on the gunwales, we came to the bluffs and a tree with a large Hair Knot sign painted white—the trailhead to Mutal. The bearers helped me into the litter and bundled me tightly, but the rocking and swaying, up and down the rooted and rocky trail made my stomach upset again. Jatz'om insisted that we all enter together, so each time I had to stop, they all stopped.

I didn't need the *aj men* healer to tell me that, like Gray Mouse, some of my *ch'ulel* had gone wondering. I could feel it. The part of me that should have been grieving for my family and deciding what to do about Jatz'om was cut off by a wall of darkness. Somehow it drew me in, down, into violent dreams. In one of them a bent-over old cigar-smoking, hooked-nose god bound my hands and feet and stuffed me into a ceramic jar that dangled and pounded against axe-shaped celts hanging from his belt. With each thunderous jolt I expected the jar to shatter. If it did, I would fall into an offering bowl, the contents of which would be burned in a god-faced censer. The rest stops that brought me out of these miserable dreams would have been welcome were it not for the *aj men* and his bleedings around my ankles, the nasty aspirations of tobacco juice and *chih*, and the brew that tasted like moss. After all that, even on solid ground the world kept spinning.

We were on the trail most of the morning when cheers, drumming, the sound of flutes and ocarinas prompted me to peek out from under my blankets. Up ahead, Sihyaj K'ahk' and a contingent of Owls had greeted our procession. I would like to have heard what Jatz'om and his dog had to say to one another, but there was too much noise. Finally, they went ahead, both in four-man litters, and we followed. Long stretches down dark and rooted jungle trails where the sunlight fell on moss-covered rocks and ferns alternated with sudden but short openings in the canopy where the brightness made my eyes burn. Much as I wanted to see Mutal, I rested back and closed my eyes.

Shouts, cheers, and applause made me sit up again. "Where are we?" I asked.

The lead bearer responded, "They are taking us to the settlement, mistress." I could see that. The faces on both sides of the trail were all Tollano—straight foreheads and broad cheeks, the women wearing black or red mantles, and shaking gourd rattles painted with cattails. Many came close to welcome us, shaking their rattles in our faces, beating on ceramic handdrums. Others sounded their ocarinas, flutes, and rasps. They came and asked if we knew their relatives or friends at Tollan. One old man grabbed the side of my litter, perhaps to slow us so he could give me several names. My throat was so closed and burning I couldn't have responded if I wanted to. I sunk into the litter and pulled the blanket over my head. Neither the noise nor the sickness, not even the jostling of the litter could stop the piercings—in my heart and throat—every time I heard or saw something that reminded me of my family and their tragic end.

Then it happened. Cowering in the shadows, engulfed in noise which at any other time I would consider the joyful sounds of welcome and celebration, the demon spoke. *This is how it is*, he said. *This is how it will always be*. When the bearers set me down I knew: I would be living the rest of my life with a hole in my heart with the greater part of my *ch'ulel* out wandering.

Jatz'om lifted me out of the litter and carried me up the terribly bright steps, into a dark, flat-roofed chamber where, after a while, an old but regal-looking woman came and gave me some hot water with chili powder, honey, and a green leaf in it. She said Gray Mouse was in the chamber next to mine, temporary quarters until we were feeling better. Judging from the lineage scar on her cheek and the jade around her neck, this woman was the wife of a nobleman or office holder. She spoke some comforting words, was gone a while, and then returned with a servant woman who kept dipping a soft, hot cloth into a brew that smelled of ginger root, squeezing it out and holding it against my forehead, wrists, and ankles until the cloth cooled. When they finished, another *aj men*—an older woman who'd been burning incense and chanting outside the doorway—came in.

Said her name and bled my legs again while her assistant, also a woman, pressed a handful of hibiscus leaves against my forehead.

Three days later I awoke in a different, much larger chamber with a high ceiling and wide doorway. The upset stomach, dizziness, and chills were gone. And my eyes were no longer burning. Still, my throat was tight and on fire. I could only whisper. The older woman kept after me to sip hot *pici,* another foul tasting concoction she said was made from guava bark. She also reported that Gray Mouse was recovering, receiving the same treatment as me, but without the bleedings.

The *pici* helped my throat, but it made me sleep so deeply it took a long while for me to wake up. The women got me up and helped me into a sweatbath that was so small I had to crawl in on my hands and knees. Gray Mouse was there with the regal woman, so we couldn't speak freely. It wouldn't have mattered much. There was so much steam we couldn't see each other. When we finally came out our knees, feet, and hands were so blackened by the soot on the floor the assistant had to wash the three of us with buckets of shockingly cold water. Around dusk I noticed that the stabbing pain in my throat had lessened. I could talk again. And the world was standing still.

Looking up at a flat, beam-and-mortar ceiling with painted likenesses of Tollan merchants, holy men, and warriors painted on the walls, it was hard to realize that I was in Mutal. Considering how far a yelling man can be heard, I was five or six yell from the Great Plaza and Father's palace. The sound of chattering spider monkeys, chirping motmots and orioles, and an occasional hawk made it easier to believe that I was close to home. All I'd seen of the Tollan settlement, besides the dirty little sweat bath and the narrow, walled-in stairway to get down to it, was the sky. Across from my sleeping bench, painted in black, red, yellow, and green, the great goddess of Tollan seemed to stare at me, scold me, perhaps for hating Jatz'om, perhaps for thinking about ways to punish him, certainly for wanting to stop him from doing elsewhere what he'd done at Mutal. I kept my back to that wall. Whenever I felt her gaze penetrating me from behind, I closed my eyes and recited over and again, Father's parting words. *Palm Flower... We are always with you... You are a daughter of Mutal...*

The Tollan Settlement At Mutal

EVERY EVENING SINCE OUR ARRIVAL AT THE SETTLEMENT, Jatz'om looked in on me. By the fourth night it became obvious that he was arranging his visits so we wouldn't be alone, arriving after the elder *aj men* and her assistant arrived, leaving before they finished with me. I was grateful for that, and for only asking if there was anything he could do to make me more comfortable.

After nine days of confinement I insisted that I was as well as Gray Mouse—who had been out walking for two days. The forest was calling and I was a prisoner of a demon without a name. The *aj men* said I was too weak to go out. While she and Jatz'om were discussing it I got off the bench and, telling them I knew more about my condition than they did, ushered them out the door. I asked Jatz'om to get Gray Mouse for me and I tied the door drape behind him.

When Gray Mouse called I was already in my sarong. I let her in and she helped me with my hair. When she held up the jewel box I reached for the *kaloomte'* necklace but stopped. If Jatz'om saw me without it, especially at the settlement, he would complain—reason enough not to wear it. Also, I didn't want the Tollanos bowing to me at every turn, so I selected the simplest pieces of shell for my neck and ears. No wristlets, no anklets. Lastly, I got out my black body-paint and had Gray Mouse paint the death sign on my cheek, a black diagonal line with dots over and under it to show I was in mourning. That the tattoo on my other cheek was a jaguar claw was unsettling for both of us.

Following Gray Mouse, I went down the steps toward the sweat bath, but turned and passed between high walls that led onto a masonry patio. I stopped abruptly when I saw Jatz'om sitting with Sihyaj K'ahk', Standing Squirrel and two other first spears—Puma and Wolf judging from their headdresses. I'd not seen Sihyaj K'ahk' since the morning he left for Mutal. Fortunately, he had his back to me. Jatz'om followed me with his eyes, but made no comment as he listened to Sihyaj K'ahk'.

Those who told me the Tollan settlement had changed since I saw it last had greatly underestimated the extent of it. There was no sign of the seven, well-spaced clusters of pole-and-thatch, flat-roofed houses that I remembered. A tall and sprawling, gleaming red apron supporting six or seven groupings of white masonry structures separated by grass-covered, multileveled patios had replaced them. White walled and red trimmed masonry houses were stacked upon houses three, in some places four levels high.

Gray Mouse took me to the side of the terrace. Below us in a square, masonry courtyard a *k'uhul winik* cast offerings into a fire on top of a little shrine surrounded by smaller box-like houses. To the South and West the forest thinned considerably so the smoke blowing east from the multi-family compounds hung in the tangled patchwork of fields where farmers were chopping the overgrowth in preparation for clearing. To the South, behind the apron, the canopy rose thick and tall above heaps of dried wood and tangled vegetation, much of it dusted with white powder blown onto it from a limestone kiln.

Closer to the great apron on the East side I recognized a clump of boulders, one of which bore the Tollan emblem, cattails in red paint. Beyond them what had been a muddy ravine, a deep cut in the ground that filled in the rainy season, was gone. In its place were four fingers of clay, channels for runoff with flattened logs over them to serve as bridges. The regal looking woman told Gray Mouse they were growing avocado, nance, guava, and papaya as well as maize, beans, and squash. The water for drinking, cooking, and washing clothes came from a separate reservoir behind the apron. Although we couldn't see it, we could well see how the runoff from the many roofs, terraces, and stairways, especially the apron, fed into it.

We went around and descended the stairs. At the bottom Gray Mouse was concerned that I was breathing heavily. She wanted to take me back. Ahead of us was a flower market, and I couldn't resist. We had nothing to trade, but just seeing the dahlias, plumeria, sunflowers, calla lilies, and marigolds made me feel better. I was taking in the scent of palm flowers when a woman sent her barefoot daughter over with an offering of a leaf packet of cashews and words of welcome. Her mother was grateful for the coming of "the prophet." Somehow, she knew who I was. On our way back to the apron a woman with three little sprouts behind her bowed with both arms grasping her shoulders as we passed. An elderly farmer walking with a stick stopped in front of me took off his reed-hat and bowed. "Do you know me?" I asked in Tollan.

"With respect dear lady, are you not the wife of the prophet, the bringer of abundance and good fortune?"

Further on, a group of unmarried men—evidenced by their black body paint—were lounging under a tree. Because they were wearing Maya headdresses I went over to them and, as they would for any noblewoman, they stood up and bowed. "I came in with the procession from Tollan," I said. "You are warriors?" They acknowledged that they were. "We heard you fought bravely." Although I was wearing my hair in the Tollan fashion, I wondered if my flattened forehead would give me away. One of the men gave out a yelp and the others agreed. The shortest of them wanted to know if I knew Sihyaj K'ahk'. "I know him very well," I said. Their eyes widened and they glanced at each other. "You and your brothers fought in the Great Plaza?" What I really wanted to know is if they saw what happened at the palace.

The tallest man shook his head. "He could not have done it without us."

"We took down the men's houses." Another boasted. "Six of them."

"Ran them into the Great Plaza," his brother responded.

"What was it like there?" I asked.

"With respect lady, too terrible to say. Much blood—."

"It ran like water," another added.

"Did you take the palace? Did you see what happened?" I finally asked.

"When the palace was cleared they sent us to the residential districts—to keep the order."

I wanted to see if what I'd been told was the truth. "I have a friend, a first spear from Tollan called Standing Squirrel. Do you know him?" They looked at each other puzzled and shook their heads.

"What was it like to fight alongside Sihyaj K'ahk'?"

"With respect dear lady," the shortest one said, "our warlords got their orders from him, but we never really fought with him."

"We only saw him from a distance," the tall one added. "Is it true he swallows fire and walks through walls of flame without getting burned?"

Rather than answer I took my leave.

Demands

NOT WANTING TO UPSET ME FURTHER, GRAY MOUSE HADN'T told me that Jatz'om and Sihyaj K'ahk' had moved into my father's house in the Central District. That was wise of her. Had I known this earlier I might have done something that would have dishonored the Ich'aak name.

Gray Mouse and I were both standing as she drew a brush through my hair, preparing me for a walk to see more of the settlement when Jatz'om pushed aside my chamber curtain. "Leave us," he said to Gray Mouse. "Close the drape behind you. See that we are not interrupted." He paced and looked at the floor until the light dimmed. "Sit," he demanded.

I adjusted my mantle so it was even across my shoulders and positioned the jade god head on the *kaloomte'* necklace so it was in the center of my chest. Only then did I sit. "I have too much on my mind to worry about you," he said. He wasn't angry. Jatz'om rarely even raised his voice. Where ordinary men might bark at their spouses or beat them, as a devout *k'uhul winik*, Jatz'om went the other way. He proclaimed that his animal companion spirit was an Owl, but his manner was more like a boa constrictor. There were times however, many times, when his gentle way of telling me what I already knew, correcting my wrongs, treating me like a child, proclaiming how things are and how they will be, that I wished he were more like other men. Now, curiously, the determination in his voice had the opposite effect. He could say whatever he wanted and I didn't care.

"You know my life is not my own," he said. "You can hide from me, even hate me if you like—. You could at least face me when I speak to you. I am your husband." I turned, but kept my eyes diverted to the goddess's dripping hands on the wall. His pacing consisted of just a few steps in each direction. "I understand. You have been ill. You lost your family and you are entitled to your grieving. But there is too much that needs to be done. There are events coming that need your attention. Yax Nuun is the Ajaw Le now. There are important people here. They need to see you standing beside him with dignity—and a smile on your face. Take three or four, five days if you must. The gathering of the new council will be seven *k'inob* from tomorrow. You will sit with us to witness the authorization of the new ministers."

Jatz'om waited for me to say something, but I remained silent. "As the seasons pass," he continued, "you will come to see that what we did what was necessary, all for the good. Until then you will provide a proper household, one that commands the respect of my people and yours. We must set an example of the *noh tzol*. You are Mistress of the Palace now. As well as the residence. I have informed the servants. Turtle Cloud will remain as Keeper of the Palace Grounds, but the others will be replaced with Tollanos. People I can trust. You made a proper home for us at Tollan and at Ho' Noh Witz. Here, it needs to be elegant beyond what we had before." Again, I made no comment.

When he sat on the bench beside me, I moved away. "Dear One, there is nothing you cannot have now," he said. "Yax Nuun will soon be seated. Mutal will prosper greatly under his rule. I will see to it." *He is too young and too full of your ways. Mutal was already prospering under my father's rule.* Jatz'om got up and walked toward the doorway. "I will be busy with Sihyaj K'ahk' and preparing Yax Nuun for initiation. You will see to the making of his garments and regalia. For the Descent of Spirits he will wear an Owl ceremonial costume—plaited headdress with eagle feathers, feathered shield, and jade collar. I want it to cover his chest completely. After the Descent of Spirits, he, Sihyaj K'ahk' and I will be visiting Siaan K'aan and other nearby centers. He will need proper attire for these visits as well, so you have much to do. Tell me how many servants you need and I will secure them." I said nothing and kept my hands folded in my lap as Jatz'om approached the doorway. "You swore an oath before the goddess that you would support me in carrying my burden. Like it or not, as my wife and Custodian of K'awiil we carry it together. You will never speak against me, my charter or the *noh tzol*."

Demand all you like. It will get you nowhere. Jatz'om pushed aside the curtain and then the doorway drape. I got up to close the drape behind him, but he came in again. "Out of respect for your family I will see that they have a proper burial. The Ich'aak were never my enemy. I know you do not want to hear it, but their sacrifice was necessary for the fulfillment of the prophecy. Instead of blaming me, you should feel proud of them for offering their lives to sustain the world. Sleep here tonight, but gather your things. Servants will be here early. A house close to the palace is being prepared for you. You can do your grieving there. Five days. No more."

When he was gone Gray Mouse came in. I could see in her watery eyes that she'd overheard what he said. She set a water jar down and followed me to the sleeping bench. Her sad eyes made me reach out to her and we cried into each other's shoulders.

The Guest House

BECAUSE JATZ'OM'S VISITORS WERE OFTEN LORDS, underlords, and ministers, they were accommodated in well furnished guest houses separate from the compounds where merchants and dignitaries, including their attendants and servants, were sheltered. Jatz'om thought that by allowing me to grieve in one of these more elegantly decorated guest houses, he could have some peace and keep me from seeing what was going on at court and in the palace. He should have known better.

The back wall of Father's palace rose atop a high, grass-covered mound forty paces in front of a row of three such houses. Jatz'om had my things delivered to the house on the end which made it easy to get to, but my view of the Great Plaza was blocked on one side by the steep palace mound, and on the other by trees. Gray Mouse and I unpacked my necessaries while her husband set a fire in the brazier. As the red clouds began showing streaks of purple beneath the blue sky, we went outside and said our gratitude for the day. After they went to the servants compound, I didn't feel like unpacking anything more, so I sat on the polished mahogany bench that butted up against the front of the house and watched bats diving and swirling around the canopy at the end of the alleyway. *Five days to grieve. How generous.*

Near to dark I heard voices coming from the palace. When they became loud and boisterous, I went inside and, not wanting to shut out the night air, kept the drape tied back. I had snuffed the torch and was nearly asleep when shouts of foul language and streams of laughter brought me to my feet. My father would never have tolerated that kind of language in the palace. Judging from the bright red glow in the arms of the ceiba that stood alongside it, the brazier atop the front steps was in full blaze, so much so it dimly lit the grassy trail that ran long in front of the guest houses. With the houses backed by forest and the palace mound rising high in front of them, the long strip of grass between made the place look like a canyon. I walked down the way wondering what I could do to shut out the noise so I could get some sleep.

As the sky darkened, the talking and laughing got louder. When they started drumming, I went over to the mound, cupped my hands and called up the back wall. "Quiet!" I hadn't shouted like that since I was little. I shouted again, even louder. Nothing changed. *Warlords and their warriors. All Tollanos. The palace is no place for warriors to be celebrating.*

Suddenly the drumming stopped. Someone was talking. I went to the mound again and listened. Sihyaj K'ahk'. His voice was harsh like a howler, but he laughed like a spider monkey. I couldn't hear everything he said, but beyond praising the leaders of the Tollan warrior houses, he and another were awarding them gifts. Weapons and trophies. The next to speak was Ajaw K'inich Bahlam. He had flowery words for the Centipede warlords, and each of them received gifts of some kind. Sihyaj K'ahk' gave a short introduction to Jatz'om which was met with thunderous applause, shouts, and whistling. His words were too soft and muddled for me to hear, but afterward they applauded, again with shouts and whistling. Their drumming and singing filled the canyon, so I went back to the house, tied the drape, got onto my bench and cupped the pillow over my ears.

On and on they went. Finally, I'd had enough. It wasn't just the noise that made my blood boil, it was the disrespect, the insult of warriors celebrating their "victory" over my father in his own palace. The kub I'd worn all day, white with standing cormorants embroidered in red around the neck and sleeves, was badly wrinkled and soiled at the bottom. But it was at hand. I pulled it over my head, gathered my hair in back, tied it with a leather cord, and stormed into the grassy canyon.

Standing barefoot in front of the grass covered mound and the white plastered wall that rose above it, I shouted again. They couldn't hear me, but the shouting felt good, so I hurled a stream of insults at Sihyaj K'ahk', even shocked myself by calling him, among other things, a dog's rectum. I screamed at Jatz'om as well, hurling punishing words at him for betraying me, violating Father's alliance, slaughtering my family, lying to me, and desecrating Father's holy palace.

Torchlight. Someone was coming. Gray Mouse. "What are you doing here?" I asked.

"Forgive me, mistress. We heard the noise. I heard you shouting when I approached. Celebrating are they?"

"A victory celebration. They think—." Someone called my name. Cave Frog stood with a torch at the corner of the palace. Having caught my attention, he gestured to ask what I wanted. I called up to him. "Tell your master to take his celebration elsewhere. He is violating my Father's palace. He is the visitor here, not me!" Cave Frog shrugged his shoulders and fanned his hands outward, a gesture that meant there was nothing he could do about it.

I took the torch from Gray Mouse. "Help me," I said. I dashed across the grass so fast I nearly trampled a little brocket deer who scampered out of the way. I went into the house, put the torch in a holder, picked up two of the nearest bundles and pointed to another. "That one! All of them! Everything—outside. I am not the guest here. I refuse to be treated like one."

Back and forth we went, carrying the lighter bundles, baskets, pouches and feather tubes, then dragging the heavy crates containing my bowls, vases, and plates, including the figurines Ix Chab' made at Ho' Noh Witz. We dragged everything that belonged to me across to the foot of the mound. Cave Frog was gone. Realizing that someone had heard me and told Jatz'om, I shouted again, loud as I could. "I am not a guest here! This is the holy palace of Ajaw Chak Tok' Ich'aak! I am his daughter! I belong here—you do not! You are violating sacred ground!" Getting no response, I went over and sat on the mahogany bench. Gray Mouse sat beside me. "Mutal is my home," I said. "Mutal is your home. Jatz'om and his dogs are violators. I will not have it."

"With respect mistress, you should get some sleep."

"Not here. These houses are for guests." Again I shouted, "I am not a guest!" The truth of it woke the demon in me. I got up and walked over to the bundles. "Bring the torch," I said. Gray Mouse followed and held the flame over the bundles so I could find the leather pouch that held my obsidian blade. "Come with me," I said with a tight grip on the hafting.

We went into the house. With Gray Mouse pointing the torch so I could see, I slashed the cords that supported the three heavy fabrics that divided the back of the house into three rooms. It was a struggle but I dragged them out the door to the center of the canyon, between the house and the palace mound. Next came a wall hanging, the not very well painted likeness of a turtle with three stars on its carapace. I flung it onto the heaped up fabrics. Rather than untie the cords that supported the thick doorway drape, I hacked at them with the blade until it fell. Gray Mouse wanted to put the torch in a holder and help, but I needed to do this myself.

Hanging straps, sashes and baskets, blankets, gourds, and bark-tubes with flowers in them, everything hanging on pegs went out the door. The feline pelts on the floor made me hesitate, but those too went onto heap. Deer cushions, tightly stuffed pillows and poles, a wood bench with wooden stools, chamberpots, calabash cups, ceramic platters, and four armloads of logs that made me sweat like never before—all of it went onto the heap. With nothing left to remove, I smashed a water jar into the brazier sending ash and coals across the smooth white plaster. The smell of ash reminded me of the cave where I had my audience with the great goddess. I decided I was performing a kind of anointing. A cleansing. I took the torch from Gray Mouse, went to the heap in front of the house and pressed the flames to the fabrics all around.

Startled, Gray Mouse couldn't believe what I'd done. Looking back and forth between me and the precious items going up in smoke, she worried what Jatz'om would do to me. But standing there with the torch in my hand and the sweat running down my face, all I could do was laugh. Mimicking the way I'd seen the *aj men* at Tollan approach the great cauldrons of fire to offer blood-splattered cloths to the gods, I strode to the middle house holding the torch with both hands as if it were a banner, entered, and offered everything that would burn to my father. When that was done I went to the last house and made another offering. I hadn't intended to do any of this, but the demon in me could not be restrained.

The smoke and the blazing reds, yellows and oranges that brightened the canyon finally got someone's attention. Sentries came running, took one look at the smoke spewing from the doorways, turned and ran back shouting, "Fire! Guest houses! Behind the palace! Water! Water!" Gray Mouse and I stood in front of my bundles with our backs to the mound. It amazed us how long it took before the alarm conches sounded—panicky patterns of two short bleats and a long one.

Concerned about my belongings as the heat intensified, Gray Mouse and I began moving them to the far end of the trail where men ran back and forth to fill and then deliver buckets of water through the doorways. After a while they too, just stood back and watched. Up on the terrace, Jatz'om, Sihyaj K'ahk', K'inich Bahlam, their warlords and others were watching. I'd faced them squarely and folded my arms when the thatched roof of the third house went up in a shower of sparks and flames. One by one the roof beams collapsed and fell in, turning each house into a sort of brazier with flames reaching nearly as high as the canopy.

Among the sixty or more onlookers who gathered at the end of the path to watch, I saw Yax Nuun, Ix Chab', and their attendants. The fire was just smoldering, so I gestured for them and a while later they came around from the other side of the canyon. Being only nine, Ix Chab' was frightened, so I sat on a box and held her in front of me, trying to explain why I did what I did. Her brother was excited by all the commotion, but he also worried what his father might do to me.

I went to the residence with Ix Chab' and spent the night in her chamber, the same one I'd slept in when I was just a flower. We were wide awake from the excitement, so I told her some of the things I remembered about my family, our celebrations, and what the palace was like when it was new. Rembering in the dark like that brought those days back for me, and it bound our hearts together more tightly.

Late the next morning Yax Nuun came asking me to repeat some of the stories I'd told his sister. In particular, he wanted to hear about the time his grandfather was punished for releasing a jaguar into the wild, an animal his father had raised from a cub to be sacrificed. He and his sister had heard very little about my father's pilgrimage to Tollan, particularly the trouble they had. I thought it best not to talk about it when they were little. The circumstances seemed appropriate, so I told how their grandfather was attacked on the way back. Forty of the seventy people who left Tollan were killed. Everything they carried was taken. One story led to another and we continued talking well into the day.

HEARING MYSELF TELL THE CHILDREN ABOUT THEIR grandfather and then listening to their confusion and questions surrounding his and their grandmother's execution made me feel more like their mother and less like their custodian. Being eleven and having witnessed the extent to which his father had been respected when he ruled at Ho' Noh Witz and then receiving a sacred charter from the lords of Tollan, Yax Nuun had considered his father near to a god. So much so, he couldn't believe he lied to me and gave the order to have his grandparents, aunt, and uncles killed. In a quieter moment Yax Nuun confided to us that, even before the attack, he was afraid of Sihyaj K'ahk'. Now he hated him. And he felt guilty. "It was my fault," he said. "They killed them so I would inherit the Mat." I pulled him close and assured him that it wasn't his fault. Although he'd never met his grandparents, he had feelings for them because of my stories. He was as excited to actually meet them. "How could Father do such a thing?" he asked. The tears in his eyes and the desperation in his voice gripped my heart.

"I am afraid, Mother." Ix Chab' admitted. "What if the goddess tells Father we are not helping him with his charter? Would he have us killed?"

"That is not going to happen." I said this trying to think of a reason why not. "Your father would never give such an order. He cherishes you both."

"Does he still cherish you?" my daughter asked.

Telling the truth was so important to my father he had us take the oath of the *winik haahil* on the day of our initiation, an oath that bound us to always tell the truth no matter how embarrassing or painful. "Once bound," I said, "always bound. You will understand when you are older. There are different ways of cherishing."

Yax Nuun leaned against my arm. "If Sihyaj K'ahk' came to establish a *noh tzol* here, why not just tell grandfather what he wanted—or send him away?"

"Your grandfather would never leave his *caah*." Yax Nuun needed to know, so I told him about the lords of Tollan wanting him to replace my father. "You were brought up in the Tollan ways, so they know you will follow their path, keep the Tollan order in the lowlands."

"I have no loyalty to Tollan," he said.

"But you are loyal to your father."

"Not to his charter. I would never—."

"Yax Nuun. You may think this in your heart, but promise me you will never let your father hear you say that. Listen to me, very carefully. If he thought you would not help him carry out his charter—. Just promise me you will never speak like this in front of him. When you are older you will come to know how important it is for you to do whatever he wants. At least until you are seated."

Yax Nuun promised. "But not Sihyaj K'ahk'. I have no loyalty to him. I will never do what he wants!"

I'd been thinking about my son's earlier question—what the lords of Tollan gained by killing my family. I remembered Jumping Squirrel saying that Waka' had been a better trading partner for Tollan than Mutal. Not wanting my words to carry beyond the walls of Ix Chab's chamber, I pulled the children close and spoke softly. "This too will be our secret. I am thinking that another reason your grandparents were killed was because of trade and tribute. The lords of Tollan depend upon Mutal because the goods and fineries from the other lowland centers are eventually traded here. Your grandfather's merchants provided Tollan with flint, chert, and cotton mantles. Salt and textiles from the north. Obsidian and *kakaw* beans from the south. All their jaguar, ocelot, and deer pelts come from here. Their ritual implements as well: bark paper, copal, stingray spines, bone, and coral. Jade and shell stones are turned into jewels here. Jade and feathers."

"Grandfather was killed for jade and feathers?" Yax Nuun didn't want to believe it.

"And Sihyaj K'ahk' cleared the way."

Yax Nuun sat up straight. "When I take the Mat I will send Sihyaj K'ahk' back to Tollan. I never want to see his face again. Not ever!"

"What should we do, Mother?" Ix Chab' asked.

My answer was less than comforting. "There is nothing to be done. Just remember that you are as much Maya as you are Tollano. You carry the blood of a long line of Mutal rulers. Your grandfather was Ajaw Chak Tok Ich'aak." I turned to Yax Nuun. "While your father is preparing you for manhood and teaching you the Tollan ways, remember that your sister and I will always be here to help you. I will help you remember your Mayan roots. They called your grandfather great because he made Mutal great. Remember how I told you the son replaces the grandfather, walks for him on the face of the earth?" Yax Nuun nodded. "Talk to your grandfather. Both of you. He is in the sky now. And he will always be with you."

"Will he show us how to make a grand contribution?" Ix Chab' asked.

I took their hands. "Here in my father's house I make a jadestone promise to you both. Whatever happens, we will make the best of it. We will find our contributions. As long as I have breath, I will always be with you. Let us promise to talk like this often—and to speak only the truth to each other in the manner of the *winik haahil*."

We put our hands together and they said in turn, "Jadestone promise."

The Prophecy

AS WHEN THEY WERE SAPLINGS, YAX NUUN AND IX CHAB' SAT with their legs under a blanket and they leaned against me, the three of us on my sleeping bench with pillows at our backs. Not wanting to frighten Ix Chab', her father and I had long ago made Yax Nuun promise that he would not tell his sister about the prophecy and its warning. Now having heard what her father did because of it, and because she was asking, I decided it was time she knew. "Tollan was just a village when it was given," I began. "They say she reached her greatness because her rulers—men whose faces, tongues, and ways were foreign to each other—took the K'awiil anointing and walked together down the road of abundance."

"What brought them together?" Ix Chab' asked.

"The Yax Hal Witz," her brother interjected. Ix Chab' already knew about First True Mountain, that it was the first to appear at the making of the world when the waters receded, that it was full maize, *kakaw*, and fruit trees, and that Chahk, the lord of thunder, split it open for the maize god to make his ascent. It was also the place where First Mother ground the yellow and white maize nine times until it became human flesh.

"As all Tollan noblemen do," I continued, "your father and I went there on pilgrimage with his father and mother. The mountain took my breath away. It was the grandest thing I'd ever seen. They said the white mantel around his neck was made of very cold stone, tiny specks that fell from the sky and bit the hands that held them. At night he vomited up fire and sparks and smoke so high it lit up the clouds. It never stopped. Even when it rained. There were many villages on his flanks. People who lived two days away could see the white mantel and his fiery breath. The chiefs and rulers had pleased the mountain lord for many *k'atunob*. In return the villages were blessed with fertile soils, bountiful harvests, and plentiful game. Water flowed down the mountain in streams and it bubbled up from the ground. As their abundance and prosperity increased, some of the vil lages became large centers — ."

"That was when the trouble began." Yax Nuun interrupted. "The rulers said they were as powerful as the gods."

"Some claimed to be their natural born sons. They wanted to be worshiped and they demanded tribute, not only for the *caah*, but also for themselves. They had singers going about singing songs to their glory. The *k'uhul winikob* shouted the rulers' titles and bathed their bodies in clouds of copal."

"The gods became angry," Yax Nuun said.

"The rulers were raising stone monuments that carried their likeness and praised their names, instead of the likenesses and names of the gods. So they held a great council at Yax Hal Witz. As your father tells it, some of the gods said the fourth world was a failure. They said it should be destroyed so they can start over. Others said that because the puffed-up rulers no longer praised their names or fed them properly, and because they were misleading their people and hoarding the bounties they received, they alone should be put down. Finally, the gods decided. They would destroy the world and make new creatures who would know how to properly feed them and praise their names.

"The goddess told them to wait," Yax Nuun commented."

"She pleaded with her brothers, asking them to give her a chance to warn the rulers, saying they would change their ways, walk a more respectful and grateful path if they knew what was going to happen. To win their approval, she agreed that if the rulers did not change their ways, she would help them carry out their plan of destruction."

My daughter pressed herself tight against me and gripped my arm. "Will we become monkeys Mother, like in the world before this one?"

"That will not happen, Ix Chab'. You need not be afraid. The goddess got her way."

Her brother couldn't restrain himself. "Now tell about the prophecy," he said. "And the destruction."

"The prophecy says that, if the rulers do not change their arrogant and selfish ways, the *chahkob* will withhold their rain for an entire season. Everywhere. After that the locust lords will send their warriors to eat the leaves. Everything green. Then the lightning lords will set fire to the forests and the earth lord will shake the ground."

Ix Chab' reached for a pillow and put it under her head. "Remember sweet flower, I said. "This is what the goddess said *could* happen, not what *will* happen."

"What else?" she asked.

"When nothing is left standing, the sky turns dark and there comes a great flood."

"The lords would all be drowned," Yax Nuun added. "Only the strongest of men would reach the top of the Yax Hal Witz. They will wash themselves with their tears and eat each others' flesh."

"That is enough, Yax Nuun. We have frightened your sister enough."

"Tell her the good happening, when the lords of Tollan heard the prophecy."

My daughter's eyes widened. "What good?"

"Your father says the goddess only got part of what she asked for. The gods said the rulers needed to be given proof that her warning was real. The Earth lord said he would provide the proof. He went to Yax Hal Witz and persuaded him to show the rulers the full force of their power."

"What did he do?" Ix Chab' asked.

"The great mountain vomited up smoke and fire and ash. It blocked the face of Ajaw K'in for twenty *k'inob*. Dark as night. And everything was covered in ash."

"What was good about it?" Ix Chab' asked.

"You will see. The villages closest to the mountain were buried. Farther out the houses and trees were all covered with ash. Because it was farther yet, Tollan still had a clean river, so people came from great distances. Yax Nuun, you tell your sister the good part."

"The chiefs and rulers went inside the mountain at Tollan. Down in a cave the goddess told them about the prophecy. She said darkness and ash was a message from the gods."

"So they were the first to hear the prophecy," I added.

"The good part is, the chiefs and rulers sat together and decided to walk the path of abundance. So they could trust each other, they took the K'awiil anointing and agreed that instead of one ruler at Tollan, there would be three, one for each of the sky stones."

Ix Chab' scrunched her eyebrows. "Is that true, Mother? Did that really happen?"

"If it happened at all, it happened a very long time ago. Still, the story is being sung and danced in many places, especially at Tollan."

"Could the bad part really happen?" she asked.

I put my arm around both their shoulders and pulled them close. "You know how I always tell the truth?" They shook their heads. "Can you promise you will never tell your father?"

"Jadestone promise," they said in unison.

"When we lived at Tollan, because everyone else believed it, I believed it. When we moved to Ho' Noh Witz I began to think differently. Now I think the prophecy is just an old story the lords of Tollan use to get their way. One thing I do know: there is no reason to worry about it. Hundreds of *tunob* have passed since the prophecy was given. If the rulers had refused to change their ways, the bad things would have happened long ago."

Yax Nuun squirmed and got down from the bench. "Father would have your head if he heard you say that."

"Your father has his beliefs. I have mine. Remember, Yax Nuun. You promised. If we are to talk openly like this, we need to trust each other."

"I remember," he said timidly.

Retaliation

FOR SEVERAL DAYS, IX CHAB' AND I HEARD SOUNDS IN THE night, shouting, sometimes screaming, always in the distance and in different directions. Often it was accompanied by faint glows of fire in the canopy. I'd heard that Sihyaj K'ahk' was going to replace the members of father's council and those who held the various court offices, but I didn't think he would remove them and their families forcibly from their homes. I could understand taking their staffs of office, perhaps even their robes, but to turn them out and burn their homes so the Tollanos replacing them could have new ones built, was an outrage.

It quickly became obvious: the noblemen that Jatz'om and Sihyaj K'ahk' had chosen to accompany us to Mutal were selected because they would make suitable replacements for the seated rulers, ministers, council members, warlords, and holy men throughout the lowlands. In conversations with these men who expressed eagerness to put down roots, start fresh, and spread the word of the prophecy, it never occurred to me that they were to be replacements.

On the fourth day of my grieving, Gray Mouse came back from the reservoir saying she heard that in addition to the members of the council and office holders — merchants, tribute counters, holy men, scribes — they would be replacing the palace servants. My servants, fan bearers, cooks, and carriers, litter bearers, grounds keepers and the attendants. One of the women at the reservoir reported that a neighbor, a tanner and his wife, were reduced to servants and sent to Siaan K'aan for speaking out against Sihyaj K'ahk'. Others said the servants of Maya noblemen were being reduced to slavery. And Jaguar Warriors refusing to serve under the Tollan banner were either being killed or sent to chop and carry stone at the quarries.

Outraged, I went to the palace and found Jatz'om in the patio with a Tollano I knew to be a builder. It was rude to interrupt, but I didn't care. "Husband," I said sternly. "If Sihyaj K'ahk' even thinks about replacing Gray Mouse or Turtle Cloud I will do something drastic. You know I will."

Jatz'om didn't bother to look up from the plaster model of a building in front of him. "Dear One," he said calmly. "Your attendant and her husband will not be replaced. You need not worry." I turned and walked away.

On the fifth day of my grieving, Ix Chab' and I heard conches at the warrior compounds sounding call-to-weapons. Three times during the day, once after dark. Again I had to rely on word from Gray Mouse and her husband to learn that the bodies of Tollan sentries and warriors had been found, axed and stabbed. In one instance, men wearing bark-cloth over their heads with eye-holes, set fire to the house where days before, Sihyaj K'ahk's choice for Minister of Water had taken up residence. When he came out of his house the rebel Maya took him down with a spearthrower.

On our walks around the central district it was obvious that the Maya and Tollanos were avoiding one another, not even talking as they passed each other in the Great Plaza or on the causeways. They wouldn't even trade with each other in the marketplace.

Growing up, I remember there were always twenty guards who patrolled the steps that led up to the palace. Another twenty guarded the residence day and night. Now there were forty guards at the palace and fifty at the residence. Instead of standing firm around the perimeter, they roamed the patios, courtyards, hallways, and steps with weapons drawn. Jatz'om said it was just a precaution. Ever since Yax Nuun could walk I worried that he or his sister would be taken and sacrificed. If that worry was like carrying the burden of two buckets of water on a yoke, it grew to four on the journey from Tollan. With what was happening at Mutal, those buckets had become rain barrels.

Firestorm

APPARENTLY MY HUSBAND HAD BEEN COUNTING THE DAYS of my grieving because, early on the sixth day, servants with muscles like stone haulers came to Ix Chab's chamber announcing that they'd come to move my belongings into the chamber next to his. I didn't want any part of it, so Ix Chab' and I went for a walk between the reservoirs. The water levels were still high and the ducks made us laugh, splashing and upending their tails.

Whenever I walked the reservoir trail I was reminded of the proclamation my father made before the *caah* on the morning of his accession. He said, "I have not come to rule; I have come to contribute." The children heard this many times, but I couldn't resist saying it again when Ix Chab' asked if I was still hoping to make a contribution to Mutal beyond my duties as mistress of the palace and residence. Her question stayed with me because I didn't have an answer for her.

Later in the day, alone and seated on my mat at the workshop, I turned to my *ch'ulel*—what there was of it—for an answer. I closed my eyes and took a deep breath. *Considering what has happened, is there anything I can do to contribute to Mutal? Have I made my grand contribution? Or is there something more I can do?*

The answer came clear: *You cannot even think of making a contribution until you speak your mind to your husband.* After some additional back and forth discussion, I called for Gray Mouse. She helped me into my full-length white gown, a Maya *kub* she had acquired from a woman said to be one of the best embroiderers in the *caah*. Around the neck was fine stitching: yellow, radiating leaves of a sunflower with darker yellow, almost brown, thread used for the inner part of the sunflower where the green seeds turn brown. This gown, together with Father's jade necklace and Mother's jade florets in my ears, gave me the confidence to do what I needed to do.

With the color gone from the sky and stars starting to appear, I approached the guards who stood in front of Jatz'om's mat-covered doorway. "I want to see my husband," I said. The more muscular of the two—whose face reminded me of a howler monkey—bowed slightly and said his master was not to be disturbed. Having anticipated this response I turned, went down the hall, took a burning torch from its holder and confronted the guards with it. What could they do? They were certainly not going to harm the mistress of the residence. Fully prepared to do whatever I had to do, even set the drape ablaze if necessary, I thrust the torch in their faces. "Let me pass!" I demanded.

Monkey Face tried to divert the torch with the blunt end of his spear, but I had a tight grip on it. I pushed the spear aside and thrust the flames at his chest. Apparently the flames licked his face as well because he yelped. He dropped the spear and crouched to the floor babbling and gripping his neck and chin. With both hands on his spear-shaft, the other guard attempted to push me back, so I thrust the torch at the hand closest to me, and then the other until he dropped the spear. Jatz'om pulled the mat aside.

"What is this?" he asked. The shorter man quickly stood. Grasping his burned hand, he was about to speak but Jatz'om ordered him to take his companion away and find someone to tend to their wounds.

With a smirk on his face and shaking his head, Jatz'om stood aside and I entered what used to be my father's sleeping chamber. I set the torch in a holder on the front wall. Jatz'om turned and raised his eyebrows. "With your hair like that and in that *kub* you look—.

"Mayan? You may have forgotten, but I have not."

"I just meant—."

"I have come to tell you, my grieving has just begun." Jatz'om made a smacking sound with his lips, turned toward the brazier and put in some ocote sticks to raise the flame. I'd avoided that chamber because it was the place where father and mother were executed, but now I was prepared to confront it. Whether because clothing now hung on the wall pegs, or because I was taller, the room was smaller than I remembered. Even the roof beams which I imagined to be rounder than the fattest of men were barely as round as me. And darker. The thatching had recently been replaced. The floor, although covered with pelts, was cluttered with Jatz'om bundles, boxes, and baskets. The walls were painted red instead of white. And the wall with the built-in sleeping bench had a mural above it, a thick band of blue water below where red and yellow fish nibbled on green lily pads, two of which cleverly disguised smoke holes in the center.

One thing familiar was the odor of stale tobacco, the reason why the air glowed orange. When Jatz'om and I began living together, I asked if he could refrain from smoking his cigars inside. He replied that, because it was a "breath-offering" to the goddess, he needed to do it inside as well as outside.

He went back to his sleeping bench and sat. "What do you intend dear one, coming here dressed like that?"

"I have come to remind you that I am not just your wife and the mother of your children. I am also my father's daughter and a woman of Mutal."

Again, a smirk. I could see in his eyes he was asking the goddess to shield him from my intrusion into their world. It made me want to slap his face. "Say what you want to say. Quietly. There is no need to wake the household."

I'd said the opening words I rehearsed, calmly and with dignity. But that condescending smirk let the demon out of his cage. Close at hand was the tall drinking cup his father had gifted to him when he received his charter. He saw me look and then reach for it. "Put that down," he said. I raised it over my shoulder, poised to throw it at him. "You are above this, dear one. I will hear what you have to say. Just put it down. Sit and we will talk." He got off the bench and put his hand out, expecting me to hand over the cup—the cup filled with precious memories of his father and the cold, sweet and foamy kakaw they shared together on that fateful day.

"You sit!" I hurled the cup over his shoulder with full force. It smashed against the wall and the pieces fell onto his blanket. "I will talk. You will listen!"

He stared at me with pursed lips and mean, squinty eyes. He inhaled deeply, probably asking the goddess if he should strike back or cage his own demon. Ever the composed holy man, he went to the bench and collected the shards, holding the larger pieces together with the hope of making them whole again with glue. "Are you satisfied?" He said. "Now remove yourself from my chamber. I will not—."

"AAAAAAAHH!" I screamed. My claws came out. "AAAAAAAHH!" I screamed as loudly as I could, not caring if I woke everyone in the residence. And beyond. Jatz'om went to the doorway and held the drape aside. Ignoring the invitation for me to leave, I shouted again. "How could you? How could you do this to me—to your children? To Mutal?" Trying hopelessly to contain my thunder so it didn't wake the children and their attendants, he quickly closed the drape over the doorway. "What kind of man orders the death of his wife's family? Who do you think you are? You are certainly no *k'uhul winik*."

He went to his bench and brushed the remaining shards—and ceramic dust—into the corner with his hand. "I am a son of the goddess," he whispered with his back to me. "You are privileged to—." With fists flailing, I struck his back and shoulder. He turned to grab my arms but I broke through his defenses and connected with his chest and clipped his ear. "You are a son of Xibalba!" I shouted. While the demon in me wanted to kill him for what he'd done, the wife in me wanted to wake him to the truth that he was also a man. "Your goddess is a demon! No mother would have her children killed. Not for any reason!" As he sunk to the floor in the corner and covered his head, I pounded at his arms and hands.

"My father—," he tried to explain.

I stepped aside. "You think because he anointed you *kaloomte'* you have the right to kill? The title gives *others* the authority to rule. Not you! You defile your titles! You are a slave to your father!"

I went over to the wooden bench, threw off the clothing that had been draped across it, and sat. "How could you do this? My father trusted your father..." Tears came and I swiped them away so I wouldn't be interrupted. "He fulfilled his promise. He kept the alliance strong. There was no reason to kill them. You could have sent them away."

Jatz'om pulled his knees up and embraced them. "He would not have—.

Wrongly, he thought I was tiring. I went and stood over him. "I will talk!" I shouted. "For once, you will listen!" He raised the palms of his hands to calm me. I slapped them down and leaned close enough to smell his tobacco breath. "Demon!" He covered his ears. "You are no *winik haa-hil*! You are a vile beast!" I dug my claws in where I knew they would do the most damage. "You stand proud and speak softly, but I know you for what you are. You are a scared little man, afraid to refuse his father, cling-ing to the mossy skirts of a cold-hearted goddess."

"Careful," he said, hiding his face.

"Or what?" The shout made me cough. I was loosing my voice. "Is she going to have me killed? Is that how she gets her way? Is that how you get your way, having your *dog* put down anyone who gets in your way?"

"Say what you will of me, but you will not —"

"I will say what I want!" I choked. I couldn't shout. I stood back, went to the wooden bench and sat. I cleared my throat and wiped my eyes with my *kub*. "Do you know what you have done? You not only cut my heart out, you cut the heart out of Mutal. She was alive and prospering. Now, she is choking. You and your Owl are choking the life out of this great tree. And the children. Ix Chab' trembled when I told her about the proph-ecy."

"No one asked you to tell her."

"She needed to know. You forced it on her. Now they fear for their own lives."

"I explained it to them—."

"They are too young! All they understand is that you killed their grandparents and you think it was for good reasons. They—and I—will never trust you."

"I would never—."

"You did! And now we know: the goddess rules your heart. If she told you to put down your own son or daughter you would not hesitate." Jatz'om got up and sat on the sleeping bench. My hair and the entwined cotton serpents that held it up had broken and covered my face. I flung them back and tucked my hair under the embroidered sunflower. "Was it not enough to execute the men in my family? Were you afraid my mother or my sister would claim the Mat?"

"They were sacrificed, not executed."

"Whatever word you use, you had them put down. They are just as dead. Tell me, why the women?"

"They could bear sons. Yax Nuun had to be—."

"The one remaining Ich'aak, groomed to favor the ways of your people." My hair kept falling in front of my face. If I'd had my blade with me I would have cut it off. "Tell me true. Was it your decision or your father's to execute my family?"

I took his pause to mean he wasn't going to answer, but he surprised me. "The lords. All of them. They decided when you and I were just saplings. When my father gave me the charter I asked that he privilege one of the other sons with it."

"What did he say to that?"

"The goddess said I had to do it. It was the reason for the alliance."

"Explain this to me! I want to understand. How does a goddess called Mother of All, order the killing of her children?"

"There are times when a few must be sacrificed so the many may prosper. You know how it is, bargaining with the gods. We feed them; they feed us. New life rises from old bones, much as new maize rises from the buried seeds."

"But you destroyed maize that had not yet matured. Sacrifices are made by *k'uhul winikob* authorized to insure fertility, bounty, and the continuation of the world. You had my family put down because your father wants to see his grandson on the Mat—increased tribute and trade."

"I understand how you could see it that way."

"Ayaahh! There is no other way to see it!" Had I not been loosing my voice the demon would have lashed out again.

"Your family was sacrificed to save the world. Theirs was a noble death. Your father was walking the path of destruction."

"How can you say that? What do you or your father know of my father's path?"

"The monuments he and your ancestors planted at Precious Forest carry their faces, not the faces of the gods. They praise their names and honor their contributions. Not the gods. The *k'uhul winikob* feed incense and prayers to these men. The gods have been neglected here. That alone—."

"You are blind, Jatz'om. Your father and the goddess have convinced

67

you that your charter will save the world and bring the dawning of abundance. What it actually does is establish a flow of bounty from the lowlands, directly into your father's hands. You destroyed my family for jewels and feathers!"

Jatz'om pulled a blanket off one of the pegs, put it around his shoulders and went back to his bench. "You are the one who is blind, woman. You misjudge my father and the other lords. You are envious of their contributions. And mine..." *Ayaahh, after thirteen tunob you do not know me.* "Your burden is slight compared to ours. We do what we do, not for jewels and feathers, but to show the Makers that we know how to praise their names and feed them what they want. Say what you like, I am devoted to the goddess because in her prophecy I see the hope of sustinance and prosperity for all men. The only way to it is to bring men into harmony with the Makers." *And you will slaughter anyone who stands in your way.* "You know I have no interest in jewels or feathers. You saw how readily I gave them up at Ho' Noh Witz." I stood and tucked even more strands of hair under my gown in back. I had to admit, Jatz'om often complained that his jewels and feathers were a burden. "Have you considered, Dear One? Your family's sacrifice is also yours. Letting them go and not resisting the winds of change may be the great contribution you have been talking about ever since we met."

Grand, not great. I went up to him and pointed my finger in his face. "You can tell your dog what to do, but not me! Not here. No longer. This is not Tollan. You are an intruder here. You should be sleeping at the visitor's compound—or with your dog at the settlement. This is my father's house. He built it." I went to the other side of the room and put my hand on the torch. Jatz'om's eyes widened. I wanted him to know that I could set the place on fire if I wanted to. "My father built this residence and the palace," I said. "My ancestors built this *caah*. They ruled here for over three hundred *tunob*. And they are still here, watching over her, protecting her. You will not destroy what they built, not in one *tun*, not in a hundred."

"It may be hard for you to accept Dear One. But under our son's rule, and with my guidance, Mutal will climb higher than was ever possible under your father's rule."

"May the gods save us—and him—from your helping."

"I cannot talk to you when you are like this."

It made me furious that he just sat there staring blankly at the floor, tolerating my words as if I were a pouting little flower not getting her way. Sitting in a niche in the wall was a shell containing ash and a half-smoked cigar. I picked it up and when I slowly poured the contents onto his blanketed lap he leaned back with his hands apart. "This is your contribution to the family," I said. "I may be living under the same roof, but you are no longer welcome in my chamber. And I will never come to you here. Not anywhere. The blade I keep in my litter will now become my nightly companion. Do you understand?" Jatz'om blinked and made a sharp clicking sound with his tongue. "And keep your dog away from me. Tell him I have a blade and I will not hesitate to use it. If I even smell his breath near me, I will slit his throat."

My gaze demanded a reply. "I will tell him," Jatz'om whispered.

My tears had dried up and I was no longer shaking. Having gotten Jatz'om's attention and having some voice left I found the courage to say what I'd been thinking. "It must be difficult, needing to puff yourself up in an Owl costume to look fierce. Having power without ever earning it must be a terrible burden."

Jatz'om pulled aside the blanket and shook the mess of ashes onto the floor. "I will not warn you again," he whispered.

"What? You will have *me* killed? Mother of the Ajaw Le?" Strands of hair fell in my face again, so I pulled it out of the *kub*, gathered it and tied it in a knot. "Without me you would have no hope of gaining the respect of my people. Kill me and you kill any chance of having your way with Yax Nuun."

"You swore an oath."

"To keep the god-bundle. And I will. For our children's sake I will stand by your side at rites and ceremonies, but I will not support your charter or the *noh tzol*."

"You should be grateful. I protected you from—."

"You protected your father and your charter." I hadn't planned to make demands, but there was more that I wanted. "I will sit with you at court and before the council. But only when I choose. I will oversee the keeping of the palace and the residence, but with Maya servants and attendants. No Tollanos."

"As you wish. But the guards and sentries will be Tollanos."

"I want a proper burial for my family. Father belongs with his ancestors, overlooking the Great Plaza. I want Mother, my brothers, and sister and the others buried in tombs at Precious Forest."

"I think—."

"I want everything proper and with sacred ceremony. And I will be the one to speak for them." Jatz'om nodded. "Sihyaj K'ahk', Standing Squirrel, the Owl and Centipede, all the Tollan warrior houses and you will have other places to be."

I walked toward the doorway. Jatz'om got up and pulled the drape aside. "I did what was necessary," he said. "For the world. If I could have done it without hurting you I would have."

Outside, there were two new guards.

The Council

ASIDE FROM DISCUSSING FOOD, SERVANTS AND HOUSEHOLD affairs, especially the preparations for the seating of the new council, few words had passed between Jatz'om and me since I confronted him. When he came to escort me to the ceremony, the little bow and the look he gave me said he was pleased that I was wearing the kaloomte' necklace and the red, ankle-length gown his mother gifted to me when we left Tollan. I would have preferred that the yellow flower designs at the bottom had been embroidered rather than painted, but it was enough that I was wearing Tollan colors, showing the new council members that, although my blood was Mayan, I was also kaloomte' and wife of their "supreme" prophet. The death sign on my cheek told them I was still mourning the loss of my family.

I thought it presumptuous that the elders to be installed in the various offices wore triple-knotted warrior headdress of white barkcloth rather than red feathers, but I could see where it could be argued that their duties involved a kind of sacrifice. Still, it wasn't their blood that they were overseeing. These men all knew each other. Most of them had come with us from Tollan. So it seemed ridiculous that Jatz'om had each man stand while he spoke his name, showered him with praise, and told about his accomplishments.

Jatz'om nodded to Cave Frog who in turn nodded to me, so I descended the steps carrying the little wooden god, K'awiil. When the drummers saw the smoke emanating from his forehead, they pounded their drums and everyone knelt. The steps were tall and although the figure was not very heavy, balancing him on his pillow required both hands. As we'd rehearsed, I walked slowly to the center of the courtyard, went up the three steps of the dais, and sat on the backless bench with the smoking god on my lap. In turn then, the ministers approached and knelt. Speaking on behalf of K'awiil and making certain the god's holy breath wafted over their heads, Jatz'om bestowed their titles, described the burden of their offices and specified the duration. I thought when the last of the ministers received his baton and blessing, that would be the end of it. It wasn't. Jatz'om neglected to tell me that Sihyaj K'ahk' was going to administer an oath that bound the ministers further: to help him "establish and advance" the noh tzol, New Order.

Shaded from the sun by an undulating patchwork of white fabrics strung together overhead, the chan aj k'in spoke after Sihyaj K'ahk', offering words of gratitude and encouragement for their assuming the burden of the *caah*, particularly, he said, at a time when the "respected and devoted emissary" from Tollan—rather than a rightfully authorized ruler—was holding the order.

For the feast I had arranged for the ministers to sit on reed-mats in a circle, the mat's being covered with a red blanket. Lime Sky and her assistants prepared maize-leaf tamales, some stuffed with paca meat, others with turkey. Four of my serving women had never been to court before, so I worried greatly that they would drop or spill something or not understand a minister's gesture.

Along with the tamales we served roasted grubs with ground beans and platters of cooked *chayote* greens topped with ground squash seeds that Lime Sky dusted with chili powder. Along with the meal, and for the purpose of toasting, we served chih. But the final offering, an extravagance usually reserved for lords and their ladies, was cold kakaw poured into outstretched calabashes from the height of the server's breast to raise a dark brown foam. Jatz'om and Sihyaj K'ahk' had easy access to my father's storehouses. Why not?

Rather than talk to Jatz'om during the amusements—men demonstrating their skill with spear-throwers, women dancing to the sound of flutes, helmeted men punching each other until one of them had to be carried off, and a macaw trained to talk — I spoke with the newly appointed Minister of Water, a well groomed and mannered man whose family we knew from Tollan. His wife was one of the women who regularly sat with us at the ceramic workshop maintained by one of Jatz'om's sisters. As the minister told about the difficulty he was having in building his house, I noticed that, aside from the servers, I was the only woman. One among forty or more laughing, belching, mouth-wiping and crotch-scratching men, drunk on ambition and all puffed up about their new offices.

With the exception of Jatz'om, Yax Nuun, and myself, when Sihyaj K'ahk' stood everyone stood. As nauseating as it was for me to be in the his presence, it was curious to see how admired and respected he was, especially considering that everyone knew about his warrior-father running from the field of battle and being stripped of his title, and his mother who, defeated by the humiliation and saddened by her husband's suicide, neglected her household and relied upon her children to keep the household together. Throughout his flowery expression of gratitude to Jatz'om for entrusting him with the burden of overseeing the "difficult but necessary sacrifices," my thoughts turned to the different ways that I could send him to Xibalba. I finally decided that strangulation would be best because I wanted to feel him gasping for breath. It gave me no pleasure, but as he praised the Owl, Centipede, and settlement warriors, none of whom were present, I imagined clubbing them with an obsidian mace, breaking their spear-throwers over my knee, and slashing their necks with my knife. Unfortunately, this only served to upset me further and tighten my throat.

Jatz'om turned to Yax Nuun and asked him to speak to the ministers. "Just stand and say whatever you like," he whispered. It upset me because he did this without his or my knowledge. And without preparation. What else could he say but what his father wanted him to say? Concerned about the distance between his father's expectation and what I knew he was feeling, particularly about Sihyaj K'ahk', I held my breath when he stood.

I couldn't believe that he began by offering gratitudes to his father for teaching him about the prophecy, and the path of abundance and the ways of the court. Without mentioning Sihyaj K'ahk', he expressed his respect for the warrior houses, not for the attack on Mutal, but for holding the order until he could ascend to the Mat. He concluded by congratulating the council members and wishing them well in their new offices.

I thought my heart would beat out of my chest. Not that he might accidentally reveal his true feelings, but that he might stumble, falter or violate the customs of oratory—respect, appreciation and word-play—such that the ministers would be embarrassed for him, perhaps even laugh. Men of power do that. They laugh at younger men for unknowingly violating customs and manners. Down deep I wished he'd denounced what his father, Sihyaj K'ahk', K'inich Bahlam, and the rest of them did, perhaps even disavow the *noh tzol*. As the Succession Lord he could have done that. He could have humiliated them all and overturned everything that happened that night. But he didn't yet know he had such power.

The applause came and Yax Nuun beamed. Jatz'om put his hand on his son's shoulder. Sihyaj K'ahk' did the same on his other side. I wanted to rush him out of the courtyard and take him to a safe place. But no place was safe. I wanted to hold him and tell him about the ways of power and the traps that come with respect and praise. Unlike his father, I wanted him to earn them—like his grandfather had.

Jatz'om's applause and his glance to me took me back to a comment he made when, at seven, Yax Nuun correctly recited four rounds of the Tollan calendar gods. He said when a farmer plants his seeds properly the maize grows strong and tall. By "properly" Jatz'om meant instruction in the Tollan ways. That Yax Nuun presented himself well was an indication to the dignitaries that he trained his son well in manners, customs, and oratory. Had he not spoken so well, he would have found a quiet way to let me know the failing was mine. Using the chill in the air as an excuse to leave, I stood, bowed to the ministers and took my leave. Jatz'om followed three steps behind. "Dear One," he said softly. I turned. "What you did to make this grand—. The banners and flowers and food, the red and black blankets, the kakaw servers, your presentation of K'awiil—and yourself. You have my gratitude. Whatever you ask for the servants will be given. I will see to it."

I took cushions to the steps outside my sleeping chamber, one to sit on the other to lean against. There were two bright wanderers in the sky, both seeming to follow the same path across the Great Tree. *Father? Mother? Do you see what is happening here? Do you see what they are doing to your grandson? Keep him and his sister safe. Make Yax Nuun strong against their ways. Help me to help him remember you and know the ways of our people. Father. I am ashamed before your eyes. I should have seen what my husband was doing. I should have insisted on knowing his charter. Forgive me. Had I not been so weak you and Mother, all of us, would be walking the reservoir trail. I have not only lost my way, I have lost myself. You said if that should happen I should talk to my ch'ulel. I tried. But so much of it has been lost. Now, all I hear inside is the voice of the demon.*

The Presentation

THE CEREMONIAL HEADDRESSES WERE TOO TALL FOR US TO stand under the portico and there were no trees on the side of the palace facing the Great Plaza, so we had to stand in the skin-tingling glory of Ajaw K'in at midday. Normally Jatz'om and I received our headdresses after the Chilam called the people to order and began reciting our titles, but on this occasion, because Jatz'om was disappointed at the poor showing, we had to stand on the hot pavement and wait for more people to come. Our only relief came from the fan-bearers and our attendants who kept wiping our faces and giving us sips of water.

When finally our titles had been announced, Ix Chab' and I followed Jatz'om to the terrace and down the palace steps to the wooden dais. Sihyaj K'ahk' came next, then Yax Nuun. Both of them wore plaited shell collars, the bulbous *ko'haw* war helmet, and the shell eye-rings that marked them as supreme Owls. Even seated in the shade of an awning and with fan bearers, the sweat ran down my face.

The chilam that Sihyaj K'ahk' chose to speak for Yax Nuun and himself was actually someone I favored. Having spent many days on the river with Banded Snake and his family, I could see how he had earned the titles, Holy One and Far Seer. Although he sent messengers out ten days in advance requiring at least one adult male from every household to attend the presentation, attendance was very poor. I could see the embarrassment on his sweaty face. Two hundred people in the Great Plaza looked less like the gathering of the *caah*, more like the gathering of a lineage.

Those closest to the steps were mostly noblemen from the settlement, recognizable by their butterfly nose ornaments and eagle feathers. Even without them they stood out from the Maya whose foreheads were tapered and hair tasseled to look like maize cobs. Tollan mothers never used headboards and the fashion for adult men was to gather their hair in back with a cord or a wooden clasp shaped like a butterfly.

Observing the fear on many of the faces farther back, especially the Maya women who kept glancing at the warriors walking among them, what struck me was the number of warriors who had cob-shaped heads but were now wearing fanged nose bars, red and yellow headdresses, and the open-frame sandals favored by the houses of Falcon and Wolf. Yax Nuun, who was seated behind me, bent forward to say the reason for the wait was that Sihyaj K'ahk' had sent Rattlesnake, Canine and Puma warriors into the residential districts to bring in more people.

Banded Snake gestured for Standing Squirrel to come up the steps. After an exchange of words the first spear went back down and spoke to a group of warriors who in turn passed word to their brothers to get the people to move closer to the steps. When they came forward and the shifting stopped, he began. "Maya! Tollanos! Whatever your tongue, wherever you came from, whatever your ancestors or lineage, we stand united—one *caah*. Men and women of Mutal..." Because Tollanos considered the goddess to be Mother of All, they prided themselves on bringing speakers of all tongues into their circle. Having sat in the circle of lords at Tollan, I think it was more that they wanted as many people as possible to adopt their gods and their ways, to pay tribute and contribute labor. I could see on the faces of my people, especially the elderly, that they found it shocking and disrespectful that the chilam began the presentation without first offering words of centering and gratitude.

Suddenly, a large group of people came from the west with warriors behind them. Moments later another group entered from the North. Banded Snake gestured again, calling for them to come forward. Ix Chab' had the count up to three-hundred fifty-six when he reintroduced himself, Jatz'om and myself, Sihyaj K'ahk' and then Yax Nuun. "I speak for those you see here in red," he said. "The honorable council of ministers. Before we came here we were men of Tollan. No longer. We have all vowed to advise the

Mat wisely, to secure what is best for the *caah*, and move her onto the path of abundance so she can become prosperous, grow tall and strong. We are now, every one of us, men of Mutal. We have come with our families to put down roots. We want you to know that our first loyalty is to Mutal. We are grateful for your patience as we learn to speak each other's tongue, and come to know each other as brother and sister. From this *k'in* forward there in no longer a Tollan settlement at Mutal. There is only Mutal. One *caah*. One people. The People of Maize." *Saying it is so does not make it so.* Banded Snake paused, perhaps expecting applause, but none came.

"We entered Mutal with open hands..." *Spear-throwers in your belts, axes strapped to your backs.* "We came to help..." *Instead you destroyed and displaced good and holy men and their families.* "We came to show you how others, with our help, are enjoying bounties and good fortune beyond your dreaming. Those who work the land know that bountiful harvests require clearing and order. By removing the weeds and establishing the *noh tzol*, centers north and west of us are already enjoying abundance and prosperity."

"Which centers?" someone shouted. "Warriors turned, but they couldn't find the man who shouted.

Banded Snake continued. "Through the ages, Tenan, our great goddess, anointed the sons of Tollan lords to carry her prophecy to those great centers..." He listed several places, gave the names of the rulers, and told how long they had been on the path of the *noh tzol*. "Your brothers and sisters in the highlands, at Chaynal, are already on that path. The rulers here are the last to receive the prophecy."

"We have no ruler!" someone shouted. This time the man stood out. Considering the slant of his forehead, the broad-brimmed hat and the dog by his side, I judged him to be a Maya merchant.

"This," the Chilam said, "is one of the reasons for this gathering. Those of us who came from Tollan are here because of one man." He gestured to Jatz'om and he stood with his eyes fixed on Banded Snake. "This is Kaloomte' Jatz'om Kuh K'awiil whose coming was foretold. He is the third son of Kaloomte' Ik'an Chak Chan, one of the three rulers at Tollan. More importantly, he is a Son of Tenan..." That was the first I heard of it. "Who speaks *to* him and *through* him."

Banded Snake turned and gestured to Sihyaj K'ahk'. "The council, guided by his emissary..." *Dog*. "...is honored and privileged to assist him in the fulfillment of his charter, most especially the establishment of the *noh tzol*." *Which will demand more of your sweat and tribute*.

Banded Snake gestured to me. "Seated beside the great prophet is his lovely wife, Kaloomte' Ix Bahlam Ich'aak K'awiil, second daughter of Ajaw, Chak Tok Ich'aak—who now resides in the sky. Next to her is their budding flower, Ix Chab'. Their son, Yax Nuun Ahiin, the soon to be anointed Ajaw Le, stands on the threshold of both manhood and rulership..."

When it came time for Jatz'om to speak he went down the stairway, deliberately taking one step at a time, holding his arms out and being careful to balance the bulbous headdress with its many shell plates and quetzal feathers rising high in back. Even with the strap tied tight under his chin, if he looked down or turned his head to the side it could have fallen. The array of eagle feathers rising above his forehead, the bright shell ear ornaments that framed his face, especially the necklace and shell rings that encircled his eyes shouted, even from a distance, that he was *kaloomte'*, a holy man and prophet above all others, one who through K'awiil, authorized those who would rule.

Walking down the steps was hazardous in other ways. He could trip on the ends of the red and yellow bead-studded streamers that hung from his belt and brushed against the steps. The belt ties themselves could break from the weight of the celts that hung from it. Then too, Jatz'om wasn't accustomed to wearing high-backed sandals with feathers front and back. The shell rings around his eyes, necessary to signify his standing as one of the few who held supreme authority over the Owl, created a glare in the bright sunlight. I held my breath until he stopped and held out his arms.

Because of his soft voice and his unwillingness to speak up, Banded Snake repeated his words louder so those farther back could hear. "Men and women, sons and daughters of Mutal," he shouted. "Our grandchildren and their children—endless generations—will mark this *k'in* as the birth of the *noh tzol* at Mutal."

Jatz'om pointed to the sun whereupon six drummers pounded the cadence for the counting of the calendar stones. "The Lord Tribute counts the drumbeats," Jatz'om said, "counts the scores of stones. After one *bundle* of stones." One loud drumbeat. "After eight *score* stones." Eight drumbeats. "After seventeen *stones*." Seventeen drumbeats. "One *score k'inob*." One drumbeat. "Eight *k'inob* since the making of the fourth world—." Eight drumbeats. "We honor and mark the journey of the bearers—Ten Tribute and his brother, Twelve Turtle. "So it is counted, so it is bound." Jatz'om gestured with both hands. "So it is established above, below, and on the face of the earth. Let it be known. Let it be recorded. The drums mark the *k'in* when Mutal entered the path of abundance and good fortune." Using a quill pen pulled from his hairnet, the scribe entered the event in the Book of Mutal. The trumpeters trumpeted and the drummers pounded their drums in a flurry of celebration. Banded Snake raised his staff and shook it. The Tollanos and their warriors applauded and yelped, but the Maya remained silent.

Banded Snake repeated Jatz'om's words: "For some," he shouted, "the coming of the *noh tzol* has meant hardship and sacrifice. These were the fires necessary to burn the brush and weeds so the seeds of the coming harvest can be planted..." *My father, my family; just weeds to him.* "All here express our gratitude for these sacrifices."

As he did on ceremonial occasions, Jatz'om closed his eyes and held out his hands palms up so the goddess would speak through him. In the silence, those of us who knew what this meant went to our knees and bowed our heads, but the chilam remained standing so he could shout the goddess's words coming from Jatz'om's mouth as whispers. "Beloved sons and daughters of Mutal!" he shouted. "Rulers of four great centers north and west of here have headed the words of my prophecy. They are walking the path of abundance. They have embraced the *noh tzol*. It is not enough. The lowland jungles have many more, even grander centers. My brothers, the storm, lightning, and earth lords are intent upon their plan of destruction. They want to make a new world. The want a world where the creatures they make will feed them properly, bend their knees before them, and praise their names. If this cannot be that world, they will destroy it." Jatz'om turned his palms toward the people. "Beloved sons and daughters of Mutal, the *noh tzol* is our last hope for this world. May you embrace it."

Jatz'om returned to his place and Sihyaj K'ahk' came forward to speak. I followed Banded Snake up the steps and across the way to the shrine that housed the god bundle. He took my headdress and replaced it with my red, serpent coil turban. Keeper of the Bundle was inside waiting.

The Presentation

He had Ch'ok Nehm K'awiil, Young Mirror Scepter, ready, sitting on his pillow with his serpent leg dangling over the front. Following the ritual I had learned at Tollan, I chanted his honorifics and passed two fingers, the sign of acceptance, across the blue-painted wood front and back to insure that everything was intact, especially the fingers and toes, and the long, foliated nose and obsidian eyes. Keeper had gowned him earlier, so all I had to do to wake him was the adornment. Jade earflares. Wristlets. The jade-bar necklace that had to lay flat over his tunic. The white headband tied high around his headdress. At Ho' Noh Witz it happened on one occasion that, although the Keeper cleaned out the ash from the slit in the little god's forehead—where Chahk, the thunderstorm god, sacrificed him—he didn't replace the white headband because he didn't think the smudge could be seen from a distance. Ever since I insisted that the headband be freshly washed in untouched rain water before every presentation.

The last thing to inspect was the god's fiery throat, the little ceramic bowl in back and at the bottom of his neck where the coals went in. Jatz'om always inspected it the night before an anointing, but it was for me to push a brush through the channels to his mouth and forehead to insure they were not obstructed. With that done I stepped aside so the Keeper could put in the burning coals. When he stepped aside I dusted the coals with beads of copal and replaced the neck-panel so the precious breath would come out his mouth and the slit in his forehead.

While I waited with K'awiil, Banded Snake went down the steps to let Jatz'om know we were ready. He nodded to Sihyaj K'ahk' and he concluded his comments. "Now it falls to us," Sihyaj K'ahk' shouted. "The k'in has come for us to show the gods that we are one people, no longer Tollanos and Maya. We are Mutal!" Again, the Tollanos applauded and the Maya remained silent.

Three trumpeters standing on top of the steps on both sides of the plaza raised their wooden horns and sounded a loud and prolonged call to announce the coming of K'awiil. Holding the little god in front of me with billows of his breath coming out his mouth and forehead made it difficult to see at times. Even with Banded Snake steading me to the side, I took the steps slowly. Those who were not already on their knees knelt as Jatz'om, doing his best to talk louder, introduced K'awiil as a lightning lord and patron of rulers, the sky god who authorizes them to speak to, and on behalf of, the Makers.

Jatz'om spoke rightly when he proclaimed that it was a day to be remembered. So many important things happened on that day: He presented himself to the people of Mutal as the supreme prophet of Tollan, son and voice of the goddess. Yax Nuun took the K'awiil anointing and was thereby authorized to carry the title, Ajaw Le, Succession Lord. Sihyaj K'ahk' received the breath of K'awiil along with the words, spoken through Jatz'om, that authorized him to serve as Regent Of The Mat until Yax Nuun was ready to rule. And by having all this authorizing witnessed by the ministers, Jatz'om demonstrated his own authority as the lowland *kaloomte'*. Sadly, it marked the day when they stopped resisting. Mutal will never be the same.

Three days after the presentations in the Great Plaza, Jatz'om sent a messenger to Tollan. Seeing him leave with an escort of thirty warriors, six merchants and as many attendants, a long line of carriers with high-packs, many score baskets, bundles, and crates along with nine covered litters, made it clear to me that he was delivering more than words to his father. While Tenan was using my husband to spread the word of her prophecy, his father was using both of them to increase the flow of precious goods to Tollan. The stream my father had established between them wasn't enough. Jatz'om's father wanted a river.

The Workshop

THE DREAD OF SEEING YAX NUUN LOOKING LIKE A YOUNGER
version of Sihyaj K'ahk' and then watching his father authorize that dog as
regent, effectively making him the Mutal ruler indefinitely, stayed with me
for days. Had my homecoming been as I'd expected I would have been
delighted to see my son standing as the Ajaw Le. I would have been eager
to help him walk in his grandfather's sandals. But now, knowing how he
felt about Sihyaj K'ahk' and considering that Jatz'om was using our son to
advance his charter, I wanted nothing to do with it. Yax Nuun came to me
asking if there was a way for him to avoid Sihyaj K'ahk', but all I could
do was assure him that I would help him to make the best of his situation.

At Tollan when I was upset, discouraged, or lonely I turned to the one
thing that helped me connect with my mother and think more clearly. Clay.
Jatz'om's eldest sister had a ceramic workshop, so when I told her how I
made figurines and bowls alongside my Mother, she invited me to come
and sit with them as a way to learn the Tollan tongue. Besides being able
to get my hands into clay again, I was able to sit with six prominent
women who helped me understand the Tollan calendar gods and rites, especially their customs regarding dress, hair styles, jewelry, and body painting.

The workshop itself was a fascinating place. I was young and so
shocked by that new world and trying to adjust to my new life, I didn't
appreciate what we had there: servants who chopped and hauled wood to

keep four fire-pits going while others were out gathering roots and tubers, ashes, grasses, cattails, and cactus plants to keep our bins full. Sister-in-law's married son saw to our tool needs. And her house-servants brought us food. The workshop was comfortable and the women were eager to show me their ways of both coiling and molding the clays. Even more, I learned about slips and different ways of smoothing and polishing my vessels from a kindly *aj jaay*, a court Ceramics Worker who frequently came and sat with us. They told me this hunched over old man with a raspy voice and scars on his hands came from three generations of "clay vessel persons." He could tell where a clay came from just by working it in his fingers and smelling it.

The best of our wares were given as gifts to distinguished visitors, particularly the lords who came to pay homage to the gods and receive the K'awiil anointing. Jatz'om's father liked to serve tamales in bowls that were incised or painted all around with figures so he could tell a story about them and then offer the bowl to his guest as a remembrance of the occasion. Unfortunately, when we moved to Ho' Noh Witz my duties as mistress of both the residence and the palace kept me so occupied I wasn't able to even think about clay.

JATZ'OM SAT ALONE ON A LONG BENCH WITH HIS BACK against the wall smoking his cigar and watching some spider monkeys in the trees at the far end of the patio. "Husband," I said. He gestured for me to sit but I chose to stand. "I was thinking about your sister and her workshop. I enjoyed what we did there. I miss having my hands in clay."

"You made some fine bowls and vases back then."

"Ix Chab' has been wanting me to teach her to make figurines. If I had a place, I might invite some of the other women as well."

Jatz'om shook his head. "Not here, not anywhere close to the residence. All that coming and going with water, the smoke and the mess."

"Not like your sister's place. Something modest."

Monkeys screeched at the far end of the patio and we turned to look. Sihyaj K'ahk' and the Ministers of Trade and Water had entered and were approaching, but Jatz'om raised his hand and they stopped.

" I cannot talk now," he said, "but I think a little workshop would be good. It ought to be close but far enough from the residence that we would not be bothered by smoke from the fire pit." *The farther the better.* "You would need servants, clay, and tools. The shelter would need to be—."

"I would rather it be enclosed rather than open," I interrupted. "To keep out of the drafts and work through the rainy season." The real reason was I wanted to have a place where Yax Nuun, Ix Chab' and I could talk in private.

"I will see what Tenan has to say about it," Jatz'om said, eager to dismiss me. "If she approves I will speak to Sihyaj K'ahk'. Meanwhile, see if you can find a suitable place. And let me know what you need. If it pleases the goddess, it pleases me." *And if it pleases you, it will please Sihyaj K'ahk'.* My old self would have smiled and expressed gratitude. Instead, I nodded and turned to go. "This could be good for Mutal as well," Jatz'om remarked. "A contribution of sorts?" I nodded again and he returned it. To avoid his visitors, I turned and went the direction I'd come.

BEHIND THE GUEST HOUSES THAT HAD BECOME MY FIRE offerings—and Sihyaj K'ahk' was having rebuilt—there was a little dirt path through the forest that led to a clearing where a storehouse once stood, a place where the servants stored water jars, wood, litters, baskets, and large rolls of matting for palace occasions. It was ideal. The view of the palace was blocked by a thick tangle of palm dwarfed by oak and wild tamarind, and the reservoir was just down the hill. That it was within the palace district meant it would be heavily guarded day and night.

Apparently the goddess approved. I told Jatz'om what I needed and he passed my request on to Sihyaj K'ahk'. Two days later men were out at the site hauling away the old support beams and bamboo walls, chopping weeds and burning the brush. While trees were being felled and the logs stripped to make new beams, others leveled and tamped the ground where I had marked the boundaries. There was a flurry of activity for six days. Then it stopped. I waited and waited, expecting the builders—somebody—to come. No one did. Three days later I complained to Jatz'om. Two days later I complained again.

Four days after that, Sihyaj K'ahk' finally sent an *aj noah* to walk the ground with me. Using his measuring cord, he had his assistant mark the corners of the platform, the placement of the steps, doorway and walls, even the hearth. Sihyaj K'ahk' told Jatz'om he would be sending nine men to build the workshop, but there were never more than six men on any given day. I nearly had to prod them with a stick to keep them moving. My reminding them that the *chan aj k'in* predicted that the rains would come early slowed them even more. They came late, left early and were not at all embarrassed to show me their disagreeable faces. Had I not been the eagle over their shoulders, showing them which trees to chop and which to save, pointing to the roots I wanted dug out so they wouldn't come up through the floor, insisting they dig the post holes deep enough to withstand high winds and secure the lashes with the thickest of tree gums, nothing would have gotten done. Not properly.

The *aj k'in's* prediction came true. And now the builders complained about needing to lash the roof beams in pouring rain. My leveled floor had become a mud pond. It took six days to get the thatching done, another twelve before the ground beneath the roof was dry enough for Gray Mouse, the children and I to sweep out the leaves and thatching and tamp it down again with stones. I thought because Sihyaj K'ahk' had ordered it, I would be able to go to the quarry and tell the supervisor what I needed for the hearth and have the stones delivered within a day or two. It took eight days and two heated arguments at the quarry before I learned that Sihyaj K'ahk' had ordered stones for the Owl compound—which took priority.

To protect the workshop from thunder and lightning, evil winds, and forest demons, I arranged for an *och k'ahk'*, the ceremony that calls a spirit to take up residence in a structure as its patron and protector. Ix Chab' had never experienced a Fire Entering ceremony, so I explained to her the difference between fire that gives heat and fire that gives life, fire that burns and fire that protects.

When finally the day of the *och k'ahk'* arrived, Jatz'om, Yax Nuun, Ix Chab', Gray Mouse and I gathered in front of the workshop with the *chan aj k'in*, now and then holding broadleaves over our heads as the Chahkob blessed us, off and on, with dove rains. After a long day of making circuits around the little house, listening to chanting, watching the *aj k'in* offering the blood of a *kox* at the center-post, placing its feathers at the four corners, and drilling new fire in the hearth—the heart of the structure—where he invited a guardian spirit to take up residence, I was relieved and surprised when he announced that a "hearty female spirit," one of my long passed ancestors, had accepted his invitation. My bamboo and masonry workshop with its compacted floor had become a *she*, a living shelter where my children and I—and any others I might invite to sit and talk or mold clay—could be warm and protected.

The morning after the *och k'ahk'* I sat by the workshop hearth sipping hot *keyem,* soaking in the quiet of the crackling logs. As unaccustomed as I was to a dirt floor and having my blue sarong protected solely by a thickness of matting, it was comforting to be surrounded by containers of possibility: fine-grained black and gray swamp clays, white limestone clay, the coarser red and brown clays from the highlands, baskets of charcoal, manioc root, cattail, dried grass, and a large jar of ash. I'd arranged my tools—cutting blade, paddle, water worn pebbles, bone, smoothing seeds—and separate water jars for my fine, medium, and coarse cloths, but I couldn't get started. The rain came. After a while the sound of the runoff dripping into the basin set under the corner of the roof had me tapping a bone on the side of a water jar. Noticing that I was doing this, I got up and paced.

I thought that having a place of my own, a place where I could be alone at times and keep my hands busy, would also calm the storms that kept rising inside me. I couldn't stop thinking about my parents, Ixway, Naway, and Kachne'. How were they killed? Did they suffer? Did I even want to know? Could they see me now? *Father? Mother? Can you see me? Can you see your beautiful grandchildren?* Pacing wasn't helping. I went to the doorway and watched the water dripping from the thatch make circles in the basin. *Why am I so—?* A thought struck me like an axe from behind. *It was me! My marriage.* Standing there on the bank of the river, watching all those Owls shove off, I knew something was wrong. *How could I have not seen it? Instead of worrying about the demons, I should have pressed Jatz'om about why only men went to Mutal in the first wave? Why did I not say anything? Had I not married Jatz'om none of this would have happened. Father forgive me. In fulfilling your alliance, I let the rats into the garden. And now they want to establish an order that increases our bounty so more of it can be delivered to the lords of Tollan.*

I turned to the hearth and spoke out loud to the flames: "Patron, beloved ancestor, if I had known what Jatz'om and Sihyaj K'ahk' were planning, could I have saved my family? Might they still be alive?" While I waited for a response or a sign, a terrifying thought struck me like an axe. My destiny, the reason I was born, might have been to prevent the attack. At least I could have warned my father. Truly, that would have been a grand contribution. Through the downpour of tears I began thinking of ways to punish Jatz'om and remove Sihyaj K'ahk', if not from the face of the earth, then from Mutal. I hated that they were turning Yax Nuun to the ways of the Owl. Aside from killing them, none of my schemes would last. Besides, the retributions I kept imagining would make me less in the eyes of my children and the ancestors, especially Father and Mother. I put on my broad-brimmed hat, went into the rain and back to the residence.

I wanted to talk to Ix Chab' but she was not in her chamber. There was still some light left in the day, but I didn't care. I went to my sleeping bench. Within moments of pulling the blanket over my shoulders I heard Sihyaj K'ahk' laughing somewhere in the distance. It made me want to take a spear and shove it through his heart. Were I a god, I would have confined him to his sleeping chamber at the settlement and removed his ability to speak or laugh, ever again. Like a dog poked with a stick, the sound of his voice kept barking at my failed attempts to find some peace. *Ayaahh. This is how it is. This is how it will always be.*

IX CHAB' HAD SEEN A NOBLEWOMAN SITTING WITH A SCRIBE at the palace. She was so taken with the woman's beauty and seated posture, she wanted to make a figurine in her likeness: scarified face, cropped hair, and a mantle that covered everything but her feet. It pleased me that she wanted to mold something larger and more complicated than the little figures that fit in the palm of her hand. And it got me started.

Yax Nuun came later in the day and sat with us. Sparked by his mention that Sihyaj K'ahk' was gathering noblemen from nearby centers to talk to him in confidence about their rulers, we had a long talk about power—how it was acquired and rightly used. As I'd hoped, the workshop soon became a place where the three of us and Gray Mouse could sit together and talk.

As the figurine of the noblewoman was nearing completion, Ix Chab' complained that because I had done most of the modeling, it wasn't turning out the way she wanted. Her brother was there, also complaining — about Sihyaj K'ahk' pressuring him to get more experience with a spearthrower. I'd had enough of their complaining. I pulled the head off the figurine and with both hands smashed it into the body. Ix Chab' and her brother gasped, startled, as I kneaded three days of work into a ball of clay. I lifted the blob and set it in front of Ix Chab'. "You saw my noblewoman. Now you can make yours. I have a jar to make."

BETWEEN HIS FATHER AND SIHYAJ K'AHK', YAX NUUN WAS kept busy most of the day. Every day. My son visited less often and our conversations were shorter, but what he had to say and the questions he brought were quite intriguing, even challenging.

On one such visit he complained not only that Sihyaj K'ahk' was doing all the talking and decision-making, but that his father sided with him. He thought that, as Succession Lord, he would at least be included in discussions concerning the *caah* so he could learn. He wasn't. Instead, Sihyaj K'ahk' kept moving him from one warrior compound to another using the excuse that he needed build his body, practice his skills with different men, and become better acquainted with the warlords and first spears at the various houses. Throughout his complaining, the jar I'd been working on sat under a cloth on top of a little wooden stand that Turtle Cloud made so I could do incising at eye-level. Yax Nuun noticed that whenever he visited, it was covered. "What is that Mother?" he asked. "I never see you working on it?"

Ix Chab' called over. "It is a secret," she said. "She keeps it covered."

I invited them both to come and sit close to me. "I will show you my secret, but only if you promise not to tell anyone else about it." Yax Nuun signed *jadestone promise* by touching his thumb to his forefinger and Ix Chab' did the same. "Remember when I told you about your grandfather building the palace?" They shook their heads. "For the dedication my Mother made a special offering jar that had a lid. I remember her taking the three of us to the house of an *aj chuwen* artist so we could watch him paint the figures and word-signs mother wanted on the jar."

"How old were you?" Ix Chab' asked.

"I was six. I remember because it was the first time I saw someone painting on stucco-covered bark paper. Mother described the figures she wanted on the wall of the jar and he painted it. On another *k'in* he painted the word-signs she wanted to go around the lid. Using the strips of paper he painted for her, she incised the figures and word-signs into the jar and its lid. On the day of the dedication they buried the jar in a hole dug into the palace steps. I remember it clear as rainwater—the jar and the lid. Along with it they put in a figurine, some jade, shells, and a little obsidian mirror."

"Is it still there?" Ix Chab' asked.

"It will always be there."

"Could we dig it up and see?"

I shook my head. "That was for the gods." I pulled away the cloth so they could see what I'd been working on. "This is how I remember it. I wanted you to see what it looked like." Using the bone shaping-tool, I pointed to the face in the center of the jar. "That is your grandfather, adorned as the Maize God. In his arms he cradles the *chan k'aan*, the Great Sky Serpent, the path the wanderers take across the night sky." They moved to get a closer look at the figures. "Over here is where your grandfather emerged from the serpent's mouth as ruler. At the end is his namesake, our namesake, a jaguar paw."

Because Yax Nuun had sat with an itz'aat for an entire season at Ho' Noh Witz and was currently learning to paint word-signs from the Mutal chan itz'aat, he asked about the signs that would go around the lid that I'd not yet started. "I was hoping you could help, Yax Nuun. I remember the words my mother put around her lid, but not the signs. I need someone to paint them for me, an *itz'aat*, a Maya I can trust to keep this secret."

"What are the words, Mother? I might know how to draw them."

I needed the hand of a skilled painter, but I didn't say so. "Ascended to his house, his holy place, his Six Sky Turtle palace, Chak Tok Ich'aak, Mutal Ajaw, ninth successor lord of Yax Ch'akte Xook." Clearly, Yax Nuun was not able to do this, and he admitted it. When I turned the jar to show them the sky serpent along the bottom of the jar, Yax Nuun asked if he, like his grandfather, would become one of the twinkling lights in the sky, or if like his father he would become a butterfly and chase the sun.

"In truth, I do not know," I said. "But I do know the blood you inherited on both sides is sacred—equally Mayan and Tollano."

"They call us 'hot bloods,'" Ix Chab' interrupted.

"We prefer to say 'sacred' because it comes from the gods."

"What gods?" Yax Nuun asked.

"From the Ich'aak you inherited the blood of Juun Ixim." Hearing myself say this it occurred to me that I hadn't spoken to them enough about the maize god, and I resolved to change that. "From your father's side you inherited the blood of his ancestors, the former rulers of Tollan. They believe their rulers all become gods when they leave this world, so they have many names."

"But why is our blood hot?" Ix Chab' persisted. She wanted to know why it didn't feel hot.

"The heat is not like the heat we get from a fire," I said. "The heat in our blood is the powers the gods gave us to carry the burden of the *caah*, powers like courage, dignity, honesty, willing sacrifice, wisdom, and the ability to learn and use word signs." I turned to Yax Nuun. "No matter what your father or Sihyaj K'ahk' or any of the warlords teach you, remember that it is *you*, not they, who carries these powers on behalf of the *caah*. When you ascend to the Mat, you alone will stand as the Great Tree. As you become layered, Mutal becomes layered. We are privileged to have sacred blood, but it is also a heavy burden, especially for one so young. Never let *anyone*, not even me, tell you how to rule."

"Father says I will find my power by walking the path of abundance. He says my contribution will be the *noh tzol*. He and Sihyaj K'ahk' are teaching me all about it."

"Learn as much as you can from everyone. But trust no one. Only your *ch'ulel* when it awakens..." What could an eleven year-old know about his spirit voice or the new order, especially when his father made it sound like the end of hardship and the beginning of abundance?

Ix Chab' was growing weary. She got up and went to the other end of the workshop where she had a mat and blanket. After covering the jar with the cloth again, I moved closer to Yax Nuun and spoke softly. "You know your father cares for you greatly. He would never purposefully harm you or guide you wrongly. But you must also know, you are not just a son to him; you are the fulfillment of his charter. He will demand your loyalty."

"I can be loyal to Father, but not Sihyaj K'ahk'."

"Your father knows that my people would never respect a Tollano on the Mat. That is why he made Sihyaj K'ahk' regent rather than ruler. They may dress you like an Owl and teach you their ways, but what makes you the Ajaw Le is blood you inherited from my father. It is because of this that no one can speak *to* the gods or *for* them as powerfully as you will when you take the K'awiil. When it comes to matters of the *caah*, Itzam-naaj, our patron and patron of Mutal, grandfather Ich'aak and the thirteen rulers before him will all be guiding you—not your father, not Sihyaj K'ahk', your underlords or ministers."

"Father does not like to talk about the Maya, especially grandfather. Is it wrong to learn Father's ways?"

In order to take a moment to think, I poked the smoldering ashes in the hearth and raised the flame with some ocote sticks. "It would not be proper to say your father's ways are wrong, Yax Nuun. They are just not my ways. Until you become a man, you and I must accept that you are bound to your father."

"I am learning from others as well. Banded Snake is teaching me how to talk to the gods and make offerings to the ancestors."

"Did he tell you what the former rulers want most?"

Yax Nuun shook his head. "They want to be *remembered*. They want us to think about who they were and what they did, not so we can praise them like gods, but because they want to hear our petitions so they can take them to the gods. And help us, help the *caah*. Remembering keeps them helping, keeps them alive."

"How can I remember people I never met?"

Ix Chab' returned with her pillow and sat beside me. "All I know about Grandmother and Grandfather is what you told us," she said. "Can you tell us more?"

Our conversation went on and because of it I couldn't sleep. I kept wishing I'd said more or differently what I told them, but I was comforted by the thought that they wanted to know more about their grandparents. It occurred to me that Father might consider this a contribution to Mutal. I must have convinced myself of this because I awoke feeling the need to learn everything I could about what my father did while I was gone.

Lords In Stone

THE MORNING BEGAN WITH THE LIGHTNING GODS THROWING
A tantrum. Their otter rains, pounding so hard I thought they would poke a
hole in the thatch, woke me in the middle of the night. Then came the
bright flashes and bolts of lightning followed within heartbeats by thunderclaps that pierced my ears. We didn't dare stand in the doorways, for
fear of being struck. Sihyaj K'ahk' and Yax Nuun were having guests that
evening, so before I could see how the workshop fared in the storm I had
to oversee the servants at the palace. I worried that if the rain broke
through the thatch, the floor would be flooded and my bins would be all
covered in mud.

Around midday the rain changed to dove and the sky lightened over
the dripping canopy. Birds and monkeys started returning, so we knew the
worst was over. We'd watched the water rise in the patio, but it was quite a
shock to see the Great Plaza flooded and empty of people.

When Gray Mouse, Ix Chab' and I arrived at the workshop, we found
the roof intact, but water had gushed so forcefully from one of the catch-
ment basins it dug a gully that ran across the walkway. We'd finished pulling away some of the fallen branches and had just sat for some of Gray
Mouse's special *saca*—she ground the maize nine times; after adding it to
the water, she stirred in marigold, honey, and chili until it became smooth.
Yax Nuun came in. Gray Mouse served him some as well, and then he told
us that his father and Sihyaj K'ahk' were preparing to leave for Siaan

K'aan. "Father is taking K'awiil with him," he said. "He is going to anoint and seat Standing Squirrel as the *yajaw*." I wasn't surprised. Jatz'om was pleased with the way the first spear was holding the order there. Yax Nuun didn't understand and there was nothing he could do about it if he did. But hearing the name 'Siaan K'aan,' the place where my siblings, father's sister and her husband had been killed, felt like a punch in the chest.

Yax Nuun persisted, telling us about the Yax Hal Witz, First True Mountain, he'd seen on a recent visit. Unlike our First True Mountain, the one at Siaan K'aan was apparently a group of shrines sitting atop an apron with faces twice as tall as him flanking a broad stairway. Yax Nuun squirmed. "Forgive me Mother, but Father says it is wrong to have faces of men carved in stone. He says the the monuments at Precious Forest are a sign that grandfather and the other rulers were walking the path of destruction. He said stone should be reserved for gods. Is that true, Mother?"

"That is what the Tollan lords teach. But it is not true that the Maya rulers are walking the path of destruction, or disrespecting the gods by having their faces carved in stone. Remember, I told you. They do it to be remembered—so they can continue to help us—and the *caah*."

"How can they help when they are stone?" Ix Chab' asked.

"When rulers take the dark road they give up their bodies, but they never give up the burden of the *caah*. Most of their *ch'ulel* goes with them into the sky, but some of it remains in the things they used or built. Your grandfather's offering bowl, his drinking cup, headdresses and regalia all have power because they carry a bit of his *ch'ulel*. Stone monuments are even more powerful because they carry words and they have eyes."

"Can they see?" Ix Chab' asked.

"Some say they can."

Yax Nuun wrinkled his brow. "If they can help, why does Father say the monuments disrespect the gods?"

"Because of the prophecy. Tollanos get very upset when they hear about rulers, alive or in the sky, receiving what should be given to the gods."

I'd had something in mind to do since our arrival at Mutal, something that required some preparation and the right circumstances. With Jatz'om and Sihyaj K'ahk' gone and the children asking about their grandfather, I decided the time had come. I told Yax Nuun and his sister to dress in bark cloth and come to the palace stairway at first light, barefoot and wearing no jewels.

WHEN I WAS GROWING UP, THE YAX HAL WITZ AT PRECIOUS Forest was the tallest pyramid at Mutal. Thirteen years later, it rose higher and was still the tallest. The god-faces that flanked the stairways on all four sides were still there and larger, but now the walls were sloped and set in frames looking much like the shrines at Tollan. Built to stand as the place where Chahk split open the earth with his axe so the Maize God could ascend, it still marked the center of the sacred district.

I wanted the children to see the place where, except for their grandfather, my family would be buried. So I took them to the eastern steps of the Yax Hal Witz. In front of us were scores of people: a man with a turkey tucked under his arm, a cluster of warriors led by their first spear, a woman with a seedling tucked tightly against her breast and a sprout following behind her holding onto her sarong, a man balancing long board on his head— mounds of maize dough covered over with a cloth. About eighty paces across the expanse of the red masonry plaza we could see the full length of the East Platform with its stairways and shrines rising nearly as high as the trees.

"Four times a *tun*," I remembered, "we got up in the middle of the night and followed a torch-lit procession from the palace to the steps of the center shrine over there. Mother and the rest of us stood here while Father and his *k'uhul winicob* went to the top of the Yax Hal Witz where they drilled new fire and performed the sacrificial rites of gratitude and celebration for Ajaw K'in reaching his turning place. The flames lit up the canopy all around." I pointed to the tallest shrine in the center. "When Ajaw K'in made his ascent over there, the drummers pounded the drums so hard my insides pounded with them. The trumpets called out from the four directions, loud and fierce, like demons scolding each other. And while the *aj k'uhuun* marked Ajaw K'in's arrival in the sky record, your grandfather and the others let their blood onto strips of cotton and burned them in god-faced censers. When we saw him again at the top of the steps, instead of wearing the jaguar cloak and the *sak huunal* on his forehead, your grandfather presented himself in the likeness of Ajaw K'in himself, turning his helmeted face to the sacred directions where he offered copal and words of gratitude."

"Grandfather became Ajaw K'in?" Ix Chab' asked.

I shook my head. "I thought so when I was little. Now I understand. By dressing as Ajaw K'in, putting on his glory face and dancing his journeys across the sky, your grandfather allowed the god to live inside him. As with the *och k'ahk'* rites, instead of an ancestor taking up residence as patron of a house or temple, the gods enter the ruler's body as patron of the *caah*. He offers the god the use of his body—his eyes, ears, and voice to show us how the Makers ordered the world and made things proper."

"I wonder what that feels like?" Yax Nuun asked. "Does it hurt?"

"Only a ruler would know. You need not worry. Your grandfather danced many gods, many times—Itzamnaaj, Chahk, Juun Ixim, Ajaw K'in, and the bearers of the calendar rounds."

Ix Chab' went up three steps and we followed her. "What was it like when grandfather stood for Ajaw K'in?" she asked.

"I wish you could have seen him. His feathered cloak was red on the inside, yellow on the outside. When the glory came streaming over the canopy and he received it with opened his arms, we could feel the holy presence. It filled us."

"Were there many people?"

"Hundreds and hundreds, all wearing white, singing, shouting, rattling their rattles, turning round and round with their torches."

Because the sun's going-down place was the place of death, the monuments to the deceased rulers were set in a long row in front of the East Shrine platform with their faces looking west. Being the rainy season, the monuments and the drum-shaped altars in front of them were covered over with thatch shelters to protect the stone and the offering fires.

Gratefully, whether because of our bark-cloth clothing, the broad-rimmed rain hats, or the crowd of people, we were not recognized. Those who'd come to pay their respects and petition the rulers formed lines behind their favored patrons, awaiting their turn to present their offerings to the holy men who, along with prayers, fed them into the fires. I'd heard that father had dedicated a monument two years earlier to mark and celebrate the completion of the seventeenth *k'atun*, so I led the children down the row, through the lines of petitioners. Thirty paces from the last and tallest stone I recognized Father's headdress. I stopped and covered my mouth, but I couldn't hold back the tears. The carver showed him from the side, but even so the shape of his nose—a bit longer than I'd remembered—combined with the slant of the forehead, folded eyelids, full lips, and broad shoulders left no doubt that, although taller and heavier, this was my father.

I pointed out the namesake, the jaguar paw, in Father's headdress. The little fish nibbling on a lily pad showed him to be the guardian of fertility. Because Huunal was the portal through which life flowed into the world, and because Yax Nuun would soon be wearing the white headband, he was especially interested to see the sacred white headband with the jade head of the god jutting out. The last time I saw Father wearing it was the day I left for Tollan.

It pleased me greatly that people were coming to honor him, offer him gifts, and ask his help. Most had brought flowers, but some offered packets of copal, and little calabashes of honey and *chih*. Within the many smokes that came our way there was the sweet smell of *kox*, but I couldn't tell if the little black bird had been offered to Father or to one of the other former rulers.

I'd brought along three packets of copal for Yax Nuun to give as his offering. Because Ix Chab' was named for honey, I had one of the cooks dip little sticks of ocote into a honey pot and wrap them individually in dahlia leaves for her offering. In remembrance of Father's favorite name for me, I brought him palm flowers. Because his most favored beverage was *kakaw* and he smoked cigars, I brought these along as well, the beans wrapped in a double thickness of dried tobacco leaves, one for each layer of the sky.

IT CAME OUR TURN AND THE ASSISTANT HANDED OUR GIFTS to his master. The old man nodded and smiled at me. As we knelt and watched him feed our offerings into the fire, I again asked my Father to forgive me for not being more forceful with Jatz'om. *If only... If only....*

Looking down the row of monuments, I leaned to Yax Nuun. "Those are the faces of your ancestors," I whispered. "Your grandfather was the ninth in his line, fourteenth since the founding of Mutal. The next monument to be planted here will be yours."

With our offerings burnt and no one behind us, the old man approached. "You are an Ich'aak?" he asked. "I noticed the tattoo on your cheek—and the mourning sign. It is for Ajaw Chak Tok Ich'aak that you morn?"

"I am his second daughter," I said softly. His eyes widened.

He reached out for my hand. "I thought it might be you." He pressed my hand to his forehead and bowed. "Then Jatz'om Kuh is—."

"My husband. This is my son, Yax Nuun."

Realizing that we did not want to be recognized, he bowed slightly and whispered to my son. "*Awinaken*," I am your servant. It was the first time I heard someone offer my son the term of respect reserved for rulers and succession lords.

"This is Ix Chab', my daughter."

The old man put his hands together. "Praise to Itzamnaaj and Juun Ixim," he said softly. Among the few teeth he had left, the two in front had jade inlays and were filed down at the sides to form the sign for breath. "I saw you from afar, dear lady. At the presentation in the plaza. Now I see even more, how much you look like your father. When they called your name it gave me great joy to see you. I thought I might approach you afterward, but you being a woman of Tollan—."

"I may have married and lived at Tollan, but I am and will always be my father's daughter and a daughter of Mutal." I'd never said that in front of the children. I was glad that they heard it. "We dressed like this to avoid notice. We came to see my father's monument."

A husband and wife approached carrying offerings. The old man passed the fire stick to his assistant and asked if he could speak to me alone. When he gestured to an amapola where we could sit on knee-high roots and be sheltered from the drizzle, I agreed and left the children to watch the assistant. "With respect daughter," he said. "I am called Naj Chan. It was my privilege to serve your father as Chan Chilam. I stood beside him for ten *tunob*..." What good fortune that was for me. As the Most High Jaguar Prophet, he'd presided over Father's rituals, recited his titles, read the auguries for him, and divined his path. Besides Mother, probably no one knew him better. "We smoked cigars together the evening before the raid."

"Did you see what happened?"

He shook his head. "The attack came in the middle of the night. I cannot understand; the gods gave us no warning. None from any direction. The gods are never quiet. But they were quiet about this. That should have been a sign to me."

"There were signs for me as well. Had I not been blinded by my dreams of coming home and fears throughout the journey, none of this would have happened. If I had known what my husband and his dogs were planning, I would have found a way to warn my father. What can you tell me about it?"

"My habit was to come to Precious Forest while it was still dark, to be with them for the dawning." He pointed to a path leading into the forest not far from where we were sitting. "I came through over there. Nearly stumbled over a body, a warrior. I held the torch up and all around..." The old man waved his hand and told about walking across the bloody, body-strewn plaza. "It made me cry," he said.

"Do you know how my parents were—?"

He shook his head. "It would do no good to tell you. All I will say is, they went quickly and honorably." I breathed deeply. "Two *k'inob* later guards came to my house. They removed us and burned the house to the ground. When I saw the other ministers and elders standing in the palace courtyard without their robes, headdresses, or batons I was certain they were going to put us down as well. Instead, Sihyaj K'ahk' came and told us some goddess had ordered the sacrifice of the Ich'aak. He said she told him to relieve us of our offices. He told us to take our families and leave the central district. If we stayed, his warriors would force us out."

"I could hear the cries in the night. The fires lit up the canopy. Where did you go? How are you living?"

"My first son has his family near Ixlu. He and his brothers are building a house for us there. "It is a long walk every morning, but the Great Trees must be fed. With all the trouble we have been having, the petitioners have almost doubled."

"I know that Father is pleased that you are doing this."

"Dear lady, he did more for me than I could ever repay. If there is anything I can do for you or your children. If I am not here you can ask at Ixlu."

"Were you here when Father dedicated the monument?"

"I watched them carve it." He led us behind the stone. "See here," he said pointing to a word-sign that contained a jaguar paw. "Your father's name."

Yax Nuun read aloud the signs at the bottom of the stone: "He completed it. The seventeenth *k'atun*. Here at Mutal Sky place."

Naj Chan gestured for Yax Nuun to follow him a few steps and he pointed to the top of the Yax Hal Witz. "Up there," he said, "is where they counted, blessed, and bound the stones. I presented the sacred bloodletter— a red-feathered stingray spine—to your grandmother. And she presented to your grandfather." He turned to me. "You know they were very proud of you. They spoke of you often. Your contribution meant much to them. And to Mutal"

"As it happened, it brought them down."

Naj Chan led us around to the front of the monument. Careful that we weren't blocking the view of those presenting gifts, we stood back and to the side of the mat. Yax Nuun pointed to an object in my father's hand, a jaguar paw with the claws extended. Because of the way he gripped the leg, he asked Naj Chan if it was an axe. "With respect Ajaw Le, that was his scepter. Your uncle Naway made it. He gifted it to your grandfather to use at the completion ceremony. That was real pelt, not painted. And the claws were pieces of white shell."

"What happened to it? Can I see it?"

"Last I saw, it was in a box in the regalia chamber at the palace. If it is not there, it was probably taken along with the other items that were taken or destroyed in the raid." Naj Chan took Yax Nuun around to the back of the monument and placed his hand on one of the word-signs. I followed. "The *aj yuxul* your grandfather commissioned to oversee the carving of this stone was a master who came all the way from Chaynal. He treated him very well, even had a shelter built at the quarry so the men could work through the rains. The stone was much fatter than what you see here. Yax Nuun had his head tilted back, looking up; the monument was at least four times his height. Frown-lines creased my son's smooth forehead. "How did they get it here?" he asked.

"They wrapped it in three layers of palm fronds. Then came a wrapping of thick matting. They tied on long cords. And while men pulled the top up using a hoist, others set a rolling-log under it. They repositioned the hoist over the bottom, lifted it, and set it down on another log. Finally they put another log under the middle and they rolled it to the causeway where they had to stop. The reservoir trail wasn't wide enough for the rolling logs, so they widened it and dug out the roots. It took several k'inob to get it to where we are standing."

"The monuments were all carved here?" I asked. "Is that right?"

"They were. Your father wanted the carving to be deeper than the others." Naj Chan pointed to Father's elbow. "See here? To make it look like he was standing in front of the temple doorway, the *aj yuxul* carved his arm so it overlaps the frame—which he said was the doorway. The dedication was grand. Many dignitaries were up there on the Yax Hal Witz, all wearing their quetzal headdresses and feeding the censers. The plaza was filled with people. As part of your father's oratory he repeated the words that earned him the title, Contribution Lord. You were a little flower then?"

"I have not come to rule," I recited. "I have come to contribute."

Naj Chan raised his eyebrows. "Ever since, I proclaimed that title whenever I introduced him."

Ix Chab' pointed to the figure of a man under Father's feet. He lay partly on his side but with his sandaled feet raising in back with his head and shoulders high, grasping a bundle to his chest. "Is that one of his captives?" she asked. The figure's artificial beard, the black mask across the eyes, the sacrificial knots on his sandal and especially the knotted burial cloths around his midsection indicated that he was an esteemed ancestor, not a captive. Naj Chan pointed to the signs in his headdress. "He held the order," it says. "He kept the count of *tuns* and *k'atuns*." He pointed to the signs alongside the figure's leg and read, "It happened at Mutal Sky place." He pointed again, this time to the bundle that the figure pressed to his chest with hands turned in, the gesture for *precious*. "It says he was the keeper of the god-bundle." The old man turned to Yax Nuun. "This is his father, Ajaw K'inich Muwaan Jol. Your great-grandfather. His name is carved on the back of the stone."

"Why is grandfather standing on him?" Yax Nuun asked.

"He is not standing on his father's back as he would a captive. He is rising above him as a maize stalk rises from its seeds. Because rulers are the   Great Trees of their centers, your grandfather wanted to honor his father by showing him as both his seed and root."

Yax Nuun went closer to the stone and pointed. "Why is the *k'in* sign on one anklet and *ak'ab* on the other?"

"*K'in* for light, *ak'ab* for darkness. It shows your grandfather had one foot in the sky, the other in the Underworld. He spoke with and on behalf of the gods in both realms."

Naj Chan's assistant needed him at the fire. An old woman was on her knees in front of the altar, crying, rocking back and forth. While the old man tried to console her, I told Yax Nuun and Ix Chab' what I'd heard of their grandfather's reputation as warrior, builder, holy man, and orator, talents he used to expand Mutal's reach by welcoming foreigners and establishing two underlords. In telling them this I realized that these were all reasons why the lords of Tollan wanted the alliance.

Naj Chan came back to us shaking his head. The rain had stopped, so he took off his hat and we removed ours. He made a ticking sound with his tongue. "It is sad, dear lady. That woman is like so many here. Without a ruler people feel adrift, at the mercy of the gods who have not been protective. They fear for their lives. They worry about the growing season and what will happen to their children. Even as I tell them not to worry, I myself worry—for them and for the *caah*." As the husband took his wife away, another family came forward and handed their offerings to the assistant. Naj Chan gestured to the holy men burning offerings down the row of monuments. "For reasons we do not understand, our petitions are not being answered. This is why our people have stopped resisting. Sihyaj K'ahk' has them convinced the gods are favoring the Owl and the other Tollan houses." He stopped to talk to Yax Nuun. "With respect Ajaw Le, do you see how we need you? The gods will listen to you. You have—."

I interrupted quickly. "There is nothing he can do, not while Sihyaj K'ahk' is the regent."

"With respect daughter, Sihyaj K'ahk' is a warrior. His blood is no hotter than mine." Naj Chan persisted with Yax Nuun. "He may be a fierce warrior and hold the order for the moment, but you are the Ajaw Le. You have the rightful authority. You need not wait for him to pass the scepter to you. Do whatever you can to move up your ascension."

Yax Nuun didn't know what to say, so I spoke for him. "First comes manhood, the Descent of Spirits."

Naj Chan looked at me. "If I may?" His gesture to Yax Nuun seemed odd, but I nodded my approval. He took his hands and to my surprise hoisted him onto his shoulders so my son was as high as his grandfather's stone face. "Look there," he said turning to the people. The lines in front of the altars snaked nearly to the back of the plaza—three or four hundred people. The rain started again, so the old man backed under the thatch. "They are all waiting for you to take your place on the Mat. As soon as your father cuts the white bead from your hair, demand that he fix the date of your accession." He brought my son down, grasped both his hands and held his gaze for a moment. I was very uneasy about all this, but for some reason, perhaps because the old man had served my father, I allowed it. "I see in your eyes young lord, you will be more powerful than Sihyaj K'ahk'. And you are wiser than your father. You know better than they how to rule. Trust your grandfather and those who came before him. They will guide you."

The seriousness in Yax Nuun's eyes and the absorption of his sister as they listened to the old man made me smile inside. Freed from the prophet's gaze, Yax Nuun went to the back of the monument again and we followed. Naj Chan saw that he was trying to understand some of the word-signs. "Dear lady," he said. "If you would allow, it would be my privilege—. I would offer to teach him to paint and read the signs." Yax Nuun's eyes widened. Ix Chab' asked if he would teach her as well. I was most grateful, so I extended a loose invitation for him to come to the workshop.

Naj Chan picked up a stick that had a feather on the end of it. He used it to point to Father's name-sign and he looked at my son.

"Great Jaguar Claw," Yax Nuun said. Across from and below the name sign, his feather came to rest on the last sign in the row. Again, he looked at Yax Nuun

Yax Nuun shrugged his shoulders and shook his head.

"His breath lives on," the old man said.

"Ayaahh. True," I said. "His breath lives on."

"What does that mean?" Ix Chab' asked.

"It means his *ch'ulel* lives on in the stone."

Yax Nuun went around and looked up at his grandfather's face. "I see

103

what you mean, Mother. I think he can see us."

Naj Chan responded before I could. "With respect Ajaw Le, he sees everything. Not only with his eyes. He knows you, your sister and your mother better than you know yourself. He knows what you are doing. He knows everything that is happening here. Now more than ever, his heart is aching to help his beloved Mutal."

We were at the front of the monument, watching the assistant cast pink dahlia petals into the flames on behalf of a woman and her two daughters. "Did our offerings help?" Ix Chab' asked.

"They all help little one. Your grandfather takes all these petitions and presents them to the gods. Because they come from him, they are received most favorably." The old man and I exchanged hopeful glances.

The Great Trees

WE WERE GOING THROUGH ONE OF THOSE PECULIAR PERIODS in the rainy season when the late mornings were dark with only occasional dove rains, those veils of mist that drip from the canopy to form little rivulets that run across the pavement, between foot-stones, and alongside thick roots. Early in the evening, when the turtle rains fell in sheets and pounded the palm leaves, we would gather inside to listen and talk and eat by the hearth. When the gods stopped throwing their lightning and thunder bolts, we stood in the doorways and watched the rain make circles in little pools while sprouts raced their sticks in the stronger currents of runoff.

Ix Chab' and I were out in the clearing behind the workshop, helping the *aj jaay* who built our fire pit stack it with wood in preparation for a firing. Because the rain the night before blew in from the side of the shelter that covered it, I was determined to get an early start. We'd put Ix Chab's figurines in the pit and I was unwrapping the dedication jar when we heard screaming and shouting in the distance.

Moments like this always gripped my heart, worrying that some lord in need of a sacrifice for his altar might have come for Yax Nuun or Ix Chab'. The sounds grew louder, but no one was sounding the alarm. Then I remembered. Yax Nuun and his father had gone south to Ixlu and were intending to stay the night. I told the *aj jaay* to stay with my daughter and continue with the firing while I went to see what was happening. I threw a mantle around my shoulders, put on my rain hat and faced toward the shouting. I wasn't alone. Others, men and women, were running to see what was happening.

I rounded the reservoir and turned south where there were even more people. A stream of men wearing black body-paint and carrying axes, apparently from one of the men's houses, passed us. I felt a little more protected with them running ahead, but my heart raced as I thought about the possibility of a raid. I kept thinking I should turn back, but my curiosity was running ahead of my feet. I recognized a man coming toward me, running as if from a burning house. "What is it?" I asked, remembering that he was one of the assistants who burnt offerings at an altar down from my father's monument.

"They are toppling the Great Trees!" he shouted as he raced by. "I need to get help!"

AS QUICKLY AS I ENTERED PRECIOUS FOREST I BACKED UP AND sought protection against a wall. Down the way and ahead of me the plaza was filled with people. Women and men were shouting, pressing against warriors who hollered back, pushing with their shields, some of them swinging axes. The warriors from the men's house who'd run ahead of me were taken down by of row of Owls brandishing spearthrowers thirty paces in front of them. Jaguars with flint-tipped thrusting spears and long, obsidian-toothed maces that could sever a head in a single swipe couldn't get close enough to the Owls to use them. Like water through a sluice, the Maya kept coming—farmers wielding axes, women throwing stones, merchants hauling their wares, holy men shouting, warriors from other men's houses running, all streaming into the plaza to do what they could to resist the Tollan warriors.

Those using slings and blowguns fared well until they too were taken down with spears, some hurled from remarkable distances. Where spears thrown by hand were snapping like twigs against the Wolf, Puma, and Rattlesnake shields, those thrown with notched throwers penetrated both shield and man. The sight of skulls being bludgeoned, flesh being pierced, and blood spurting from necks, legs, and stomachs made me want to run back as fast as I could. But I had to see if what the assistant said was true.

I went up some steps to see beyond the people clashing with the Wolf and Rattlesnake. In the distance a long row of Owls, two deep with their backs to the Yax Hal Witz, held back another crowd of people who pressed hard against their shields and spear points, shouting and waving their fists, not at the warriors, but at the men behind them—stoneworkers wearing leather straps who pulled cords wrapped around the throat of a monument, attempting to topple it as they had three others that were being chopped into marl. Even as the monument fell, others moved to the next one in line and began the termination of its *ch'ulel* by hacking at the stone face with long-handled axes. Others broke up his altar.

I ran down the trail twenty paces and went alongside the platform wall, only stopping when a spear hit the pavement and slammed into the wall four paces in front of me. The thundering sound of yelps, grunts, and clashes made me run even faster, halting to go around or step over bodies, occasionally screaming to avoid being trampled. In the midst of all this it began to rain hard. And the blood began to run in rivulets across the lighter red masonry.

From the corner of the Yax Hal Witz I could see how the protesters, mostly women, were being held back by the long rows of warriors pressing them with their shields. Up on the central stairway at the level of the first terrace, a fierce looking Wolf, a first spear, called to the men below. Although we'd never spoken, I recognized him from the settlement. Having no thought about what I would say or do, I went around the back of the great pyramid, climbed the steps to the first terrace and made my way along the side. Even before I reached the front, the guards standing between the corner and the first spear saw me and barked. Quick as lightning they pointed their spears at me, one at my neck and the other between my breasts.

With all the commotion below and his calling down to get more men to chop up the toppled monument, the Wolf leader hadn't noticed my approach. It was only when he stopped shouting and turned to the men who were bringing in more cords that he saw me. I'd attended a banquet with Jatz'om the night before, so fortunately, my hair was still up on the sides. Although I wasn't wearing the *kaloomte'* necklace, I looked more Tollano than Maya. I couldn't move toward him, so I had to shout. "With respect, first spear, may I speak with you?" He ignored me and waved his arm to hasten the men below. I shouted again, "My husband is—."

"I know who you are," he shouted back, not taking his eyes off the men taking turns hacking a monument as if they were felling a tree.

Trying to remain calm while raising my voice I asked who had ordered the termination of the monuments. He gave a quick gesture and I looked up. In deference to the spears they kept trained on me, I moved to the front of the pyramid so I could see. At the top and in the center of the stairs, Sihyaj K'ahk' stood with two other Owls, all of them wearing triple-knotted headdresses with quetzal feathers streaming high and in back. I turned to the leader. "What are you orders?" I shouted but he ignored me. "How many monuments?" I called again, even louder, and got no response. "Tell Sihyaj K'ahk' — ."

"Go away!" he snapped. The guards holding me at spear point looked at each other and smirked. Ignoring them I went to the edge of the terrace and gestured to Sihyaj K'ahk'. When he looked at me I signed my demand that he stop the destruction, adding that I was speaking for my husband. He folded his arms and looked away, intent on the happenings below. His refusal, together with the guards' smirk, confirmed what I suspected.

WITH JATZ'OM AND YAX NUUN NOT EXPECTED UNTIL EARLY evening, Gray Mouse and Ix Chab' spent most of the day helping me become presentable as the wife of the great prophet, complete with his mother's red gown, the cattail headdress, and *kaloomte'* necklace. To prepare myself for the coming storm, I told Gray Mouse what I wanted to say to Jatz'om while she ran avocado through my hair. As if to give me courage, Itzamnaaj, the "Far Seer" and Lord of Lords, pounded the world outside with thunder and lightning.

Except for a reddish break in the clouds to the East, it was turning dark. The canopy and roofs were silent except for the runoff and dripping cold. Having told Jatz'om that I would never enter my father's sleeping chamber as long as he slept there, I arranged for Cave Frog to deliver him to the rebuilt guest house where we could talk in private. It took an argument, but I insisted. No matter how weary or wet he was I wanted to see him immediately. And alone.

Jatz'om came, accompanied by two guards carrying torches. Stomping the mud off his sandals, he dismissed the guards with words in private and they stayed outside.

"I expected this," he said. "Could it not wait until—?"

"Then you admit it," I said. "You ordered the termination of the monuments."

Jatz'om removed his cloak, went to the brazier and faced his palms to the flames. "*Terminate* and *remove* was the order," he said calmly.

"All of them? My father's stone as well?"

"One insult to the gods is too many."

"Both our people petition the gods through the ancestors. Yours kneel before their shrines. Mine kneel before their monuments as well as their shrines. How would you feel if we destroyed your shrines?"

Jatz'om sat on one of the mahogany benches and pulled his cloak over his knees. "You forget, dear one. Your people and mine—everyone—will perish if they continue in the old ways. Stone is reserved for the gods. It was necessary. Do you not want your people, all people, to continue to walk the face of the earth and prosper?"

"Have you been to Precious Forest? Have you seen the bodies and blood?"

Jatz'om shook his head. "We just arrived. Sihyaj K'ahk' is following his orders."

"How many *sacrifices* does your goddess require? When will she be satisfied?" Jatz'om gave no response. "What can I say to get you to stop this?" Again, he remained silent. "Why not let the Maya remove them, give them a proper burial? There would less resistance, no more killing—."

"You know better. They would resist either way."

"I saw noblemen and their wives are out there. Many women. This is just the beginning. More are coming. I know my people. They are willing to give their lives so the Great Trees may live."

"All that attention and devotion should be going to the gods."

"You chose the height of the rainy season to do this? Why now?"

"The situation became urgent."

"Urgent? How?"

"When you took Yax Nuun and Ix Chab' to see their grandfather's monument. Yax Nuun told the servants he made offerings."

"Ayaahh, you are that vindictive?"

"When Yax Nuun takes the Mat it will be the enforcement of the *noh tzol* that demonstrates his commitment to walking the path of abundance, not paying homage to his grandfather. His burden is to lead Mutal forward, not backward."

It was useless to say anything more. Suddenly, there came a downpour of otter rain and he turned to the doorway.

"You have made your decision," I said. "I have made mine."

"What does that mean?"

"It means I am going to stand with my Father. To get to his monument, they must get through me first." I went to the door, got one foot on the threshold and backed away from spear points.

"Forgive me dear one. Until Sihyaj K'ahk' carries out his orders, you will remain here."

"You cannot hold me here. I burnt this house to the ground once. I can do it again. And I will."

"I will send Gray Mouse to attend your food and comforts." He turned to the guards. Now there were four. "Do not speak to my wife," he told them. Take no orders from her. She is not to leave this house until I say so. Use force if you need to. If she sets fire to the house, she will perish in it. Do you understand?" They nodded. "Convey this to your relief. Her only companion will be her attendant. Gray Mouse may come and go for necessities, but I want one of you to follow her wherever she goes. Admit no one else into this house, not even my son or daughter." He turned to me. "When Precious Forest has been cleared of its monuments and your people, you may return to the residence and your workshop."

Jatz'om went through the doorway and two of the guards lit his way with their torches. The other two remained inside and faced each other with crossed spears. I paced a while and then sat. Although I could no longer hear the frightful sounds at Precious Forest, I kept seeing raindrops splashing in pools of blood and axe heads smashing against stone faces, hands, and word signs.

Exhausted, I gathered some cushions and pillows and took them into the back corner where I could be close to the hearth and as far from the guards as possible. Despite the growing lump in my throat, I refused to cry. I clutched a pillow to my chest and stared up at the thatch. *How long does it take for a memory to die? At least Yax Nuun and Ix Chab' got to see*

Father's monument. But will they remember it enough to tell their children and grandchildren? The sound of the runoff outside brought to mind the blood I saw flowing across the plaza. And the men hacking the stone into gravel. *What happens to a* caah *when her former rulers, the Great Trees have been toppled? What is a forest without her fallen trees? Who are we as a people? What are we, without our ancestors? What happens to Father's* ch'ulel *when it leaves the stone? Where does it go? Does he gather it back or does it just die?*

I must have been six or seven when Father took us to a place in the forest where men on a scaffold high above the flutes of a gigantic amapola took turns chopping at the tree. I remembered it because of the groan the tree made when it was about to fall. Whether for the groaning sound or the tree crushing other trees when it fell, I cried. Waiting for Gray Mouse to come with my food, I recalled what Father said that day: The reason he named Mutal's ritual center Precious Forest, what made it precious, was the living presence of the Great Trees, the former rulers who made and sustained her.

The Sweeper

THROUGHOUT MY CONFINEMENT IN THE GUEST HOUSE, before going to sleep each night, I put a little piece of charcoal in a calabash. Besides listening to the rain, taking naps, and stoking the fires that kept raging inside me, I had nothing to do but wait for my attendant's visits.

One of my dreams, likely encouraged by the thunder and lightning, was Sihyaj K'ahk' tearing out my heart and hurling my body down the temple steps. When I awoke I realized that having the life pulled out of me wasn't nearly as bad as the helplessness I felt bounding from step to step, and then lying at the bottom of the steps, a bag of skin and bones, feeling that it didn't matter. Nothing mattered.

When the guards released me I counted eleven pieces of charcoal in the calabash. The first thing I did was to take a long sweat with Ix Chab' and Gray Mouse. Afterward, I wanted to see for myself what had happened at Precious Forest. They said there was nothing left of the monuments, but I hoped to find some remnant of my Father's monument, if even a piece of gravel or dust, for my altar.

It was not to be. Guards had been posted to keep people away from the plaza. The only way to tell where the monuments once stood were patches of fresh paint on the red pavement. Tollan holy men paced the entrances in their red and yellow robes, calling out warnings about the "curse of agonizing death" that a sorcerer put upon anyone who attempts to mark or revere the places where the Great Trees stood. Listening to the details of the curse made me realize that Jatz'om fully understood that it was the *memory* of our rulers that kept them alive. And that's why he had to destroy every trace of them.

Days later Gray Mouse and I were walking the reservoir trail when an old man called to me from behind. He was limping and hurrying to catch up, so we stopped. "My lady," he said with a bow. "Forgive an old man for calling out so and following you." He looked ahead and back to see if anyone was coming. "I saw you up on the terrace at the Yax Hal Witz—when they were terminating the monuments. When you passed back there I thought I would ask." The old man was missing his teeth and his odor caused me to step back. "I am on the doorstep of Xibalba," he said. "I tend bees in the forest—alone now, except for my dog. So I care not about the curse. If you want to know about the monuments, I can tell you what I saw."

"I would be very grateful for anything you can tell us," I said.

"It is my privilege to keep the steps of the Yax Hal Witz clear of leaves and wash off the bird droppings, so I am up there every *k'in*."

"You are a sweeper?"

He chuckled. "There is no end to it, dear lady. My wife and I witnessed the ascension of two rulers: K'inich Muwaan Jol and his son Chak Tok Ich'aak. May the gods bless them both."

"Chak Tok was my father," I said.

The old man eyes widened and he stepped back. He covered his mouth and started to kneel but I stopped him. "With respect dear lady, your father is how I came to sweep. When he took the Mat he said he came to contribute rather than rule and that stayed with me. It made me want to do something more than tend my garden and the bees. I have been sweeping ever since."

"He made us all want to contribute. What can you tell us about the monuments?"

"I saw it all, first to last."

"My father's monument was the last in the row."

"They started fierce, probably because of the crowd. But once the warriors cleared the plaza the stoneworkers tired quickly. After three k'inob they were only up to the ninth ruler. The last five stones were fatter and taller than the others, so after they were toppled instead of chopping them into marl, they rolled them out on logs."

"Did you see where they took them?"

"Forgive me, dear lady. I do not wish to add to your heartache, but you should know: those five were all chopped into pieces before they rolled them out. They rolled easily. It only took—."

"Which direction did they take them?"

"Same as the marl. They went along the causeway and turned onto the reservoir trail. After that I could see no more. Even from the top of the Yax Hal Witz the trees blocked my view." The rains had washed away any indication that logs carrying heavy stones had passed along the reservoir trail, but the sweeper found a gouge in the dirt and some branches that looked to have been hacked recently. As we looked for more such signs, three men wearing purple-stained leather aprons approached, so we stepped aside. When they were passed us the old man continued. "Beyond the reservoirs, if you keep to the trail going west you will come to a clearing where they are building a plaza and a great pyramid. My guess is the builders are using the gravel and stones for the fill-pens."

The old sweeper had risked his life in telling us this, so I gave him the only thing I had with me—my obsidian blade. He bowed, we exchanged gratitudes and he turned back. I wanted to continue on to the construction site, but there was a reception that evening for Yajaw K'inich Bahlam—Father's traitor from Waka'. Much as I hated even the thought of it, Jatz'om said it was necessary for me to sit with his wife. Getting cleaned and gowned wouldn't take that long, but because Gray Mouse had to undo my serpent-turban and shape my hair into Tollan ear-rolls with straight bangs, we had to turn back.

Gravel

THE RECEPTION FOR K'INICH BAHLAM AND HIS FAMILY ONLY served to show me how divided I was. On the outside I was pleasant. I even smiled and was courteous to Jatz'om's guests—who included the underlord's ministers of water, trade, and tribute, and two warlords who surely had participated in the raid on Mutal. Inside I called them the foulest of names and, while listening to them talk, imagined the most agonizing ways of sending them to Xibulbu.

Throughout the evening their pleasantries, wordplay, and laughter left me cold. I could smile but I couldn't laugh. Nothing amused me in the least, not the orator and his story about the sky crocodile, not the dancers who bent their bodies in impossible ways, not even the singer with a deep voice who had everyone clapping to his drumbeat.

The night was long and the next day even longer, made tedious by needing to sit under a shelter at one of the larger training fields for warriors—a circle of mud—where Maya and Tollan hunters tried to best each other by capturing a tapir barehanded. Warriors competed for distance with their spearthrowers. Helmet-wearing boxers punched each other with stones in their hands until one of them could no longer stand. This and the other bloody games were so disgusting I kept looking away.

So it went for four long days and nights. All the while, I yearned to go to the construction site. The longer it took to get there, the greater was the likelihood that the pieces of Father's monument—if any had survived—would be chopped into marl and dumped into fill pens. When Sihyaj K'ahk' went to center and delivered his oratory on the *noh tzol*, his pretentious manner stirred the already raging winds within me and his comments created wave after wave of disgust and resentment. The storm grew even stronger when I saw Yax Nuun being puffed up by the false praise of the Waka' visitors. On the fourth night I had Gray Mouse offer my excuse for not being able to attend the farewell banquet. The illness she reported was real.

BECAUSE OF THE SHAPE OF OUR HEADS, ALL GRAY MOUSE AND I needed to do to be regarded as Maya was to gather our hair in cob tassels and wear either sarongs or *kubs*. Wanting to present myself as a noble-woman to the men at the construction site, Gray Mouse painted my shoulders and neck red, left off the mourning sign on my cheek, and dressed me in a full-length white *kub* with pink flowers around the neck and sleeves. Hers was plain, but I gave her a ribbon for her hair and I let her borrow modest pieces of shell for her ears and neck. With white sarongs and white mantles over our shoulders, we looked like highly placed mother and daughter.

We were on the reservoir trail, further along than where the sweeper had stopped us, when we saw two young men coming toward us. Normally we would divert our eyes in the presence of men not known to us, especially commoners splattered with white powder, but these men were Maya and I put custom aside. "Glorious *k'in*," I said with a nod.

I surprised them by speaking, even more by stopping in front of them. The tall one bowed slightly and touched the brim of his hat. "Pray Chahk to pour rain and wash off more of this powder," he said.

"May I ask young man? We were told there is a grand pyramid being built further on. Can you direct us to it?"

"We can noble lady," he said. "We just came from there."

The shorter man had a deep scar down the side of his face. "We are stonecutters," he said. "Apprentices," his brother was quick to add.

"I would not put you at risk by asking about the stones that were removed from Precious Forest, but I wonder if the master at the site would allow us—."

"You are not the first. People have been coming to the site ever since. They find ways to not talk about it, but we all know what they want. One old man had us blink our eyes if what he said was true."

"The curse only applies those who *speak* about it," the shorter man said.

The older brother nodded. "That is why we cannot..."

I pulled my net bag around for them to see. "As I said, I would not put you at risk. A curious thing however, some say *kakaw* beans can cause a man to blink when he is asked a question." The brothers glanced at each other and grinned.

This is how we learned that both gravel and large, carved stones had arrived at the construction site. When I asked if the carved stones had been broken up, my heart sunk when both brothers blinked. "Were there pieces large enough to show any carving?" I asked. Neither man blinked.

"No carving?" Gray Mouse asked. They both blinked.

"Broken into gravel?" Again they blinked. "We are on our way to the site. Do you think the master will let us look?" she asked.

"He and the supervisors are all Maya," the shorter one said. "They turn their heads when people come to look, but they are not allowed to take anything, not even the gravel. It is very dirty."

"There is nothing to see. Just mounds of broken stone," the other said. I gave them each more beans, expressed my gratitude and we went ahead. Even if there was nothing to see at the construction site, it felt good to walk the ground where Father, Mother, my brothers and Ixway had walked together. Because the reservoirs on both sides were so deep it always amazed me that, what looked like lakes were actually dug out canyons lined with clay well before my great-grandfather took the Mat.

The construction site was fronted by enormous heaps and tangles of fallen trees, vine, and vegetation waiting to be burned. Behind it lay an expanse of limestone bedrock where hundreds of slaves chipped and carried stone to a central area where supporting pens had been erected. The only indication of the structure it was to become was four red-painted poles that marked the corners and green ones that likely marked the placement of stairways in all four directions. As we were told, on the far side of the tangled trees and brush, there were some people walking around mounds, picking up stones and sifting gravel through their hands.

The New Order

I'D FORGOTTEN HOW MUCH WATER COULD POUR FROM THE jungle sky. And how hard. At Tollan lightning was generally far off and spread out, flashing mostly above the clouds. All day sometimes and often through the night, the lightning lords threw their fiery spears at the canopy with startling, chest pounding thunderclaps. Father said it was during the rainy season that we came closest to feeling the power of the Makers.

The disappointment of not finding even a piece of Father's monument and then having all but two of my vases crack because they weren't fired properly, left me sitting in my workshop watching the rain pound the stones in front of the doorway.

Although I missed them, it was good that Yax Nuun and his sister were being kept busy at the residence, he with his preparations for the Descent of Spirits, she at her loom weaving a *kub* to wear at the ceremony. Becoming a man of the *caah* only happens once. I didn't want my brooding and complaining to take away from it, so I kept Gray Mouse at the residence to look after the servants while I sat and thought my miserable thoughts, knowing that I was neither suffering my children's sympathies nor their attempts to make me feel better.

Naj Chan had introduced me to an *itz'aat*, a Maya artist and sage named Long Stroke Macaw who, as it turned out, provided me with a strip of coated bark paper containing the word signs I needed for the jar similar to the one Father cached when he dedicated the palace. For some reason, perhaps because Yax Nuun was disappointed that he hadn't been able to find someone to do the painting, my heart wasn't in it. I'd barely started the incising when I stared dreaming how it would be if I commissioned a carver to make another stone like Father's and have it set in the workshop. Of course, it was impossible. But I enjoyed the dream. Finally, I covered the lid, put it aside, and re-folded the strip of bark paper.

With my back to the wall and flames from the hearth licking the bottom of a water jar hanging above it, I stared out the doorway. It was a day for dreaming. *How could this have happened? Am I being punished? My husband is a demon, enslaved by his goddess. My son is preparing to walk his path. Ix Chab' will likely marry a Tollan warrior. Father's* ch'ulel *is gone. I will remember him, but without his monument will anyone else? When we are gone his memory will die and his contributions will cease. By then Mutal will have turned into another Tollan—if she survives at all.*

Naj Chan came down the path and waved at me. I took his wet hat and cloak and offered him a cloth to dry his arms and legs. Shivering, he apologized for coming unannounced. I gave him a blanket for his shoulders and had him to sit close to the hearth. While we spoke again of the tragedy at Precious Forest I served him some hot *keyem.* "Your mother served it this way," he said. "Very tasty—honey with a bit of chili powder."

"I like more than a bit," I said. "If it is too strong—."

"With respect daughter, I thought you should know. Our people are taking up weapons. Even the young ones at the men's houses are making spearthrowers and practicing with them. The Jaguars and Quetzals who pledged themselves to Sihyaj K'ahk' are talking against him now. I keep watching the sky. The way the wanderers are aligning, this could be the unraveling of the *caah.* It could come soon."

"Because of monuments?"

He sipped the hot maize and nodded. "The *noh tzol.* Farmers and tradesmen, even their sprouts, are making weapons and shields. The *k'uhul winikob*, my brothers, are enflaming them. Everyone is talking against Sihyaj K'ahk'. They want to put him down. With respect, your husband as well. I thought you should know."

"You have my gratitude, Naj Chan. I hear very little of what is happening. Jatz'om has cut me off from the council. He has been keeping the children close to the palace. The servants and attendants do my bidding, but they are not talking to me."

"Sihyaj K'ahk' is trampling our ways. He says he speaks for your son. We do not want to believe him, but with respect, Yax Nuun just stands and nods his agreement. The *noh tzol* is like an axe, chopping down everything your father and the Great Trees before him established. Instead of fixing rituals and festivals on the *haab* which is the counting of the *k'inob* since the making of the world, he says they will now be fixed on the round of two-hundred sixty *k'inob*, the count used by farmers and midwives to mark Ajaw K'in's journey north and south. With respect dear lady, is this something you understand?"

"I know the Tollanos favor shorter rounds and their calendar honors Ajaw K'in, rather than Juun Ixim."

"That is changing as well. Since the beginning, the sacred rounds have always ended on Eight Ajaw. That is the order, the proper order, established by Juun Ixim himself at the beginning of the world. The Tollanos say the only rounds that matter are those ending on Thirteen Ajaw."

"Thirteen is a sacred number for the Tollanos. Are they not letting you keep to your calendar?"

"The *aj k'inob* can keep the count as before, but all the rites, festivals and writings of the *caah*, they want them rooted in the Ajaw K'in count and the Thirteen Ajaw ending. What will Juun Ixim think when he arrives for his festivals and sees the plaza bare? With respect dear lady, the winds brought in by the Tollanos are choking us."

"These changes, the *noh tzol*, are they coming from my husband or from Sihyaj K'ahk'?"

"Both. But we rarely see your husband. Sihyaj K'ahk' ordered a gathering of the former ministers, council members, warlords, first spears, the *k'uhul winikob*, even the long-distant merchants. By my count eighty men faced him at the settlement." I shook my head. I knew nothing of this. "The messengers told us we were 'invited,' but what kind of invitation comes with spears?"

"What happened?"

"They were all there—Sihyaj K'ahk', your husband, the council and the ministers. They greeted us with smiles, even gave us tamales with turkey meat and *saca* to drink. While we ate, your husband delivered the

120

prophecy—the same as at the presentation in the plaza. Sihyaj K'ahk' told us what the *noh tzol* required—the calendar changes, the reordering of the marketplaces, how Tollan-style frames and slopes would be built on the terraces of all new buildings, and how only the likenesses of the gods may be carved in stone or painted on walls. The only monuments they will allow are those that mark the journeys of the gods burdened with the calendar rounds, especially the *k'atun* endings. Also, rather than *healing* those who commit evil deeds, they will be *punishing* them. Even worse, they are binding all the warrior houses, Mayas and Tollanos, into one house, one house with many compounds—with Sihyaj K'ahk' at the head and all wearing red and black."

I shook my head. "That will never happen. The warrior houses all have different patrons."

Naj Chan's gesture said he didn't understand. "Apparently he expects only one to prevail."

"That would be the Owl. Jatz'om's father is the supreme Owl."

"There is more. Sihyaj K'ahk' said we can expect the burdens of both goods and labor to be increased. Instead of one visitation to the counting house by the *head* of the household, they want *every* adult male to sit before the tribute collectors—three times a *tun!*" Unusual for a holy man, Naj Chan was raising his voice. "As for my brothers and me, including those of the K'alk'in Brotherhood, they are requiring us—even at my age—to make a pilgrimage to Tollan."

"I am not surprised. One of their patrons is a feathered serpent, a god of fertility. The lords of Tollan need pilgrims to come and bring him gifts. They say he favors salt, cotton, *kakaw* beans, green obsidian, and jade."

"He finished his speech saying we needed to go and tell everyone what we heard. Daughter, some of us were hoping you could talk to your husband. He is the only one who seems to have power over Sihyaj K'ahk'.

"It was good you came to me, Naj Chan. You have my gratitude for telling me this, but my husband does not listen to me. His father chartered him to establish the *noh tzol* in the lowlands and Sihyaj K'ahk' is carrying it out. There is nothing more I can say or do. I tried."

The holy man got up, gripped the blanket tight at the neck and paced. "Entire lineages have already left. The only men not talking about leaving are those talking about fighting. Sihyaj K'ahk' kept assuring us he had not come to turn Mutal into another Tollan, but that is what he is doing."

"I sat with the lords of Tollan. They are so determined to save the world, they will do *anything* to restrain the wrath of the gods. Because the *noh tzol* brought abundance to Tollan, they see it as the only path."

"Then you believe the prophecy?"

"I did. Now I trust no one, especially not a goddess who orders the slaughter of her children."

Naj Chan sat again, held his hands to the hearth and sighed. "Why would the gods tell the Tollanos they were going to wipe clean the face of the earth and not tell us? What makes the Tollanos so favored that they alone are given the authority to make gods and rulers—and come here and tell us how to live?"

I didn't have an answer. As our conversation continued and the sky darkened, the old man's manner changed from humble petitioning to despair. I had to get back to the residence before dark, so I offered that he could stay the night in the workshop and wait for me in the morning. "If I can talk to my husband about this, what would you have me to say to him?"

"With respect and gratitude dear lady. If instead of requiring the changes at the point of a spear, could take council with him—without Sihyaj K'ahk'—to understand the reasons for these changes? How do they save the human beings? How it is in other places? In what ways are changes in the calendar, in monument building and tribute obligations going to bring abundance to the *caah*?"

"I will try to speak to my husband, but I can make no promises. I learned more about the *noh tzol* from you just now than I ever did from him."

"Daughter, speaking for those who were privileged to serve your father, we are grateful that you are willing to try."

I WAITED A WHILE AT THE RESIDENCE FOR JATZ'OM, BUT WHEN Cave Frog came and said his master was at the palace with Sihyaj K'ahk' and some ministers I decided to wait and speak to him in the morning.

Gray Mouse helped me undress and I settled onto my sleeping bench. The thought of talking to Jatz'om about the new order made my stomach growl. I was near to sleep when the demon that had taken up residence in me put a question in my head which, delightful as it was to consider, I knew I couldn't carry it out. He asked: *What would happen if Jatz'om and Sihyaj K'ahk' were to suffer a fatal, accidental fall down the palace steps?* With pleasure, I imagined Yax Nuun taking the Mat with Naj Chan and myself among his closest advisors.

As it happened, my conversation with Jatz'om was short that morning. It was nearing midday and raining hard when I went to the workshop. Naj Chan greeted me in the doorway. "I tried but he would not listen," I said. "We talked about Yax Nuun and the Descent of Spirits and that brought up the changes in the sacred calendar. When I asked how it was being changed he held up his hand and dismissed me."

Seeing the water in my eyes, the old man extended his arms and I fell into his embrace, sobbing. "He destroyed my family. He has my children. He chopped down the memory of the Great Trees. Now Mutal is falling." I wiped my eyes with my sleeve. "What will you tell the others?"

"I will tell them you tried. What else can we do? I will never accept that Itzamnaaj and Juun Ixim have abandoned us. I will offer what I can and pray even more fervently to your father."

"Do you expect violence?"

He nodded. "And we will loose more families."

"What of your family? Will you leave?"

Naj Chan removed the blanket from around his shoulders, found his hat and turned. "Mutal is the only world I know. Our roots here grow nearly as deep as yours. Whatever happens my branches and I will be here, standing as tall as we can, as long as we can." In the doorway he snugged his hat. "When the rains stop my sons said they would help me clear a field next to theirs. Farther north." He held up his walking stick. "Given what is happening, I think I can do more with a planting stick than I can with a staff." The old man expressed his gratitude again, bowed, and entered the veil of rain.

Lady White Gourd

JATZ'OM AND I HADN'T SAT TOGETHER FOR AN EVENING MEAL since I confronted him in his sleeping chamber, so I was surprised when Cave Frog came to say his master wanted Gray Mouse and me to join him for some paca tamales. I'd never seen him take food with a servant before, so I was very suspicious. Nonetheless, after hearing that Sihyaj K'ahk' would not be present, I accepted.

We hadn't seen the bright face of Ajaw K'in for ten days or more. The clouds were so thick and low above the canopy, at midday the sentries and guards carried torches, as did the servants who came to escort us to the palace. All through the meal Jatz'om tried to put Gray Mouse at ease. Although he'd known her for as long as he knew me, he knew next to nothing about her family.

With the platters removed, cups refilled and servants removed to the cookhouse, I finally learned the reason for his invitation. He turned and put his hand close to mine. "Dear one," he said. "I speak now with a desire to assist you, to ease your burden." *Now what?* "Your unhappiness has not gone unnoticed. What I mean to say—. I understand your upset over recent events..." For him to be saying this in front of Gray Mouse was highly inappropriate and it made me uncomfortable. "People are talking," he said. "Not just the servants."

"Who is talking? What are they saying?"

"You have not been yourself..."

You destroyed my family and crushed their memory. Now you and your dog are preparing my son to rule in ways that are tearing him and the caah *apart. And you complain that I am not myself?*

"I want you to see a healer. Your gloom has been casting a shadow on both the residence and the palace." I started to comment but Jatz'om held up his hand. "Gray Mouse found an *ix men*, a woman who treats—."

"Gray Mouse?" I turned and she nodded, obviously embarrassed that she had kept something from me. "You and she—?"

Jatz'om interrupted. "I ordered her not to say anything to you—or to anyone else." He nodded to Gray Mouse, inviting her to respond.

"With respect mistress, I was told I would be replaced if I didn't—."

"Just tell her what you found," Jatz'om insisted.

Gray Mouse averted her eyes. "With respect mistress, I found a healer, an *ix men*. A Maya woman called Ix Sak Tzu'. She works in the white way and casts out demons. She moved to Ixlu from Chaynal to be with her daughter."

"I sent a messenger," Jatz'om said. "She does not know who you are or who sent the messenger, but she said she would be willing to receive you."

I turned to Jatz'om. "No *ix man* can make me forget—."

"It would be good for you to get away for a while."

"Good for whom?" I didn't care that Gray Mouse heard me talking this way. "Now it is my fault?"

Jatz'om's gesture to calm me made it worse. I got up to leave. "Just listen to what Gray Mouse has to say about this woman. No one is forcing you, Dear One. Whatever you decide."

Mid way across the patio I stopped and turned. "If I would decide to go, Gray Mouse would need to accompany me."

"As you like."

"I would present myself as a Maya and I would walk all the way. No litter. No guards." He repeated himself with a wave of the hand.

Although I had no reason to scold Gray Mouse, I said nothing to her on the way back to the residence. Jatz'om sounded too sincere and eager, but I understood: that's how he got his way with people. *He wants me gone. Whatever the reason, it does not matter. Nothing matters.*

I LISTENED TO WHAT GRAY MOUSE HAD BEEN TOLD ABOUT THE healer, and I bore her many apologies for keeping the search for her a secret. Still, I decided not to go. With my duties as mistress of the residence and palace completed, I just wanted to be left alone to stay warm and dry in my sleeping chamber, under my blanket, with the drape across the doorway.

Late the following morning, Yax Nuun and Ix Chab' came in, obviously sent by their father. Yax Nuun said I looked defeated. I felt defeated. After a while I couldn't resist the concern in their eyes, so I decided to go. Ixlu was just a morning's walk from Mutal. If I didn't like the healer or approve of her methods, I could return the same day.

Once there, everyone I asked was eager to guide me to the healer's compound. A curving mound of eight or ten stone steps led up to a dirt patio surrounded by four pole-and-stone thatched structures painted white. Normally I was wary of dogs and gave them wide berth, but because the brown, scruffy-haired brute that had finished urinating on the top step backed away without so much as a growl, we went up the steps. When he started barking, a plump woman with full cheeks and hair parted down the center clapped her hands and he leapt away. "Welcome," she said with a smile. "You are seeking Ix Sak Tzu'?" I nodded, watching the dog circle back. "I am her daughter. They call me Muwan. Just Muwan." The dog came and sniffed our feet. "He is friendly. He just wants to know you. This is your first time here, is it not?"

"It is," I said. "We came from Mutal."

Gratefully, Muwan patted the dog on the shoulder and the scruffy beast ran off. "This way," she said. "I will see to your comforts. Then you can join the others." The "others" she spoke of consisted of a line of ten people waiting to see the shaman, all standing along the wall of the longest building, the only one with an extended roof. The women in front and behind us confirmed what Gray Mouse had heard—the shaman took the name Ix Sak Tzu', Lady White Gourd, because she swore an oath only to practice white healing. As a sign of it, she always wore white. They said she'd come to Ixlu only recently, but was already widely known and respected, especially for treating fractures of the heart: *ch'ulel* loss, stomach aches, skin conditions, nervousness, sadness, and madness. I was encouraged when they mentioned the last two.

One of the women in front of us had an adolescent daughter who hid behind her and seemed never to have passed a brush through her hair. This was their second visit to the shaman, and they'd traveled two days. Watching the comings and goings around the compound, I noticed four women who seemed to live there. One of them was with child. Another, intent on her threads, had her backstrap loom attached to a doorpost across from us. A man I was told was Muwan's husband, sat in the doorway further down, apparently telling stories to three little sprouts while he tied a torch.

When finally we were admitted, the shaman, whom I judged to be in her late thirties, bowed to us. After I conveyed the reason for my visit, she politely asked Gray Mouse to wait outside. On the way to Ixlu I had imagined her to be a bent-over old woman whose features would resemble a reptile. Instead, she stood a head taller than me, was well proportioned and quite handsome. Her voice was deep for a woman, a bit raspy, as if she needed to cough. The little lines that radiated from her eyes and those that creased her cheeks seemed to have come more from smiling than age.

She held both of my wrists and squeezed, as if to determine their ripeness. As she gazed into my eyes in silence, I noticed the patches of gray and black hair coming out from under the black shawl that covered the back of her head. Because the shawl fell well below her waist in back, I imagined she also used it to carry produce home from the market. Apart from the red paint on her shoulders and a bird tattoo on the side of her neck, her only adornments were pink shell-tubes drawn through her earlobes. She felt the top of my head, put her hand on my chest to feel my heartbeat and then gestured for me to sit on a little bench that faced an altar. It was good to get off my feet and rest my back after standing so long on pavement. On one of the red-painted walls there were long rows of dried herbs hanging on hooks. In silence she broke off several pieces of varying kinds, lengths, and colors.

In the shadows behind the altar, on two levels of long planks, there was a grouping of ceramic figures. All men—painted, clothed, and surrounded with fresh flowers. I judged them to be her healing patrons rather than gods because their features were all human and they didn't have jewels in their eyes or god-markings on their bodies. Whoever they were, their constant gaze made me feel uneasy.

The altar itself consisted of a waist-high plank, deeper than my arm and twice as long, resting on four red logs positioned on a bed of dried pine needles. On the male side of the altar, sitting on a bed of green needles, there were separate baskets for colored stones, feathers, beans, copal and four colors of maize kernels. In front of them, a wisp of smoke rose from a little hand-censer that had the head of a serpent on the handle. A flat ceramic circle that showed the charred remains of previous offerings marked the center of the altar. Mixed in with the smudges of burnt wood and ash were green leaves, bits of broken stone and bone, twigs of herbs, a piece of crystal, and pink flower petals. Around the offering plate, maize kernels had been mounded in the four directions: red marking the East, white the North, black the West and yellow the South. On the female side there were the little rows of beans and crystals, apparently used in divinations.

White Gourd stood behind me. "Just stay still," she said. I waited for her touch but it never came. Instead, she moved around me facing her hands toward every part of my body. "Show me your hands," she finally said. She looked at both sides, went to the altar, took a crystal and a handful of red beans. These she placed in the flat of both my hands and she put her hands face down on mine. She chanted in the highland tongue. Rather quickly I felt my hands becoming warm. Then hot. Continuing to chant, she took the beans and crystal from me and laid them on the offering plate so the crystal was in the center and pointing east. Above and below it she arranged four rows with the beans and fed some copal into the little censer. When the smoke rose she waved the crystal through it then gave it to me. "Hold this to your heart," she said. As I did, she pulled up another bench, placed it in front of me and sat with her eyes closed and her palms facing me. Her lips moved but she made not a sound. She opened her eyes, took the crystal from me, laid it on the plate and then turned back to me. "Daughter, it appears you have been choked and smothered," she said. "The choking fractured your *ch'ulel* and much of it, perhaps most, has scattered—quickly." She smacked her hands together. "Like sparks from a fire."

"Will it come back?" I asked.

She squeezed the flesh at the bottom of my throat. "Is it tight here?" I nodded. "It is an effort to speak, is it not?"

"Everything is an effort."

She sat back. "It is good you came to see us, daughter. The darkness will grow if it is not treated. There is a storm raging inside you. If it does not calm you could find yourself on the dark road."

"In truth, I would prefer that to battling those storms. I am weary of it."

She put her hand on mine. "We hear this often. It feels like the smothering heaviness will never leave. Does it not?" I nodded again. "Your flame is weak, but as long as you have breath there is hope."

"Is there anything you can do? The storms keep raging. I think there is a demon in me stirring them up. I was never like this."

"What do you do when the storms come?"

"My blood boils and I think terrible thoughts. I dream violent dreams, even with my eyes open. I want to lash out. Sometimes I wish I were a warrior. Other times I take to my sleeping bench and cry. Even then, the demon screams and spews hateful words at—certain people. If my thoughts were axes, these people would be dead."

"How often does this happen?"

"When does it not?"

"Now we must ask: Do you truly want to be healed?"

What an odd question. *Why else would I have come here?* I thought of Yax Nuun and Ix Chab', what their lives would be like without their mother. "I need to be here for my son when he becomes a man, for my daughter when she takes a husband. But only if I will not be a burden to them."

"If you would like to think about this and come back—."

"No need. I can say now, if this *can* be healed I want it to be."

The shaman nodded, turned and took the crystal from the offering plate and gave it to me to hold in my fist. "Then tell us now, aside having the storms calmed, what is it you want?"

My thoughts rooted like a peccary digging for termites. "I cannot have what I want," I said. "Learning that it was destroyed is what choked me."

"Then that is gone. What do you want now?"

Again I had to root for an answer. I couldn't tell her I wanted to make a grand contribution to Mutal. Family heirlooms came to mind: father's offering bowl, his jade pieces, and the paw scepter. I wanted spacious and clean sleeping quarters as well, but none of these satisfied me. "I want my children to be safe and happy."

"That is for your children. What do you want for *you*?"

"I want things to be as they were when I was a flower. I want to be as I was then."

"This is what happens when the *ch'ulel* goes wandering. We grieve for the loss of ourselves; yearn for the way things were. You feel adrift, do you not?"

I nodded. "I am not the woman I thought I would to be—or wanted to be. Far from it. I was raised in—. Very differently. My husband has high standing in the *caah*. There are many expectations put upon me."

"We see you have a noble bearing and you speak well. You are the one who sent a messenger from Mutal, are you not?"

"My husband sent him. My brooding is an embarrassment for him, but I cannot help it. Terrible things have happened recently—beyond imagining."

"Did the changes in you happen before or after these terrible things?"

There hadn't been anyone standing behind me when I entered, but I expressed to the shaman that I was taking too much of her time. She assured me that I was last, and that we could talk until her husband called for her. Relieved, I settled myself on the bench, even crossed my legs. "I was twelve when my father sent me a great distance to marry. My husband, his family and his people were very different. They dressed differently and spoke a different tongue. I tried to be pleasant and I accepted their ways on the outside, but on the inside I found them disagreeable. Shocking at times. I saw things that terrified me. They treated me with respect—some more than others—but I was always an outsider."

"Did your husband know this?"

"He knew. There was nothing he could do about it. He was so taken with his father and his brothers—. My life only began for me when the children came. Of the four who touched the earth, two survived. I have a son, eleven. My daughter is eight. They are the reason I came to see you. They are frightened for me."

White Gourd nodded. "They were right to send you."

"You said I choked. It was my husband who made me choke. In just the last nine moons I learned he is not the man I thought he was. When my head was turned he destroyed—. Everything I cared about, even the dreams we had together for our children."

"He was striking back at you for something you did?"

"It had very little to do with me. His father told him to do something he knew would trample my hopes and dreams and he did it."

"Is your husband still alive?

"Our sleeping quarters are separate but on the same compound."

"Do you speak?"

"Only when necessary—which is often. My husband is a powerful man in the *caah*."

"You were raised in the lowlands, were you not?"

The shape of my head made that obvious, but she was asking something deeper. "Once bound, always bound," I said, reciting the common expression. "I could never leave him. He could never leave me."

She nodded. "Does he beat you?"

"He is not like that. Can I tell you something in confidence?"

"Nothing you say goes beyond these walls."

"My husband is a *k'uhul winik*. Because of his standing and due to circumstances above him, he has become a destroyer. He—." The words caught in my throat.

"He is ruled by a goddess. If she would tell him to have our chil dren—or me—sacrificed, he would order it."

She lifted my chin so she could see into my eyes. "With respect daughter, he is not your concern here. Not now. Being bound does not mean you must walk the same path."

I sobbed. "But he is the reason I am so miserable."

Someone coughed at the doorway. "That is my husband," White Gourd said. "You and your attendant will stay the night. We will take a sweat in the morning. Later, we will try to call back your *ch'ulel*. White Gourd stood and I followed her to the doorway. I expressed my gratitude for taking so much time with me and I asked how she is compensated. She patted me on the shoulder and said we would speak of her compensation after the winds and waves have calmed.

The White Flower

GRAY MOUSE AND I WERE IN THE SWEAT BATH TALKING WHEN White Gourd entered, naked but for a blanket draped over her shoulders. She removed the blanket, smiled and sat across from us. "Not enough steam," she said, dunking the dipper into a bucket of water and sprinkling the coals. Two more dippers-full and the world went white, burning my nostrils with every breath I took. I waited for her to say something but she remained silent, taking in deep breaths then letting them out. After a while we matched her pace and I became less startled by the drops of hot water falling from the ceiling.

Ten paces beyond the sweat lodge we followed the shaman up a steep grassy hill to a shelter where we spread our blankets on reed-mats and lay naked, looking up at a thatched roof supported by poles braced with cross poles. Even in the shade, I could feel the hot air sucking away the wetness. Again, we remained silent. I was near to sleep when raindrops on the thatch made me sit up. White Gourd said her daughter was expecting to feed us and it would be best not to keep her waiting, so we went to the house and got dressed.

The *uhl* that Muwan served had chili mixed into the balls of maize dough and water, as did the black beans. Afterward, Gray Mouse and I munched on roasted and generously salted grubs that had also been sprinkled with chili. Salt from the north was a rare treat, even at Mutal, so we were most appreciative.

The White Flower

I sat on the little bench again, facing White Gourd's altar. "Now we will call back your *ch'ulel*," she said with hopeful eyes. From a stoppered jar she poured water into an open-top gourd. "*Zuhuy ha'*," she said. "Pure, untouched. From the throat of the Underworld." From a basket she took a handful of salt, dropped it into the water and swirled the gourd with both hands. From other baskets she took kernels of red, black, white and yellow maize and added them to the salted water. Looking in, she observed, "the number of grains whose "mouths," the part of the kernels that were attached to the ear, are pointed up show us the lost parts of the *ch'ulel*. The others, the ones that are "seated," resting quietly on the bottom of the gourd are the parts still residing in you." White Gourd reverently lifted the gourd with both hands and turned toward the doorway. "Come," she said. Outside, Gray Mouse was talking to two women. She stood when she saw me and was prepared to follow, but I gestured for her to stay.

White Gourd took up her bamboo staff, her sign of office, and I followed her across the compound, past the sweat lodge and up the hill, past the shelter where we had dried ourselves and quite some distance along a narrow path to an outcrop of stones blackened by years of burnt offerings. "It is best to do this where your *ch'ulel* went wandering, but we will try this first." Setting the gourd on a high stone, she explained that she'd converted the old hunting shrine into a healing shrine when she came to Ixlu. Under one of the stones was a ceramic whistle in the shape of a bird. I held it for her while she went to two trees and asked them to forgive her for taking a branch that she needed for the calling. She had me kneel to the side of the shrine and remain silent. With the whistle in her mouth and blowing an eerie, high-pitched sound, she beat the ground with the wand of pine and oak brush calling in a loud voice, "Come, please! Come please! Come and enter gracefully. It is safe now. Come please!..."

Back at her altar, she had me sit beside her and hold out my arm. "This will not hurt," she said. "This is how we prepare the blood to receive the *ch'ulel*." She drank from the gourd and, keeping a little water in her mouth, she sucked noisily on the palm side of my wrist and then under the elbow. She swallowed the water and then turned to the altar where she fed copal into the burning censer. Throughout her whispered chant I was pleased to hear her invoking Itzamnaaj, not only because he was lord of the gods and patron of Mutal, but also because he was Father's personal patron.

White Gourd took a little piece of white bark-paper from her altar. I'd noticed it because it was cut in the shape of a four-petaled flower. She brushed the ash and other offering remains from the ceramic circle, set the paper flower on it, took four crystals from a basket and placed them on it so they pointed inward from the four directions. She held her hands over them and prayed in silence. When that was done she removed the crystals and placed the paper in the palm of my hand. "Until your white flower is whole again, keep this close. Wear it inside your clothing, over your heart, as often as you can. Keep it open and flat. Do not soil it or pierce it. Especially do not loose it. White flower attracts white flower, the parts of your *ch'ulel* that went wandering."

"This little paper can do that?"

"Your eyes see a paper flower. Our eyes see the tree from which it came. We use amate because the tree stands firm against the winds that blow through its branches. When the destructive winds blow, remember the amate and stand firm within yourself. No matter how ruffled your leaves, stand firm. Until your white flower is whole again, bend but do not break. In the midst of a storm, try to just stand and watch. Let it pass. That is what storms do, they pass. Whatever your husband says or does, stand and watch. The amate neither blames nor scolds the wind. It thinks not of lashing back. It knows it has deep roots and trusts they will hold."

"By 'roots' you mean my ancestors?"

"Call to them by name. Ask them for strength when the dark winds blow. You are Maya. You were brought up trusting as well as revering your ancestors, were you not?"

"I was. But I was also taught to speak up, and not let a man treat me like a dog."

"The greater part of standing and watching is knowing who you are and what you stand for. The warrior has his shield, the turtle has its shell, the house has a roof. Human beings hold to the truth of who they are in order not to be crushed."

"I have become so busy with the household, the children, and my husband's—torments—I have lost the truth of who I am. Whatever he says or does, you want me to just stand and watch? Say nothing? Do nothing?"

The shaman nodded. "Until your white flower is whole again. When your husband sings a song or dances a dance that offends you, stay steady inside yourself. Allow it and listen, but do not loose yourself by fighting against it. Stand firm. Remember your roots. As soon as you can, remove yourself to a quiet and beautiful place. Offer words of gratitude for what the gods have given you—and name them. And then ask the ancestors to guide you through the storm."

"You sound like my mother. She talked to me like that when I was a flower. But I get—distracted. And upset, perhaps too easily. When I see something out of place I have to speak up. I am the mistress of two large households. I supervise servants..." I explained that if I didn't scold them and constantly show them the proper ways to behave and do the things that needed doing, those places would not reflect the high standing of the residents—that they deserve and visitors need to respect. As I spoke White Gourd put her hand on my knee and looked into my eyes. "With respect daughter, do you hear yourself? Do see how you are stirring the wind?"

"Ayaahh, I did not realize. I forget myself."

"The first step in healing *ch'ulel* loss is *not* to forget yourself. The storms that passed, have passed. Dwelling on them just keeps them alive in your heart."

"I see that now."

White Gourd stood and I followed her to the doorway. "We have great concern for you, daughter. Keep the white flower close to your heart, say your gratitudes and ask for guidance. Come again soon."

"Will I know if the wandering *ch'ulelob* has returned?"

"That is why you must come again."

135

Yax Nuun's News

BREEZES AND A MISTY DOVE RAIN SEEMED TO SAY WE'D SEEN the last of the otter downpours, but according to the aj *k'inob* the rains would continue for at least two more moons. That was good for the reservoirs and the crops, but we had to be careful of mudslides, snakes, mold and mildew.

The wife of one of the dignitaries that passed through showed us a figurine she made, a young Tollan woman with arms that moved, and Ix Chab' set out to make one like it. We were arguing about whether the woman should be seated or standing, hadn't even gotten the clay on the stand yet, when Yax Nuun came rushing through the doorway. He pulled off his dripping hat and set it alongside the others along the wall. His cloak and legs were soaked, so I got a cloth for him to dry himself and then a blanket for his shoulders. He and his father and Sihyaj K'ahk' had just returned from one of their many trips to Siaan K'aan.

"Mother! You will never guess!" he said, coming to the hearth. His eyes were wide with excitement. "Father said I could tell you. We are going to Tollan! Just him and me! On a pilgrimage. Like grandfather. A messenger came, just to say the goddess is calling for me. Is that not amazing?"

I hadn't even heard about a messenger from Tollan. "I can see you are excited. When will you leave?"

"After the rains but before the harvest, when the rivers are favorable.

After I take my initiation, Father says he can arrange for me to take the K'awiil anointing at the *wi te' naah*—in the presence of the Storm God and the Feathered Serpent."

Ix Chab' crossed her arms and rested back on her cushion, disappointed. "But my gown for the Descent of Spirits is almost finished," she remarked.

"You can wear it to my ascension," her brother replied. "We will be gone close to a tun. When we return Father says I will be ready to take the Mat. He wants Sihyaj K'ahk' to move on, widen the reach of the noh tzol. Everything is happening so fast." *Too fast. Stand and watch. Stand and watch—like the amate.* Ix Chab' got up and moved to the other end of the workshop. Understandably, she didn't want to hear more about her brother's excitement.

"Mother, I know how you feel about Sihyaj K'ahk'. I hated him too— for what he did. But we were wrong about him." I handed Yax Nuun a little cup and poured him some warm *saca*. "He is amazing in many ways. Did you know he became an Owl when he was thirteen? They raised him to first spear when he was seventeen."

I nodded. "Your father and I oversaw it. As the Supreme Owl, your grandfather presented his shield and mirror." When I glanced at Ix Chab' the disappointment on her face said what I was trying hard not to say.

"I will never forgive him for what he did to you, but he and I had some long talks. I need to look ahead, toward the *k'in* when I take the Mat. He has been teaching me. I hate him for what he did to you, but Father could not have found a more powerful and loyal emissary for sowing the seeds of the *noh tzol*."

"Your father calls him 'emissary,' but you must never forget, Yax Nuun. Above all, he is a ruthless man trying to overcome the humiliation of his family."

"That may be what makes him so powerful. I have not seen anyone more fierce..." I wanted to respond but he didn't give me a chance. "On the way to Siaan K'aan we talked about what he was going to say to Standing Squirrel. It was an awkward situation." *Awkward?* I'd never heard him use that word before. "The great surprise was, when we got there he let me do the talking. All he did was agree with me—everything I said. On the way back he said my power was increasing, and that I conducted myself with good manners and speech."

Ix Chab' overheard and called to her brother. "He wants Standing Squirrel to take a wife?"

Yax Nuun ignored her. "Mother, you will not like this, but I think you should know what is happening." I nodded my appreciation and held my son's gaze. "One reason for going to Siaan K'aan was to tell Standing Squirrel that after my ascension, Sihyaj K'ahk' will replace him on the Mat."

"You think it will happen?"

"I know it will. But there is more to it—something you will not like." Yax Nuun glanced at his sister then took up his cup and turned to me. "Before he takes the Mat he will marry your aunt's third daughter."

"Ix Sacha'?"

"I met her. She has a handsome face." Lady White Water touched the earth well after I left for Tollan. Standing Squirrel introduced her to me, but I only saw her that once. "How could anyone give a woman, any woman, to the man who killed her parents?"

Yax Nuun shrugged his shoulders. "My path is finally coming clear, Mother. Initiation and anointing at Tollan, ascension to the Mat and then the *ajaw* title." He set the cup down and let the blanket fall from his shoulders. "While we are away, Sihyaj K'ahk' will be visiting with the rulers within three *k'inob* from here. When I get back I will authorize them as my *yajawob*—at the ascension ceremony. What a sight that will be!" *More underlords to provide your grandfather more tribute, more often.* "What father and you dreamed for me is coming true."

Not like this, my son. Not like this. It took everything I had to hold my tongue. *He is becoming his father's son.* I thought of my paper flower and wished I hadn't left it at the residence. *Stand and watch. Just stand and watch. Remember the amate.* "Standing Squirrel must have been disappointed," I said.

"I wish you could have been there. I told him how it would be and I allowed no discussion—just as Sihyaj K'ahk' taught. It worked. It was amazing. Standing Squirrel wore the *sak huunal* and sat on the jaguar bench, but he gave no resistance."

"He could not. You are the Ajaw Le and soon to become his overlord to whoever holds the Mat at Siaan K'aan. To refuse would not have been wise." *Deadly, if it rubbed Sihyaj K'ahk' fur the wrong way.*

"All the way back we talked about what it will be like when I take the Mat. He told me the ways of the tribute collectors and long-distance merchants. I know how they bargain. I know their stops and the names of the rulers where they trade. I already know some of the ways to show my power. On the way to Tollan, Father is going to teach me about the goddess and how to talk to her. I can speak the prophecy now, and I am learning how Sihyaj K'ahk' has been planting the seeds of the *noh tzol.* I will be training with the Owls at Tollan..." I couldn't take much more of his excitement. "I need to distinguish myself as a warrior before I take the Mat." I nodded. He was right about that but my heart was torn. Yax Nuun got up and straightened his tunic. I got his hat and held it out to him.

"It is good to see you so happy," I said.

"When I am seated it will go well for all of us, you will see. Sihyaj K'ahk' will be gone. I will make you proud." When he was gone I told his sister I wanted to go back to the residence. She knew that his news was too much for me. Gratefully, she didn't say anything about not being able to start the figurine with arms that move.

Outside my sleeping chamber, Gray Mouse fed some wood into the brazier, tied the drape over the doorway and left me alone on my bench. Curled under the blanket, I pressed the little paper flower to my chest. I wanted to cry but couldn't. My throat had tightened again, making it diffi cult to swallow. Although it was good to see Yax Nuun so excited, it sickened me to see how completely his father and Sihyaj K'ahk' had bent him to their ways. That he would be gone for a year and I would miss his initiation made me feel like I'd already lost him.

I pulled the blanket over my head and in the darkness prayed my most fervent prayer. *Wherever you are Father, I would rather be with you and Mother now. You called me into this world. It would be a kindness now to show me the way out. I have done all I can here. I am becoming a burden to my children. They will do better without me. Besides, I have made my contribution—to you and to Mutal. Forgive me for opening the door to the Tollanos. Forgive me for not being able to stop the termination of the Great Trees at Precious Forest. I miss you, Mother, Naway, Kachne' and Ixway more than I can say. I ache to see you, all of you. The shaman asked what I wanted. What I want most is for us all to be together again.*

139

Hope

EARLY ONE MORNING JATZ'OM INFORMED ME THAT A MAN, AN
aj noah from the settlement, would be coming to present the final plaster
model of the regal residence he wanted built for Yax Nuun while they were
away. Inconsiderate as it was to commission such a grand undertaking
without inviting my recommendations, and rude as it was to request my
presence just moments before the presentation of the model, I was less
than grateful to finally be included.

Situated just north of Precious Forest and occupying vastly more
ground than the current residence, the platform the *aj noah* designed was
twice a high with taller and longer buildings that enclosed a masonry
patio. The courtyard beside it was expansive enough to be considered a
plaza. A broad stairway faced the much larger plaza at Precious Forest.
Another broad stairway permitted descent from the patio in back of the
residence. The facing walls of the three long buildings situated on the front
and sides displayed the typical Tollan sloping supports with framed walls.

Unlike Father's residence compound where the houses all had thatched
roofs that rose to a peak, the model showed the new residences as having
flat, beam and mortar, roofs. Three doorways provided access to reception
chambers, each with built-in masonry benches. Yax Nuun and his family
would occupy the entire west range. Our chambers were located on the
East side at ground level, beneath and in front of a narrow shrine that
would have a vaulted ceiling. "Yax Nuun deserves the finest," Jatz'om

said. "He will rule like none before him. Already I see the fire in his eyes."
I'd seen it too. It made me sad. Jatz'om stooped to eye-level with the
model and put a finger through the central doorway. "What do you think of
your new home?"

"I will need more servants," I said.

"And you shall have them," Jatz'om offered. The *aj noah* was a pock-
faced man with hair braided long down the back of his cloak. He'd come
to Mutal with us in the second wave. Jatz'om spoke mainly to him, asking
questions and nodding his head, occasionally turning to invite my agreement. Overall, he said he was pleased with the platform but he wanted the
entire structure located twenty paces closer to Precious Forest so he could
see the steps of the Yax Hal Witz from our doorway. He also wanted the
reception chamber doorway to be wider and stairway leading up to it two
strides longer on both sides. "I will talk to Sihyaj K'ahk'," he said. "He
will offer you and your brothers the commission to build. Most important
is that it be finished before we return from Tollan. That gives you eight or
nine moons."

I asked the *aj noah* to excuse Jatz'om so I could have a word with him.
Politely he bowed and walked away. I turned to Jatz'om and gestured to
the model. "Where will Sihyaj K'ahk' have his quarters?"

"Dear one," Jatz'om said, "you need not worry. Until he takes a wife
and becomes seated as Yax Nuun's *yajaw* at Siaan K'aan, he will continue
to live at the settlement. You will not be seeing much of him. He has too
much to do. While we are gone, anything you need to say to him can be
conveyed by to him by Gray Mouse. Because he is regent, you will need to
stand with him at ceremonies." I turned and left him to talk with the
builder alone.

SOMEHOW, WHILE I'D BEEN SITTING BY THE HEARTH listening to
the rain, gazing out the doorway and helping my daughter mold figurines,
some with moving arms, there came and went the passing of three moons.
It wasn't until Ajaw K'in's wispy glory came streaking through the canopy
that I noticed how the everyday rains that alternated between turtle and
dove had stopped altogether. Were it not for the constant heaviness, and
now the foreboding that clutched my insides, I would have been delighted

to finally go out without a hat, and walk the paths without getting my feet muddy. Especially to put on dry clothes.

I kept hearing the shaman's voice in my head saying I needed to see her again soon, but I lived for the possibility that Yax Nuun would come through the doorway and tell me that for some reason they were not going to Tollan. The rites and preparations for harvest and then the rites of gratitude that followed would also have passed without notice had it not been for the moments I stood beside my son, even if it meant listening to speeches given by his regent and the ministers.

Finally, the dreaded day of my son's departure arrived. The procession was long, consisting of so many Owls I wondered if there were enough left to protect the *caah*. Added to the loss of my son and the certainty of his embracing his father's ways, was the heartbreak of seeing the enormity of the tribute they were taking from Mutal's—Father's—storehouses: obsidian cores, crates of incised and painted ceramic wares, thick bundles of bark paper, fat ones filled with *kakaw* beans, quetzal feathers in long bark-tubes, boxes of salt, shells to make purple and red dye, feline hides, caged animals and birds and stacks of smaller boxes some containing stingray spines and bone perforators, others jade beads, ear ornaments, necklaces, wristlets, and carved effigies. Being right was not at all satisfying. Jatz'om was making this journey, not only to present the next ruler of Mutal to his father and the other lords of Tollan, but also to deliver to them a taste of the bounty they could expect to flow to Tollan regularly as the new order spread across the lowlands. Seeing all those crates, cages, hide-covered poles, bundles, and high-packs snaking into the forest on the backs of slaves, it felt like Jatz'om was draining the blood from my father and our beloved Mutal.

Wearing our red-painted Tollan gowns and burdened with our heaviest jewels, Ix Chab' and I stood in the hot sun atop the palace steps throughout the long procession. My final wave to Yax Nuun was not returned. He'd asked me to be happy for him, so I turned away thinking of the glorious welcome he and his father would receive when they entered Tollan.

IX CHAB' KEPT AFTER ME TO GO AND SIT WITH THE SHAMAN again. "It seemed to help the last time," she said. If it had I wasn't aware of it. The least little thing that went wrong fed the flames of anger and blame, sometimes rage. I lashed out, complaining and blaming whoever was involved. Afterward I felt bad about myself. Always, it roused the demon whose voice persisted well beyond the incident: She knew very well... *How could I let this happen? Why should I care? Nothing I do... I just make things worse. Something terrible is going to happen. Nothing I could ever do would... I should have know better... I shouldn't be around people.* There were days when I couldn't eat. If I forced myself, my insides would grip me all through the night. Mornings, as Gray Mouse dressed me, I braced myself for the coming disappointments and irritations of the day. I became vigilant and guarded.

Avoiding my duties at the palace, no longer raising my voice to the servants, and day after day watching Ix Chab' make figurines, the shaman's voice became more persistent. Finally, Gray Mouse shamed me into going by saying my father would be disappointed in me for sitting around brooding. Had any of the other servants said that to me they would have been dismissed.

I decided to present myself to the shaman this time, not only as a fellow Maya but also as a *noblewoman* and mother of the Mutal Ajaw Le. After applying red body-paint to my chin, neck and shoulders, Gray Mouse parted my hair down the center, cut the sides into steps and tied the rest high in back, letting it hang long in a tassel. It was pleasant to just sit and be attended to again, selecting the clothes and jewels I wanted to wear and those I wanted packed. Gray Mouse slid the white *kub* over my head and tugged at the embroidered sleeves and hem with a damp cloth to pull out the wrinkles. Finally, she adorned me with the jewels: jade florets for my ears and the *kaloomte'* necklace, a beaded turban and wristlets with tiny pearls sewn onto the stays.

On the trail in my litter with two bearers, Gray Mouse and two carriers, I seemed to breathe better, more deeply. Seeing spider monkeys chasing each other in the trees and a mother jaguarundi on the side of the trail with her three pups made me grin. Although there wasn't much life left within me, I was encouraged by the life around me, even a flock of black vultures that darted with wings flapping, pecking at a dead snake.

As it happened, perhaps as the gods ordered it, we arrived on one of the days when White Gourd was not seeing patients. Had it not been for

Gray Mouse announcing me by name and the dog squirming at me, begging for a pet, Muwan would probably not have recognized me. Instead of leading us across the patio, she asked us to wait while she ran to her mother's doorway. Moments later, White Gourd and I were greeting each other as old friends. Whereas Muwan was uneasy about being in the presence of a noblewoman, her mother regarded me as if nothing had changed.

As before, White Gourd performed the ritual of walking around me, feeling my hands, selecting the herbs and attending to the offerings while I sat behind her on the bench facing the altar. I had questions and wanted to tell her what had happened, but again I waited for her to talk.

She came and sat in front of me, took my hands, looked into my eyes and confessed she already knew who I was. "My husband and I attended the closing of the harvest rites at Mutal. We saw you standing with your husband and children. It was not too surprising. The Tollan in your voice, the jaguar claw on your cheek. Your long fingernails."

"I wanted you to know the truth of my situation."

"I still feel a great darkness within you. Heavy, as before."

"Jatz'om, my husband, took my son to Tollan. I am missing his initiation. Even worse, he will turn to his father's ways. Already he is persuaded that Sihyaj K'ahk' is a great man." I asked if she'd heard about the *noh tzol* and she said she had. "He is excited to be learning its ways and how to establish it throughout the lowlands. He calls it *establishing*. I call it *imposing*. I thought the darkness weighing me down was as heavy as it could get. Now that my son is gone—."

White Gourd nodded. "This is *their* dance," the shaman commented. It is for them to judge whether or not it is proper for them. If they believe it is, we allow it and bless them on their way. So it is with all men—and women." I couldn't accept that. "My husband can dance all he wants, wherever he wants, as long as he wants. What I cannot abide is turning our son to his destructive ways. More than not seeing him and missing his initiation, I grieve for the loss of the temperament and customs that make us Maya—beauty, respect, gratitude, the sacred calendar round, honoring our ancestors and keeping them alive. Not so long ago, he hungered for stories about his grandfather."

"Your son has a youthful face," the shaman remarked.

"Two moons from now he turns twelve. No one agrees with me, but I think he is too young and inexperienced to shoulder the burden of the *caah*."

"Even younger men have inherited the Mat elsewhere."

"When Jatz'om announced that we would be moving to Mutal, I thought Yax Nuun would learn how to rule by observing his grandfather, that he would replace him and continue the Ich'aak tradition of making what Father called, 'our grand contribution.'"

For no apparent reason, White Gourd winced as if from a sharp pain. "As *ajaw* all his contributions would be grand, would they not?"

"My worry is that they would be grand for Tollan, not so grand for Mutal."

The shaman took a finger-length crystal from her altar and held it across her wrist. "As you were talking we felt a tinge of lightning at the back of our neck." She closed her eyes. "The ancestors want you to know: if you remain here—in the middle world—you will dance a great dance with your son. Many of his contributions will be grand—for Mutal. They will please you. One in particular will make you very proud." Anticipating that I would ask, she held up her hand so I wouldn't speak. Moments passed in silence. Then a curious thing happened. I hadn't noticed the thin, nearly straight line of smoke rising from the censer off to the side. Now, it was bending toward me, wavering like a finger and only then did I smell it. "Contribution?" she asked. "Son?" she asked. Apparently she was talking with the ancestors. Mine? Hers? I didn't know. "Grand Son," she whispered. "Grandson. Is that it?" The finger of incense fluttered, seemed to disappear then rose again as it had, toward the ceiling. White Gourd opened her eyes and nodded knowingly. "Ah ha," she said. "It seems a grandson could be your grand contribution." She paused and opened her eyes.

"What did they say about it?"

She shook her head. "We saw a seed taken up from the depths and planted in the ground. It became a tree and we saw a sprout kneeling in front of it, casting flower petals. White flower petals. Then came the words: 'grand' and 'son.' When we put them together the lightning came strong. Heat lightning. That was all." White Gourd stood, turned, and shook her hands as if to shake away the remnants of the lightning. She walked around me vigorously three times—I assumed for the same reason.

What she said was not very encouraging. While a blessing for certain, a grandson was not the kind of contribution I'd hoped for. "With your husband gone it will be easier for you, will it not?"

"A bit," I said. "Between the palace and the residence I regularly supervise twenty-seven servants—."

The shaman came around and sat facing me again. "They stir the winds as well?"

"Standing and watching is not my way. I was gifted with eyes that see everything. And I know what is proper. I cannot have leaves that have blown onto the palace floor gathering in the corners. I will not have my husband serving his guests tamales that fall apart or salt that clumps. Mud on the palace steps makes me want to scream. Walls need plastering. Thatch needs replacing. The door-drapes need to be washed. Every morning the braziers and smoke holes have to be cleaned out. Tollanos do not understand or appreciate the things that set a palace and regal residence apart—the touches of beauty at every turn, the reflections of caring, the ordering and proper handling of objects, the arrangements and placements that show respect. I find beetles and other insects under the cushions and between blankets. One of our guests, a *yajaw*, had a scorpion in his sleeping chamber!" I was becoming short of breath just talking about my everyday annoyances, but I couldn't stop, perhaps hoping that White Gourd would offer a solution. "As often as I scold the beverage servers for grasping the drinking cups where our guests put their lips, they continue to do it when they think I am not looking. I find broken feathers on banners, chipped serving bowls, hair tangled in combs and splatters of lime powder next to the chamber pots. Even worse, pots that have not been thoroughly cleaned. This is not proper and I will not have it..." It amazed me that White Gourd let me go on, even more so that she listened intently. I apologized for talking so much.

"Did you bring your white flower?" she asked without comment. I kept it between thin pieces of leather that hung from my neck on a cord. When she took it, she placed it on the offering plate and performed the ritual with the crystals. She recited a prayer over it, and then she handed it back telling me again to always keep it close to my heart.

"With respect Ix Sac Tzu', has any of my *ch'ulel* returned?"

"To know that we must repeat what we did on your last visit. We will take a sweat in the morning and talk—just the two of us. Then we will visit the shrine." As part of my preparation for our talk she told me to go down the hill and across the way to the lake when it was dark. She wanted me to sit by the water, hold the white flower to my heart and ask the remaining *ch'ulelob* certain questions. To keep me safe from the night demons, she said she would caste a cocoon of glory around me that would protect me until first light.

THAT NIGHT, GRAY MOUSE WALKED ME ACROSS THE TRAIL TO a masonry platform at the water's edge, a place where women set their jars and fishermen kept their nets. After sitting for a while with our feet dangling over the edge, watching the broad and shimmering path of moonlight on Lake Peten narrow through an inlet to our feet, and wondering what it would be like to live in one of the houses high on the hills where the torchlight flickered, she went back to the compound.

I'd never been alone in the open at night, not even as a flower. Gripping a blanket tightly to my neck, intent on watching the water in case a demon would raise its monstrous head in the path of the moonlight, I clung to the hope that the shaman's protective cocoon of glory was real—even though I couldn't see or feel it. I sat upright a long while before I was able to rest back on a bundle of netting, loosen my grip on the blanket, and close my eyes. I tried matching my breath with the sound of the water lapping the sand, but couldn't sustain it.

Ch'ulel? Can you hear me? The shaman wants me to ask: What do I want? As always, I paused after asking the question. Father said it was important to listen immediately, so the voice would come from the *ch'ulel* in my blood, not from the thoughts in my head.

First, do you know who you are?

Who I am? I lost who I am—who I was. I told the shaman that. Now I am asking you: Can I ever be the woman I wanted to be—before all this happened?

Would you build a house identical to the one you tore down?

The plaster model of our new residence—all Jatz'om's choices—came to mind. *I would want it to be better.*

Then make your house your own.

I do not understand.

What the shaman said: Walk your own path. If the path others are tak-ing offends you, allow it and continue on your way—on your own path.

What they are doing is not just offensive. It gets me so upset I—.

The winds and waves are of your own making. To calm them, stand and watch. Allow the dancers around you to dance—as they must. You dance as you must, as the woman you want to be. And begin now. No one needs to give you permission.

You make it sound easy. How can I stand and watch when terrible things keep happening?

Open your eyes now. Do you see the path of glory streaming from the moon? I opened my eyes. *Do you see how it leads to your feet? You stand at the center of the world. Ix Chel is pointing to you. Her brightest glory shines not on the hills, but on you. That is how it is. Know that you are the center of your world.*

If my husband were here, she would shine on him as well.

The center that matters to you, the only one you are responsible for, is you. Live from your center, no other.

It occurred to me that at that moment, somewhere on the bank of a river, gazing into a campfire or watching the same moon, Yax Nuun was probably listening to his father tell stories about how it will be when he becomes the Mutal lord. I closed my eyes again.

I lost my father, my family, father's monument, my dream for Mutal, and now my son.

The response came before I could even ask my question. *Nothing is ever lost. Up and down the Great Tree there is layering. Children prosper and layer best when they see their fathers and mothers prospering and layering. We each have our own path, our own dance. We loose ourselves when we get off our path; dance someone else's dance. Your father, your mother—their destiny was theirs. Your son has his path. You have yours.*

I was happiest when we were all dancing together.

Nothing stays the same forever. There is a reason why you entered and walk the face of the earth. Know that reason and find joy in the walking. Whatever happens along the way, as long as you keep to your path—what gives you joy—you will meet your destiny.

I was growing weary of all this talk about paths, dancing, and destiny.

With respect, ch'ulel, the shaman will be asking me what I want. What should I tell her?

Answer first: Who am I? What is my path?

Somehow, hearing it put that way I was able to answer. *I am my father's daughter. According to my birth prophecy, my path is the path of the jaguar. Can you tell me what that means?*

Now you can ask: What does your father's daughter want? What is her dance?

Ayaahh. I couldn't answer that, but the question struck like a lightning bolt in the clouds that covered my heart. What it left was the hope of an answer.

AS BEFORE, THE SHAMAN AND I LAY NAKED ON THE HILLSIDE after our sweat, the only difference being we were out from under the shelter with our mats on the grass allowing the heat of the sun to singe our skin. With a cloth over my eyes I told her what my *ch'ulel* said about walking my own path and remembering that I was my father's daughter. After explaining what that meant to me, she asked what I thought would happen when Jatz'om and Yax Nuun return.

With my eyes closed I could almost see it. "Jatz'om will sit with the rulers that Sihyaj K'ahk' will have brought into the *noh tzol*. After he authorizes Yax Nuun and he ascends to the Mat, my husband will journey to other lowlands centers to deliver the prophecy. As mother of the *ajaw*, I will be required to go with him. Yax Nuun will be enforcing the *noh tzol* at Mutal, distinguishing himself further as an Owl. My son knows me well. We will talk of seasons and ceremonies and gossip about the ministers and other members of court. He will be very polite and treat me kindly. But like his father, he will not speak to me about matters of importance."

"Following your husband around and talking to your son in this manner, is that your path?"

"What other path is there for the wife of a *k'uhul winik* and mother of an *ajaw*?"

"The guidance you received at the lake—it was helpful, was it not?"

"It was. But now I have more questions."

"Keep asking. This is how we find the path that is right for us."

"How do I know if I am not on my path?" I suspected her answer, but I wanted to hear it.

"The tightness in your throat, the heaviness in your heart, all the things you told us."

"Standing and watching did not help much. I am not as strong as the amate. Is there anything else I can do?"

"When the wind blows strong and the waves of anger keep coming, it can be helpful to change the way we see. Eyes that *only* see a deer as food want to kill it. They haul it off in pieces without so much as an apology or gratitude. Eyes that see the same deer as a beautiful son or daughter of the forest let it live so it can bring abundance. If they have need of it, they ask permission. If the Forest Lord gives it, they offer their apology before hand, and their gratitude afterward. How we see changes how we are. Instead of seeing the leaves on the palace floor as disorderly and dirty, you might try to see them as a blessing from the trees. Broken tamales and salt that clumps present opportunities for you to teach the cooks. As we see, so we become. Do the servants know *why* you want things a certain way?"

"They would not understand. I have to keep after them. Otherwise nothing would get done. Not properly. We do not live like other people—." In her position White Gourd knew about dignity and that rulers, daykeepers, and holy men like my husband had not only to keep their eyes on the sky, they also had their hands occupied with rites and rituals to secure the safety and prosperity of the *caah*. What she didn't know and I had to explain, was that both the palace and the regal residence were not just living presences like all the other houses in the *caah*, they were *sacred* presences, established, ordered, and anointed after the ways the Makers established, ordered, and anointed the world. Lime powder splattered on a wall was not just dirty or an assault to the eyes. It was disrespectful, a sullying of the sacred presence and a disregard for their contributions. Left alone and increased in like manner, the disrespect could threaten the well-being of the *caah*.

"If the servants knew this, we think they would surprise you." I heard her turn to me, so I removed the cloth from my eyes and turned to her. "Did you ask your *ch'ulel* what you want?"

"I did, but it got confusing." I rested my head on my hands. "I know I need to find my own way. And I do need to change the way I see things.

But for now, all I really want is not to be upset all the time. I go along for two or three *k'inob*, but then something happens and the storm rages again." White Gourd turned on her back again and replaced the cloth over her eyes.

Not knowing what else to do, I laid back and did the same. *Itzamnaaj? This would be a good place to leave my body. Can I just leave now? I could find a new path but I am too tired and too old to begin again. I am becoming more of a burden to my husband and children. Let this beautiful place be the place of my final resting. I touched the earth wearing nothing, so it would be proper to leave it that way.* Somewhere on the hill across from us a bird sang a loud and long, most amazing song.

"*Xwukpik*," White Gourd said sitting up. I pulled the cloth from my eyes and sat up. Neither of us could locate the black-feathered creature. "Has anything ever made you feel that chirpy?" she asked.

I had to think. "Clay," I said. I drew my knees up and locked my arms around them. "When I was at Tollan I made bowls and jars and cups—decorative ware. I have a little workshop at Mutal but I use it mostly to get away from—everything. I made a jar recently, but it was disappointing."

"What were they like, the ones you made at Tollan?"

"The bowls were well rounded and heavier than most. I like to make things big, so I made thick coils. The vases were also thick, but with straight walls. Most of them stood on three feet, three for the hearthstones in the sky. The ones I was most proud of had molded animal heads on the lids—mostly warrior patrons. They served as handles. My hand was never very good with a brush, but I painted legs and feathers down the sides. For the bird bowls I painted feathers and claws."

"They sound beautiful."

"The banquets at Tollan were beyond imagining. Some went on for five *k'inob*. There, all I had to do was present myself, smile, and agree with everything my husband said. Here, nothing gets done without my pushing."

"Will your son be hosting banquets?"

"Many. Each new underlord will require a feast in their honor."

"Your son will need gifts for those so honored, will he not? Instead of wolf and owl bowls, could you make jaguar and quetzal bowls?"

Just the thought of it exhausted me. "Never again. The jar I just made showed me showed me I have been away from it too long."

We got up and wrapped ourselves in blankets. I had not responded very well to her questions, or her suggestion. "Sometimes," she said, "having our hands busy can help us change the way we see."

Walking down the hill a thought came into my head and I stopped. "With respect Ix Sak Tzu', your lineage. What is it called?"

"B'aatz'," she said.

"If I were to make a bowl and paint the likeness of a howler monkey on it with its head for a handle and have an *aj k'in* call for the spirit of one of your ancestors to enter and live within it, would that be something the elders would want?"

White Gourd's eyes widened. "Like an offering bowl? They would cherish it forever. It would be a memorial."

"A memorial bowl!" I repeated out loud. "Might they use it to honor and petition the ancestors?"

"The would. It would have a place of honor I would think—in the lineage shrine."

After getting dressed and sharing a meal, White Gourd read the maize kernels to see if any of my *ch'ulel* had returned. As I expected, it hadn't. I took my leave and on the way back to Mutal I told Gray Mouse that I'd decided to make a Monkey vase as part of my compensation for White Gourd. If that would go well, then in secret I would make vessels for each of the Maya lineages at Mutal and gift them to their heads at a Fire Entering ceremony. To offer such a gift to the esteemed elders who sat with my father would be a great honor for me. And it would keep my hands busy while I tried to find my new eyes, hopefully my path.

"They will become heirlooms," Gray Mouse said.

"The new branches will remember the old ones, keep them alive."

Gray Mouse's excitement made me quicken our pace.

Memorials

THE PROSPECT OF MAKING VESSELS TO HOUSE THE SPIRITS OF deceased ancestors made me want to get my hands into the clay immediately. While it wasn't the kind of contribution I'd hoped to make, it was better than staring out the doorway and worrying about Yax Nuun.

I sent Ix Chab' to help Gray Mouse collect the items I needed—various clays, cattails, *kante* roots, cording, stucco-coated bark paper, wooden paddles, some blades, marl, and lime powder. When they returned from the storehouse and Gray Mouse told me the keeper wouldn't release either bark paper of clay without permission from Sihyaj K'ahk', I became furious. I should have known. Tollan keepers held onto their goods as if they were their children.

Over my embroidered red gown I covered my shoulders with the black mantle. With jade in my ears and the *kaloomte'* necklace around my neck, I approached the master of the ceramic yard with four bearers and told him that my husband instructed Sihyaj K'ahk' to provide me with everything I needed for my workshop. While he spoke with another keeper, apparently the one who kept the clays, I walked the many rows of crates, occasionally asking the workers the purpose of the various stones and added them to the list of clays and other items I needed. Although I didn't need the bearers, I came away with a promise from the master that he would speak to Sihyaj K'ahk' regarding my needs.

Fortunately I was at the palace when, two mornings later, seven bearers arrived with everything I requested. I led the bearers to the workshop, compensated them for their labor, and asked their leader to express my gratitude to their master.

Using a piece of charcoal from the hearth that I sharpened to a point, I drew some outlines for the Monkey vase on a slab of plaster-coated masonry. After washing off several attempts and arriving at one I liked, I more carefully drew the details of the head and the sides of the bowl onto strips of stucco-coated bark paper.

Jatz'om's sister liked to get into the clay after finishing her drawing. I was never that confident. I needed to let the drawing sit, sometimes for five or six days, so I could add or take away a line or feature to make it better. Wanting to give my hand more practice while I was considering the drawing, I turned to a vase that I had in mind to make for Yax Nuun's ascension. Since my hands were already black with charcoal and the slab freshly cleaned, I drew the shape of a vase that I had made at Tollan. My son's head would be filled with the glories of Tollan when he returned, so rather than an animal or a bird, I thought I would incise the scene of his homecoming with ministers presenting him gifts and warlords presenting him with the *ko'haw* war helmet. As it happened, I became so engrossed I finished the vase in five days.

With that vessel set aside for firing, I turned to drawing the Monkey vase and realized I had much to think about before I could even set up the clay. Should I or should I not tell the lineage heads what I was doing? Considering the animal and bird heads on the lids, would it be wise to seek their counsel on the design? Should the mouths and beaks be open or closed, the heads big or little? Should they all be bowls, or might some be lidded vases? Should they be the same size? I knew I wanted them to be colorful, but that meant having them painted after the firing and my hand was not steady enough for brushwork. I would have to find someone I could trust, not only to do the painting well, but also to keep it secret. I didn't want Jatz'om or Sihyaj K'ahk', not even Yax Nuun, to know what I was doing. What would I say was the reason for spending so much of my days at the workshop? Surely the ministers and council members would ask.

Because it held memories of my family, the reservoir trail had become my favorite place to go and think, particularly at dawn and dusk when there were fewer people. Early one morning with a thin blanket of fog resting on the still waters of both reservoirs, I sat alone on the stump of a tree talking to my *ch'ulel* about the vases when a tall, strikingly handsome young man with a severe, cob-shaped head approached. At first I though he was carrying a staff, but it turned out to be a stick painted yellow. Judging from the tonsured hair that hung below his waist in back, his cotton loincloth, and high leather sandals, I judged him to be the son of a nobleman, perhaps an apprentice to a holy man, but he bore neither scars nor tattoos and his only jewels were jade florets in both ears. Unmarried men and warriors his age wore black body paint, yet this man's flesh was unpainted and fair beyond any I'd seen. Almost pink, like the inside of a shell.

His appearance was so striking it was difficult to keep my eyes on the water as he approached. After taking several strides beyond me, he turned, faced me and approached. I thought perhaps he recognized me, so I stood. Then the oddest thing happened. He came up to me and we looked at each other, but neither of us spoke. If he was unmarried, which was likely considering his youth, this was a blatant breach of manners. Even so, we just stood there in silence and held each other's gaze. Without expression. I certainly had never seen him before, yet something about him made me feel at ease. We must have stood there for a hundred heartbeats, perhaps more, before his mouth curled into a little smile. "I know you," I said.

"I know you," he replied. He nodded slightly, turned and went his way without looking back. I stood a while and watched as if the sun were setting at the end of the trail, wondering what had happened and what it meant. I sat on the stump again and looked across the water to where a dog running along the shoreline made ducks take flight.

Down the trail and in front of me I noticed through the trees that some of their roots overhung the cliff, pointing their dry and gnarled fingers toward the water. Suddenly, I burst into tears. I cried hard and long and deep, all the while wondering why. I thought I had cried all the tears I could for the loss of my family and the destruction of the monuments, but here they were again. I'd caught my breath and composed myself by the time a mother, a Maya woman with three barefooted little ones wearing bark cloth passed behind me, all bent over with firewood carried on their backs with forehead straps. When they were gone and the tears came again, they seemed to come more from gratitude than loss.

Back at the workshop I couldn't stop thinking about the fair young man with the tonsured hair. Whoever he was, whatever he was, his deeply folded eyelids and penetrating gaze had somehow assured me that all was well and that everything I needed to know about the memorial vessels would come clear. Bubbling up from inside was a knowing that I was on a proper path. Whether or not it was *my* path was uncertain. I tried to name it—the path of clay, of standing and watching, the path between reservoirs, the path of new eyes. Unfortunately, none of the names I could think of had anything to do with *jaguar*, the path predicted at my birth.

NAJ CHAN, THE FORMER CHILAM WHO SHOWED US FATHER'S monument, took me to the house of a bony *aj k'in* who, before he went blind, had also served my father. Although I didn't remember Shining Flint, perhaps because he'd aged so poorly, he remembered me. The daughter who attended him said he lived to talk about his days at court, his circle of daykeepers and how they observed the journeys of the sky wanderers. He couldn't stand for very long, so we went to the side of his house where there were benches in the shade of a palm grotto. He insisted I sit on a bench, but because he'd become accustomed to sitting on mats he preferred the ground.

I told him about the memorial vases and he recommended that I add a bit of copal to the clay to make it especially delectable to the ancestor spirits. He said the firing itself would peak their interest even before the Fire Entering ceremony. We talked about my family and my father's ministers. He was especially interested to hear about Yax Nuun and his sister. As his daughter served roasted squash seeds, cashews and limewater sweetened with honey taken from their hives, we decided that he would perform the Fire Entering rites for all nine vessels, all at once—and on his land where the lineage heads could come and have privacy. I readily agreed to the only compensation he wanted, a vessel for his own lineage, the Trogon.

Having Jatz'om gone had several advantages, one of which was not needing to ask his permission for everything. I had Gray Mouse tell Sihyaj K'ahk' that I needed an addition built onto my workshop, and three days later the men came to talk about building a stone chamber behind the workshop with the only entrance inside. I needed it both to protect the vessels and keep them out of sight as I worked on them. When it was finished and the builders were gone, I began molding the vase for White Gourd. The monkey head on the lid took shape rather quickly, as did the vase itself, but I struggled for days trying to shape the supports into monkey hands and feet. It wasn't working. Monkeys have four, not three appendages, so I decided to have them painted on, leaving the supports plain so dots within an oval—the sign for a monkey's wrinkled skin—could be painted on them.

While I was shaping the monkey head, I realized that when Yax Nuun became the head of our lineage at his accession he should have a memorial vase for our lineage, the Jaguar Claw. There were considerations: he wouldn't be present for the Fire Entering rites, and I still wanted my gift for his ascension to be the black vase I incised with his reception scene. On what occasion would I present him with a memorial vase? With his head so filled with Tollan ways, he might not even appreciate a memorial of the Ich'aak. Still, the prospect of having a vessel that would contain the spirit of an Ich'aak, perhaps even my father, so excited me I turned to making it as soon as I finished the Monkey vase. White Gourd would have smiled. I'd finally found something I wanted—for myself.

When decorative bowls sit on mats to the side as they did at the palace, it was hard to see what was painted on the sides, particularly by torchlight. For that reason I decided the Ich'aak vessel would be a broad bowl with bulging sides and a lid large enough to accommodate the jaguar's barred claws as well as his snarling head in the center. Viewed from a seated position and in dim light, the entire jaguar could be seen. As I wound the first coils of clay, Ix Chab', Gray Mouse, and I expressed our most fervent hope that it would contain Father's *ch'ulel*. Any of the Ich'aak ancestors would have been welcome, but to have something of my father present in the palace looking after Yax Nuun, was my best dream.

I had no difficulty shaping and smoothing the bowl, but the lid gave me trouble. The jaguar's teeth needed to be large, so the mouth had to be wide open. That meant his head needed to be bigger than I expected and tilted back, which required a thicker neck to support the weight. Where the Monkey vase took me seven days to complete, the Jaguar head alone took five.

I'd asked Naj Chan if he could recommend an *aj tz'ib'al,* someone with a steady hand and great experience with painting on stuccoed ceramic wares. He needed to be a Maya and someone I could trust. As it happened the man he brought me had also served my father. Aptly named, Long Stroke was a Macaw nobleman whose family had left Becanokol Nal when, because of a long and severe draught, there was talk of terminating the *caah.* We had an enjoyable talk about my father and some of the vessels he and his brother made for him. After seeing him draw with a piece of charcoal, I decided that he would be the one to paint the memorials.

I was smoothing the underside of the Jaguar bowl when it came to me. Considering that it might house my father's *ch'ulel,* it needed to be *entirely* Ich'aak. I had to paint it myself. If not the others, I would at least paint that one.

I'd been disappointed by my brushwork at Tollan so I went to see Long Stroke, hoping to persuade him to teach me the ways of the brush while I was working on the other vessels. He would have agreed were it not for his wife who kept insisting that it wasn't possible to learn in several moons what took her husband a lifetime to learn. Still, Long Stroke appreciated what I was doing and he offered to come to the workshop to show me some "secrets" on mixing the plaster and preparing the surface of the bowls for painting. After his second visit, Long Stroke's wife changed her mind. She said he convinced her, but I think it was because I compensated him with *kakaw* beans as well as fabrics and salt from the north.

Rather quickly I got into the habit of attending to the servants early, while it was still dark. First at the residence, and then the palace. Ix Chab' and I spent the better part of the day at the workshop, she molding figurines of young noble women, while I rolled thick coils of clay and shaped them into bowls and vases.

Long Stroke came to the workshop every third or fourth day. He brought brushes, paints, and pieces of clay that had been fired and plaster-coated so I could practice my hand. The first thing he showed me was soon to become my greatest challenge: painting black lines with a single fiber brush so they would be long and consistent—a necessary skill for outlining an animal's form, bird feathers, eyes, ear ornaments, and paws. He showed me how to load the brush and hold it with my hand resting on a stick to maintain the long and steady strokes. Equally difficult was learning how to apply the paint with an even pressure against the stucco which, because the thickness varied in places, drank up the paint differently.

Long Stroke had me make a plain but well-rounded bowl for a trial. He took it to his brother's house and had it fired. When he brought it back I painted feathers all around it — just the outline, with black paint. Over this I brushed on a coat of plaster thin enough so the black lines would show through, yet thick enough that the plaster would stay wet so I could repaint the feathers and quickly filled in the open spaces with red using a softer, paca-hair brush. When it dried the color became part of the plaster.

The decorated vessels we brought out for banquets at the palace were mostly those father had commissioned. Among the finer painted bowls and vases reserved for calendar rites, I found several that had been made by Long Stroke and his brother. The painted wares for burials were among the finest, but I only found one of the seven that Long Stoke described. Apparently the others had been traded or gifted by various guests and dignitaries. Of the ones we had, I admired their deep red and brown tones and the occasional white and cream colors, but I wanted the memorial vessels to be different, not only in shape but also in color.

Having seen the finest of Tollan wares, I went to the settlement and talked to an *aj jaay* who not only answered my questions, but gave me several baskets of minerals they used to make pink, green, and yellow. Long Stroke, Gray Mouse, and Ix Chab' spent many days and great effort grinding them into fine powders, but it was worth it. The colors on the practice bowl were very close to those I remembered from Tollan.

TEN MOONS LATER THE VESSELS WERE ALMOST READY TO BE ensouled and gifted. After several discussions and for a variety of reasons, when the shaping and molding was completed, we carefully moved them to the House of Macaw where Long Stroke and his brother did the firing. Because their compound was well north of the central district and sat on a rise surrounded by dense jungle and swampland, it afforded privacy. Also, because his wife was right about how long it takes to master the way of the brush, I commissioned Long Stroke to paint six of the nine vessels. The Cormorant memorial, a tall-standing vase that I painted, was the most difficult but also the most satisfying. I worried that the long, curving neck and head of the bird rising taller than a hand above the lid, was too delicate. The slightest bump could break the neck. Ix Chab' wanted me to make it shorter for that reason, but I finally decided the Cormorants would just have to be more careful with it.

It was a hot morning when the lineage heads and their families gathered in the shade of a cedar that overhung the steps at the Macaw compound. I'd already had private conversations with them, so they knew to bring incense and offerings for their respective ancestors. Shining Flint, aided by his daughter, led us along the path to the clearing where the Macaw brothers had a fire going in a pit they sometimes used for cooking. They'd arranged the vessels on mats placed around the pit, so the elders went first and I had them sit next to their vessels. The family members arranged themselves behind them on blankets. When the great circle was fully formed I counted thirty-eight people.

So it happened that Shining Flint Trogon, an *aj k'in* to my father, performed the daylong Fire-Entering rites, calling forth the ancestors, in some cases the founders of the Cormorant, Crocodile Eyes, Quetzal, Tapir, Agouti, Turtle, Resplendent Turkey, and Heron. I sat for the Jaguar Claw. At my request, Ix Chab' sat for the Monkey, accepting the vase for White Gourd's lineage. Shining Flint's daughter sat for the Trogon. In all, eleven vessels were ensouled that day.

Afterward, the celebration at the Macaw compound was made special by the many gratitudes I received, several with watery eyes. Most moving for me was when I held up the Jaguar Claw bowl and Shining Flint put his two fingers in front of the jaguar's mouth. Listening from the heart takes a while. Finally, he announced with raised eyebrows that my father had answered his call. People were so moved they bowed their heads. In the silence, I cried tears of welcome and gratitude.

That evening, kneeling before the altar with the bowl in front of me, I offered incense and flowers to my father along with further gratitudes—for his coming to live with me, for showing me the path of memorial vessels, and for guiding my hands to make them. Although I heard nothing back, by his presence in the bowl I knew he regarded it a contribution to our people. To keep Jatz'om from seeing the Jaguar Claw memorial, Gray Mouse and Ix Chab' helped me dig a hole in the workshop floor, on the eastern side of the hearth. We tamped the dirt, lined the bottom and the walls with matting and added ceiba tuft all around. With a sturdy board laid over the crypt and a blanket over the board, the vase remained hidden beneath the very place where I sat.

I took it out rarely, always in the dark of night, sometimes when the full face of the moon shown brightly outside the doorway. On those occasions I talked to Father and made my gratitudes and petitions hoping for a response, but none came. Shining Flint said the bit of Father's *ch'ulel* that resided in the vase was probably not strong enough to form words. I accepted that. It was enough to feel his presence.

AS JATZ'OM HAD PROMISED, SIHYAJ K'AHK' ARRANGED A ceremonial burial for my father that was proper, respectful and regal. Happily, Sihyaj K'ahk' honored my request and chose to be elsewhere on that day. My only regret was that Yax Nuun was not there to witness the countless numbers of people who came, many from great distances, to show their respect and offer gifts of flowers and incense to his grandfather.

The tomb was set into the floor of one of the temple-shrines Father had commissioned. It overlooked the Great Plaza and was higher but in line with the tomb of Mutal's founder, Yax Ehb' Xook. The holy men cleansed father's body and then dusted it generously with cinnabar, the color of blood and life. After laying a jade mask over his face, an *itz'aat* painted his name and titles on the wall of the tomb, including a proclamation that his smoke and mist, his fame and honor, would live on.

Ix Chab', Gray Mouse, and I gathered up flowers from the hundreds of bundles and took them to the temporary graves at Precious Forest where Mother, my brothers, sister, and her husband and child were buried. Jatz'om said he would respect my wishes regarding their disposition but he didn't. I wanted them all buried next to each other, and in a shrine built specially for them. Instead, he and Sihyaj K'ahk' decided the greater honor for them would be to rest in tombs dug into the existing shrines atop of the eastern platform. Walking around the scaffolds and talking to the workers only served to stir up my anger toward Jatz'om and Sihyaj K'ahk'. They could have built another shrine. They just wanted an excuse to raise the existing shrines higher so they could redo the façades with slope and frame walls similar to the shrines at Tollan.

At least they were making progress. The walls of the tombs were all in place, the bins for the expansion of the platforms and stairways were filled, and the stonecutters had started on the facing stones. When that was done, all that remained was the plastering and painting.

On the way back to the palace we visited the site of the new residence where men, heavily dusted with white powder, brought in stone from the southern quarry while women with tall jars on their heads brought water from the reservoir. The all-masonry structure was twice the size of the current one: two long buildings joined at the corner with a two-story building opposite. The walls were all up and plastered. On the North side, men on scaffolds painted long red bands along the top. Jatz'om was finally going to have a place where he could talk to his guests about the prophecy and the *noh tzol* after their more formal gatherings at the palace. For me it meant supervising more servants with fewer and shorter days at the workshop.

An Owl warrior was waiting for us at the palace steps. "With respect, Ix Bahlam Ich'aak," he said with a slight bow. "Master Sihyaj K'ahk' sent me to tell you. He received a messenger saying your husband and son are on the river. They are three *k'inob* from the bluffs."

Rapids And Shoals

SIHYAJ K'AHK' ARRANGED A HOMECOMING FOR JATZ'OM AND Yax Nuun that was loud and grand—scores of drummers on the steps beating the deep-voiced standing-drums with antler horns, musicians blowing conches and long wooden trumpets, many others sounding reed-flutes, ocarinas, and whistles. Unmarried women shook their gourd rattles while older women scraped their frog and crocodile rasps. Fire-dancers twirling and throwing torches led the crowd of commoners down the western causeway to the Great Plaza where Yax Nuun and his father got out of their litters and onto a red and black palanquin where they stood holding onto the ear flares of a man-sized medallion—the face of the Tollan storm god.

Ix Chab' and Sihyaj K'ahk', his Chilam, the red-robed underlords and I watched from the palace as Jatz'om and Yax Nuun were carried up the steps, past the courtiers, holy men, warlords, and ministers who greeted them with smiles and words of welcome. Jatz'om had put on considerable weight and somehow seemed shorter. In spite of the eye-rings, I could see that Yax Nuun's face had filled out and his skin was a deeper red. His muscular mass bore little resemblance to the young man who had left us eleven moons past.

After an exchange of greetings, we followed the Chilam to the patio where we took our comforts and afterward got into litters that took us to the Yax Hal Witz. From a dais set on the third terrace, we watched as the

nine warlords led their black painted warrior-bands in front of us, all wearing red loincloths and yellow headbands, carrying spearthrowers and
Storm God shields, with darts strapped across their shoulders, and mirrors
attached to their belts in back. Except for their tapered heads, Sihyaj
K'ahk' had somehow managed to make even the Maya warriors look the
same as the Tollanos. With warriors framing the plaza on all four sides, the
Chilam Bahlam introduced the quetzal bedecked underlords, eight of them,
each coming up the steps, kneeling before Yax Nuun, offering their gifts,
and speaking words of respect and commitment. I thought it curious that
the gifts were either carved jade pieces or quetzal feathers. Someone,
probably Sihyaj K'ahk', had to have arranged that. The entertainments that
followed began with displays of loud and fast drumming. There were acro-
bats, singers, bird imitators, and spear throwing contests. It was the first
time I saw Maya and Tollanos enjoying themselves together.

Toward evening we went to the new residence where, as arranged, our
belongings had been moved. Near to dark we were sitting in the patio and I
finally got a chance to have a moment alone with Yax Nuun. Although he
had much to say about his initiation, his audience with the goddess, and
the taking of the K'awiil, the reserved manner of his speaking combined
with frequent words of gratitude and respect for his father and the lords of
Tollan told me that he would no longer be coming to me for advice.

With my head sunk into the pillow and the little paper flower pressed
to my chest, I prayed to Itzamnaaj and my father asking them to somehow
help Yax Nuun to remember and respect the ways of the People of Maize.
Having seen how completely he'd adopted the Tollan dress and manners,
in particular the Owl stance with their legs apart and arms folded. I also
asked Ix Chel, the Maya goddess, to soften the hardness in his heart and
keep him from harm as he enters the path of the warrior-ruler.

FOR THE NEXT YEAR AND A HALF SO MUCH WAS HAPPENING IN
and around the residence and the palace, I had to clear the workshop floor
of everything having to do with ceramics to make room for the six Tollan
women who joined me in the making of costumes, headdresses, and regalia
for my family's funeral ceremony, Yax Nuun's marriage which came two
moons later, and his ascension to the Mat which came six moons after that.

The funeral for my mother and siblings was well attended; all my people; no Tollanos. Although I was not pleased that they were being laid to rest well apart from one another, at least they were all on the same platform. Yax Nuun said very little, allowing me the opportunity to speak my words of respect. Even more, he surprised me with a vase Mother had made for Father, the top of which she incised with his head wearing an elaborate serpent headdress with signs all around it. It pained me to part with it, but I set it beside her in the tomb.

Again, as Jatz'om promised, he and Sihyaj K'ahk' removed themselves to Siaan K'aan for the day. I thought they were just honoring my wishes, but there was more to it. While there, they arranged for Yax Nuun to marry Ix K'inich, Lady Sun Eyes, who'd been introduced to Jatz'om and me as my half-niece. Despite her name, she was quite beautiful—and four years older than Yax Nuun. By having Yax Nuun marry the daughter of my half-sister, my father's granddaughter, the Ich'aak bloodline would remain intact for at least one generation after Yax Nuun. So it happened that, five moons after celebrating my son's return from Tollan, we went up the steps of the Yax Hal Witz to witness the tying of their garments.

SIX MOONS LATER, THE CHAHKOB WITHHELD THEIR RAINS long enough for the *caah* to witness Yax Nuun's ascension. After a long and smoky circuit around Mutal to plant the trees that marked her new boundaries, Jatz'om anointed Yax Nuun with the smoking K'awiil. Although the lords of Tollan had anointed him as the Mutal Ajaw Le, K'awiil now spoke through his father, authorizing our son to "speak to the people on behalf of the gods," the anointing that established him as the Mutal Great Tree. Because of his fascination with the beast, he took the name, Ajaw Yax Nuun Ayiin—First Crocodile, Lord of Mutal.

For my part, I presented the sacrificial bowl and its implements. Yax Nuun took the feathered perforator from the bowl, turned and let blood from his foreskin onto strips of cotton. He placed the strips in the bowl and I took them to the *chan aj k'in* who burned them in the sun-faced censer. With the smoking K'awiil cradled in the crook of his arm, Yax Nuun went to the steps and presented himself to the *caah*. The drummers pounded their drums hard and fast as the red-robed *aj k'inob*, daykeepers, fed incense into the rows of god-faced censers that stood on both sides of the Yax Hal Witz stairway.

With clouds of smoke rising up, the *chan aj k'in* approached Yax Nuun holding up the *sak huunal*, the jeweled White Headband that identified him as the *ajaw*, Lord and Ruler of Mutal, the living portal through whom life flows. Yax Nuun handed me the K'awiil and I took my place behind and on his female side. Nine trumpeters, one for each layer of the sky, raised their long wooden horns to the four corners of the world. All through the tying on of the sak huunal and positioning of Huunal god on the front, they sustained their loud call for the gods and ancestors to come and witness

Seated on the sumptuous, deeply carved jaguar bench that was situated on a tall dais, Yax Nuun received the long line of dignitaries—red-robed council members, white-painted holy men, and warlords wearing their animal-patron helmets. Last to kneel in his honor were the twelve under-lords that Sihyaj K'ahk' had "secured." Watching Yax Nuun receive their words of respect and gifts, I wondered: *Who is this young man dressed like Jatz'om's father?* The bright shell-rings around his eyes and with the greenstone plated war helmet nearly half his height, together with the back-mirror and spear-thrower identified him as an Owl warlord, yet he wore the quetzal sprays, jade jewels, and the *sak huunal* of my ancestors.

Yax Nuun came down from dais. Careful not to break the long feathers streaming from his helmet, the Chilam untied the *sak huunal* and held it back so his assistant could remove the helmet. When his master retied the headband over the Crocodile headdress, I noticed the care with which he tied the knot in back—so it would lie flat against his head with the ends hanging long. It was the knot at the back of the head that had come to distinguish Mutal rulers from the other lowland rulers, so I was glad to see it.

Attendants substituted his white cloak for a full-length jaguar pelt, painted his feet with the blood of the captive lord who'd been sacrificed earlier, and they escorted him to the cloth-covered scaffold where he climbed up nine rungs of the ladder, leaving dark bloodstains on the white cloth. At the top he turned and presented himself with open arms. *My little sprout—running to me in tears when he bloodied his knee. Now look at him, seated and tied, looking fierce and lordly.* I glanced at Jatz'om. His heart was so filled with pride he knelt with his shoulders back, looking up at our son with the same expression he wore when we knelt in front of the

Great Goddess at Tollan.

While they were away, Sihyaj K'ahk' had carried out his charter even better than expected. The twelve underlords, all Tollanos except for two, knelt beneath the bloodstained ladder with their arms across their chests, listening to their master tell about the prophecy and the new order. I seemed to be the only one mourning the fate of the Maya rulers who they replaced. Their palaces and residences may not have been destroyed, but without the Maya lords and ancestors who grew their centers into forests of Great Trees, they might as well have been terminated and buried. The whole time I stood there, watching and listening to the underlords recite their oath to establish and defend the *noh tzol* in their respective *caahob*, I could feel the dark clouds gathering in and around my heart.

NEARLY A YEAR LATER, AFTER TWO ROUNDS OF MY TAKING ILL and tending to Ix Chab' after she suffered a snakebite, Gray Mouse and I were out on the reservoir trail. We sat side-by-side on the stump watching two men in a canoe lower a long knotted cord with a rock on the end of it into the water. Jatz'om and I had had a heated argument that morning, so I wondered out loud: "Why is life so easy for him? And difficult for me? He gets everything he wants. He sets his canoe in the water and it glides so smoothly he barely has to paddle. Mine is either in the rapids, bumping over shoals or going aground. I am always paddling hard, against the current, and there are boulders everywhere." Gray Mouse commented that it was not fair.

It wasn't. He wanted my family out of the way and he made it happen. He wanted the monuments destroyed and that happened. He wanted Yax Nuun to take his initiation and the Ajaw Le anointing at Tollan and that happened as well. He wanted a new residence and he got it. He wanted Yax Nuun to marry a Maya woman and he did. He wanted him seated on the day of Tenan's feast and that happened. He wanted Sihyaj K'ahk' to marry a Maya woman, so he chose the sister of Yax Nuun's wife. According to his wishes, Sihyaj K'ahk' replaced Standing Squirrel as the Siaan K'aan ruler, anointing him with the new scepter he called Young Mirror, made especially for that occasion. The gods—he would say the goddess—gave him everything he wanted

167

"Gray Mouse," I asked. "How is it that a man can be so greatly blessed while his wife is so—? Am I cursed?"

Gray Mouse thought for a moment. "Not cursed, mistress," she said. "Perhaps differently blessed?"

Prophecy And Fever

WITH SIHYAJ K'AHK' INSTALLED AT SIAAN K'AAN AND VISITING only occasionally, Jatz'om became Yax Nuun's principal advisor, *telling* him what to do, where to go, what to commission and not, even how to dress. To some extent I understood. Even for one raised in the shadow of palaces, thirteen was too young to know what was best for the *caah*. Together, he and his father and the council of ministers imposed the *noh tzol* on every aspect of life at Mutal. As Naj Chan had predicted, rather than pay the higher tribute and sweat labor demanded by the new order or stand up to the warrior bands, families of both noblemen and commoners began moving away. And it kept happening. Overnight, a thriving compound of fifteen or more people would become deserted without a word about where the families had gone.

One of the boldest things Jatz'om told Yax Nuun was less like advice and more a prediction. He said he would have a son. When three moons later it happened, I began to think my husband was not only taking orders from the goddess, but giving them as well. One of the things I learned from the standing and watching I was able to manage was how he made things happen. Upon hearing him make this prediction, and realizing that it was likely to come true, I wondered if I could make something happen as well, just by predicting it. "Husband," I said. "If Yax Nuun is going to have a son, the seedling will need a name suitable for the next ruler."

"Tenan will give us a name," Jatz'om replied.

"Have you or Yax Nuun arranged for a *k'uhul winik* to do the welcoming ceremony?"

"You need not concern yourself, dear one. Any of the ministers would be honored to do it."

"What about the tainting? Have you spoken to Yax Nuun about it?"

Jatz'om turned and his eyebrows bent forward. "Tainting? What tainting?"

"You remember—the precaution about foreign hands."

Jatz'om took a long drink from his cup, probably to hide his eyes. "Remind me," he said.

"If a sacred-blood seedling is touched by foreign hands within ten *k'inob* of touching the earth, it taints his blood. The heat goes out and the blood is no longer *zuhuy*. My people take this very seriously. Remember? We talked about it, even took precaution when Yax Nuun and Ix Chab' were born? That was why I had a Maya midwife—and why you had to avoid us for ten *k'inob*.

"I remember the avoidance," he said.

"Ix K'inich will be delivering soon. Have you or Yax Nuun arranged for a midwife—a Maya?"

"That is for you women to decide." Jatz'om waved his hand dismissively. "Do whatever is necessary. The seedling's blood must remain *zuhuy*. Everything must be proper in the eyes of your people and mine." I got up and took my leave.

I knew that Jatz'om would want to do the naming. Having Yax Nuun marry a Maya woman wasn't enough to insure that my people would never challenge his grandson's right to rule. For that reason alone, he would want to give our grandson the name of my father's great-grandfather: Sihyaj Chan K'awiil, "Sky-Born Lightning," eleventh in the line of the Jaguar Claw. Another reason for his choosing that name was because Sihyaj Chan was the first to allow immigrants from Tollan to settle at Mutal. The only source of water for the *caah* in his day was one reservoir, so it was both risky and generous of him to share it with foreigners.

The name didn't matter to me. As long as it was Mayan. Even more, I wanted a Maya holy man, not a Tollano, to conduct the welcoming rites, especially the rite of prophecy. With Jatz'om's permission to secure a midwife for Ix K'inich, I also decided that Naj Chan would do the welcoming.

So it happened. With all of us gathered in a circle, Naj Chan touched our grandson's little hand to the earth and said the greeting and gratitude. As arranged, he called upon my ancestors, the Ich'aak alone, to give the prophecy. Speaking so all could hear, he repeated the words that they — and I — gave him: "The seedling before us, blood of our blood, will live a long life. He will have many sons. In one arm he cradles the serpent. In the other the jaguar. With one foot rooted on the path of the Owl, the other rooted on the path of the Jaguar Claw, the tree grows strong and rises high in the forest of men."

IN THOSE DAYS A NEWBORN WAS NOT CONSIDERED VIABLE until after forty days. For that reason we held two additional celebrations after the welcoming. The first of these was a daylong feast where Jatz'om and I hosted Ix K'inich's parents and their extended family. Apart from Yax Nuun and Ix Chab', the only blood relative on my side was my half-sister from Siaan K'aan.

At the end of the forty "holding" days, it was customary for the father of the seedling to host *both* families in a feast of venison, but because Yax Nuun was the *ajaw*, Jatz'om had him invite the entire *caah* — ministers, nobles and commoners, including the underlords and their families. The Keeper of Counts said his men counted seven hundred sixty-three heads in the Great Plaza that day.

I went to my sleeping chamber early. It was hard to believe that at twenty-eight, I was a grandmother. Equally hard to believe was how quickly I'd given my heart to a *kakaw* colored, baldheaded seedling no longer than my forearm. Kneeling in front of my altar, I asked Itzamnaaj and the ancestors to keep him from harm and to never let him forget his Maya roots.

Three days after the feast, Ix K'inich complained of feeling weak and aching all over. Her head was throbbing. To relieve her I bundled the little one into my shawl and we went for a walk around Precious Forest Plaza. When we returned I found her lying on the floor, sweating and shivering, holding her head with both hands. She didn't have the strength to get up and I couldn't lift her, so I went to the doorway, shouted for help and tucked the little one tightly in his crib.

I'd pulled the blankets from Ix K'inich's sleeping bench and was just covering her when Gray Mouse entered. "Yax Nuun is at the Tollan settlement," I said. "Send someone to get him, then find my husband and tell him we need a healer. Hurry!" Two blankets weren't enough. I got three more and heaped them on. While I was covering her, Ix K'inich brought up everything she'd eaten that day. The mess was all down her neck and shoulders, on the blankets and it puddled on the floor. I hollered again and this time one of the cooks came in. Stunned by the vomit and seeing Ix K'inich writhing in agony, I had to yell at her to get more help and bring water.

Another cook came through the doorway, so I sent her to get some clean blankets, as many as she could carry. When a guard came he lifted Ix K'inich and took her to the sleeping bench. Nothing I did seemed to help. She kept complaining about her head and twice again she vomited into the calabash I held under her chin. When the healer finally arrived he looked into her eyes and chased us out of the house. His assistant came out with us, drilled a fire and set a smudge to burning, which he took inside. Fresh blankets arrived, and I was taking them in when the *aj men* pointed to the floor. "Drop them!" he shouted. "Away with you! Keep everyone away from here." People were gathering, so they followed me into the patio where I explained what had happened. The healer's assistant came out and said they needed a litter. The guard knew where there was one, so he and a companion ran off to get it.

Yax Nuun came running. I told him he had to stay away, but he went in anyway. I followed him to the doorway. The *aj men* shouted. "Away! Out of here!" he demanded.

"Not until I know how she is!" Yax Nuun demanded, brushing off the assistants gesture.

"With respect, your wife is in the grip of a terrible demon," the *aj men* said. "I have seen this one before. He attacks all who come near. The only thing protecting us now is the smoke. If you want to help, find a secluded place where she can be warm and dry, a place where we can keep the smudges going night and day."

"This demon, will it kill her?" Yax Nuun asked as he backed into the doorway.

"She is young," he said. "Still master, it will take all her strength. You should go now! Quickly! This demon will put down any who come within twenty or thirty paces."

Gray Mouses's husband apparently overheard them. When Yax Nuun came to the steps he knelt in front of him. "With respect, Ajaw Yax Nuun Ayiin, *awinaken*. I know a place, a clean place where no one goes." He pointed west to the trees. "The path over there leads to an abandoned building..."

I knew that building. Ix Chab', Gray Mouse, and I had considered it for the workshop. It was long with six little chambers on each side. Because the bamboo pole-and-mortar roof was flat and the chambers without benches, we guessed that it had once served as servant quarters. Before they went in to get Ix K'inich, Turtle Cloud, the litter bearers, and the healer were heavily smudged. When they came out, the assistant preceded them with two smudge bundles, waving them all around and calling for all of us to stay back. Ix K'inich, still holding her head and moaning, was covered with several blankets and carried off in a cloud of smoke. Yax Nuun and I wanted to follow, but the *aj man* insisted that we remove ourselves from the area. Two more assistants with smudges were already pulling the fabrics, pelts, pillows, cushions, feathers, and clothing from the house so they could burn it. Afterward, the chamber itself would be generously smudged with a drape over the doorway. Someone said, and I agreed, it was fortunate that the little one had been with me when the demon attacked.

TWO MORNINGS LATER THE *AJ MEN* CAME AND TOLD US IX K'inich was still in agony. The rash he found on her hands was now coming out on her face and forearms; a sign the demon was attacking her blood. In addition to his aspirations and bleedings, he said her grandmother was providing the annanto, gumbolimbo, and amaranth brews they needed. That was all he could tell us. And there was nothing we could do to help.

On the fourth day after the attack, the demon struck me. I was sitting on a wicker bench in the patio, talking to the house servants about a banquet when I felt nauseous. Within moments I was on the ground, sweating and shivering with a pounding headache. Everything that happened to Ix K'inich happened to me. According to the *aj men*, the demon entered when I was attending her and it waited inside me, building up strength for the attack. Like her, they smudged me until I choked. And they moved me into the chamber farthest from hers and on the back side of the building.

I never felt so bad, worse even than when I entered Mutal. I prayed to Itzamnaaj, Ix Chel, Father, and all the Ich'aak. Three days later the rash appeared on my face and the demon was still pressing my head as if between boulders. No matter how many blankets they laid on top of me, I couldn't stop shivering. Ix K'inich seemed to be recovering, but even if the *aj men* was telling the truth, I was older than she and not as strong. The rash spread to my stomach, even to the soles of my feet. My entire body ached, especially my back. On the fourth night it got so bad I prayed for Itzamnaaj to come and show me the road to Xibalba.

I OPENED MY EYES AND SAW A WHITE BLURRY SHAPE LEANING over me. "Greetings daughter," the voice said. "You journeyed far and long. Twelve *k'inob*."

Ix Sac Tzu'

"The *aj men* said he thought you would take the dark road." I couldn't respond. My eyes were filled with water and my lips seemed crusted shut. "Your blood is raging less," White Gourd said. I moved my fingers to my mouth and lifted my head a bit to ask for water. As I drank I noticed that the shivering and the pounding in my head had both stopped. It was true what the *aj men* said: Ix K'inich and I had fought hard. Our prayers had been answered. Unfortunately, not those of the first cook and the guard who helped me with Ix K'inich. Like a warrior after a battle, I felt bruised all over. I couldn't even lift my arms.

When next I awoke the brightness in the doorway made my eyes hurt. The *aj men* pressed the back of his hand to my cheek and went outside. Moments later White Gourd came in and I asked her to cover the doorway. "I thought it might be you," I said. "What are you doing here?"

"Ten guards, three carriers, and two bearers came to our little compound. Your son sent them. How could we refuse? We have never before been carried."

"But they need you at Ixlu—the line outside your doorway."

"Muwan was glad to see us go. The others will just have to wait." We spoke a little more, and then I had to sleep.

Three days later White Gourd was preparing to leave. I wasn't moving very fast, but I was well enough to sit on the bench in the shade of a lime tree and wait while the servants gathered her bundles. "Do you believe the prophecy?" she asked. "The prophecy of Tenan?"

"Living in Tollan with the man she burdened to deliver it made it hard not to believe. You have been talking to my husband?"

She nodded. "We had some long conversations. What if it is true that the fate of the world depends upon their establishing the *noh tzol*? It happened before, did it not? Three times. From what we saw at Chaynal, we can see how the Makers would be angry." It wasn't a question that needed an answer. Watching the carriers load her bundles into their high-pack baskets reminded me of the journey from Tollan.

"It sounds like you believe the prophecy," I offered.

"Only because of the dream we had last night. Very disturbing."

"May I ask what happened—in the dream?"

"It came very clear," White Gourd said. "Too clear." She crossed her wrists in front of her chest and closed her eyes. "The animals are killing each other. Jaguars, monkeys, deer, tapir, dogs, paca, raccoons—running, and howling, barking, yelping. The forests are burning. Houses and temples are burning. The ground shakes. People are screaming, running, pulling each to run faster. The rains come down hard, fiercer than otter. Rivers rise up. They roar like thunder and overflow their banks. Snakes and tarantulas, jaguars, monkeys, and birds scramble to the top of the canopy but the water overtakes them, plunging all creatures into the Underworld. All that remains is dark sky, lightning, and black water." Hearing this from a shaman was especially frightening. She opened her eyes and took a deep breath.

"Terrible," I said. There was no other word for it.

White Gourd shook her head. "Dark sky above, black water below. Not a bird. Not a tree. Not a mountain peak. Not a sound."

"So you think the prophecy is coming true? Is that why the gods or your ancestors showed it to you?"

"There is much to ponder here," she said shrugging her shoulders. The guards and carriers had arrived, but we were waiting for the bearers to come with a litter. "Your husband told us what happened here. He said it was a necessary sacrifice. Your son sees it that way as well." I didn't want to talk about it, especially if she was leaning their way. "What do you think?" she probed. "If you knew the gods were going to destroy the world and you had the power to change their minds, would you do it? What would you be willing to sacrifice?"

I didn't want to answer. I couldn't. "What would you do?" I asked.

"Praise Itzamnaaj," she said. "That is not the dance we have been given. Ours is to heal. We cannot worry about the animals or the birds—or the world. There are too many people on our doorstep."

The bearers arrived with the litter, so I walked her over to it. She expressed her gratitude for the Monkey vase and asked that I extend her appreciation to Yax Nuun for the accommodations at the guesthouse. Although she didn't say how, she told me that Jatz'om had compensated her generously for attending to me both at Ixlu and Mutal. She had more to say, so I asked the bearers and the others to wait in the shade of the lime tree.

"Had you not come," I said, "the demon would surely have devoured me."

"Him or the smoke. The body is healing well, daughter. But inside, you are still stirring up the winds. The wandering *ch'ulel* has not yet returned because it knows this."

"What do you advise?"

"As before, stand and watch. When someone dances a storm in front of you, know that it is *their* dance, not *yours*. Dance your own dance, whatever it is."

"I thought—hoped—it would be the memorial bowls. Now that they have been gifted I do not know what to do."

"Have patience, daughter. Your roots are guiding you. Keep the white flower close and go off by yourself to dream the world you want."

She'd never said that before. "What do you mean?"

"The dream about the world being destroyed? The meaning and the reason it was given is yet to be revealed, so we stand and watch. We pay attention to what is in front of us, watching what the gods and ancestors provide as we walk the path that makes us feel good about ourselves—."

"I felt that way when I was making the memorial bowls."

"Our teacher at Chaynal used to say, 'Inside world makes outside world.' It was his way of saying what we said about seeing with new eyes: what happens to us in this world depends largely on how we see it—and ourselves. Especially how we respond. We could stir up a powerful storm inside worrying about the destructions that were given in the dream. But does that help us on our way? More helpful is to attend to those waiting on our doorstep. If the dream was intended to help us down that path, the meaning will be revealed."

"I worry about everything."

"Distractions. Remember? That is why we asked you what you want. Without that knowing we walk this way and that, of the path of expectation or recommendation. It takes us this way and that, does it not?"

"And we end up nowhere."

"Know the destination and the path to it will appear. The forces be yond and within us can then guide us. Do you see?"

"I understand. But knowing what I want is not so easy when you have been through what I went through."

" Knowing comes from dreaming, seeing the person you want to be, dreaming of the life you want, the world you want. And then walking the path toward it as best you can.

"I am afraid to dream again. What if—?"

"Dreams of what we want have a way. If we cannot find them, they will find us. You will see. We were sent here to dance the dance we must, not to fall victim to the dances of others. Seek the dream and it will come to you."

"And when the distractions come?"

"Distractions can be trials, even blessings. Wisdom is gained when we see where they fit. Meanwhile, stand and watch. You told us that at your birth the *aj men* said yours would be the path of the jaguar, did you not?" I nodded. "Jaguars stand and watch. They do not pounce until they know what they want—and how to get it. Like the jaguar, you will know when to pounce when you know what you want."

"And how to get it." Thirty paces beyond, without turning in the litter, White Gourd raised her arm and waved. "We look forward to your next visit" she called back. "Bring your best dream!"

Purification

SMOKE FROM THE BURNING FIELDS BLANKETED THE *CAAH*, ITS
bluish haze hanging in the trees with shafts of light brightening patches of
brown leaves, verdant fern, and bared roots. Although a wonder to see, the
odor stung our nostrils and watered our eyes. Most of us stayed inside with
the drapes pulled across the doorways. Gray Mouse and I were folding
gowns when a familiar voice called out.

Standing behind a sentry was a round-faced and barefoot woman wearing a bark-cloth sarong. He said she wanted to speak to me but she
wouldn't tell him what it concerned. Normally I would never receive such
a person, not even a Maya woman, especially not at the residence, but her
frightened smile and unwarranted show of respect with both arms crossing
her chest made me curious. Gray Mouse was with me, so I expressed gratitude to the sentry and allowed her to enter the reception chamber.

"With respect my lady," the woman said. "Gratitude for allowing me
to speak with you. I am called Ix Chak Kaab. I have come—. I am embarrassed to tell you—. I know the rule that forbids entry into the reservoir.
My husband and I—. We have four little ones. Nakal is my oldest. He is
thirteen. His brother Nakoh, is eleven. You know how they run."

"They got caught in the reservoir?" She nodded. "Were they in the water?" Again, she nodded. "The punishment can be severe, but I am not the
one you should be talking to." I turned toward the doorway. She took a few
steps in that direction, but stopped.

"With respect Ix Bahlam, I came not only for my sons. We heard you were looking for pieces of the stone—. Forgive me, a curse does not allow me to say more—."

"The stones taken from Precious Forest?"

"Nakal, my eldest, he found a stone under the water, a large one. It had carving on it. I thought you might want to know."

I backed away from the door and gestured for the woman to take a place across from me on one of the occlot cushions. She nodded, smiled nervously and sat, tucking her sarong tightly under her knees. "What can you tell me about it?" I asked.

Gray Mouse offered her some limewater and honey, but the woman raised her hand. "Gratitude mistress, my husband is waiting at the sentry post. He is worried that you will report our sons to the Minister of Water." I gestured and Gray Mouse took her place on the mat by the hearth.

I touched the woman's hand. "I am pleased that you came, Ix Chak Kaab. You can speak freely. I assure you, I will not report your sons—or what you have to say—to anyone. Tell me about the stone."

"That relieves me greatly, mistress. Nakal is the one who went into the water. He said he saw a stone with a foot carved in it. The stone was covered in mud so that was all he saw."

"The stone is under the water? How deep?"

"He took us to the overlook, but all we could see was a shape. The water level is very low. The drop over the cliff is very steep. We had to hold on to the trees, but we could see the shape. Nakal was telling the truth."

"Was part of the stone sticking out of the water?"

"No mistress. The wind was high, so all we saw was the light shape."

"What was he doing down there? How did he get down? The drop must be thirteen or fifteen men deep in places."

"He climbed down on a vine. The other sprouts helped him. Apparently they make a game of it. If I had known they were going..."

I needed to see for myself. Immediately. At the sentry post the woman introduced her sons and her husband who apologized for their soot-covered feet and soiled loincloths. The odor of sweat and smoke told me his wife had pulled them away from his field. The eldest son wore black body paint and didn't have a white bead in his hair, so I asked why he was not with his brothers at the men's house. He explained that the master of the house released him to help his father with the burning.

We were midway across the reservoir trail, about thirty paces beyond the stump where I often sat, when he stopped, went up a little rise and pointed down. Holding onto a sapling I leaned over, enough to see the muddy bottom where footprints led to a shape that was lighter than the dark green water. I judged the stone to be five or six strides out.

"Your mother said you climbed down on a vine?" I asked.

Nakal and his brother went to the other side of the trail and we followed. From behind the brush they pulled up part of a thick and menacing tangle of double twisted vine. I was certainly not going down on that, so they dropped it and pushed it back into the brush with their feet.

The father, Nakach Kaab, had been looking over the cliff and came back to the trail. "Nakal" he asked in a stern manner, "You know it is forbidden. Why would you go down there? If you'd fallen or drowned—."

Embarrassed to be scolded in front of strangers, Nakal kept his head bowed and eyes to the ground. I assured his father I was not going to report him. "Nakal," I asked. "What is the game you play? I am just curious."

"We come here when the water is low, mistress.

"You have done this before?" the father asked.

"Since I was ten or eleven. We all come and help, but no one goes down until the season before their initiation. Until then we hold the vine and keep watch. We post lookouts up and down the trail. When no one is coming, the one going down turns his back to the water so he cannot see the one who throws a white-painted rock as far into the water as he can. Bringing it up proves we made our descent into the Underworld. We only do it when the water is way down."

"What do you do when people or the guards come?" I asked.

"We keep the vine tied to a tree. If someone comes we go to the other side of the trail and act like monkeys to keep them from seeing it."

"There are never any guards," his brother offered. I expressed my gratitude to Nakal Kaab and his family and invited him or his wife to come to the residence the next day so I could give them something for telling me about the stone and showing us the location.

Leaving them where the reservoir trail met the causeway, Gray Mouse and I and continued around the elbow of the reservoir to see if we might reach the stone by going down the steps the women used to fill their water jars. Several women were down there, so we knew the clay was solid where they were walking.

Down thirty or forty steps, vegetation growing high on the floor blocked our view of the ground in front of the cliff in the distance. Even if I had some men to chop a path through the vegetation, there could be deep water or mud further on.

Gray Mouse and I spent several days talking about what, if anything, to do about the stone. Given its size and shape, it was either a small monument, a piece of one, or not a monument at all. Still, the young man said he saw a foot. The palace reservoir was the first to be dug, so the stone could have been dumped there long ago.

Gray Mouse suggested I find some Maya stone-haulers and compensate them well to take a closer look and tell us what they found. I started on that course, but when I heard myself telling the men what I wanted them to do, I changed my mind. However they were going to reach the stone, I had to go along.

ON THE AGREED UPON MORNING, AT FIRST LIGHT AND WITH A heavy mist filling the reservoir basin, Gray Mouse and I met Nakach Kaab and his sons, Nakal and Nakoh, at the top of the steps. With heavy cords on their shoulders and carrying a slasher for the vegetation, we went down the steps and onto the clay. Had a guard or sentry seen me walking barefoot and wearing a bark-cloth sarong I borrowed from Gray Mouse, they would never have believed that I was the wife of the Great Prophet of Tollan. The black clay was hard, so it was easy to get to the cliff wall.

Nakach led the way with his sons, occasionally swiping at the vegetation, some of it rising well above our heads. The wall rose on our male side to a height of about fifteen men if they were to stand on each other's shoulders. Around the bend the ground rose and from there, through the mist, we could see the darker edge of the pool we needed to reach. To get to it we had to cross a strip of water where we sank into mud up to our ankles.

Crossing over mounds that looked like weed-covered turtles, we came to the edge of the pool and made our way down a long strip of clay that was only two arms length between the water and the wall. Finally, we came to the place where with the footprints. Beyond them the light patch in the water lay about an arm's length beneath the surface of the water. Calm as it was, I could see that we were looking at the corner of large slab. Nakach pointed up to the rooted cliff. "It must have been dumped when the reservoir was full. Otherwise it would have fallen closer to the wall."

Not wanting anyone to stir up the mud before I could get a closer look, I had Gray Mouse steady me with a hand until the water came up to my knees and my feet were covered in mud. The stone was still out of reach. Because the flat side faced away, I couldn't see any carving.

With my permission, Nakal, the elder son, swam out and went under the water to show me where he saw the carved foot. When he came up about three strides out, he said he said it was directly under him. "Come, I will show you," he said, treading water.

"Did you see any other stones?"

"I will look again," he said, plunging down.

I turned to his father. "I never learned to swim," I said. "As long as I can remember, I have been deathly afraid of the water. I have never been deeper than my waist."

"With respect, the father said. "I could look as well—if you like?"

Nakal surfaced, panting. He swam over and grabbed hold of the stone's edge. "All I could see is the one," he said rubbing his eyes. "I wiped more of the mud off. The foot is wearing a sandal and the leg is bent up at the knee."

I nodded to his father. He went out to his son and together they plunged in headfirst. I turned to Gray Mouse who had her hand over mouth. "Did you hear?" she asked. "The leg is bent up."

I'd heard. The tears were already pooling in my eyes. The figure at the bottom of Father's monument, the founder of our lineage according to Naj Chan, was wearing sandals and had his leg bent up. "It has to be," I said.

Nakal broke the surface with a splash, coughing and rubbing his eyes. His father came up, swished his hair back and followed him to where they could stand. "The side facing up is all carved," Nakach said. "Below the leg there are word-signs. Farther down is the face of a small jaguar. Across from it there is a wider leg and a jaguar paw with the claws pointing up.

That was all I could see."

"The back side seems to be all word signs," Nakal said.   I was out
of my head with delight. With no thought at all, arms full out, grasping at
air, and forgetting my fear of the water I leapt to the stone like a frog on a
lily pad. Down I went. Cold and dark. Thrashing and kicking, gulping-in
water, my foot hit the stone. I got hold at the top, but my hand slipped and
I slid down the bumpy face of the stone, deeper into blessed darkness. A
hand grasped my wrist and pulled. Another took my arm. Choking and
gasping for breath at the surface, Nakach and his son pulled me onto the
muddy bank. Oddly, after catching my breath and sitting up, I looked at
myself and laughed. In spite of the mud on my legs and the sarong, I felt
thoroughly cleansed on the inside.

WHEN A RULER DIED IT WAS SAID HE "ENTERED THE WATER,"
began his ascent into the sky by first descending into the watery Underworld. I was reminded of this because my descent into the reservoir pool
turned out to be an ascent of sorts—I would never before have gone into
the water like that, but having done so a burden had been lifted. Whether it
was acting in spite of my fear or just touching Father's monument again,
for the first time since leaving Tollan, I got a taste of confidence—and
hope. The knowledge that Father's monument, at least a large piece of it,
was still intact made it easy to forget the little scrape on the bottom and
side of my foot.

EXCEPT FOR THE ATTENDANT STANDING BEHIND AND WELL off
to the side, Yax Nuun sat alone beside the patio brazier tying owl feathers
onto the neck of a ceremonial spear. "Mother," he said as I approached. I
took the bench across from him. It was a pleasant day and a rare opportunity for us to be alone together. If he or his father or Sihyaj K'ahk' knew
that a piece of Father's monument survived, they would have it chopped
into marl for certain, so I was careful not to mention it.

Yax Nuun repeated that he'd enjoyed his conversations with White
Gourd. I responded saying how blessed his wife and I were to have had
such good healers. "It helped that Father and I burnt offerings and prayed

to the goddess for your recovery," he said. "Tenan told Father you would both be spared." Apparently they hadn't prayed hard enough for the guard, the cook, and two others who fell victim of the demon.

"Your father says a special visitor is coming to celebrate the *tun-ending*," I said. "You must be very pleased."

"Can you believe it? For a Tollan lord to come this far is a great honor."

"To journey forty *k'inob* and be away from Tollan that long for a calendar celebration is most unusual." Jatz'om had told me the real reason for his father's visit, but I wanted to hear it from my son.

"There is more to it, Mother. In addition to witnessing the *tun*-ending, he will be celebrating the establishment of the *noh tzol* in the centers. He wants to give my *yajawob* his blessing."

The last I'd heard, the count of underlords was up to twenty-one underlords. "What is the count now?"

"Twenty-five. If all goes well there should be thirty when Grandfather arrives." Something Jatz'om said before he left for Siaan K'aan led me to believe that the reason for his visit was to have Sihyaj K'ahk' arrange a way for Yax Nuun to further distinguish himself as a warrior. Nothing would make Jatz'om more proud of his son than having his father witness the offering of his grandson's captive, especially if that offering could be a ruler who refused or was reluctant to adopt the new order. "Does that mean you will be going on raids with Sihyaj K'ahk'?"

"I am surprised father told you. There is no reason to worry, Mother. I trained with the Owls..." Suddenly, there came a loud and bubbly, flutter-like sound that ended in a quieter clucking, like *kyuk, kyuk, kyuk*. When we stood they were over our heads: ten or more oropendolas, large black birds with bright yellow beaks and tail-feathers. It was unusual to see so many of them together and to hear them in flight. More often the sound of just one or two of them could be heard in the plazas. These were flying north, apparently to the reservoir where their palm fiber nests hung from cedar branches like black sacks of stones. When we sat again, Yax Nuun turned to me. "Mother," he said. "I have been thinking—. May I ask a favor?"

"Always," I said.

"I know there is still bad blood between you and father." I blinked my eyes slowly to say he was not wrong. "You have every right. I try not to think about it..."

"What is it?"

"When grandfather comes it would favor me greatly if you and Ix Chab', if the two of you would dress and wear your hair in the Tollano manner — like you did at Ho' Noh Witz."

I thought a moment. "Are you asking for yourself or your father?"

Yax Nuun raised his hands as if the answer was obvious. "Just me. Only while grandfather is here — ten or twelve *k'inob*. I want his visit to be special in every way. He does not know that you and Father are —."

I took a deep breath. "You know I would do anything for you, Yax Nuun. This will take some deliberation. It has more to do with your father than you."

"You stand with him as *kaloomte'* and Keeper of K'awiil anyway."

"I have and I will. But if I dress as I did at Ho' Noh Witz, particularly now, my people will think I have adopted the Tollan ways."

"They have seen you, Mother. They know better. You could talk to them if you like, some of them. Explain that you are just being respectful, just for this visit..." The more my son spoke the more I realized how much this meant to him.

"You are asking me to present myself as something I am not."

"I am not asking you to adopt the Tollan ways, just to show respect for my grandfather. You presented yourself as one of them at Ho' Noh Witz. Why not here, just until he is gone?"

"That was before your father..." The disappointment on Yax Nuun's face reminded me how, on his sixth birth anniversary, I wouldn't let him play with the throwing-knife his father gave him. I turned away. "Ayaahh," I breathed.

"What is it?"

By exasperation told him I was hiding something. I wished I'd kept quiet. "I cannot say. Your father would be furious."

"Is it about grandfather's visit? Whatever it is you can tell me. You know I will not repeat what you say to Father."

I sat closer to the edge of the bench. "You will not get upset? Jade-stone promise?"

He touched his forefinger to his thumb. "Jadestone promise."

"Do you remember when I took you and Ix Chab' to see your grandfather's monument?"

"I remember. What about it?"

"A large piece of it survived."

I could see in his eyes he did not want to believe it. "That cannot be. The monuments were all chopped up, even the ones they rolled away. Sihyaj K'ahk' oversaw it himself."

"Somehow, the bottom survived. I have seen it."

"Where is it?"

"Very well hidden."

"You know there is a curse on anyone who talks about those stones? Are you not afraid?"

"I care not at all about the curse. I have been talking about it with the people who found it. They even showed me where it is, and nothing happened."

"You are right. Father would be furious if he knew. He would have it destroyed."

"That is why I bound you to secrecy."

"What are you going to do?"

"I would like to give it a proper burial, but it would take many stone workers and several *k'inob* to move it."

"Father might not object to that, not if I ordered it. If the stone is out of sight no one could venerate it."

"But it *needs* to be seen. It could keep your grandfather's memory alive—so he can continue to contribute."

Yax Nuun got up. He circled twice around the brazier, thinking. He took his seat again. "Consider this Mother. We could make a pact, just between us. If you present yourself as a Tollano and speak to Grandfather in his own tongue while he is here, I will order the stone raised and give it the burial you want."

"You would do that?"

"I am the *ajaw*, remember?"

"I could not survive another disappointment, Yax Nuun."

"Father is not a minister, not even a member of the council. When it comes to matters of the *caah*, he has no standing. He only advises."

"Still, he could order someone to destroy it."

"I will protect it. If for any reason it would be destroyed, I would not hold you to our agreement."

Agreement? Is this my son or the Mutal ajaw? I got up and walked to the far end of the patio where one of the older indoor servants was washing the floor with a wet cloth. She bowed and I nodded. I returned to the brazier and sat again. "I will agree to present myself and Ix Chab' in our Tollan attire and speak in your father's tongue while your grandfather is here, if you will give the stone a respectful burial. As part of our agreement, you will protect the monument with guards from the moment it is uncovered until the moment it is buried. Also, it needs to be cleaned and handled carefully by stone carvers so it suffers no further damage—."

Yax Nuun nodded. "That is acceptable. I will—."

"There is more. I want a Maya *k'uhul winik*, a man of my choice, to perform an *och k'ahk'* to see if he can restore your grandfather's *ch'ulel* in the stone. That may not be possible, but I want him to try. Also, I want it buried in the Eastern Shrine at Precious Forest, somewhere close to my mother. And I want it buried in a tomb with a little opening so my people and I, you and your sister if you like, can enter to pay our respects."

The pause and the expression on Yax Nuun's face told me he was thinking how he would present all this to his father—and then enforce it. "This is a grand favor, Mother. So I will add another favor as well." I nodded. "I want it so Father will never know about this—our agreement. I want him to think that *you* decided, out of respect for him and his father, to present yourselves as Tollanos."

"I understand. I can agree to that, but it occurs to me that your father could have the monument destroyed *after* it has been entombed. The entryway could be used as well by someone who wants to hack it to pieces."

"Once the stone is entombed it will be protected by standing order. You know the penalty for desecrating a shrine." I did: loosing both hands or descent into slavery. Bargaining that way with my son, especially in opposition to his father, was like walking on a muddy vine. I had to be careful. And I didn't like it.

The Precious Bundle

I WAS WALKING THE PALACE GROUNDS WITH SERVANTS WHEN Yax Nuun arrived. Before his litter was even set down, his *caluac*, Full-Of-Knots, came to me saying Yax Nuun wanted to see me.

The guards at the bottom of the steps bowed and stood aside for me to pass. Those on the terrace did likewise and two of them escorted me around to the doorway where Full-Of-Knots—whose composure and impeccable dress were nothing like his name—gestured for me to enter the spacious chamber. Yax Nuun rose to greet me. "Mother?" he said. Ever since his return from Tollan he spoke the word as if he were surprised to see me. He gestured and I took my place, facing him on one of the jaguar cushions on his female side.

We exchanged words regarding my request to dump trash in one of the old quarry depressions. Then came the real reason for his wanting to see me. "Regarding our agreement, you were right. Father said I had no choice but to have the stone destroyed. He could not believe that I was even considering the prospect of a burial."

"He was insistent?"

Yax Nuun raised his eyebrows. "You know how he is. He said the goddess would be displeased. He said if the Maya were to venerate even the burial place, she would punish me."

"Did you tell him where I wanted it buried?"

He shook his head. "That would have been too much."

"How did you leave it?"

"I think he is mostly worried that it would interfere with Grandfather's visit."

"Then you will hold to our agreement?"

"I will—as long as you hold to yours."

Later that evening Jatz'om and I sat with Yax Nuun and his wife for a meal of roasted iguana, bean and maize dumplings, and cooked squash with ground chili. Gratefully, not a word was spoken about the monument or the upcoming visit. Afterward, while Jatz'om was trying to coax a smile from his grandson, Yax Nuun and I took a walk. "I ordered Full-Of-Knots to arrange an audience with the master stone carver and the *aj noah*," he said. "They built the tombs, so they know the best place to set another one. I will tell them about the stone and talk about their compensations, but you need to tell them what you want done. You should supervise them. Because of Father, the less I know about this the better."

"I understand. I am sorry this adds to your burden, even more sorry that it is causing trouble between you and your father."

"He does not worry me, not nearly as much as the goddess."

"Are you speaking to her now?"

"I talk but she does not answer. Father says I am still too young. But you know her power."

WITH THE MASTER STONE CARVER AND THE *AJ NOAH* MAKING preparations in secret, I visited with the blind old *aj k'in*, Shining Flint. He said it would be his privilege to invite my father's *ch'ulel* to take up residence in the stone again, but when he divined the beans and crystals to determine the most auspicious day to do it, the ancestors warned him strongly against breaking ground at any of the eastern platform shrines. Apparently not enough days had passed since we buried my family. To dig into the shrines sooner than the calendar date called Five Wind Two Harvest, would not only be disrespectful, it would disturb the *ch'ulelob* that had not yet completed their period of adjustment. That meant a wait of one hundred and forty-six days.

That was not acceptable. The rains were coming in six days. If Shining Flint's prediction was right—and it always was—the rain would be deepening the pools at the quarry, so that meant the stone had to be removed within ten to fifteen days at the most.

Gray Mouse and Ix Chab' and I talked and talked. Finally, I went to Yax Nuun, revealed that the stone was in a pool at the reservoir and told him we had to get it raised before it became impossible. "If you wait a *tun*," he said, "the water might even be lower."

"It could also be higher," I said. "I cannot risk it. Meanwhile, what is the water doing to the carving? I want it raised now."

"We cannot have it out in the open where people can see it. Father would—."

"Then raise it and cover it. Or bury it—put it in a temporary grave."

Yax Nuun paced and thought. "No matter what I do, Father is going to hate it. I cannot hide this from him. He is here every day. He knows everything. He will keep asking about it."

"What did I teach you, Yax Nuun?"

He shook his head and grinned. "Always the truth, I know."

"You are the *ajaw*, the Great Tree. Your allegiance is to Mutal, not your father. I trust you will do what is best for the *caah*."

"If only it were that simple."

JATZ'OM DID WHAT HE ALWAYS DID WHEN HE WAS UPSET. Nothing. By not speaking at all about the monument, I knew he had appealed to the goddess and put the situation in her hands.

Three days had passed since Yax Nuun told his father he'd decided to bury the stone in a temporary grave. It might have been his assurance that the reservoir trail and Precious Forest Plaza would be closed while the stone was being raised, or that the grave would be plastered over, but he didn't even purse his lips when he overheard one of the servants ask another about the many stone haulers taking heavy beams and long cords down the reservoir steps. Then too, his mind was mostly on the preparations for his father's visit.

I expected it would take three, perhaps four days to raise the stone, move it to Precious Forest and bury it. It took nine. Four just to build the hoists—one at the pool to raise the stone, the other on top of the cliff—and three to get the rolling-logs in place. The stone-haulers already had the cords they needed for binding and hoisting, but they had to make one long enough to reach the bottom of the chasm from the top of the cliff. And it had to be strong enough to bear the weight of the stone.

Early on the morning set for raising the stone, four men were already in the water when I arrived. Their going under to secure the cords had muddied the water all around, so I couldn't see anything. They pulled and tugged and got three more men in the water, but the stone wouldn't move. Finally, the master called for logs to be used as a lever. "Be careful!" I shouldn't have shouted but I couldn't help it. They were shoving the longest log hard and into a place where they couldn't see. They could have broken the stone or damaged the carving.

By prying the lever up and down, the shoulder of the stone rose above the water briefly. And then it slipped and the entire piece sunk. My heart sunk along with it, but the men said it would be easier for them to tie the cords around it now that it was free from the mud. After several men kept plunging down with cords, they pulled the heaviest two over the hoist. With men standing on both sides of the hoist, some in water up to their necks to balance the stone it began to rise. Eight of their brothers pulled and pulled. Finally, covered in mud except in the places where Nakach and his son had wiped it off, the stone broke the surface. Even from a distance I could see the foot and leg—and then the jaguar claw scepter. I also saw how it was broken. Father's belt and everything above it, the larger part of the monument, was gone. "Can you clean it off?" I shouted. "I want to see the carving." While the men in the water struggled to balance it so others could tie cords full around it, two others went in and wiped the mud off with the flat of their hands, splashing water across the surface and digging into the crevices, drawing the mud out with their fingers and swishing water down the carved channels.

First to be revealed was the part closest to me, the bearded face of our founder, my grandfather, Ajaw K'inich Muwaan Jol. Clutching each other's arms, neither Gray Mouse nor I could hold back the tears as the other details were revealed. The men in the water were straining and the master was eager to lift it onto solid ground, but the revelations that came with every swipe of the hands held me captive. It was like they were conjuring my father—his hand, legs, and fancy anklets with the signs for "night" and "day," his feet and sandals, the ends of the celts and the fob that hung from his belt—completely gone. The jagged edge showed that the monument had been brutally hacked at the waist leaving only a few traces of Father's hip and hand. They had even hacked his feet off, probably because it showed how his power was rooted in the line of his ancestors.

I stepped back. The master stone-hauler gestured to his man. He in turn shouted to the pullers. The hoist bar bent under the weight. Up it went, muddy water streaming over the sides. Waterfalls and then spray. They set it down gently on the harder clay. While they prepared to right it for the lift to the top of the cliff, several other men went into the pool as I'd requested, to see if they could find any other pieces. I was hoping they might find the upper part or pieces of it, but they found nothing. The master guessed that the men hauling off the piece we were raising were tired and eager to be finished. Without a supervisor watching, they dumped it over the cliff.

With the stone righted and tied to the hoist on the cliff, the master gestured and it rose. As we watched, he came close to me. "With respect mistress," he said softly. "That day in the plaza, when we broke them up? I hated that we had to do it, but we were under orders. I and many other Tollanos grieved for your people. I often walked from monument to monument with my sons, to teach them about the carving." He paused as Father's stone halted before going up again. "Whoever supervised the carving of that one was not only a master, he had to be a man of great wisdom."

Despite the reservoir trail being closed and guards posted to keep watch through the night, when Gray Mouse and I arrived the next morning a crowd of Maya men and women bearing torches, had gathered at the trailhead. As I passed, they asked about the monument. Somehow, they even knew it was the one my father had dedicated. They wanted to know what was going to happen to it. I told them we were going to bury it temporarily until later, when we could give it a proper burial. To honor my agreement with Yax Nuun, I didn't say where.

The haulers were in position, waiting for me to give them permission to move the stone. Wrapped in thick layers of palm and then covered with matting, the stone had been tied to two planks that rested on four rolling-logs. Two more were at the ready. So with men lighting the way on both sides with torches, I gave my permission and the rolling began.

By the time the stone reached the trailhead the sky had brightened enough to snuff the torches. Even more people had gathered. Held back by long rows of guards, there were comments and occasional shouts, but there was no resistance.

As the hauler crews rotated their positions, removing the log in back and quickly moving it forward to place it under the planks in front, people complained that they could not see the carving because of its wrappings. In the distance between the causeway and Precious Forest, I saw the Ministers Of Tribute and Water standing with an Owl warlord and some Tollan noblemen. I worried that there might be trouble, but they just nodded as we passed. I kept my eyes on the monument.

Yax Nuun had succeeded in keeping people out of the plaza. Warriors stood at weapons-ready guarding all the entrances to Precious Forest. Slowly and with hands guiding its movement, the haulers pulled the cords over the hoist that had been erected beside a shallow hole dug just strides in front of the central shrine's steps. The bundled stone rose above the planks and was gently set down on the ground. With the hoist repositioned, they raised it again and lowered it into the hole. While the hoist beams were being unlashed and carried away on rollers, the hole was filled with dirt and well tamped. Cut stones were then laid on the dirt to make the surface as flat and even with the surrounding pavement as they could make it.

True to his word, Yax Nuun had ordered a rotation of guards to stand watch. Tollanos. Six of them. Standing tall and grasping long-spears and Storm God shields, they appeared to be there more to honor the stone than to protect it.

Visitors From Tollan

FOUR MOONS OF QUIET HAD PASSED, AND THEN EVERYTHING happened at once. Quiet that is, except for the thunder rumbles that continued into the days of planting.

Along with the dying breezes and the first days of harvest there came a messenger from Waka' to tell Jatz'om that his father had arrived there safely with a contingent of two hundred Tollanos. "Two-hundred! Ayaahh!" I blurted so loudly I frightened Ix Chab' who was across the patio. The messenger said they would be taking the overland trail rather than the river, and if all went well they would reach the western *ahkantuun*—the turtle stone that marked the boundary of Mutal—in seven days. Yax Nuun became excited and nervous, insisting that he be informed of all the arrangements I was making, particularly regarding the accommodations and feasting for his grandfather and the other dignitaries.

With the help of Sihyaj K'ahk', he had made a capture—as I expected, a ruler who refused to adopt the new order—and he wanted everything to be proper. He said he wanted the ceremony, the sacrifice, and the feast afterward to be an event his grandfather would never forget, a story he would tell often, particularly to the other lords of Tollan. Jatz'om and I were less excited: he because the arrival was too close to the date the *aj k'in* marked as the only one fitting for a burial at the eastern shrines, me because—for that reason—he insisted that the burial be postponed until the *aj k'in* could divine a date for the ceremony after his father left.

In my presence, Jatz'om scolded Yax Nuun for being too soft. "You bend to anyone who has your ear," he complained. *Mainly me.* "Tenan says you are not to be distracted... This is the first visit of a Tollan to the lowlands... The celebration of a *tun*-ending is one of the most important things you will ever do.... Everything that happens while your grandfather is here, will be taken back to Tollan... You cannot have anything to do with that stone until he is gone..."

The extent of my husband's concern on a topic could always be gauged by the amount of his talking it required. When finally Yax Nuun had an opening, he pointed out the Maya were standing vigil around the patch of stones day and night. "Scores of them are sleeping in the plaza," he said. "And they keep coming."

Jatz'om took a puff on his cigar. "What are you going to do about it? Their noise keeps us awake at night." That was true. They were singing and playing flutes and ocarinas. "The trees are all lit up over there, One thing for certain, you must put a stop to this before my father arrives."

"They will not stop," I said. "It shows how much they hunger for the memory of the Great Trees."

Ignoring me, Jatz'om pointed his cigar at Yax Nuun. "You are the *ajaw.* Demand that they leave! Show some strength! If they will not leave, send the Owl."

I stood. "No more!" I shouted. "Both of you! My people have suffered enough." I faced my husband. "If warriors go in, I will go first and stand in front with my people. Is this what you want? Do you want your father to see us at war with each other? Have you seen how many people are out there? How reverently they sing over a patch of stones covered with flowers. If you postpone the burial, what kind of welcome do you think the *Maya* will give your father?"

We argued back and forth until Yax Nuun offered a solution. He said if the events coincided, as it appeared they would, Jatz'om could take his father to visit Sihyaj K'ahk' sooner than planned. Because Siaan K'aan was the best example after Mutal of how the new order was being enforced in the lowlands, and because Sihyaj K'ahk' deserved the honor of providing a feast for his father, they would be gone a full day and a half, time enough for Yax Nuun and me to oversee the burying of Father's stone and the removal of the trappings. The only problem was explaining to

Jatz'om's father why Yax Nuun, his sister and I, would not be accompanying them to Siaan K'aan. I could see that Jatz'om was not liking what he heard, so I offered a suggestion: "Yax Nuun and I could talk to the people. I could explain how important it is for the *caah* that the visiting Lord of Tollan be welcomed and shown respect. Yax Nuun can strike a bargain with them: If they are willing to give your father a grand welcome in the Great Plaza and conduct their vigil in silence and without fires and torches, not even at night, he and I would be able to stand and witness the burial as planned."

"And if they do not agree?" Jatz'om asked.

"Then Yax Nuun will tell them the stone will remain where it is, perhaps for another *tun*." There was more discussion. Finally, reluctantly, Jatz'om agreed. The very next morning Yax Nuun and I made our appeal to the crowd at Precious Forest — about three hundred people. After listening and a round of questions, Naj Chan stood and spoke for them, saying they would honor our request.

From then on, between the preparations at the palace and the residence, I had not a moment's rest. Most difficult was gathering the bands of hunters and arranging which would go out when, to insure a steady supply of meat or fowl over the course of twenty days. Yax Nuun and Jatz'om knew the compensations we were promising might bring Mutal to her knees. We went ahead anyway, hoping that the gifts coming from Tollan might make up for it.

Through the days of final preparation the only cloud over the residence was Jatz'om. His usually calm, relaxed, and aloof manner changed. We seemed to have changed places — I the calm one, he the irritable one. He even brushed an attendant aside who was having trouble arranging the eagle feathers in his headdress.

Although it wasn't loud, the constant music, singing, and chanting from Precious Forest made it worse — as did the torchlight at night. Whereas the singing lulled me to sleep, it fueled Jatz'om's anger. He didn't trust that my people would hold to their promise. In truth, I doubted they would as well.

WE KNEW WHEN THE PROCESSION FROM TOLLAN REACHED the western *ahkantuun* because the conch trumpets began to blare. Yax Nuun had arranged for fifty trumpeters spaced a yell apart, to sound their shells as soon as the Tollan banner came into view and sustain it until the palanquin carrying Kaloomte' Ik'an Chak Chan Kuh was set down at the bottom of the palace steps. As the conch sounds increased to the point of becoming disturbing, we took our places atop the steps leading up to the palace.

Wearing a white robe embroidered with yellow owls on the shoulders, Jatz'om took his position at arm's length next to Yax Nuun on his male side. Ix K'inich stood on his other side. Ix Chab' and I stood next to her. In fulfillment of my promise o Yax Nuun, we wore our hair up in back, fanning out to the sides with cattail reeds prominent in our headdress. Just as a flat knot tied behind the head was the sign for Hair Knot, Mutal, cattail reeds were the sign for Tollan, The Place of Reeds. Ix Chab' wore jade ear spools, florets similar to mine but smaller. Befitting her age, over the yellow gown adorned with storm god faces framed in cattails, a white shell hung in front from her beaded waist-cord. I wore the same yellow gown, fringed on the sides, with sleeves that reached to the wristlets. Showing beneath our gowns, the hems of our red sarongs covered our ankles. As always, when Jatz'om and I stood together on ceremonial occasions, we wore the *kaloomte'* necklaces.

Yax Nuun startled me when he came out wearing my father's headdress, a large jaguar head with an open front allowing his face to protrude from the gaping mouth. Instead of quetzal streaming out the top, there were eagle feathers fitted with cattails behind the *sak huunal*. It didn't surprise me that he wore the combination of red apron and yellow kilts which the lords of Tollan often wore, but I was surprised to see the jade-beaded cape that covered his shoulders and chest because they were distinctively Maya—as were the oyster-shell ear ornaments, incense pouch, jade wristlets, and the ancestor mask attached to his belt in back. Jatz'om was very smart. By omitting the eye-rings, back-mirror, and the storm god shield, he was showing his father that Yax Nuun a ruler with Maya and Tollan blood, not just a warrior. The offering of his captive would establish that.

The Great Plaza became a sea of bobbing heads, men, women, and children, nobles and commoners, merchants, tradesmen, and holy men. Tollanos and Maya. On the terrace below us, Sihyaj K'ahk' stood in the center of the steps with the underlords he'd "persuaded" and Yax Nuun authorized, all wearing quetzal headdresses with cattail reeds rising above their jeweled white headbands. All but four of the twenty-five men were Tollanos, mostly Owls. Gathered below them and talking in clusters were the red-robed ministers who tended to be elderly, and the purple-robed council members who were younger men, all carrying their staffs of office and wearing the headdresses of their respective lineages. The holy men, all gowned in white with white headbands, gathered on the lower terrace. Among them, and first to greet our visitors, were seven men with faces painted blue. The serpent scars on their foreheads, together with their serpent scepters identified them as members of the ancient and revered K'alk'in, "Voices Of The Sun," brotherhood.

The first to enter were the drummers. Where my people had the deep voiced drums enter second to last in front of the dignitaries, Tollanos bought their drummers in first. So it was that we heard them before we could see them. Macaw, toucan, and other birds took flight. Spider monkeys screeched and scrambled into the canopy. Our trumpeters stood on the tallest structures sounding the welcome with their long wooden trumpets. Below us, the nine warlords who'd been talking casually with their men, now shouted commands and they scrambled to their positions around the perimeter of the Great Plaza. It was impressive to see our different warrior houses, each wearing different colored loincloths and battle-jackets, but all carrying storm god shields, back-mirrors, and the red headbands tied flat in back. Because of the netted caps surmounted with their respective animal totems, it was impossible to distinguish Maya from Tollano head shapes.

Four abreast the Tollanos came—black-painted warriors after the drummers, pounding down the western causeway with conches blaring, stomping their ankle rattles to the beat of the drums. I glanced to the side where, out of respect for those who'd served at Father's court—and without permission from Jatz'om or Yax Nuun—I provided Naj Chan and several others with tall and white, bark-cloth mitres so they could stand with their Tollan counterparts at court—the *aj k'inob* day-keepers, *aj noah* builders, the *aj tz'ib* artisans, *itz'aat* wise men, the *ek' chuwaj* merchants, *aj yuxul* stone carvers, *aj yum ak'o*t dance masters, the *ajk'uhuun* keepers of records and holy books, and the *caluacob* tribute collectors. By his nod

I knew Naj Chan was grateful for the honor. Not so grateful were the seven captives painted blue and tied in kneeling positions to posts on the ritual platform across from us. Yax Nuun's captive stood out because, unlike the others, he still wore his sandals and a necklace of jade beads.

There seemed to be no end to columns of warriors, all wearing red battle vests with back-mirrors and triple knotted headdresses and carrying obsidian tipped darts with spearthrowers tucked into their belts; warlords wearing shell eye rings and green ear spools and their first-spears with painted white spots on their jaws.

The procession and greeting took the entire morning. Then came the reception that took even longer because we were obliged to personally welcome each dignitary and his family. I never liked speaking Tollan. The words were long and often had several meanings depending upon how they were spoken. It was exhausting, but Jatz'om and Yax Nuun were pleased.

The banquet that evening went smoothly except that Yax Nuun was served a chipped platter. He hadn't noticed, but I noticed. He was more concerned that the male servers were having trouble diverting their eyes from the female guests, some of whom wore see-through gauze. Much more to my concern, there were no sounds coming from Precious Forest. To keep Jatz'om's father and the other dignitaries out of hearing range, I'd arranged for them to sleep in the guest houses behind the palace. Still, I worried that the silence might not hold.

As tired as I was, the possibility of seeing torchlight in the canopy or hearing noises across the way kept me awake. And I couldn't stop thinking about an incident that occurred toward the end of the feast: although they were seated on the other side of the patio, I noticed that Sihyaj K'ahk' and an Owl warlord introduced to me as K'uk' Mo', were talking about me. They kept looking at me while they talked. I kept looking away, but whenever I glanced back they were gazing at me. Not only was it a breach of manners, it was very unsettling. Disrespectful. Because this warlord with a mouth like a frog came second to last in the procession, I'd asked about him. Jatz'om said he was the "Exalted Owl." And curiously, he'd touched the earth at Mutal and lived there for ten years before moving to Oxwitza, a center six days east of Mutal, where his father—who served my father as Minister of Trade for a time—took the Mat. I had no recollection of him or his father. As Jatz'om told it, the father entered the water—died—soon after his ascension and K'uk' Mo' inherited. In his second year he made the pilgrimage to Tollan to take the K'awiil and receive the emblems of office at the wite' naah, but instead of returning to Oxwitza, he stayed there and rose to prominence as an Owl warrior. For me, the most interesting part about all this was hearing that he would be staying behind to take counsel with Jatz'om and Yax Nuun because his "privilege and charter" was to deliver the prophecy to Oxwitik, a center far to the South, not far from the mountains where jade was being mined.

When K'uk' Mo' stood and spoke, his slight build and parrot-like voice made him seem an unlikely warrior. Up close, without his nose-pendant and eye-rings—and besides his frog-like mouth—I judged him to have the face of a hardened woman. Still, his oratory about the abundance that was coming to the lowlands as result of our rulers "praising the gods in one voice," was spoken with exceptional confidence and enthusiasm—without once mentioning the new order.

Change Of Plans

BAREFOOT AND BARELY AWAKE, I USED THE CHAMBER POT and made my way to the doorway in the dark. The servants had not yet lit the torches, and except for the sounds of dripping rain and water running through the ground-troughs, all was quiet. No singing. No ocarinas or flutes. I returned to my bench and pulled the blanket over my ears, grateful that, judging from the darkness outside, I could get more sleep before the chacalacas began calling for the day.

"Mistress! Mistress," Gray Mouse called. "Forgive me. I overslept."

My eyes were heavy and everything was a blur. "Are the torches lit?"

"The glory face is already cutting the fog."

I turned, pulled back the blanket and sat up. "Jatz'om and his father? Still sleeping I hope?"

"There is smoke coming from the palace," she said. Gray Mouse fixed my hair and got me into the red sarong that had small, brown cattail heads painted around the hem. Because Jatz'om and his father were to be served at the palace—to keep them as far away from Precious Forest as possible—I'd told the cooks that, even if the master and his guest slept late because of the long day they'd had, the food needed to be there early—and hot. Before the chacalacas. The smoke was a good sign.

Rounding the corner to the palace patio, I was shocked to see Jatz'om, his father, and K'uk' Mo' already there, walking the patio. I was somewhat relieved when I saw them sipping from gourds. Not wanting to interrupt what seemed to be an intense conversation, Gray Mouse and I continued on to the serving chamber.

Among the strict rules I set down for serving guests at the palace, was the requirement that one of the three *master* cooks had always to be there. The cookhouse was well away from the patio and behind the trees, so they had to supervise the cooking and the servers, three to attend to each guest: the food and beverage-servers, and a comfort attendant who provided damp cloths, fly-sweeps when necessary, cigars, and anything else our guests might need. I personally selected and trained these women, all un-married daughters of noble families, even provided them white sarongs and had them tuck the fold so a hint of their breasts would show at the top.

Lime Sky, an exceptional cook who came with us from Tollan, greeted me when I entered the serving chamber. "Deepest gratitude," I said, "for honoring my wishes. I thought my husband and his father would sleep late."

The men were still walking back and forth. "I was surprised as well, mistress. The three of them were here when I arrived."

"It was dark then?"

"Dark and damp. I had to move quickly to get the water boiling."

"Could you hear what they are talking about?"

"It seems important, mistress. Your husband put a log on the brazier himself, so I had the servers run out with more."

Seeing Yax Nuun enter the patio and the bearers setting his litter down, Jatz'om and his companions went over to him. As they made their greetings, Lime Sky filled a gourd with hot maize porridge and sent a server out with it. I was too far to hear, but as their conversation went on Yax Nuun began to speak louder. Something they said upset him. I was about to send another server to refill the other gourds—and see if she could hear what they were saying—when another litter arrived carrying Sihyaj K'ahk'. Lime Sky filled another gourd and took the serving bowl out to them. When she came back she said they were talking about the fog but it was obviously more than that. Sihyaj K'ahk' and K'uk' Mo' were doing most of the talking. Yax Nuun, his father, and grandfather were lis-tening. Finally, Yax Nuun bowed to his grandfather, glanced over at me, nodded, got into his litter and went back toward the residence.

Jatz'om led the others to the bench where I was standing. He set his gourd down for the servers and nodded his gratitude to me, as did K'uk' Mo' and Sihyaj K'ahk'. Rather than set it down, Jatz'om's father handed the gourd to me. "Best *uhl* since we left Tollan," he said turning to me. "What gives it the flowery taste?"

"With respect Kaloomte' Ik'an Chak Chan Kuh, awinaken," I said. "I am pleased that you enjoyed it. Lime Sky was standing close, bowing from the waist with her arms across her chest. I gestured to her. "Cal Chan here, our ixwaaj, powders vanilla bean and mixes it into the maize dough before cooking it. When it is ready to serve, she crosses it with a honey stick to honor the sky and the sacred directions. The men have it that way often."

Jatz'om's father turned to K'uk' Mo'. "That gives us another reason to rise early," he said. As with the other Tollan lords, he referred to himself as a multiple—he and his ancestors—so I didn't know if he was including the exalted Owl, or just talking to himself out loud. Without his tall head-dress, eye-rings, and face-paint, the Tollan lord was an older and heavier version of Jatz'om but with a sad, drooping mouth and an expression that seemed to ask, "Who do you think *you* are?" Having sat with him and his wives often and under less formal circumstances, I knew there was a soft-ness behind his deeply folded and imperious eyes, but I never saw him laugh.

Sihyaj K'ahk' got into his litter and, after a word to the bearers, they rushed him off. Jatz'om walked his father and K'uk' Mo' to the side of the palace where they took their leave and went around to the guest houses. When he came back he did something I'd never seen him do before: he sat on the steps. My curiosity was too much, so I went over and sat beside him.

"Yax Nuun was upset?" I asked.

Jatz'om leaned back against the cold stone and interlaced his fingers across his chest. "There has been a change of plans," he said. "I told you —. I told Yax Nuun. Now it has happened. Somehow Sihyaj K'ahk' heard about what was going on at Precious Forest. He told K'uk' Mo' and they went to see after we left them last night."

"In the dark? It was late when I looked. There were no torches. Not a sound."

"That made them even more curious: hundreds of people sitting in the dark, huddled under their blankets. K'uk' Mo' said he never saw anything like it—a great circle sitting around a mound of flowers. All they heard was whispering."

"What did your father say?" Jatz'om took a deep breath and leaned forward. He clenched his hands and stared at the pavement beneath his feet. "Go and prepare yourself," he said. "When Ajaw K'in is high we will receive my father and K'uk' Mo' at the residence. The plan is to take our comforts and then go across to Precious Forest. My father wants to see for himself. Ix Chab' will remain in her chamber. Yax Nuun is calling out the warlords and their warriors—all the houses. I can tell you, their weapons will *not* be ceremonial."

My heart began to pound. "Why? What are they going to do?"

"Sihyaj K'ahk' and K'uk' Mo' worked it out. The warriors will surround the plaza and keep the order. Yax Nuun will have the stone raised and destroyed, hauled off as gravel."

My throat tightened. Pressing my hands against my chest reminded me that I'd left the white paper flower on my altar. Jatz'om inhaled deeply and let it out slowly. "Do you see?" He shook his head.

"Yax Nuun will not do it," I said.

"He will. He said he would. He is arranging it now. Your meddling in the affairs of the *caah*—. Now your people will suffer along with you."

"They will not let it happen. There are too many of them."

"Against nine warrior houses poised with spearthrowers, maces, and axes? The only good in this is that Yax Nuun will demonstrate his commitment to the *noh tzol* in front of his grandfather. If the need arises, he will show his strength before the *caah* by putting down any who challenge his decision." Jatz'om got up and walked toward the palace.

"You know what this means!" I shouted. "My people will fight. They will not let you do this! Not again!"

"If there is bloodshed," he said calmly, "it will be yours alone to drink."

FROM THE MOMENT JATZ'OM'S FATHER AND K'UK' MO' arrived at the residence I started feeling sick. I had only a moment alone with Yax Nuun in the back of the audience chamber. Even so, we couldn't speak without being heard, there being so many dignitaries around. Having caught his eye, I made a small gesture to ask what happened. He shook his head and showed me the hand-sign for forgiveness. I shook my head and shaped the words with my mouth, clearly asking him not to do what he was intending to do. The shrug of his shoulders and raised eyebrows told me nothing could be done.

Stand and watch, Ix Bahlam. Just stand and watch. This is their dance. You do not have to dance it with them. At each place where Jatz'om stopped to proudly show his father and the others the opulence of the residence he'd built, I stood back. *Stand and watch? I stood. I watched. What has it gotten me? What good did it do?* Jatz'om wasn't particularly interested in showing his guests the front terrace, but in crossing it K'uk' Mo' stopped and pointed. Ahead, about six hundred paces through the trees, there was an unmistakable crowd of people, some seated, others milling around. "With respect *kaloomte'*," he said pointing. "Over there, that is Precious Forest."

Along with the Tollan lord, everyone moved to get a better look through the open forest. "Much larger than I thought," Dawn Red Snake commented. "Let us go there now. We would like to see what they are doing."

"With respect father," Jatz'om said, "we have food set out."

His father turned to me. "Is it urgent, or could the food wait?" he asked.

My heart pounded and I shivered. "The food can wait *kaloomte'*, but I will need to tend to it."

The Tollan lord gathered the end of his robe and started down the steps. Jatz'om glanced at me with a blank face and that was the end of it. Ignoring the litters I had standing ready, he and the others followed the *kaloomte'* across the grass. I went around back and told Lime Sky to do whatever was necessary to keep the food fresh until their return. Thinking to follow the dignitaries I went around to the front again, but seeing them approach the crowd was more than I could bear. *Ix Bahlam, this is their dance. Let them dance. You do not need to dance with them.* A cascade of what if possibilities raced through my head as I stood watching. Finally, feeling sick to my stomach, I turned, ran up the steps to my chamber, dropped my headdress to the floor, and fell on to sleeping bench. Moments later I jumped up again and darted to the chamber-pot where I brought up what little I'd eaten.

With gown, jewels, and all but my sandals, I crawled onto the bench again, covered myself, and pressed the paper flower against my pounding heart. *Itzamnaaj. Father. Mother. Let this not happen. Scatter the people. Get them out of there before anyone gets hurt or killed.* Again, I went the chamber pot and heaved, squeezing and retching, bringing up little more than pain and tears.

Gray Mouse called from outside. When I didn't answer her, she came in and found me on the floor, hunched over the pot. She wanted to help, but there was nothing she could do. When I could, I rested against her and she stroked my hair.

Inside World — Outside World

THE SCARLET MACAW THAT I KEPT IN A CAGE OUTSIDE THE audience chamber, a gift from Naj Chan, kept squawking loudly. He knew there was trouble in the house. Lying on the bench, I tried not to think about the stone being chopped to pieces. Worse, the warriors putting down any who tried to stop them. I thought about White Gourd and her asking what world I wanted. *I can tell you now, not this one.* The storm raging within me was made worse by the persistent squawking *Stand and watch. I would rather they chop off my leg than watch them hack away at Father's stone.* I sat up and screamed. "Someone quiet that bird!"

"Sorry mistress," came the reply. I laid down again and stared at the ceiling. *Plaster and beams are for Tollanos, not me. I want a world without ceilings, a world where the roof-beams rise to the sky and are well thatched. I want a world without killing. I want to sleep until midday and not hear that my husband or his dog have destroyed something I care about. I want a world where the gods and goddesses just stand and watch—and not threaten to destroy what they made. I want to not worry that my son or daughter will be taken and sacrificed. I want the world I had when I was a flower.*

I rose up on my elbows. *Not even an amate can stand in winds such as this. If all I came to do is fulfill Father's promise and make some bowls—.* Unwanted tears fell from the corners of my eyes, so I lay back and wiped them with the blanket. Turning on my side, I noticed the little flame in the brazier beyond the doorway. I thought of my birth prophecy, how it said that, amidst powerful winds and waves I would battle a mighty demon. *If Jatz'om, Sihyaj K'ahk', Ik'an Chak Chan and now K'uk' Mo' are the demons, then I surrender. What more can they do to me? I am not a warrior, I am a—.* I couldn't finish that thought. *I want a world without demons. No wind. No waves. No trials.* I turned onto my other side, faced the wall, and pulled the blanket over my head to block the light coming through the doorway. With my eyes closed and the macaw no longer squawking I hoped for some peace but my heart kept pounding. *What did she say? Inside world makes outside world? Shaman talk, who knows what it means.*

I heard a crashing sound and lifted my head. Something had fallen on the pavement outside. Apparently it was nothing important but the sound gripped my insides. At that very moment they were destroying what was left of my father's monument, chopping it into gravel—for fill. *I want a world where people are allowed to honor their ancestors, and the gods, however they like.* I pulled the blanket back and sat up, straightening my gown and sarong so my feet could dangle over the side. That there weren't sounds coming from Precious Forest I took as a sign that my people weren't resisting. Feeling the coolness of the leather between my breasts, I remembered the white flower and took it out. I waved it a little to help it dry, and then just held it between my fingers. I whispered, "Little flower, have you anything to say?"

Palm Flower?

Ayaahh. I breathed in and let my breath out slowly. On the chance that those words came from somewhere other than my memory of Father speaking my name, I stared at the paper and asked again if it had anything to say.

Palm Flower. Remember, you will always be my daughter and a daughter of Mutal.

I controlled my breathing so not to disturb the voice. Like an empty canoe floating on calm water, I let my thoughts go.

I am with you, Palm Flower. Your mother is with you. All of us, the entire Ich'aak forest is here. We are standing and watching.

Forgive me Father, I am so ashamed. I took a deep breath, then another. I swiped hard at the water blurring my eyes. *Father?* The tears would not stop. *Can you help me? What should I do with myself? These storms —. Father, what would you do?*

I didn't need an answer. I returned the white flower to its leather sleeve and centered the neck cord between my breasts. "Gray Mouse!" I called, getting up. "Gray Mouse!" I screamed. I didn't know what I was going to do, but I had to move. I ran to the top of the steps. The crowd was still over there, larger and more clustered than before. Still quiet. But surrounded by warriors.

"Gray Mouse! Where are you?"

I went inside and straightened my sarong. I'd run a brush through my hair and tucked in the strands when she came in panting. "Forgive me mistress, I was —."

"Help me with the headdress. Quickly!" She reached to tie the bands under my chin, but I turned away. "Get the bearers," I said. "Run!" She was nearly across the courtyard when I called for her to come back. "That will take too long! Come with me." I lifted my gown and sarong to my knees, pressed the *kaloomte'* necklace against my chest, and raced across the grass.

THE PLAZA WAS COMPLETELY FILLED WITH PEOPLE, ALL trying to get closer to the base of the middle shrine at the eastern platform. I couldn't get through anywhere. One look at how I was dressed and people purposefully blocked my way. Above the heads I could see the hoist straining and the cords moving across it. That meant the stone was still intact. I needed to get higher, so I went around the crowd, some of whom were standing on the steps at the Yax Hal Witz. Gray Mouse followed me up another ten or twelve steps.

When I turned I couldn't help myself. "Ayaahh!" Gray Mouse held out her hand and I pulled her up. "They just raised it!" Quetzal headdresses blocked my view, but I could see stoneworkers lowering the stone onto a brown fabric on the pavement. A ring of Owl warriors standing with crossed spears, kept the people back.

"They are just watching," Gray Mouse said. "Why are they not doing anything?"

"They still think they are going to entomb it in the shrine — as Yax Nuun promised."

"Why then would there be so many warriors?"

I wondered myself. People were looking around, anxious that the black-painted warriors standing an arm's length apart enclosed the entire plaza. They'd even closed off the sides of the eastern platform. All Tollanos: Eagle, Wolf, Rattlesnake and the others. No Jaguars or Quetzals. I pressed the *kaloomte'* beads hard against my chest and shuddered like never before. "They never stand with darts and spear-throwers in their hands unless they intend to use them."

"I cannot look, mistress. We should not be here."

"You may leave if you like. I need to stand and watch. I just pray they do not resist."

"If you stay, I am staying. We should go higher."

"Ayaahh!" With the stone laid flat, the haulers chopped off the cords, each of them sending pieces of stone flying. One of them even stood on top of it to chop off a knot. The crowd groaned, but no one resisted. I was glad for that—until the stoneworkers tore off the wrappings and exposed the carving. The onlookers raised their voices in expressions of awe and pressed against the guards.

Then it happened. Three of the more muscular stoneworkers took up their hefty, long-handled axes and approached the stone. "STOP!" I screamed. "STOP!!" Even louder. Suddenly, hundreds of faces turned toward me. "STOP!!" I pointed to the stone. "DO YOU SEE? THEY ARE GOING TO DESTROY IT!"

Gray Mouse steadied me down the steps as fast as I could go. I forced my way into the crowd, much like I plunged into the water at the reservoir, arms thrashing, reaching again for the stone, now with more breath and muscle than I knew I had. "STOP! LET ME THROUGH!..." The faces looked shocked. When some men wouldn't let me pass, probably because they were afraid my hysteria would cause the warriors to attack, I went around them. "LET ME THROUGH!" I screamed and I pushed. "I AM IX BAHLAM, DAUGHTER OF CHAK TOK! LET ME THROUGH!" When I said Yax Nuun was my son, some women made an opening and I saw a familiar face. Naj Chan held out his hand and I took it. He pulled me forward and widened the way by sweeping his arm and backing into the crowd. "They want to destroy it," I said panting, "chop it into gravel."

Naj Chan glanced at me with sad eyes. "We know," he said. "The warriors came during the night. When we would not leave, they surrounded us."

A ring of warriors blocked my way with locked shields, but Yax Nuun gave the order and they let me through. I wouldn't let go of Naj Chan's hand, so the warriors looked to Yax Nuun. He nodded and they let him through as well. Gray Mouse was held back. "Mother, you should not have come," Yax Nuun said. "I am doing what I must. If you care for your people you will step aside and let these men—."

"Yax Nuun, I am your mother. I am asking you to wait. Just wait. I need to catch my breath." The expression on Jatz'om's face seemed to say he regretted not having me "sacrificed" along with my family. His father peered at me through his menacing eye-rings, then turned to Yax Nuun. K'uk' Mo', looking equally fierce in his Owl helmet and collar, stared at me and made a pitying sound with his tongue while shaking his head. Sihyaj K'ahk' was also staring at me, his hand resting on the haft of a thick obsidian blade tucked into his belt. A nod from Jatz'om and he would have gladly taken my head off.

My heart pounded and I gasped for air. Looking around at all those men, perhaps because they were arrayed in black feathers, I suddenly felt like a jaguar surrounded by vultures. On the other side of the stone, the daughter of Shining Flint Tapir, the blind man who'd called the spirits of the ancestors into the memorial bowls, was guiding his outstretched arms. Supporting his weight on a staff, he touched the jagged edge of the stone and explored with his fingers. I didn't hear what he said to his daughter, but he was trying to reach farther, to touch the carving.

Sihyaj K'ahk' made a move toward him but I got there first. I helped his daughter get him up so he could reach the little jaguar head that dangled from Father's garter. While his fingers explored the round face and tufted ears, I reached ever farther. The blow that just moments ago had cut the knot, also chopped off Father's hand, so I placed my hand on the paw scepter. Like a flint-spark falling on dried kapok and ocote tinder, my doing this ignited a firestorm of shouting. "Bury it!" a voice cried out. "Bury it in the shrine!" Then another: "You gave your word!" Yet another: "It deserves a proper burial!" The shouts rose like a thunderhead with fists striking the air above their heads: "Bury it! Bury it! Bury it!..."

Yax Nuun's grandfather turned to him and raised his chin as if to see better through the eye rings—and ask what he was going to do to quell the commotion. He turned to his father and Jatz'om spoke. I couldn't hear the words, but his lips said, "You know what to do."

Yax Nuun got up on the mound of dirt and stones that had been dug from the grave. He raised his arms and shouted. "Enough!" Three times more he shouted, before the crowd lowered their arms and quieted. "There is nothing here but stone. It once housed the spirit of my grandfather, but no more. He is not here. He cannot help you. Petition him at your house-shrines, not here. This stone is empty. The *ch'ulel* is gone, terminated long ago." He picked up a stone from the heap and held it up. "Rather than waste it, we will use it to support the new temple." He let the stone fall and it tumbled under Father's monument. "Return to your homes. There is nothing to be gained—."

"With respect my son," I said in loud voice, "The spirit of your grandfather may no longer reside in the stone, but it keeps his *memory* alive, the memory of the *caah* as well." Beyond but including the ring of warriors, some of the onlookers were shocked that I, a woman, would dare to interrupt the *ajaw*, even if I was his mother. I went around the monument and faced Yax Nuun. "When they destroyed the monuments, they not only took the breath from the Great Trees, they took our breath, the breath of the *caah*, the spirit that gave life to this forest—Mutal."

Ignoring Jatz'om's disapproving gaze, I went and stood between two guards so I could talk to the people. "My father and those who held the Mat before him had their likenesses carved in stone, not to be praised or stand as gods. They wanted the record of their contributions to live on, so when the bearers of the calendar periods return with tragedy and hardship, the rulers know what to do." I walked along the arc of warriors, ignoring their stolid faces and speaking over their shoulders. "To see the likeness of a Great Tree in stone, if even a hand or foot, is to remember and appreciate what he did for the *caah*. Your memory of the Great Trees and your petitions to them on behalf of your family is what keeps you safe and healthy—and this forest alive." My heart was pounding. "Your memory is their heartbeat, the heartbeat of the *caah*. When they chopped our Great Trees into gravel they choked us. I feel it. Do you feel it?" Again, there arose a mountainous noise, people shouting over and again, "Bury it! Bury it!..."

A glance back told me that Yax Nuun, against his father's wishes, was allowing me to speak. I held up my hands and the people quieted. "My father—," I said. "My family—. They were all sacrificed for the *noh tzol*. Because my father and the other Great Trees take council with the gods and goddesses now, I believe they can do more to secure the strength and prosperity of the *caah* than they ever did when they held the Mat." Judging from the voices, people agreed. Here and there I saw a familiar face. "There has been much talk about the path of abundance. My son is on that path. No one walked it with more devotion and determination than my father—Ajaw Chak Tok Ich'aak."

Far beyond, a man shouted: "No one!"

"We will remember!" another shouted.

"All of them!" a woman shouted.

As I passed to address the people close to Jatz'om's father, I could feel his eyes on me. I felt like Father and Mother and the entire line of Ich'aak ancestors were watching me, so I was determined to speak my heart. "My father held the Mat for eighteen *tunob*. Whatever happens to his monument—what is left of it—as long as you and I remember him, he will remain in our hearts and in our prayers, not only because he was a Great Tree among the many who built this forest. He was the grandest of the grand contributors."

Someone shouted, "That he is!" The crowd started shouting again, building to a thunderhead of: "He is! He is! Bury it! Bury it!..." I turned and went over to Yax Nuun. He'd come down from the mound, so I took his hand and held it to my side until there was quiet. "My son," I called out, "is giving his life to this *caah*—to you and your families—that we may all enjoy abundance and be free from harm. I know that, like his grandfathers, he will *do* everything, *sacrifice* anything, and *petition* the gods and ancestors on our behalf so Mutal will grow strong and prosper. If in his heart he truly believes that the *caah* will be better served by using his grandfather's monument to provide fill for the new temple, then let it be done." I looked up at Yax Nuun, squeezed his hand and let go.

Shouts from the crowd began again: "Bury it! Bury it!..." I could see in my son's eyes that he was considering, directing his gaze to the stone and the blind man whose fingers were still exploring the depressions as if nothing was more important. Jatz'om saw it too. He shook his head and leaned to his father to say something. Judging by the way he jerked his head back, the old lord didn't want to hear it. Yax Nuun went over to the men with the long-handled axes and told them they would not be needed. When one of them set his axe so it leaned against the step, K'uk' Mo' grabbed it and went over to Yax Nuun. "With respect Yax Nuun, you gave the order!" he said. "Now let it be done!"

"We will bury it," Yax Nuun said. "Properly. Mother is right. It is good for these people to remember their—."

K'uk' Mo' went to the stone. Quickly, the *aj men's* daughter pulled her father back. After a tug on his headdress to snug it down, the warlord grasped the axe handle with both hands and made a forward-to-back sweep to add power to his swing. Yax Nuun took up a piece of broken pavement and darted to block the axe. The slab was too heavy. Instead of hitting the axe, it smashed against the warlord's forearm. K'uk' Mo' shrieked and fell to the ground grasping his bleeding arm. Yax Nuun was first on his knees beside him, asking for forgiveness and saying he only meant to deflect the axe. K'uk' Mo' shoved him back with his foot.

Yax Nuun fell back, startled. The onlookers, including the warriors and myself, were horrified. Jatz'om told two of the warriors to help. Immediately they dropped their spears and got K'uk' Mo' to his feet. Dripping blood on the pavement, they led him off toward the causeway. Jatz'om's father followed after them, as did Jatz'om after shaking his head at me. Yax Nuun picked up the axe, handed it to the master stoneworker, and they went their way alongside the platform.

Yax Nuun was looking at his dusty white hands when I approached. The stone had scraped his male hand and it was bleeding. I looked for something to wrap but there was nothing. "Mistress!" Gray Mouse shouted, "Here!" She tore off a strip of cloth from the side of her sarong and held it out. Yax Nuun nodded to the guards in front of her and they let her pass.

There being no water, I grabbed a handful of the flowers that had been scattered, mashed them between my palms and wiped the dust off as best as I could. "I just wanted to stop him," Yax Nuun said.

"I am proud of you. You did what you thought was best for the *caah*." Wrapping the cloth around his hand, I remembered again when he scraped his knee. I looked up at him and smiled, but he was looking away. People were just standing there watching. The warriors too. The quiet was unsettling. They didn't know what to do. With his hand tied, Yax Nuun went over to the Owl first spear. "Release your men," he said. "Tell the others they will not be needed."

On his way to the shrine, he leaned down and touched the head of the blind man's daughter as she went to her knees and bowed. About ten steps up, he turned. Before he could say a word, everyone—the hundreds of my people and the hundred or more warriors—all took to their knees. As did I. And for a moment, my son let the sky and the trees and the birds have their say.

In the manner of rulers making proclamations before their people, he faced the palm of one hand to the sky and the other to the crowd. "Here at the center," he said. "Here at Mutal. Let it be established. This monument, what is left of it, was planted here by my grandfather, Ajaw Chak Tok Ich'aak. It will now, before Ajaw K'in makes his descent on this very *k'in,* be buried in the tomb that was built for it. Once the stone is buried and the workers are gone, now and forever, all are welcome to visit, offer gifts, and pay respect. "In the name of Itzamnaaj, our patron, so it is established."

Yax Nuun lowered his hands and nodded to the master stone-hauler. He in turn called to his men to run and get the rolling-logs while others retied the cords around the stone, and still others got the wooden step-fillers to build the ramp. It took the rest of the day to hoist the stone onto the rollers, get it up the ramp, and lowered into the tomb, but they did it. Only then did the crowd disburse.

So it happened: Father's stone was buried in the center shrine atop the eastern platform, just three strides in front of his tomb. With Ajaw K'in making his descent behind the western canopy, Yax Nuun and his wife, Naj Chan and his wife, Shining Flint Tapir and his daughter, Gray Mouse and I went to the residence, leaving it to the builders to repair the shrine floor. Although we walked slowly to accommodate Shining Flint and his daughter, they were well behind us, so I dropped back to ask if he thought it possible to coax some of Father's *ch'ulel* back into the stone. "Your Father may be eager," he said. "But the stone is broken. Would you come to live in a house that had broken walls and no roof?"

"I would be grateful if you would try anyway."

Shining Flint pawed the air, reaching for my hand. And I gave it. "You are truly your father's daughter," he said. "We will do our best."

I nearly cried. I could not have received a greater compliment—and I told him so. "Seeing you touch the carving is what started the shouting," I said.

"Did I tell you I performed the sacrifice at the dedication of that stone?" He had told me, but I didn't say so. "You spoke of memories, daughter. I may have forgotten what your father said on the occasion. He gave many oratories. But I will never forget the *way* he spoke. Most powerful."

"I have not come to rule—," I began.

"I have come to contribute," the old man completed. Repeating my father's words gave me the same kind of comfort as smelling the tobacco he used.

Shining Flint reached for my arm, pulled me close and whispered, "Your father was not only a worthy ruler, he was a good man. He once told me he would rather help commoners build a house, than sit and talk with foreign dignitaries. He was happiest when he was helping."

"He helped me just now," I whispered back. "Had he not reminded me who I am, I would *never* have gone out there and did what I did."

"Had you not they would be sweeping up gravel back there."

Yax Nuun stopped and waited for us to catch up. "Now I have to face Father, grandfather, and K'uk' Mo'," he said.

"You do not answer to either of them," I said. "You did what was best for the *caah*. Whatever they say, you are the Mutal Great Tree and I stand with you. *Awinaken*." By proclaiming myself his servant, I made it clear that I now respected him as a ruler.

Naj Chan, Shining Flint, and his daughter needed to take the northern path off the causeway, so we stopped to say farewell. Naj Chan went up to my son, knelt on one knee, bowed and crossed his arms over his chest. "With respect Ajaw Yax Nuun Ahiin, I ask your forgiveness for not trusting you, for resisting the *noh tzol*. Tollan ways are not agreeable to me. You have my deepest gratitude for what you did."

Yax Nuun released him and I walked with the old man to the side of the causeway. "I have not the words to tell you what it meant to me, that you took my hand and led me through the crowd."

"It was my privilege, daughter," he said. "Until you called out your name I did not recognize you. With your hair like that, and dressed as you are, you looked like the mother of all Tollanos." We laughed.

Typical of Jatz'om and his father, through the evening feast and the amusements, it seemed nothing unusual had happened. They were cordial with everyone, but they kept their distance from me. Ix Chab' and I sat to the side and behind her brother and Ix K'inich. They were avoiding them as well.

During the oratory given by Jatz'om's father, Full-Of-Knots came from behind and whispered something to Yax Nuun. In turn, he whispered it to Ix K'inich and she whispered it to me. K'uk' Mo' had suffered a broken bone. In spite of the Morning Glory the *aj piltec* gave him to ease the pain, he bit through the stick in his mouth when it was reset. It was his spear-throwing arm.

Once Bound, Always Bound

IT WAS A GLORIOUS DAY WHEN JATZ'OM'S FATHER LEFT FOR
Tollan. Glorious because the bright face of Ajaw K'in warmed the cool
breezes coming from the East. Glorious because the guest houses were
empty and no more visitors were expected. Glorious because I awoke for
the first time since my return, grateful that Itzamnaaj had not answered my
prayers to show me the road to Xibalba. Glorious mostly because the Lord
of Tollan was no longer sitting in judgment of every move we made, word
we spoke, and the food we served. It wasn't that he voiced his disapproval; he
was too holy for that. It was his obsidian eyes and an occasional twitch at the
corner of his mouth that jabbed us in the heart. The day was also glorious because Yax Nuun and I had had a more open talk. His father, in his soft yet
stringent manner, had made a passing remark about his humiliation at Precious Forest. After that, Yax Nuun was more reserved in his conversations
with his father. Less interested in his advice.

In the days that followed, Ix Chab', Gray Mouse, and I made a circuit,
first to visit Father's tomb at the Great Plaza, then to Precious Forest to
pay our respects to Mother, my older sister Ixway, my brothers Naway and
Kachne', my aunt, her husband and their unborn child. After that we took
flowers and incense to the monument tomb. The little chamber only had
enough space for two people at a time, so if we came late in the morning
we sometimes had to wait for others to come out. I was delighted when, at
the Fire Entering rite, Father gave Shining Flint powerful lightning in his

legs to let him know that a bit of his *ch'ulel* had taken up residence in the stone. Sometimes, when I knelt alone and talked to him, I could feel his hand on my shoulder.

I'D JUST FINISHED WITH THE SERVANTS AND CHANGED INTO my most comfortable sarong when Jatz'om called from outside. I met him in the light at the doorway. "Walk with me," he said. "Show me where you found the stone."

"There is nothing to see," I said. "The reservoir is full."

"I know. I have something to tell you. I just thought it would be pleasant to walk there." Much as my insides tightened at the prospect of hearing *anything* from Jatz'om, curiosity had me follow him.

Jatz'om liked to begin serious conversations with a compliment, so even before we reached the causeway I was dreading what he had to say. "Dear One," he began, "I want you to know that, apart from what happened at Precious Forest, I am grateful for all you did to make my father and the others comfortable. I know it was difficult for you, speaking Tollan and presenting yourself and Ix Chab' as you did. You have my gratitude for that."

"The servants surprised me," I said. "It was good that Yax Nuun compensated them well." Jatz'om nodded. "Did your father say anything? Did he enjoy his visit?"

"I think the best part for him was the *Tun*-Ending ceremony and the celebration afterward." *True. And the mountainous bounty that Yax Nuun, Sihyaj K'ahk', and the now twenty-eight underlords heaped on him when he left.*

The reservoir trail was covered with leaves. I kicked them ahead of me. Jatz'om crunched them under his sandals. "Did he say anything about my speaking out?"

"He was more concerned about K'uk' Mo'."

"He had to know it was an accident."

"He did. K'uk' Mo' doesn't fault Yax Nuun." I knew that. "Before he left Father commented that he did not realize how strong you are."

"Strong?" The word enflamed the tinder in my heart, but I kept my mouth shut. *There is a storm coming, so just stand and listen. Let him dance his dance.* Three women carrying water-jars on their heads approached. Seeing our jewels they nodded and diverted their eyes. When they were passed us, Jatz'om stopped and picked up a large, yellow, deeply veined leaf. He held it to the sky and it brightened. "We have done well here," he said. "Yax Nuun has much to learn, but he is well on the path of abundance. Father was pleased to see how the *noh tzol* is taking root."

I couldn't resist. "Like his grandfather, our son wants to contribute."

Jatz'om plucked little pieces off the leaf and threw them aside. "What I have to tell you — ." I clenched my teeth. "Father has honored me greatly. He has given me a new charter. Yax Nuun can manage on his own now, so we will be moving on."

"Moving? Why? Where?"

"Sihyaj K'ahk' has been chartered to establish the *noh tzol* to the East. As my Father planned, K'uk' Mo' will remain here. He will take counsel with Sihyaj K'ahk' and Yax Nuun in preparation for his charter which involves a long journey south. By then his arm will have healed. Father wants him to celebrate the turning of the *bak'tun* as ruler of a place called Oxwitik. You and I will be going north to Maasal."

"Maasal? What is there? How far is it?"

"Merchants count it a six *k'inob* journey, entirely over land. No more canoes. I am told they have a fine residence... *Stand and listen. Let him dance.* Talking to myself did little to dispel the clouds that were gathering in and around my heart.

"One of the warlords going with us will take the Mat. Standing Squirrel deserves it. I have yet to decide... This begins the wider expansion. With me in the North, Sihyaj K'ahk' bringing in the East, K'uk' Mo' the South, the entire lowlands will... Finally, we will put down roots."

"Maasal." I said. "Where have I have heard that name?"

"While we were in Tollan your father led an attack there. He took the ruler captive and brought him here to be sacrificed. His son rules now and his alliance with the Snake Lords has turned Maasal into a respectable center."

"Is he expecting you?"

"There are some Tollanos already there, not enough to call a settlement. Sihyaj K'ahk' will honor my father's request to smooth our way. We will not leave until..." *Like he did here? Execute the ruler and his fam-*

ily—is that what you call smoothing?

I stopped at the place where we raised Father's stone and pointed out the filled holes where the hoist-beams had been planted. Jatz'om wasn't interested. He didn't even ask how the monument was found. As he talked about him and Yax Nuun escorting warriors to Siaan K'aan, warriors that Sihyaj K'ahk' would train and then take to Maasal, I went to the rise, held onto a tree and looked over. "Careful," he said. "The dirt could be loose there." The water was three or four arm-spans below the cliff, clear and dark blue. He waited for me to respond, but I didn't. "Of course Gray Mouse and Full-Of-Knots will come with us. Lime Sky as well. Others if you like. I leave that to you." I came back from the rise, went down the trail to the stump and sat, remembering the handsome young man with the tonsured hair and yellow stick—especially his eyes. "Yax Nuun said he would —."

"I will not be going," I interrupted.

"What—?"

"I will not be going to Maasal. My home is here."

"Dear One, your home is wherever the goddess directs me. You carry the *kaloomte'* title. You are—."

"I am my father's daughter—above all. My roots go deep here. My family, what is left of it, is here. My ancestors are all here."

"Dear one, listen. I understand that you have suffered greatly. I regret that it had to happen as it did. You must put all this behind you? I have grown comfortable here, but you know how it is. The goddess—."

"And your charter."

"We have no choice. Father says we go and we go. That is the burden and privilege of our station. You know that."

I turned and faced my husband. "You may not have a choice but I do. I am my father's daughter first, a woman of Mutal second, and your wife third—."

"You keep saying that—"

"I will keep saying it until you hear me. This is where I choose to make our home."

"Yours is to keep the household, mine is to say where it shall be."

"No longer. You put my family, my roots, in the ground. You set my son on the Mat here. My grandson is here. In every way, I am bound to

Mutal."

"You are bound to me."

"I have kept your household. I will continue to keep it. Here." I got up and waited until a family passed by, apparently carrying bundles of food and cording home from the market. "Come or go as you will," I continued. "If you want to be part of this family you will find us here."

Jatz'om spun around. "You have always been a pebble in my sandal! Must I remind you? A woman is nothing in herself or before the gods without her husband. Once bound, *always* bound." His blood was boiling. Strangely, it calmed me. I kept looking him in the eyes. "True," I said. "Same for a man. He is nothing without his wife. You are the one who took an axe to the cord that bound us, not me. It almost destroyed me, but I am still here. Now you want to split the family we have left? I will not have it!"

"So this is your way of punishing me."

I stepped closer to him. "Husband," I said calmly. "You had my family killed, *sacrificed* if you prefer. You replaced my father's ministers and deposed his council. Except for the piece of his monument that I saved, you destroyed the memories that kept the Great Trees alive. You turned our son against the ways of his people. Now you expect me to make a new home six *k'inob* from here? For the children's sake—and mine—I am trying to forgive you, Jatz'om. But I will never forget."

Jatz'om went to the stump and sat. My heart was still pounding but a weight had been lifted. "You do not know what it is like." He spoke so softly I had to go closer to hear what he was saying. He seemed to be talking to the water. "To be guided by the goddess is as much burden as privilege."

"For everyone around you."

"Remember at Tollan, standing high on the Serpent Pyramid with my father and the other lords—the sky like this?"

"It was windy and cold."

"The great valley. All those people. The great causeway running from Mother Mountain to the river. All that, including Mutal, will be lost if we loose the lowlands."

"I cannot worry about the world—or tomorrow. I am worried enough about my family and Mutal—today."

222

Jatz'om shook his head. "You do not believe the prophecy. My own wife." I went up the rise to where Jatz'om could see me, but did not answer. "I do not just believe it, I know it. Tenan talks to me."

"Then *you* must do what she says. I cannot. Besides, the thorn in my foot is not the prophecy. It is the way you are delivering it—and the *noh tzol* that establishes it. Alliances. Betrayals. Killing. I want no part of it."

"Like it or not, that is the way of men. Neither Tollan nor Mutal would have risen from the forest floor without them. The jungle must be cleared for the seeds of order to be planted and nourished."

"Then go to Maasal and clear the jungle for your *noh tzol*. But I will not be going with you. That is not my path. Should my Father and my ancestors want me to save the world from the wrath of the gods, they will show me another way—here."

Jatz'om got up slowly and shook his head. "So it is clear between us, you are saying you will make our home here, even if my permanent residence is in Maasal?"

I nodded. "Once bound—. Our garments were tied. You will always by my husband; I will always be your wife, your *principal* wife if you should take another woman under your roof. I will keep your chamber open and clean. As for myself, I am not comfortable in the new house. As soon as I can arrange it, I will have Ix Chab' and our things moved to my father's house."

Jatz'om turned toward the causeway. "Are you coming?"

"I want to stay a while," I said.

To calm myself I sat on the stump and watched the little breezes making ripples on the water. Over across the reservoir an oropendola called loudly for his mate, and I was reminded again of the pale young man with the long hair—who by his look seemed to welcome me home.

Epilogue

NINE DAYS AFTER MY CONVERSATION WITH JATZ'OM AT THE reservoir, Nuun received a messenger from Sihyaj K'ahk' calling for the warriors he would train and lead to Maasal under the blade and banner of the Owl. Yax Nuun and Jatz'om had a heated argument over which houses and how many warriors he should send. In the end, Jatz'om escorted only forty of the sixty Owls he wanted, the other sixty consisting of Wolf, Puma, Eagle, Falcon, and Rattlesnake—all men with straight foreheads.

Three moons later the procession that left to join them at Siaan K'aan included noblemen, holy men, merchants, tradesmen, stoneworkers and farmers, all Tollanos, all believing so devoutly in Jatz'om's charter that they were willing to move their families to a strange place and start over, some for the second time in two years. If a column of leaf-cutter ants heard Jatz'om talking about the prophecy and how the new order was restraining the wrath of the gods, they would turn in their tracks and deliver their burdens to his feet. Such was my husband's power to turn people's heads. Such was the power of the goddess to turn *his* head.

It wasn't so much that my *head* had been turned, as my *eyes* had been opened. The loss of my family and the long grieving, the lost *ch'ulel*, and the longing for the return of the life I'd had so clouded me that I became blind and fell into a pit of regret, anger, and bitterness. Whether it was the shaman's healing, our conversations, or remembering Father's parting words to me, the foolish, uncontrollable lurch into the reservoir and then the outburst at Precious Forest had the effect of washing that muck away, enough that I could see what I'd been missing. And what I wanted—life as it *could* be.

Whether at court or council, presenting himself to the people, or conducting the round of calendar rites, Yax Nuun continued to present himself as an Owl, but always wearing the jeweled headband with the knot tied flat in back. He spoke often and openly about the goddess's prophecy, and he strictly enforced the new order, requiring his underlords to do the same. Whenever he could, usually at my urging, he tried and often succeeded in blending the best of the old ways with the best of the new.

As planned, Sihyaj K'ahk' defeated the lord of Maasal. Several moons later Jatz'om sent a messenger to Yax Nuun to tell him that he seated a first spear Owl on the Mat there, positioned himself as his overlord, and took the title, Kaloomte' Of The North. Jatz'om and Yax Nuun sent messengers back and forth occasionally, but Yax Nuun only told me about his father's health and accomplishments relating to the new order. When one of the ministers revealed that Jatz'om had taken another wife I was not surprised. He visited us occasionally, mostly to talk to Yax Nuun about how the new order was progressing in the lowlands. Rightly, as *kaloomte'* and Lord of Maasal, he had to celebrate the major feasts and calendar rites there.

Within a moon of his father's leaving for Maasal, Yax Nuun granted my request and appointed the wives of two ministers to care for the residence and the palace. Relieved of those duties, I invited noble women and their daughters, Maya and Tollanos, to come to the workshop and make bowls, vases, and cups for their husbands and fathers to give as gifts. Ix Chab' was very helpful in this and she made some bowls, but events turned and she was drawn more to weaving than working clay. After the Descent of Spirits, Yax Nuun and I arranged for her to marry one of Naj Chan's grandsons, a handsome and hardworking young man with a cob-shaped head who could read word-sign. Eventually, they gave me six grandchildren.

After Ix K'inich presented Yax Nuun with his second son, she took ill again. Her eyes and hands turned yellow. She recovered but she was never the same. Known for telling made-up stories about the gods and Underworld demons, she spent her days weaving in the patio and telling these stories to the older flowers, including Ix Chab' and her friends. Watching her work is how it happened that Ix Chab' took to the backstrap loom.

All through her illness, Ix K'inich's servants tended to my grandsons. When it became apparent that she would no longer be able to care for them, I stepped in. I was not going to have my grandsons raised by servants. As it happened, the task of tending to the little ones was more than I expected. Sihyaj Chan, now four, ran like a spider monkey on *chih*. He demanded and pouted to get his way. When he didn't, he cried—not unusual for a child at that stage. On occasion he lashed out at me. At the same time, there was never a child any sweeter or more observant. Bugs, birds, monkeys, and servants, even clouds, nothing could move without his taking notice. His brother was the opposite. The only way I could get him to move was to take him by the hand or pick him up.

White Gourd visited occasionally. On her first visit she verified what I already sensed, that my *ch'ulel* had returned and that the dark clouds that had choked my heart for so long had dissipated. "What happened?" White Cord asked. "You seem no longer to allow the winds and waves to grow into raging storms?"

I told her about my plunge into the Underworld and what happened at Precious Forest, both being situations where I had to do something. "You'd stood and watched," she said. "When who you are became threatened, you had to pounce."

"I couldn't help myself. When they pulled me out of the water I felt—. I do not have a word for it. Released? Relieved? Purified? Like a butterfly finding its wings."

"You learned to trust."

I had to think about that. *Trust what? Trust who?* "I just know it is easier now to stand and watch when those around me are kicking up a storm."

"Even the most violent storms happen for good reason. *Everything* that happens happens for *good* reason." Like having a bucket of water ready to douse a stray flame, it comforted me greatly to have White Gourd sleeping nearby.

THERE CAME A DAY, AN EXCEPTIONALLY *HOT* DAY, WHEN Sihyaj Chan ran around the patio like a monkey, chasing a pretend monster with a stick. His brother was sleeping in the shade, so I asked Ix Chab' to watch him while Gray Mouse and I took the little monkey for a walk to tire him out so he too, would take a nap. A friend of Gray Mouse's daughter happened to be crossing the plaza and they wanted to talk, so I continued on with Siyaj Chan to Father's monument, eager for the cool that the tomb provided.

A little game we played in the chamber was to take the little ones to the back of the monument, hold them up or sit them on a knee, so when they touched one of the sign, we would shout the word and clap hands. The loud, hollow sound made them giggle with delight. On this occasion when I lifted Sihyaj Chan onto my knee he wriggled off and ran around to the front of the stone. There, he reached out and I called, "Foot!"

"Foot!" he shouted and clapped.

He touched the knot on Father's garter. "Knot!" I shouted.

"Knot!" he repeated.

"Smoking Axe!"

"Moking Axe!" he shouted, wriggling in my arms.

"Dark!"

"Dark!

"Jaguar!..."

Before leaving the tomb it was my habit to place my hand on the stone where Father's hand had been, and recite his words about coming to contribute. "Me! I want to touch!" Siyaj Chan said with his arms raised. "Pick me up!"

I lifted him, positioned him in the crook of my arm, and stepped close so he could put his little paw on the cold stone. He jerked his head and looked at me, expecting me to shout. Instead, I put my hand on top of his little hand and said, "I have not come to rule—."

I looked at him. "I have not come to rule," he said softly.

"I have come to contribute," I said.

"I have come to—tribute," he tried to repeat. He patted the stone as he'd seen me do many times. Hearing those words spoken so sweetly in that little voice hit me like a lightning bolt. Joy beyond measure. I set him down and he ran to the doorway where Gray Mouse met him. "Could you take him?" I asked, lifting him over the masonry rise. "I would like another moment alone."

"Come and see?" she said to Siyaj Chan. "There is a fox out here. Someone is feeding it."

I went to the monument and placed my hand on the place where Father's hand had grasped the Jaguar Claw scepter. "Did you hear your grandson?" I asked. "He is in my care now. I will teach him to put contributing ahead of ruling. This will be my contribution — my *grand* contribution. I see now. As long as I have breath, I will sow the seeds of your ways in the fields of my grandsons. They will know you and what you did here. My contribution to the *caah* — and to you — will be great-grandchildren who remember you and your deeds, all the Great Trees and their ways. When Siyaj Chan ascends to the Mat, I want him to see Mutal through *your* eyes."

Having complete confidence in the Tollan goddess, Jatz'om believed — and often said — that everything that happens, happens for the best. Lacking that confidence and having experienced the worst, I didn't believe it. But when White Gourd kept remarking that, "Everything that happens, happens for good reason," I began to allow that they could both be right, but "the best," could take a very long time, and "good reasons" were usually not apparent. Considering my impatience and hunger to make all things proper, the advice to stand and watch had been very helpful. When Jatz'om went off to Maasal and I moved into my father's old residence, I found my confidence was in knowing who I was and what I wanted — a grandson who in manhood would honor and respect my father and the Great Trees before him, perhaps even restore some of the ways of my people. Kneeling before my altar every night I expressed gratitude, not only for the day and the safety, health, and prosperity of those I loved, but also for having found my grand contribution.

True to my birth prophecy, amidst powerful winds and waves, I had battled — and continued to battle — a mighty demon, a demon within, a demon of my own making. The only part of the prophecy that eluded me throughout this lifetime was what the ancestors meant when they said my path would be the path of the jaguar.

Historical Information

THE NEW ORDER OF TEOTIHUACAN IMPERIALISM HAD A profound and lasting affect on Tikal (Mutal). Although the inscriptions say little about the intrusion and its aftermath, the situation was intense for at least thirty years. What they do say is that eight days after Sihyaj K'ahk' performed a "fire shrine" ceremony at the *wi-te' naah*, Root Tree House, at Waka', he arrived in Tikal on January 15, 378. "Arrivals" in the hieroglyphic inscriptions generally imply military action. On the very same day, the Lord of Tikal, Ajaw Chak Tok Ich'aak "entered the water." He died. His family line was surely killed, so it's likely that he was killed as well.

Sihyaj K'ahk', Born of Fire, was a vassal of a Teotihuacan lord called Spearthrower Owl (Jatz'om Kuh). Soon after his *arrival* in Tikal, he went north eleven miles to Uaxactun where he killed two royal women, one of whom was pregnant, and two children, taking the captured ruler and his son back to Tikal where they were sacrificed. While serving as regent—to rule and prepare Spearthrower Owl's son for the throne—he brought twenty-eight lords of outlying provinces under the banner of the Tikal polity, establishing them as Yax Nuun's underlords when he ascended to the Mat (throne). A year later Sihyaj K'ahk' married a Maya woman. He ruled at Uaxactun for approximately seventeen years (AD 379—396).

Spearthrower Owl served for three years as ruler of a site called Ho' Noh Witz, Five Great Mountain—which could possibly be the ancient name of Teotihuacan. His title there was *kaloomte'*, which carries the sense of regional overlord or emperor. Much later, he became the overlord at Maasal (Naachtun, Guatemala). He was eighty-nine when he died on June 10, 439. This is most exceptional considering the average lifespan at that time was between thirty-five and forty.

Yax Nuun Ahiin, "First (?) Crocodile," the son of Spearthrower Owl, was three years-old when Sihyaj K'ahk' *entered* Tikal. Although his father was from Teotihuacan, bone analysis indicates that he was raised in a lowland climate, not central Mexico. And his name is distinctly Mayan. At twenty, he ascended to the throne on September 12, 379, receiving then "the burden of" twenty-eight underlords, all "the doing" of his regent, Sihyaj K'ahk'. Throughout his reign, Yax Nuun introduced strong Teotihuacan imagery in dress, architecture, and art. He added Tlaloc, the central

Mexican storm god, to the Maya pantheon, and solidified vigorous trade with Teotihuacan. He may have married a daughter of the former ruler, his grandfather. The back side of a monument he dedicated (Tikal Stela 31) contains information about gods and time-periods including a history of the dynasty leading up to and including aspects of the intrusion in 378. The front side of this well preserved monument shows him dressed as a Teotihuacan warlord complete with plated helmet, spearthrower, and storm god shield. His reign lasted forty-seven years (AD 379-426).

His son (the protagonist's grandson) Siyaj Chan K'awiil II, Born of Sky K'awiil The Second, ascended to the throne on November 26, 411. He ruled for forty-five years (AD 411 to 456). While he retained many of the Teotihuacan traits promoted by his father, he reestablished continuity with his Maya ancestors and returned to the ways of a traditional Maya king. He not only took the name of a king who ruled Tikal a hundred years before and asserted his connection to Yax Ehb Xook, the city's founder, he reinvented the symbols of power in ways that in the modern era define "Classic" Maya civilization. Arguably, it was during his reign that Tikal reached the zenith of its influence. Once again, the monuments erected to celebrate period endings depicted *rulers* and their *deeds*, not just gods.

K'uk' Mo', Quetzal Macaw, went south and became highly venerated in later years as the founder of Copan in Honduras. Upon his ascension to the throne he took the name, K'inich Yax K'uk' Mo', Resplendent First Quetzal Macaw. The scientists who studied his bones noted that he'd suffered a broken arm.

Also pertinent to the story, Tikal Stela 1 shows the protagonist's grandson, Siyaj Chan K'awiil II, wearing the regalia of his *matrilineal* ancestry. On other monuments he pays homage to his grandfather, Ajaw Chak Tok Ich'aak. The bottom half of Stela 39, the monument featured in the story was found entombed in Structure 5D-86 at the Mundo Perdido. It now "lives" in the Tikal Stela Museum. The memory of Ajaw Chak Tok Ich'aak is alive and well.

Photographs of Tikal Stela 39
<research.famsi.org/schele_photos_list.php?_allSearch=stela%2039>

Drawings of Tikal Stela 39
<research.famsi.org/schele_list.php?_allSearch=stela%2039>

Glossary

ahkantuun: "Turtle Stone Marker." Large stones, likely painted, set up to mark the four directions of a village or city. They marked boundaries between man-made settlements and the wilderness.

Aj Jaay: "Clay vessel person." One who makes and trades ceramic vessels. Murals at Calakmul in Campeche, Mexico show these individuals wearing very tall hats with wide brims and storing vessels in large baskets.

Aj K'in: "He of the Sun." A calendar priest devoted to the sun god Ajaw K'in, Lord Sun. Part of the responsibility of the *aj k'inob* was to keep the count of days—possibly by binding sets of stones as well as painting glyphs on paper—to maintain the sacred and secular calendars. The *chan aj k'in* was their master.

Aj Men: Shaman. These ritual specialists were the equivalent of medical doctors, but they also used advanced spiritual skills in their healing.

Aj Noah: "He the Builder of Walls." Architect. These men would design the structure and make measurements—"the laying of cords"—to establish the dimension and layout of walls and other architectural features.

Aj Piltec: "He Who Opens The Eyes." An accomplished shaman-healer who dealt with more serious injuries such as snake bite. They set bones, treated severe wounds, and performed surgery.

Aj Tz'ib: "He of the Writing," or "He of the Paint." Scribe. Scribes were likely to be members of the royal household or members of the nobility.

Aj Yum Ak'ot: "He the Dance Master." One who teaches sacred and ceremonial dances. It's likely they also commissioned the costumes and regalia that went with the dances, coordinating with drummers and musicians.

Aj Yuxul: "He of Carving." Stone sculptor.

Ajaw: "Lord." In the Early and Middle Classic periods this title was applied to rulers and gods. In the Late Classic, it was also bestowed upon high ranking noblemen who were close to the ruler.

Ajaw K'in: "Sun Lord." The sun god. Later in the Classic period, his name became K'inich Ajaw, "Sun-Eyed Lord."

Ajaw Le: "Succession Lord." The individual designated as heir to the throne. Inheritance normally passed from father to a son, but there are instances of brothers and women inheriting depending upon circumstances.

Ajk'uhuun: Trained in both hieroglyphics and symbolic communications (perhaps alongside scribes), these individuals kept the polity records, holy books, and advised other artisans on these matters.

amate: The tree from which bark cloth is produced.

awinaken: "I am your servant." Used in the story as a term of respect accorded solely to rulers.

Bahlam: "Jaguar."

Becanokol Nal: "River-Entering Place." A mid-to-large Late Preclassic site on the Bay of Corozol in Belize, close to the eastern coast of Yucatan. Today it is called Cerros.

caah: "Town," or "Village," or "City." For the ancients the term included all its people, structures, trees, animals, and patron spirits—everyone and everything that contributed to its identity as a functioning whole.

Caluac: A personal steward. Also a title for the individuals who collected tribute.

c*h'ulel*: "Soul," or "Spirit." The life force. The animating essence in gods, people, and animals. The ancient and many modern Maya regard the soul as having multiple parts, any one of which can go wandering. When that happens, the result is an illness called "soul loss." If the condition is not treated, madness or death can result.

chak patan: "Grand Contribution," "Great tribute." Every adult owed tribute to the Mat (throne) annually in the form of both goods and labor.

Chahk: God of thunder rain. These four patrons of the cardinal directions had long noses that bend downward, wore shell-shaped ear ornaments, and in some instances had snakes protruding from the sides of their mouths. Rain was the result of water poured from their vessels. Thunder and lightning resulted from the clashing of their enormous flint axes.

chaak: "Great." "Rain."

chan: "High" or "Esteemed." A prefix relating to the title of a leader, the head man.

Chan itz'aat: Master of writing.

Chaynal: "Fish Place." Fictitious name of a large site known today as Kaminaljuyu located in a suburb of Guatemala City. Into the Classic period the city was situated on a lake which, in the Late Classic dried up. The author chose the name because on many of its structures archaeologists found the image of a fish.

chih: An alcoholic beverage made from the maguey plant. Pulque. The fermented juice is a less refined form of tequila.

Chilam: "Prophet" or "Speaker." A high ranking holy man who spoke to the people on behalf of the ruler. Along with serving as a prophet generally, he could serve the ruler as his personal oracle.

copal: Incense. The resinous sap of the copal tree.

Chuwen: Artist.

Ho' Noh Witz: "Five Great Mountain." Hieroglyphs on a stone feather standard found at Tikal cite this location as the place where, in AD 374, Spearthrower Owl ascended to rulership. That was four years before Siyaj K'ak' entered Tikal. This could be the ancient name of Teotihuacan; more likely it's a site located somewhere between Central Mexico and Waka' in Guatemala. Since bone analysis shows that Yax Nuun Ahiin, was not raised in Central Mexico, the author places Ho' Noh Witz closer to the lowlands.

Huunal: "One Headband." This is the name of a deity referred to by scholars as the "Jester god" because of his three-pointed cap with beads on the ends. The three beads represent the three stars in Orion that constitute the cosmic hearth. When his head is worn as a jewel on the *sak huunal*,

234

White Headband, it marks the ruler as the central living portal from which the life force flows.

Itz'aat: "He of the Writing." Artist and wise person. The *chan itz'aat* would be the master artist.

Itzamnaaj: "Lizard House." A creator deity. *Itz'* refers to precious or sacred fluids such as nectar, dew, sap, sweat, semen, or tears. As a sorcerer or enchanter, Itzamnaaj could manifest *itz'*. This old creator god with a hooked nose and flower-bedecked headdress was the Maya supreme deity.

Ix Chel: "Lady Chel." A Mayan moon goddess.

Ix Men: A female shaman. A healer.

ixwaaj: "Cook."

k'ak': "Fire"

K'alk'in Brotherhood: "Voices of the Sun." A fictional title of an ancient brotherhood of astronomer-priests established at Izapa, Mexico in the Early Classic period.

k'atun: A period of 7,200 days. Approximately 20 years.

K'awiil: "Scepter." The god, Ch'ok Nehm K'awiil, Young Mirror Scepter, is the most prominent deity in Classic period imagery. A fire god, he is depicted with a flaming celt (axe) in his forehead. One of his legs is a serpent and serves as the handle when he is presented as an idol or scepter. As a source of power in the form of fire, he conferred the authority to rule and signified the ruler's control over lightning. He was linked to ideas of fertility and abundance.

k'in: "Day." "Sun."

k'uhul winik: "Holy Man." A man of god. Priest.

kakaw: "Cacao." Chocolate.

Kaloomte': The meaning of this title is not yet known. It was accorded to an overlord who had powers above and beyond those of a ruler—somewhat like an emperor. His powers were regional rather than restricted to a city. The author has this title originating in Teotihuacan, but that has not been established. Also, because there is evidence to suggest it, the *kaloomte'* has the power to anoint and confer the authority to rule. In our terms, he was a king-maker. Wives shared the title with their husbands.

kapok: A soft, fibrous material similar to cotton only finer. It grows on the arms of ceiba trees. Among other things, the ancients used it to stuff pillows and cushions.

keyem: A beverage made of cooked maize and water. Served at home and for entertaining guests, honey, chili, or cacao was added. Farmers and hunters going out for the day took balls of maize dough wrapped in leaves. They added water to it to make a gruel.

ko'haw: A large war helmet worn by Maya rulers in imitation of Teotihuacan warlords. It was made of jade or shell platelets and was sometimes accompanied by a short cape of the same plates covering the chest. It can be seen on Piedras Negras Stelae 7 and 8.

kox: A black bird with long shiny tail feathers. The meat is said to be sweet, somewhat like chicken.

kub: A huipil, a single full-length gown worn by women. Two pieces of large cloth were sewn together allowing holes for the neck and arms.

lakamtun: "Big stone." A stela. The tall, carved monuments that stand in ceremonial centers.

Maasal: A site in Northern Guatemala known today as Naachtun.

Mat: Throne. (When capitalized). The symbol of the authority to rule was a plaited mat woven with cattail reeds. When a man ascended to the throne is was said that he "took the Mat." Literally, he climbed up a tall scaffold situated on top of a temple and presented himself as ruler by sitting on the mat of authority. Thereafter, as long as he ruled, he always sat on a mat, even if it was covered with a jaguar pelt or cushion.

Mutal: "Hair Knot." The site known today as Tikal in the Peten forest of Guatemala.

noh tzol: "New order." The order of Teotihuacan imposed new gods, more stringent requirements regarding trade and tribute, a different emphasis on calendrical cycles, conformity in dress among certain elites and warriors, a different perspective on the purpose and placement of monuments, new colors and symbolism in every artistic medium including architecture. And more.

och k'ahk': "Fire-Entering." A ceremony performed to ensoul a new temple or house (temples were god-houses). New fire was drilled and the hearth lit fresh. The blood-sacrifice of a bird was offered at the center-post of a house to attract a protector spirit. Consistent with most indigenous people, the ancient Maya believed that everything is alive. When a house or vessel became ensouled in this ceremony, it was infused with the spirit of an ancestor.

Oxwitik: "Three Roots." The ancient name of the site known today as Copan in Honduras.

Oxwitza: "Three Mountain Water." The ancient name of the site known today as Caracol in Belize.

patan: "Service." "Tribute." As part of the tribute owed to the ruler for his protection, generosity, and bargaining with the gods, adults were required to offer an agreed upon service to the community. Usually this amounted to labor on community projects that alternated and rotated according to calendar cycles.

Peten: A large lake with an island on it, located about seven miles south of Tikal. In ancient times the city on the island was called Nohpeten, "Great Island." Today the lake is called Lake Peten Itza', named for the Itza' Maya who lived there at the time of the Spanish invasion. The city is Tayasal.

saca: A refreshing beverage made of cooked maize. The maize is ground raw, without powdered limestone, and dissolved in cold water.

sak huunal: "White Oneness." The name of the white headband of kingship. A jade jewel on the front depicted Lord Hu'unal wearing a peaked hat with a bead at the end. Because of the resemblance, scholars refer to him as the Jester god.

Siaan K'aan: "Born In Heaven." The site known today as Uaxactun in Guatemala. It's within a morning's walk, fourteen miles north, of Tikal.

siyaj: "He is born."

Tenan: In Nahuatl (Aztec), "Our Mother." Two large, monolithic sculptures of a water goddess were found near the Pyramid of the Moon. One of them wears a diamond-patterned jade skirt. Also, the image of the "Great Goddess" was found on the wall of Portico 2, Tepantitla at Teotihuacan. Scholars have viewed her as the personification of Cerro Gordo, the mountain that rises behind and above the Pyramid of the Moon. The iconography strongly suggests that she was the patron of abundance and prosperity.

Tollan: The Maya name for Teotihuacan, an enormous site in central Mexico. Maya hieroglyphs render the name as *Puh*, "Place of Cattails," the Aztec equivalent of which was "Tollan," a Place of Origins, perceived to be the birthplace of the gods. What's more, the Aztec spoke of it as a "Place of Emergence," where *men* became gods. Teotihuacan may or may not have been the first among many legendary Tollans.

tun(ob): "Year(s)." A *tun* is a period of 360 days. It is equivalent to the Gregorian year, except the Maya added five additional days to make a complete annual cycle.

uhl: Ground maize balls are mixed in water and then cooked to reduce them into a thick liquid. This made a porridge or thick jelly depending upon proportions.

unen: "Infant."

Waka': A site in eastern Guatemala known today as El Peru/Waka'. It lies close to the San Martir River which was the main east-west waterway connecting Central Mexico with Chiapas and the Peten—the ideal route to and from Teotihuacan.

Wi Te' Naah: "Root Tree House." A fire shrine and origin (lineage) house. "Root" is a reference to lineage ancestors.

winik haahil: *Winik*, "Holy." *Haahil*, "Man." Together, the phrase refers to a "Man of Truth." Used in the story to designate holy men and rulers who vowed to either speak the truth or not at all.

Xibalba: "Place of Fright." The Maya Underworld. The world under the ground and under water.

xwukpik: The Mayan word for a brown-backed solitaire, a bird of the thrush family that's plain in appearance but sings one of the most remarkable songs in the world.

yajaw: "Underlord." A vassal ruler. A lord authorized to rule by an overlord of a larger polity. For instance, upon Yax Nuun Ahiin's ascension to the throne, he "assumed the burden" of twenty-eight underlords, all of whom owed him tribute in the form of goods and labor.

Yax Hal Witz: "First True Mountain." The mythical location where Chahk, god of thunder and rain, split open the earth—perceived as a great turtle—with his axe. In the Maya creation story, Chahk split open the earth so Juun Ixim, the Maize god, could ascend from the Underworld. First True Mountain is also the place where First Mother fashioned human beings from blood and maize dough. The Lost World Pyramid at Tikal in the Mundo Perdido complex was considered to be a replica of First True Mountain. It was Chak Tok Ich'aak who named the plaza surrounding it Precious Forest. In the Early Classic period the pyramid in the center of the plaza was the tallest structure at Tikal.

zuhuy: "Virgin." A reference to purity. Water from caves and springs was considered pure and was reserved for ritual purposes.

About The Author

David L. Smith is Emeritus Professor of Communication at Xavier University in Cincinnati, Ohio. Academically, his focus is on mass media and the Anthropology of Visual Communication. He enjoyed a thirty year career in broadcast television as a multi-award winning documentary filmmaker and television producer. He exhibits and publishes fine art photography.

Since 1967 he has been a student of Mesoamerican art, archaeology, and anthropology, with an emphasis on the ancient Maya. He conducted research at the principle sites featured in this story.

Made in the USA
Charleston, SC
23 November 2011